Fran

The History of Normandy and of England

Volume 3

Francis Palgrave

The History of Normandy and of England
Volume 3

Reprint of the original, first published in 1864.

1st Edition 2022 | ISBN: 978-3-75259-296-2

Verlag (Publisher): Salzwasser Verlag GmbH, Zeilweg 44, 60439 Frankfurt, Deutschland
Vertretungsberechtigt (Authorized to represent): E. Roepke, Zeilweg 44, 60439 Frankfurt, Deutschland
Druck (Print): Books on Demand GmbH, In de Tarpen 42, 22848 Norderstedt, Deutschland

THE
HISTORY OF NORMANDY
AND OF
ENGLAND,

BY

SIR FRANCIS PALGRAVE, K.H.

VOLUME III.

RICHARD SANS-PEUR—RICHARD LE-BON—RICHARD III.
—ROBERT LE-DIABLE—WILLIAM THE CONQUEROR.

Narratione autem historica (ait Augustinus) cum præterita etiam hominum instituta narrantur, non inter humana instituta ipsa historia numeranda est; quia jam quæ transierunt, nec infecta fieri possunt, in ordine temporum habenda sunt, quorum est conditor et administrator Deus.

LONDON

M.DCCC.LXIV.

TO THE RIGHT HONOURABLE

SIR JOHN ROMILLY, K.B.,

MASTER OF THE ROLLS

———

MY DEAR SIR,

You have honoured me with your kind permission that I should explain, in a few words addressed to yourself, the circumstances in which the Third and Fourth Volumes of this History are now published.

The Fourth Volume was printed throughout (with exception of the "Summary") several years since. Some corrections in it were afterwards planned by my father; but it represents, on the whole, his maturest judgment on the events narrated.

The completion of the Third Volume (postponed for personal reasons to the composition of the Fourth), had formed the author's occupation during the leisure hours of the last four years of his life. Great part had been written previously; and it was his wish to revise the whole, incorporating in it the fruits of additional study and of visits to the scenes of the principal events described. Death, however, in July 1861, stayed his hand when this revision had been completed only to the end of Chapter III.

From this point onwards (Chapters IV to XV), the book has been edited by me. From a task for which I did not feel myself qualified, I should have shrunk, had it not been for the advice which you kindly gave me, to print the remaining manuscripts with the least possible amount of addition, and for the encouragement which you held out, that the work, if so performed, would be better done by a son than by any abler or more accomplished man, not connected so closely with the author. I trust that this explanation may procure pardon for the want of complete finish in some passages, and for the errors which my best care has been probably unable to avoid. However imperfectly I may have practised it, one who, more than most sons, had the privilege, during many years, of living with his father as his most intimate and dearest friend, could hardly fail to learn the lesson, how History should be written.

For those who may wish to know the exact amount of the Editor's responsibility, the following details in regard to the Third Volume are added.

Chapters I to III were completed by the author. IV was printed, but not finally arranged, by July 1861. V (as stated on p. 271), has been put together, partly from fragments in type and in manuscript, partly by a reprint from the author's small Anglo-Saxon History. VI continues these extracts. It had been doubtful to my father (I may add) whether to adopt this plan himself, or to omit from this book what he had described before, or to rewrite the narrative. But it was his intention to make use, for the next portion of the history, of an article published in the *Quarterly Review*, of October 1844 (No. 148). Chapter VII has been, therefore, composed partly from this article, in part from manuscript sources.

The whole reign of the Conqueror in England, Chapters VIII to XIV, has been printed from the almost perfect manuscript prepared originally for publication, but destined, as noticed before, for a revision which was never to be accomplished. Chapter XV is a selection from the materials which the author had hoped to work up into a more complete and continuous survey.

The Appendix has been reproduced from a privately printed, but not finally corrected, pamphlet, in the formation of which my father was, I believe, much assisted by the lists drawn up by M. de Gerville. I have added this, in hope that it may, in some degree, serve to replace the authentic catalogue (so far as such could be compiled), of the Conqueror's companions, which it was the author's wish to give.

For almost all the dates, for the division into paragraphs, for the marginal notes and headings, from Chapter V to XV, Books Second and Third, with the "Summary" from Chapter IV to the end of the Fourth Book, I am responsible. A very few additional words and corrections have been inserted, and are distinguished by enclosure within angular brackets.

These indications will, I hope, make it clear that the volumes now published have not suffered much by the author's death. Except in one chapter, the work was, by that time, substantially completed. What has been lost lies principally in the additions which would have been made on the effects of the Conquest, and in the Notes, which were, I believe, to have given references to the authorities employed.

A few words of more personal nature may, I trust, be permitted me in conclusion. It was my father's hope that he might live to make the book of which these volumes form the most important portion, his best contribution to the history of England. He therefore dedicated it to the Friend who (in his judgment) had beyond all others advanced our knowledge of that history, and whose high and noble nature he had proved in an almost life-long friendship. They have been both called to rest from the labours which only advanced age, in Mr. Hallam's case, and death, in my dear father's, could suspend. I may now, therefore, be allowed to connect these volumes with your name, as one of the friends to whom, during his latter years, my Father was indebted for constant kindness, at once in private life, and in regard to the official duty which he performed under your Keepership.

—— His saltem accumulem donis, et fungar inani Munere.

I remain

yours with much respect

FRANCIS TURNER PALGRAVE

5, York Gate, London:
9 May, 1864.

CONTENTS.

BOOK II.

CAPETIAN NORMANDY.

CHAPTER I.

ROBERT, KING OF FRANCE—LAST YEARS OF RICHARD SANS-PEUR—ACCESSION OF RICHARD LE-BON—OPENING OF HIS REIGN—REVOLT OF THE PEASANTRY.

987—996.

A.D.		PAGE
987	Richard Sans-peur, his family and connexions during the concluding period of his reign . . .	1
—	Ivo de Belesme, and his son William	1
—	Espriota, her marriage with Sperling the Miller,—their son Raoul, his famous battle with the bear . .	2
—	Duke Richard, Raoul's half-brother, grants to him the County of Ivri	4
—	Illegitimacy—perplexities connected with the question	5
—	Tudor and Braganza	6
—	Marriage antiently a bargain and sale . . .	7
—	Missions and civilization	8
—	The Rechabites	9
—	Anglo-Saxon form of wedding	10
—	Richard Sans-peur and Guenora	11
—	Legitimation of their marriage	13
—	Richard Sans-peur's children	14
—	Marriages of his daughters	14
—	Prospect of family troubles	15
—	Apprehension of Richard Sans-peur as to the succession	15
—	Disorders of the Norman Church	16
943—994	Hugh, Archbishop of Rouen—his scandalous conduct	16
994	Richard appoints his son to the Archbishopric . .	17
—	Robert ineligible by reason of his bastardy . . .	17

CONTENTS.

A.D.		PAGE
994	Bastards legitimated by the subsequent marriage of the parents	18
(1235	Parliament of Merton—Prelates and Barons of England refuse to adopt the civil law) . . .	18
—	Marriage of Richard and Guenora	18
—	Archbishop Robert marries and becomes Count of Evreux	19
—	Richard Sans-peur's natural gifts	19
—	French or Romance language cultivated in Normandy	20
—	Coin struck by Richard Sans-peur	21
—	Fécamp built by him	21
—	Gothic architecture	22
—	The stone chest across the pathway	23
996	Richard's sickness and death	24
—	Appointment by Richard of his son Richard (le-Bon) to be his successor	25
—	Intermural interment, not practised in the early ages of the Church	26
—	Directions given by Richard for his burial without the walls of Fécamp Abbey	26
—	Richard le-Bon performs homage by parage to the King of France	27
—	Rise of the Norman nobility	28
—	Apanages of Richard Sans-peur's children . . .	28
—	Geoffrey Count of Eu, and Seigneur of Brionne . .	28
—	Mauger Count of Mortagne: he obtains Corbeil by marriage	28
—	William in the first instance Count of Hiesmes, subsequently receives another endowment . . .	28
—	Robert the married Archbishop of Rouen, and Count of Evreux	29
—	Archbishop Robert's sons	29
—	Richard the Archbishop's eldest son, Count of Evreux	29
—	Ralph Wace, or Gace, the Archbishop's second son, Tête-d'étoupe, or Tête-d'âne	29
—	Guillaume, the Archbishop's third son, the companion of Robert Guiscard	29
—	Herfastus, Richard's uncle, and Guenora's brother, ancestor of the FitzOsborne family . . .	30
—	Adelina, one of Richard le-Bon's maternal aunts, marries Osmond de Balbec	30
—	Gueva, another aunt, marries Therrold the son of Terf, Baron of Pont-au-de-Mer	30
—	Norman nobility originating or arising in the reign of Richard le-Bon	31

CONTENTS.

A.D.		PAGE
996	No information concerning the antient jurisprudence of Normandy	32
—	None known anterior to the reign of Philippe Auguste	33
—	Theory of Howard, that the Norman costumes were borrowed from England	33
—	Bourgeoisie of Normandy—her commercial prosperity	34
—	Norman peasantry	36
—	Hereditary aristocracy, not necessarily exclusive	37
—	Heraldic gentility favoured by Richard le-Bon	38
—	Oppressions of the peasantry, in consequence of encreased notions about gentility	39
—	The Norman forests—game laws	40
990—1000	Confederation of the peasanty suppressed, and with great cruelty, by Raoul Count of Ivri	43
—	Ultimate result, not unfavourable to the villainage	44
—	Servitude obsolete, at an early period	44
—	Position of Richard's brothers and nephews	45
—	Geoffrey Count of Eu and Brionne	45
—	Gilbert son of Geoffrey	45
—	He quarrelled with his cousin Tête-d'âne or Wace	45
—	William, an illegitimate son of Richard Sans-peur	45
—	Hiesmois or Exmes granted to him	46
—	Falaise, its commercial opulence	46
—	Fair of Guibray	47
1002	Count William refuses to render his services: he is taken prisoner by Raoul Count of Ivri	48
—	Kept in captivity in the Tower of Rouen, whence he escapes	48
—	Pardoned by his brother Richard, who grants him the County of Eu	49
—	His descendants—their high position in Anglo-Norman history	50

Chapter II.

ROBERT, KING OF FRANCE, AND RICHARD LE-BON.

996—1024.

CLOSE ALLIANCE BETWEEN NORMANDY AND FRANCE—ROYAL AND DUCAL MARRIAGES—WARS AGAINST FLANDERS, BLOIS, CHARTRES, CHAMPAGNE, AND BURGUNDY.

| 1002 | Entente cordiale, between King Robert and Duke Richard | 51 |

CONTENTS.

A.D.		PAGE
1002	Hugh Capet's anxiety to associate his son Robert with him in the royal dignity	51
—	Robert's education	52
—	Conjoined with his father in the royal authority	52
—	Endurance of the male progeny in the Capetian line	52
—	Hugh le-Grand's policy grounded upon feudality	53
—	Tranquillity of the realm under the first Capet	53
—	Fortifications raised by him throughout the realm	54
—	Right of advowson	54
—	Cast of French historical characters	55
—	Hugh Capet's dealings as patron	56
—	Foundation of Abbeville	56
—	Tranquil accession of Robert	57
—	His character as a poet	57
—	Robert's humouristic simplicity	57
—	He quizzes the pope (Bishop of Rome)	58
—	Robert's trust in Normandy	58
—	Uncertainty of the extent of the obligations resulting from the Carlovingian homages	59
—	Norman Dukes hold *en parage*	59
—	Feudal obligations incurred by Normandy to Hugh le-Grand	61
—	Richard of Normandy a Capetian Peer	61
978 (?)	Death of Thibaut le-Tricheur	63
—	He is succeeded by Eudes or Odo	64
—	Extent of Eude's possessions	64
—	He assumes the name of Comes Ditissimus	64
995	Death of Eudes	64
996	Marriage between King Robert and Bertha, Eudes' widow	65
—	Contrary to the canons of the Church	65
—	Gregory V., first Transalpine Pope	66
998	Council at Rome—Robert and Bertha commanded to separate	67
—	Gerbert exercises his influence against Bertha	67
—	Inconsistency of public opinions in these matters	68
—	Robert repudiates Bertha and marries Constance	69
—	Robert's patience and humour	70
—	Eutrapelia	71
—	New School of Chroniclers	72
—	Richness of the Norman Chroniclers	72
999—1000	Eudes le-Champenois threatens France	73
—	Melun	73
—	Burchard of Anjou	74
—	Burchard marries Count Aymon's widow	75

CONTENTS.

A.D.		PAGE
1000	Melun and Corbeille, granted to Burchard	76
1002—1003	Burchard obtains Melun by treachery	76
—	Duke Richard assists the King in recovering Melun	77
—	Lyderic the forester, first Count of Flanders	78
1006	Bandouin la-belle-barbe, or Bushey-beard, Count of Flanders	79
—	Geoffrey of Rennes, first Duke of Brittany	80
—	The Norman damsels	80
—	Alliances of Richard Sans-peur's daughters	81
—	Godfrey of Brittany marries Hawisa	82
996	Richard le-Bon marries Judith or Ivetta, Godfrey's sister	83
—	Sons of the marriage	83
—	Daughters of Richard le-Bon	84
—	Richard le-Bon's second marriage to Estritha, the daughter of Canute—she is divorced by Richard, and marries Jarl Ulph the Anglo-Dane	84
—	Richard le-Bon's third marriage to Papia	84
—	William, Count of Arques, and Mauger, Archbishop of Rouen	84
—	Complication of Norman History—its fourfold tangle	85
—	Marriage between Ethelred and Emma	86
936—986	Partial conversion of the Danes	86
936	Expulsion of Harold Blaatand	87
966—973	Otho the Great, the Ottensund	87
972	Swein's baptism	87
936—1014	Blaatand and Swein, their success in the British Islands	88
—	Christianity and civilization	89
—	Heekee the Maori	90
—	Richard Sans-peur, scorned as the Dux Piratarum	91
—	Harold Blaatand in the Cotentin	92
—	Objectivity and subjectivity	92
—	Commercial character of the Normans	93
—	Richard le-Bon's dubious neutrality	94
—	Departmental division of France	95
—	Department of La Manche, equivalent to the antient Avranchin and Cotentin	96
—	The Cotentin, its natural strength	97
—	Parts of the Cotentin—Barfleur	98
—	Cherbourg	99
—	Bravery of the inhabitants of the Cotentin	100
—	Oslac, settled in the Cotentin by Rollo	100
—	Barony of Saint Sauveur created by Rollo	101
—	Nigil, Count thereof	102

xii CONTENTS.

A.D.		PAGE
—	Castles of the Cotentin	102
—	The Cotentin, the nursery of the Conquerors of Apulia and England	102
—	Ethelred declares war against Duke Richard	103
—	Landing of the English in the Cotentin	104
—	Their defeat by the inhabitants	104
—	Peace said to have been concluded by the intervention of Pope John (XV.)	105
—	Ethelred's family	107
—	His courtship of Emma, and marriage	109
1001	Emma returns to Normandy	111
—	Burgundy	112
965—1002	Henri le-Grand, first Capetian Duke	114
—	Otho Guillaume	114
1003	King Robert—his invasion of Burgundy	115
—	Aid given by Normandy	115
—	Siege of Auxerre	116
—	Siege of Avalon	117
1015—1032	Henry, first Capetian Duke of Burgundy	118
1027	Renaud, Duke of Burgundy, the trouble his descendants gave to the Conqueror	119

CHAPTER III.

RICHARD LE-BON AND HIS SUCCESSORS, RICHARD THE THIRD AND ROBERT LE-DIABLE.—EARLY INFANCY OF WILLIAM THE BASTARD.

1024—1035.

—	Hostilities between Richard and Eudes le-Champenois, by reason of the County Dreux	120
1007	Tilliers — importance of the place, source of the dispute between Normandy and France	121
—	Marriage between Eudes le-Champenois and Matilda of Normandy	122
1015	Refusal of Eudes to surrender Tilliers according to agreement, Maude having died without issue	122
—	Niel de Saint Sauveur,—Ralph the Toeny chief amongst the Norman Baronage	123
—	Tilliers, attacked by the Norman forces	123
—	Defeat of Eudes—he flies	125
—	Narrow escape of Hugh, Count of Maine	125
—	Richard invites Olave, King of Norway	126
—	Tooley Street	126

A.D.		PAGE
—	Northmen land in Brittany, probably sailing from England	126
—	Defeat of the Bretons at Dôl	126
—	The pit-falls	127
—	Danes sail up the Seine, great alarm created	128
1020	Treaty of Coudres	128
—	The Champs d'Argent	129
—	Dreux, Castle and Chapel	129
—	Stephen of Blois	129
—	His marriage with a Norman Princess	129
—	Burgundy—Renaud, son of Otho William, marries a Norman Adeliza	130
—	Hugh, Bishop of Auxerre, and Count of Chalons	130
—	Renaud captured by him	131
—	Richard, the son of Richard le-Bon, his good qualities	131
—	Invasion of Burgundy by the Norman and French forces	131
—	La Mirmande	132
—	Count Bishop of Chalons, bridled and saddled	133
1026	Richard le-Bon appoints his son, Richard the Third, as his successor; and dies	133
—	His interment at Fécamp	134
—	Sources of early Norman history	134
—	Prose authorities	134
—	The Trouveurs	134
—	Traditional history	135
—	Richard and Robert, no information concerning them till the Burgundian campaign	136
—	Their quarrels	136
—	Richard III. performs homage to King Robert	137
—	Espouses the daughter of France	137
—	Settlement made upon the intended marriage	137
—	Ermenoldus the Breton	138
—	Encrease of population amongst the descendants of the Scandinavian races	139
—	Havelock	139
—	Norman population encreasing beyond the means of subsistence	140
—	Robert rebels against his brother	140
—	Richard besieges Falaise	140
—	Pacification between the brothers	141
1027	Sudden death of Richard attributed to poison	141
—	Accession of Robert	141
—	Illegitimate children of Richard III.	141
988—1036	Baudouin à-la-belle-barbe	142

A.D.		PAGE
—	Robert's soubriquets	142
—	His liberality	143
—	Falaise and its tanneries	144
—	Robert or Fulbert, the tanner and brewer	144
—	His daughter Arletta	145
—	Skinners, a degraded caste	145
—	Union of trades, of Tanner and Brewer, prohibited	146
—	Duke Robert keeps company with Arletta	146
—	One child, William, acknowledged as his offspring	147
—	Public offence given by Robert's connection	147
—	Premier families of Normandy	148
—	Guillaume de Belesme or Talvas	148
—	He curses the baby	149
—	The dislike against the child continues unabated	150
—	The Conqueror's bastardy never condoned, because he was the Tanner's grandson	151
—	William always a bastard	152
—	Great offence given to all members of the ducal family	153
—	Robert, Archbishop of Rouen, breaks out first—he flies the country	153
—	Hugh, Bishop of Bayeux, follows the example of the Archbishop of Rouen	154
—	Robert attacks Talvas, who is beat, and compelled to bear the saddle	155
—	Political importance of Duke Robert	155
—	Baudouin à-la-belle-barbe takes refuge in Normandy	156
—	Revolt of the Flemings	156
—	Robert mediates between the Norman and the Flemish Dukes	156
1031	Death of King Robert	157
—	Contested succession of King Henry	158
—	Henry expelled by his vixen mother	159
—	Treason—what constitutes treason	161
—	Wallace	161
—	Duke Robert continues his exertions on behalf of Henry	162
—	The Vexin—Drogo, Count thereof	163
—	Drogo's marriage with Ethelred's daughter	164
—	Brittany—its importance in Norman History	165
—	Political and feudal relations between Brittany and the crown of France	166
—	Geographical extent of Brittany	167
—	Duke Geoffrey and his achievements	167
1008	Geoffrey killed by an old woman	168

A.D.		PAGE
1008	Alain, his son, succeeds	168
1010	Revolt of the Armorican peasantry	168
—	Dissensions between Count Alain, and Alain Caignard, Count of Rennes	169
—	Alain's courtship of Eudes le-Champenois' daughter	169
—	The Armoricans despised by the Frankish race	170
—	Peace between the two Alains	171
—	Alain Caignard carries off the lady, presents her to Duke Alain, who marries her	171
—	Duke Alain restores Belle Isle to Alain Caignard	171
—	Pomp and pride of Duke Alain	172
—	Alain repudiates the homage due to Normandy	173
—	The Normans of the Cotentin invade Brittany	173
—	Niel de Saint Sauveur, and Alfred the Giant; their exploits	174
—	The English Athelings, Edward and Alfred, placed under Duke Robert's protection	175
—	Canute and Emma	176
—	Duke Robert prepares for the invasion of England—frustrated by a storm	176
—	Archbishop of Rouen mediates between Robert and Alain	178
—	Antipathy entertained against the child William	178
—	Duke Robert, le-Magnifique, suddenly determines to go as a pilgrim to the Holy Land	179
—	Solemn confirmation of the Bastard's right	181
—	The Barons perform homage and fealty to the Bastard	181
—	King Henry accepts William as his liegeman	181
—	Regency appointed by Duke Robert	182
—	Robert commences his pilgrimage	183
—	Drogo, Count of the Vexin, accompanies him	184
—	Robert's mode of travelling	184
—	Robert at Rome	185
—	Robert at Constantinople	186
—	Robert's health fails	188
—	Contest of liberality between the Emir of Jerusalem and Robert	189
1035	Robert dies poisoned	190

Chapter IV.

WILLIAM THE BASTARD, FROM HIS ACCESSION TO THE BATTLE OF MORTEMER.

1035—1054.

A.D.		PAGE
1035	William's reign divided into three acts	191
—	Alain of Brittany appointed guardian by Robert	192
—	Anarchy on news of Robert's death	193
—	Partly caused by the legal interregnum	193-194
—	Partly by the lax rule of Robert	195
—	Indelible stain of bastardy on William	195
—	Claims of Guido, Count of Burgundy, to the duchy	196
—	Regency during William's minority	197
—	He is placed in Vaudreuil	198
1036	Attempt against him by Montgomery	199
—	Presaged the troubles of his life	200
—	Miserable state of Normandy	200
(1042)	Truce of God instituted	201
—	William's enemies: Mauger; Ferrers	202
—	Roger de Toeni	203
—	William's character	204
—	Chronological perplexities of the period	205
1037 (?)	Baronial conspiracy	206
—	Henry's feeling towards William	207
—	Development of William's destiny: several years of comparative peace	208
—	Henry attacks William	209
—	Takes Tilliers	210
—	Guido of Burgundy asserts his claim	210
1047	Rebellious spirit of the Barons: Niel de St. Sauveur	211
—	They attempt to seize William in Valognes	212
—	He escapes to Falaise; then to Henry	214
—	The barons seize Normandy	214
—	Henry supports William, who summons his supporters	214
—	William and the rebels meet at Val des Dunes	215
—	Battle of Val des Dunes—conduct of Tesson	215
—	William completely victorious	217

CONTENTS.

A.D.		PAGE
—	Fate of Grimwald and Guido	218
—	Anjou: governed by Geoffrey Martel	218
1048	He takes Alençon, and threatens Normandy	219
—	William's siege of Alençon	221
—	His success: makes an alliance with the Emperor	222
—	Yet the stain of his birth indelible	223
1050	Plot of William the Warling	224
—	William takes Mortaigne	224
—	Importance of Ponthieu: Saint Riquier	225
—	Abbeville: the Vimeux	226
—	Rebellion of Counts of Arques and Ponthieu	227
—	William blockades Arques	228
—	Brittany: minority of Conan under his uncle Eudes	229
1040—1047	Conan recognized in Brittany	229
—	Intrigues of William in Brittany	230
—	And of barons against William	231
1054	Henry supports them: invades Normandy	231
—	Plan of the campaign	232-233
—	William's caution	235
—	Battle of Mortemer	236
—	Defeat of Henry	237
1054	Troubles begin from Anjou	238
—	Importance of Maine: its early history	239
—	Herbert Wake-the-dog	241
—	His successors	242
—	Geoffrey Martel in possession of Maine	242
—	William occupies Maine	243
—	Hostility of French to Normans	244
—	Normandy again invaded	245
1058	William defeats Henry and the French at the Gué Berenger	245
—	Henry makes peace	245
1059	His marriage: crowns his son Philip	246

Chapter V.

PREPARATIONS FOR THE CONQUEST.

1054—1066.

—	William's marriage	247
—	Condition of Flanders	248
—	Flemings in Scotland	251

A.D.		PAGE
—	Activity of the race	252
—	Character of Matilda	253
—	Her children	254
—	Lanfranc	255
—	His youth	256
—	Settles at Avranches	257
—	And Bec	258
—	Herlouin and Lanfranc	259
—	Cabals against Lanfranc	262
—	Enmity and friendship with William	264
1061	Hostility of Gautier and other barons to William	266
—	Robert de Giroi	267
—	Death of Geoffrey Martel	268
—	Maine surrendered to William	269
1063	The Manceaux resist	270
1064	William captures Mantes	271
—	Holds court at Lillebonne	273
1062	Council at Caen	274
—	Mauger, Archbishop of Rouen	275
—	Is deprived	276
1063	Harold in Normandy	277
—	William attacks Brittany	278
—	Death of Conan	279
—	Resumption of English affairs: death of Canute	279
—	Harold Harefoot and Hardicanute	280
1042	The Confessor: Normans in England	281
—	Norman law: Romance language	283
1051	William visits England	284
—	Divided state of the country	286
1052	Domination of the Godwin family	287
1057	Edmund Ironside	288
—	Dispute as to the succession	289
—	William and Harold	291
1063	Harold in Wales	291
1066	Edward dies	292
—	Harold's claim	293

Chapter VI.

THE INVASION.

1066.

1066	Competitors for England	295
—	Harold seizes the crown	296

CONTENTS.

A.D.		PAGE
1066	William claims it: Harold refuses	299
—	Parliament at Lillebonne	300
—	Invasion determined on	301
—	William publishes his reasons	302
—	Harold's preparations	303
—	William's fleet	304
—	Lands at Pevensey	306
—	Harold learns the news	307
—	His measures	309
—	The two camps	311
—	Arrangement of the forces	313
—	The Battle of Hastings	314
—	William the Conqueror	318
—	Battle Abbey	319
—	Fate of Harold	320
—	Henry I. and Harold	321
—	Uncertainties of the event	323

CHAPTER VII.

ENGLAND AT THE TIME OF THE CONQUEST.

Physical aspect of England	325
Temperature in early times	326
Changes in the sea line	327
In the Flora and Fauna	328
Celestial phenomena	331
Decayed state of the Saxon realm	333
Abuses amongst the clergy	334
The slave trade in England	336
The country ripe for dissolution	337
Territorial divisions of England	338
Danelagh	339
Earldome	340
Burghs	341
Winchester	342
London	343
Wessex	344
Lincoln	345
The South East	346
Northumbria	347
East Anglia	349

	PAGE
Scotland	350
Strath Clyde	352
Cumbria	354
Malcolm Canmore	355

[BOOK III.]

THE CONQUEROR.

Chapter VIII.

THE CONQUEROR, FROM HASTINGS TO THE CORONATION.

1066.

A.D.		PAGE
1066	Anarchy after Hastings	356
—	Claimants to the throne	357
—	William's operations	359
—	In Sussex	360
—	And Kent	361
—	Canterbury taken	363
—	Kent submits	364
—	William moves on London	365
—	London submits	367
—	Reasons for Saxon submission	368
—	Necessity for a king	369
—	Abeyance of law during vacancy	372
—	Position of an English king	373
—	William assumes the crown legally	374
—	Promises to maintain the law	376
—	His coronation	378
—	Receives Saxon homages	381
—	His engagements to his army	382
—	Limits to his recognition	383
—	Policy of Denmark	385
—	William's first progress	386
—	Confirms the rights of London	387
—	His administration: fortifications	389
—	The Tower	391
—	Ralph Baynard	392

A.D.		PAGE
1066	Shire divisions	394
—	Negotiations with Denmark	396
—	Copsi placed in Northumbria	397
—	East Anglia	398
—	Builds Norwich Castle	400
—	William's grants of land	401
—	Mitigations of his grants	402
—	Examples of them	404
—	Foundation of Battle Abbey	405
—	The Roll	407
—	Traditions of the Abbey	408

Chapter IX.

WILLIAM RETURNS TO NORMANDY—HIS TRIUMPHANT RECEPTION—OPPRESSIONS EXERCISED IN ENGLAND BY ODO OF BAYEUX AND FITZ-OSBERN—GREAT TROUBLES—THE ENGLISH INVITE EUSTACE OF BOULOGNE—WILLIAM RETURNS TO ENGLAND—REBELLION OF THE WEST—DEATH OF COPSI—WILLIAM SUBDUES THE INSURRECTION—MATILDA IN ENGLAND.

1067—1068.

1067	Government of Normandy	409
—	William's arrangements for England	411
—	Returns in triumph to Normandy	412
—	Display at Fécamp	413
—	William's glory	414
—	Men of intellect about him	415
—	Guido of Amiens	416
—	Disturbances in England	417
—	Bad conduct of regents	419
—	English emigrate	421
—	Others form alliances	422
—	Eustace of Boulogne	423
—	Wales in ferment	424
—	William returns	425
1068	Is resisted at Exeter	426
—	Takes Exeter and conquers Cornwall	428
—	Matilda is crowned in England	429
—	Henry Beauclerc born	430

Chapter X.

WILLIAM'S POLICY—REVOLT OF EDWIN AND MORCAR—FIRST NORTHUMBRIAN CAMPAIGN—DEATH OF ROBERT COMYN—EDGAR ATHELING'S FLIGHT TO SCOTLAND—MALCOLM'S MARRIAGE WITH MARGARET — DANISH INVASION — THE ATHELING RECOGNIZED AS KING OF NORTHUMBRIA — WILLIAM'S SECOND NORTHUMBRIAN CAMPAIGN — FINAL REDUCTION OF THE NORTH — REVOLT OF HEREWARD AND EDWIN — FURTHER CONFISCATIONS — CHURCH MATTERS.

1068—1072.

A.D.		PAGE
1068	Godwin invades England	432
—	William in Wessex	433
—	Quarrels with Edwin	434
1069	The North revolts	435
—	William's methodical campaign	436
—	Takes York	437
—	Malcolm submits	438
—	Castles built in many places	439
—	Further seizures of land	441
—	The Saxon royal family in Scotland	442
—	Margaret marries Malcolm	443
—	The Danes prepare an invasion	444
—	The Normans are discouraged	445
—	William leads a new campaign	446
—	Wessex pacified	447
—	Difficulties in the North	448
—	Comyn killed	449
—	William regains York	450
—	Danish fleet sails	451
—	The Danes reach York	452
—	The castle holds out	453
—	But is taken	454
—	William now goes to the North	455
—	His stern policy	457
—	Holds his court at York	458
—	Grants land to his followers	459
1070	The Danes about Ely	461

CONTENTS.

A.D.		PAGE
1070	William in perplexity	462
—	Secures Durham	463
—	Marches on Chester	465
—	And Sarum	466
—	The English party in the fens	467
—	Hereward and Sweno	468
1071	Peterborough plundered	469
—	Sweno bought off	470
—	William blockades the fen	471
—	Edwin is slain	472
—	English starved out	473
1072	Malcolm aids them	474
—	William invades Scotland	475
—	Malcolm does him homage	476
—	Gospatric	476
—	His earldom given to Waltheof	478
—	New confiscations	479
—	William becomes more tyrannical	481
—	The English in Byzantium	482
—	Church matters	483
—	William censured	484
—	Penance imposed on the Normans	485

Chapter XI.

AFFAIRS OF FLANDERS—WILLIAM SUBDUES MAINE—DISTURBANCES IN ENGLAND—RALPH GUADER'S CONSPIRACY—EXECUTION OF WALTHEOF.

1073—1075.

1051	Flanders	487
—	Baldwin and his family	489
1070	Frieseland	490
—	Richilda	492
1071	Battle of Cassel	493
—	Robert the Frizon	494
1069	Le Mans revolts against William	495
—	The country offered to Albert Azzo	497
—	Further changes in Le Mans	499
—	Sulley; Geoffrey; Gersenda	500

CONTENTS.

A.D.		PAGE
1073	William returns to Normandy	502
—	Takes Le Mans	503
—	William's sons	504
—	Memorial monasteries built at Caen	506
—	New dissatisfactions in England	507
—	The Bretons are discontented	508
1075	A cabal formed: Waltheof	509
—	Waltheof implicated in the plot	511
—	The Normans and English unite	512
—	And the rebellion is put down	514
—	William's vengeance	515
—	Waltheof tried	517
—	And executed	519
—	And venerated	520

CHAPTER XII.

WILLIAM RETURNS TO THE CONTINENT—SIEGE OF DÔL—QUARRELS BETWEEN ROBERT AND HIS FATHER—BATTLE OF GERBEROI—ROBERT'S SECOND OUTBREAK—DISTURBANCES IN NORTHUMBRIA—BISHOP ODO'S IMPRISONMENT—MATILDA'S DEATH.

1075—1083.

1075	Guader's activity against William	523
—	William invades Brittany	524
—	Is repulsed by Fergant	525
—	Marries his daughter to Fergant	526
1081	Adela marries Stephen	527
1078	William and Robert	528
—	Robert's party: Belesmes	530
1075	William invades Perche	531
—	Quarrel of the sons	532
—	Robert goes into opposition	533
—	And leaves his father	535
—	His wanderings	537
1078	William and he in combat at Gerberoi	539
1079	Troubles in Northumbria	540
—	Liulph; Walchere; Leobwine	541
—	Liulph murdered	542

A.D.		PAGE
1080	Walchere and Leobwine also	546
—	Odo pacifies the rebellion	546
—	Malcolm plunders the North	547
—	Robert retaliates	548
—	William de S. Carileph	549
—	See of Durham established	550
1081	Northumbria and Wales	551
—	Odo is led away by ambition	553
—	Aims at the Roman See	554
1082	William jealous	555
—	Odo tried and imprisoned	556
1083	Matilda dies	557

Chapter XIII.

REVOLT IN MAINE—STATE OF DENMARK—DEATH OF CANUTE—CONSEQUENCES OF THE THREATENED DANISH INVASION IN ENGLAND—FORMATION OF THE DOMESDAY SURVEY—GENERAL IMPOSITION OF THE OATH OF FEALTY.

1083—1086.

1084	Affairs of Maine	558
—	William unsuccessful	561
—	State of Denmark	562
—	Canute	563
—	Collects a great fleet	565
1085	William's preparations	566
1086	But the expedition comes to nothing	567
—	Internal position of Denmark	568
—	Olave	569
—	Osbern; Canute slain	571
—	Conclusion of Danish attacks on England	572
—	Administration of England	573
—	Domesday survey	574
—	The book framed	575
—	William imposes fealty on the landholders	577

Chapter XIV.

WILLIAM'S EXPEDITION AGAINST BRITTANY—THE SIEGE OF DÔL—DISPUTE WITH FRANCE ABOUT THE BEAUCASSIN—SIEGE OF MANTES—ILLNESS AND DEATH OF THE CONQUEROR.

1086—1087.

A.D.		PAGE
1086	Affairs of Brittany	579
—	William's unsuccessful invasion	580
—	Quarrel with the Manceaux	581
1087	William fires Mantes	582
—	Is thrown: carried to Rouen	583
—	His dying dispositions	585
—	And death	588
—	The burial of the Conqueror	589

Chapter XV.

RESULTS OF THE CONQUEST.

NEW POLITICAL POSITION OF ENGLAND—SOME CHANGES CAUSED RATHER BY TIME THAN BY CONQUEST—CONTINUITY OF LAW IN ENGLAND—SO-CALLED FEUDAL SYSTEM—WILLIAM'S ADMINISTRATION: IN CHURCH MATTERS: IN THE LAW—MILITARY SERVICES—JUSTICE—EFFECTS OF WILLIAM'S IGNORANCE OF ENGLISH—HIS CHARACTER—POSITION AS LEGAL HEIR TO THE THRONE—FALSE IMPRESSIONS AS TO HIS INNOVATIONS: EXEMPLIFIED BY THE COURSE OF THE ENGLISH LANGUAGE—THE CHURCH IN ENGLAND—LANFRANC—MAMINOT—WILLIAM'S ECCLESIASTICAL APPOINTMENTS.

England, how affected by the Conquest	592
Brought into communion with Europe	593
Specific effects in England overrated	596
Correlative changes elsewhere	597
The law remained substantially unaltered	599
Proofs of this	600

Norman law influenced by English	602
Feudal system: what does it mean?	603
Feudal tenures	605
William's ecclesiastical policy	607
Land tenures in England	610
William as administrator of justice	613
Fails to learn English	614
Effects of this on the law	615
The Court of Chancery	616
Regent Justiciars	618
General attitude of William towards the Constitution	619
Despotism of his administration	621
Compared with his legal position	622
William's general character	624
Popular errors as to the effect of the Conquest	625
Law	626
Curfew	627
Language	628
William did not bring French into England	629
"Anglo-Saxon" language	632
Linguistic changes elsewhere	633
Romance dialect spreads in England	635
Church system under the Saxons	637
William's policy to ecclesiastics	639
Stigand: Saxon bishops	641
Lanfranc's appointment	643
Maminot	645
Remigius	646

APPENDIX.

The Baronial Castles of the Cotentin, Avranchin, and Bessin	649

BOOK II.

CAPETIAN NORMANDY.

Chapter I.

ROBERT KING OF FRANCE—LAST YEARS OF RICHARD SANS-PEUR—ACCESSION OF RICHARD LE-BON—OPENING OF HIS REIGN—REVOLT OF THE PEASANTRY.

987—996.
996—1003.

§ 1. ERE we again approach Richard Sans-peur's grave, let us recapitulate the domestic events and internal affairs occurring during his last years, but whirled away from our pages by the driving storms which wrecked the Carlovingian dynasty.

987—996
Position of Richard Sans-peur, during the concluding period of his reign, ending 996.

Towards the close of the first Richard's lengthened reign, almost all his youth's companions and friends had departed—he might reckon the survivors upon the thumb and fingers of his left hand. Famous Ivo de Belesme was living; but he was soon succeeded by a son, the active, sanguinary, and rebellious William, Count of Alençon. Possibly Osmond de Centvilles, valiant Aymon supporting his old father, may also have hobbled by the side of *Richard le-Vieux,*—for such was the genuine appellation given to the heir of Longue-épée in his own country.—I am almost angry with myself, for having adopted the comparatively modern conventional fashion of denominating him by the more romantic epithet.

Espriota, Richard's mother, her husband Sperling, and their son Raoul.

As to Richard's relatives, first of all must be noticed his mother, Espriota. Since she married Sperling, the rich Miller of Vaudreuil, whom she took to, when discarded for the venomous Liutgarda, by her fickle faithless husband, we hear but little concerning her, until the iron-handed, stony-hearted, resolute Raoul, her only son by her second consort, comes before us.

With respect to the connexion between the Miller and the Duke, and their respective families, we have strong inferential evidence that their mutual intercourse was conducted discreetly on either side. They behaved themselves as sagacious people are wont to do, when a very great disparity in rank exists or arises between near connexions:—either party avoiding rubbing against the other. The bon-homme Sperling, his matron and house-folk, and the Duke and his circle, each kept themselves to themselves, and therefore continued good friends. Sperling was very wealthy, and he bestowed an excellent training upon his son Raoul; the son of Duke William's widow. The education which the young man received fully qualified him to be engrafted upon the stem of Rollo; and the clerkship manifested throughout the Norman Line was equally exhibited by the engrafted Raoul Fitz-Sperling.

Ivri,—Ivri la-Bataille, so picturesquely recollected by the *panache blanc* waving above the

Royal Hero's helm, adjoined Sperling's possessions. The forest abounded with wild animals, as well the weak and harmless, who are therefore persecuted as the legitimate objects of the chase, as those whose ferocity necessitates their destruction; and it came to pass, that when the Duke's courtiers hunted the forest, the strong and supple young Raoul joined the party.

Pursuing their sport in the wildest dells, they roused an enormous bear. Geologists and Zoologists may be interested by this anecdote, testifying that in a zone, where the race has been so long extinct, the ursine genus still survived after the commencement of the era vaguely and unphilosophically termed the "historical period:" a period, which in each particular case, is simply determined by two chances, witnesses able to testify, and the preservation of their testimony. Had not the tribute of wolves' heads been imposed by Edgar upon the recalcitrant Britons, we should know nothing concerning Isengrim's endurance in England until the reign of the Anglo-Saxon Basileus.—His bones, found in the lime-stone fissures, would have grouped him with the hyæna of the tertiary formation.

The huntsmen took flight. Not so the sturdy stripling; he kept his ground, and battled with the monster, whom he slew. The gallants who had fled, returned when the danger was over, honestly relating to Richard Sans-peur the exploit his half brother had performed: and the denomination of *Val Orson*, which the locality acquired, commemorates the achievement, even unto the present day.

Richard I. grants Ivri to Raoul.

Raoul's prowess delighted the Duke: and, as a token of approbation and admiration, he granted to his uterine brother the noble domain of Ivri.—Ivri Forest, and Ivri Town, subsequently to be defended by that awful Castle, which became the wonder and the horror of the country. The Ivri territory was erected into a County: and, loosely as the transaction is noticed, we may, considering the form which the Norman policy was receiving, call attention to the circumstance that this grant is amongst the first recorded creations of a territorial dignity.

Raoul's great ability—Norman history preserved by his exertions.

The ability evinced by Raoul, subsequently to his elevation, was such as to testify that the wise and prudent Sperling had duly estimated his own parental duty. Raoul's encouragement of literature resulted from the direction his mind had received. The Northmen of Normandy were losing the reminiscences of their ancestors; but Count Raoul, raised up when the memory of antient times was fast gliding away, deeply appreciated the dignity of national history.

Raoul the instrument of preserving the antient traditions of the Northmen.

Raoul became the depository of the family traditions: and, at this critical juncture he rescued them from the danger of falling into oblivion. Raoul's patronage gave to Normandy her first historian. It was Raoul who excited Dudo to his task, and dictated the text as it now stands. The honour rendered to the past kindled the imagination of the Normans.

Their old language was yielding to the speech of the land, for the *parlance Danoise* was generally,—even in the Cotentin and the Bessin,—becoming silenced by the polished Romance which had now fully obtained the name of *Norman*,—the badge of a new nationality.

The cultivation which the Norsk language had received from the Skallds was extended to the adopted dialect; and, if the Trouveurs of Normandy took precedence over all their fellows throughout the Langue d'oil, let Raoul be honoured as a main inciter of their energy.

An able statesman, faithful Raoul acquired and deserved his brother's confidence; and, maintaining an honourable station in the world's recollection, continued that fidelity to his brother's children.—But he was stern,—even to cruelty, never allowing his views of policy to be mitigated by mercy.

Raoul becomes his brother's Prime Minister.

As for Albereda, or Aubrée, his wife, her talent suggested the construction of the awful Castle, the edifice through which she acquired an unhappy renown. The real cause of her violent death remains a mystery. She possessed great talent, but contaminated with such extreme violence and bitter ferocity, that her conduct may be considered as indicating insanity.

Albereda, the wife of Raoul—her cruelty.

§ 2. The invidious questions grounded upon lawfulness of descent, often cloud the mediæval annals; and, even at later periods, occasionally perplex the judgment of posterity. In some memorable instances, the stain on the Royal

Legitimacy of birth— perplexity connected with the question.

Standard has been discharged by loyalty, or the bar-sinister effaced from the Royal shield by the valour of the bearer. True it is that the parchments, under which the House of Tudor claimed the English Crown, must have been as rotten rags in the secret judgment of the Lawyer. But the defeat sustained on Bosworth field condemned the claim of Richard, and the dubious graft of the roses flourished in the sunshine of national opinion. Or, if we look to the South, we may equally discern how the infirm pretensions of Braganza were welcomed as affording the means of escape from Castilian tyranny.

The dynastic succession in Normandy continued by bastards.
In Normandy the same question of that condition which we may term spurious legitimacy, enters into the very core of the Ducal history, but receives its solution from the national verdict: and, during Normandy's heroic era, the dynastic succession was continued by the progeny of Ducal Concubines, or females so termed. But the explanation, or rather the cause of these irregularities, may be found in the subsisting influence of the customs prevailing amongst the Belgic, German, or Scandinavian Races, ere they became incorporated in the Christian Commonwealth:— primeval usages, uncouth in aspect, and in themselves somewhat liable to evil report, though neither really reprehensible nor necessarily repugnant to morality.

Marriage amongst antient nations a matter of bargain and sale.
§ 3. Marriage amongst these antient nations was, for the most part, perhaps in all, a cheapening, a purchase, a bargain between the parties

or their friends. Nor should we deride those rough Teutons, for entertaining a principle which they held in common with antient Greece and Rome. It is no satire upon human nature to say, that the seeking to better yourself in marriage is an universal and indelible feeling.—The *Sensale di matrimonio*,—a broker on the Rialto, and sometimes something more,—who figures in the old Italian comedies, followed his vocation openly and lawfully in England, until the days of Queen Anne, when the statute prohibiting "marriage brokage" attests equally the existence of the practice, and the opinion that the usage had given rise to abuse.

<small>987—996</small>

<small>The marriage broker.</small>

Laws cannot alter sentiments, and when Roger North, as plenipotentiary on behalf of his brother, conducted the amatory negotiation for the marriage treaty between the future Lord Keeper, and the Alderman's daughter, the match went off because the civic Magnate stipulated that the full amount of the portion should depend upon the produce: that is to say, that the full payment should be postponed till the appearance of the first Baby. Nor is it an improbable conjecture, but that the gentleman of the long robe, whom in the first scene of *Marriage à la mode*, we see sharpening his pen, may have received a handsome per centage for having managed the ill-omened union.

If a man buy a Maiden with chattels,—as the Dooms of Ethelbert declare,—the bargain must stand, if it be without guile. Let the

<small>Antient Teutonic forms of marriage.</small>

"Capitale," the Cattle driven in by the Bridegroom—sheep, cows, or beeves—be truly told, and free from murrain and rot, or the silver, (equivalent to the value of the heads,) of sterling standard. When Clovis betrothed Clotilda, his ambassadors bought the royal Damsel, by tendering as earnest a Solidus and a Denarius, or, as we should say, a silver shilling, and a silver penny.—Whether the King's daughter or the Shepherd's, the price of every Virgin was equal in the eye of the Salic law.

§ 4. It has been assumed as a fundamental principle of modern missions amongst the Heathen, that Christianity and Civilization should march hand in hand. The advancement of our national interests is proclaimed to be an inducement no less cogent than the diffusion of the Gospel: or, quoting the very words uttered whilst these pages are passing through the press, "the British Flag should ever precede the Missionary, and the Missionary be followed by the bale of merchandise."—We now hold as a clause in our creed, that Evangelization and Civilization should be inseparably combined—yet an enquiring Berean might wish to know how the Preacher who labours to create "artificial wants" is consistent in his doctrine with the Teacher who enjoins us, that, having food and raiment, the Christian should be content.

But the mediæval Church, the Church of the "Dark ages," practically pervaded by gospel spirit, adopted a different principle. Instead of running a muck against antient customs and manners, the primitive Missionaries endeavoured to preserve all practices and usages which were antient and innocent, as tokens of the veneration rendered to the Forefathers by the children. National faith is never firm until it becomes traditional. A Disciple of the Apostolic age might more than doubt whether "Progress," using the term in the sense of its universal employment amongst us, be really a state of mind harmonizing with the humble and childlike obedience inculcated by the whole tenour of Sacred Writ. Even in garb or food, adherence to ancestorial customs is a confession of submission to the will of the Most High, not the less forcible,—perhaps the more,—because rendered by the Living to the Dead, by the Visible to the Invisible.

Those who drink no wine, and plant no Vineyard, and sow no seed, and live in tents, as their Progenitor commanded them, simply rendering obedience to the behest of their Ancestor, have received that blessing which has enabled them to preserve their identity and vitality even to the present day.

The most recent amongst our archæological travellers, encountering the children of Jonadab the son of Rechab,—as faithful now, as in the days of the Prophet,—bears testimony to their prosperity in the Marches, where they were settled by the Babylonian Sovereign. And, whatever may be the individual crimes which stain that mysterious Race, who have adopted "the first Commandment with promise," as the foundation of their Commonwealth, this simple obedience has multiplied the numbers and prolonged the existence of the most numerous amongst the children of Noah; one-third (as it is reckoned) of the Human race, beyond that of any other people on the face of the earth.

Anglo-Saxon form of wedding retained by the Church of England.

§ 5. How the mediæval Missionaries acted with respect to any ethnic custom, innocent and of good report, is still evidenced in the Church of England. When the Bridegroom presents the golden ring,—which, until comparatively recent times, was always accompanied by the silver coin,—as the symbol of the Bride's participation in his worldly goods, he follows the example of Clovis and Clotilda. Even in the simple and affecting wedding words :—" I take thee Mary to my wedded wife, to have and to hold, for richer, for poorer, for better, for worse," —we listen to the echo of the rythmical flow and alliterative resonance of the earliest age. This complete incorporation of an antient and impressive form with the offices of religion, is peculiar to the Anglo-Saxon Church. We may discern in the practice the living kindness of Gregory the Great, fructifying through Saint Augustine's wisdom. The Blessing hallowed the legal form, which thus became binding upon the Christian's conscience, testifying at the same time, his respect for his forefathers.

See Rise and Progress of the English Commonwealth, Vol. II. 135.

A course, somewhat less satisfactory, was pursued in the other Latin Churches. Four

Carlovingian Capitularies direct, that the marriage should receive the Benedictio Sacerdotis; but, it is very probable, that, in many cases, the wedding parties contented themselves with the betrothal according to the Teutonic tradition, without requiring the sanction of the altar. The Church might frown, but the civil marriage satisfied their conscience; and we apprehend that many children who are termed illegitimate by historians, were not thus stigmatized by the opinion of society. This was peculiarly remarkable in Normandy, where the espousal, *more Danico*, was generally accepted by the Laity, as not needing further corroboration.

§ 6. Richard conducted himself kindly and respectfully to the childless and solitary Emma; and, when she departed, he notified the event to her father, Duke Hugh, requesting the despatch of some of the Damsels and Matrons of the French Court, to aid him in distributing her charities. But, whilst Emma's life, since her unhappy espousals, had been wearing away in solitude, Richard ran riot, and a plurality of unknown paramours presented him with a goodly progeny.

Richard's fluttering affections were ultimately fixed on the celebrated Guenora,— a damsel of pure Danish descent; and Dudo's rhetorical language, happily ambiguous, may be construed into an assertion, that her lineage was distinguished by nobility. The details of Richard's adventures with Guenora are such as delight

987—996

Guenora, her parentage and connexions.

the free spoken merry Trouveur; but it is more seemly that they should be elided by the historian. Guenora's father's name is not recorded, though we know all about her. She had a brother, Herfastus, and three sisters, Sainfrida, Gueva, and Adelina. The eldest of these damsels, distinguished by her beauty, became the wife of Richard's Forester, who dwelt at Secheville near Arques. The report of her loveliness reached the Court: and Richard visited the Forester's lodge with a dishonest intent. Sainfrida, wise and chaste, escaped the snare, and the adventure terminated by the lusty Duke taking to Guenora, not less attractive than her sister.

Circumstances of the courtship and marriage.

We receive the narrative of Richard's amours with Guenora from two informants. The one presents us with a tale of intrigue more credible than creditable—the second and graver narrative, we owe to the Dean of Saint Quentin, who is discreetly silent concerning any incidents which might offend the family. When Guenora was first introduced as the sharer of Richard's affections, he reserved the privilege of fickleness, avoiding any permanent engagement which might be binding, whether according to the municipal jurisprudence, or the precepts of the Church. But his Nobles were mindful of the national interests. Richard must neither live heirless, nor die so; and this was one of the rare cases when a state marriage can be sweetened by affection. The Normans were proud of their progenitors. The adoption of French manners and French customs did not diminish the worship due to ancestry; and they urged the Duke to contract a legitimate marriage, which tie he had hitherto avoided. They therefore earnestly exhorted him to espouse the Damsel, as a measure tending to popularity. Guenora would give him children of pure Danish blood—father and mother belonging to the conquering race. Thus would he gratify the popular appetite for pleasant illusions; a policy constituting an essential element in the science of government. When the Monarch is inclined to be gracious, a very small tincture of concession accomplishes the end. George the Third declared to his Parliament, that he gloried in being a Briton: an assertion, poetically admissible in the days when Britannia ruled the waves. And, if at Hanover, the "Churfurst Georg" had gloried in being the descendant of Arminius, the effect amongst the Germans would have been the same.

987—906

Richard urged by his nobles to contract a lawful marriage.

§ 7. Guenora's first born received, at his mother's request, his father's name. This Richard is known, dynastically, as Richard le-Bon, or Richard the Second.

Children of Richard Sans-peur.

Robert, Guenora's second son, died young; his curious memorial was discovered at Fecamp, towards the beginning of the last century. The tomb has been since destroyed; but if admitted as coeval, we have to lament the loss, since the Revolution, of the earliest certificated sepulchral

967—996 monument in Normandy, the more interesting as it exhibited a Lion, apparently employed as a device or bearing.

Further account of the children. Robert thus prematurely cut off, another Robert was in due time nursed upon Guenora's knee. Long did he live, and in common language, prosperously; but he would have left a better report, had he, like his brother, died an infant.

Richard's immediate descendants were numerous, but the antient authorities and the modern genealogists are at variance amongst themselves and contradictory to each other. The *status* of adventurous William, the bastard of Normandy, is disclosed by his epithet.—Geoffrey, said to be the ancestor of the Earls of Clare, falls in the same category. Mauger, who acquired much importance in French affairs, was assuredly legitimate. *The daughters of Normandy.* Richard's daughters contributed as much as their brothers to the brilliancy of the family. The fine well-grown Norman women of Rollo's lineage, wooed by grandees and sovereigns, were renowned for their comeliness. It became a species of proverb that the race of Rollo gained as much by the fascinations of the damsels as by the prowess of the sons. The daughters of Guenora inherited their mother's bright charms; Maude, Countess of Tours Blois and Champagne; —Havisa, Duchess of Brittany;—and the brisk, buxom, commanding Emma, the "Alfgiva Emma" —twice the Regnant Queen, and twice the Dowager of England.

Royal heirs,— heirs apparent,— are not

always comforts to their parents; Richard's *987—996* father and grandfather had each in their turn much cause for anxiety.—Troubled was Rollo when he resigned his authority to the blooming son, the only son, Guillaume Longue-épée. Sorrowfully, and with many cankering cares, did Guillaume Longue-épée provide for securing the succession to his only son Richard: and Richard Sans-peur, in his turn, might anticipate a troubled and clouded future. The right of Primogeniture, though admitted, was not indefeasible, even in the Royal Family. A bevy of stout and growing youths might contest the Coronal; and, like the Carlovingian Empire, the House of Rollo be distracted by fraternal enmity. It was a difficult problem how to satisfy the expectations of the brothers. But a way opened through which Richard's uneasiness might receive a partial sedative, if not a cure: one son, at least, could obtain a competent provision, without impairing the integrity of the Duchy. *Claims of Richard's sons for proper provisions.*

§ 8. The Norman Church, at this period, presented a most unedifying aspect. The disturbances of the country, the Danish devastations, the irregularities of a mixed and floating population, and the absence of any moral restraint, had disordered the whole system. Provincial Councils or Synods, had wholly ceased; nor were any held in Normandy until the Conqueror's reign. Had they assembled, they would have been mischievous. The forms of ecclesiastical government, when they have lost their hold on the national conscience, are mere delusions; *Church of Normandy— disorders thereof.*

16   DISORDERS OF THE NORMAN CHURCH.

987—996 nor can the principles or the practice of any Church ever acquire stability, except when she firmly demands obedience from her members. When she hesitates, she is next to lost. Her gentlest persuasions should be accepted as commands. Unless the Priest can lay down the law like the Judge, he had better let the law alone.—The Monks, with few exceptions, were destitute of discipline, the regular Canons, worse. Tosspots they would have been called in old Latimer's language, constantly lapsing into drunkenness and disorder.

942—994 Hugh Archbishop of Rouen. All observance of canonical election had disappeared. It did not tell for much any where; but in isolated Normandy the principle was wholly ignored. The rights of the Regale were rampant; and whether by management, but oftener by direct and absolute power, it was the Duke's Clerk who ascended the episcopal throne. Hugh, who, placed in the See of Rouen by Guillaume Longue-épée, held the dignity till nearly the close of Richard's reign, wasted and dissipated the property of the Church, and surrendered himself wholly to gross sensuality. Richard acted as patrons are accustomed, and therefore he, the Sovereign, determined to provide for his son Robert in the Church. Yet he had some regard for decency. At an early age the lad was put to book, and trained for his future vocation as carefully as his father's opportunities would afford. At length Hugh's expected death ensued, and Richard presented his son

994. Upon Hugh's death Richard

to the dignity. He possessed as much authority as any King of France; nay, greater. Time had not yet matured those usages and practices, which, enshrined in an antient Monarchy, convert the exercise of prerogative into an institution, modified or restrained by precedent, at the same time that they strengthen the hands of the King. The Norman Duke was a constitutional Despot. No need had Richard to consult his Nobles in this affair of patronage: nor does it appear that the Citizens of Rouen retained any prescriptive right of participating in the nomination of their spiritual Chief, approximating to the influence enjoyed by the antient Municipality, who guarded the Shrine of Saint Remy. Yet, in this case, an exception was taken by the Clergy. Not that they contested the Patron's power, nor were they scandalized by the Candidate's nonage, but they denied his eligibility, on the ground that he was incapacitated by bastardy.

§ 9. According to the Civil law, the injury inflicted upon the innocent offspring by the erring parents who gave them birth, is not irreparable.—A subsequent marriage legitimates all the previous concubinary issue.—Such is the subsisting law in Scotland, England being the only portion of the Western Church, where this charitable doctrine never did prevail.—The proposal made, in the reign of the third Henry, for catholicising our common-law jurisprudence, was repudiated under circumstances which rendered

VOL. III. C

967—996 the sturdy resistance of the Temporality to the dictation of the Clergy, an era in our Constitu-

1235 20 Hen. III., the Prelates and Barons in the Parliament of Merton refuse to change the laws of the Realm.

tional history.—For when the Archbishop of Canterbury, and his Bishops and Suffragans, and the Earls and Baronage of England, were assembled in the famous Parliament of Merton, and the law was settled upon various important points requiring amendment, all the Bishops thereupon instanced the Earls and Barons, that they would consent that all such as were born afore matrimony, should be legitimate, as well as they that be born after matrimony, as to the succession of inheritance, forasmuch as the Church accepted their legitimation.—And then did all the Earls and Barons reply with one thundering voice, they would not change the laws of England, which hitherto had been used and approved.—"*Nolumus leges Angliæ mutare, quæ usitatæ sunt et approbatæ.*"

Richard and Guenora marry canonically, whereby their children are legitimated.

But, in Normandy, the way was open for removing the canonical difficulties in this particular case. Richard forthwith assented to the suggestion made by the Priesthood. A marriage between him and Guenora was celebrated before the altar : and, according to a symbolical usage which still obtains in Scotland, all the children of the hitherto unsanctified union were sheltered beneath the flowing mantle of the matronly bride. Robert, the disqualification thus removed, was forthwith seated on the Archiepiscopal throne. Hugh, Robert's predecessor, was so far decent as to be a Priest in garb. Robert did not make even any pretence [987—996] to the clerical character. He married a wife, and obtained in due time the County of Evreux: —and from him, as after mentioned, came the Devreux family.

§ 10. Great were Richard Sans-peur's natural gifts, manifest and manifold his pleasant qualities; urbane, and fairly right-minded as a Sovereign, or seeking to be so. Happy with the hawk on his wrist, or the leash in his fist; kind, though his kindness did not always restrain him from cruelty. Jovial with the Jougleur, popular with the Priest, singularly had the education bestowed by his father's forethought profited to him, adapting him for the peculiar condition, presented by the political as well as the social state of Normandy.—Richard Sanspeur, first of the name, must be contemplated as the last Duke of Danish Normandy, whilst his son Richard, the second bearing that name, is the first Duke of Norman Normandy; the State holding the highest position in the political Hierarchy of the French Monarchy.

[Richard Sans-peur's natural gifts.]

A man is as many times a man as he knows many languages, quoth Charles-le-Quint,—speaking to us in the old books of moral apophthegms and wise saws, now discarded from the educational series,—perhaps not much for the better.—There are, at all events, those who begin privately to suspect,—for they dare not speak out,—that the lessons upon stocks and stones are not quite so fruitful as the study of mankind and man. The saying of Charles-le-Quint is, however, true or untrue, according to the recipient's capacity. If the student be wise, linguistic knowledge becomes a sure encrease of wisdom to him; if unwise, he is rendered a polyglot of folly.

Diffusion and cultivation of the French or Romance language in Normandy.

Equally was the second Richard versed in the venerable dialect of his ancestors, and in the Romane speech, now vernacular, though the need of the first qualification had become less urgent. Men could speak Norsk, but Norsk was not much spoken; and the pleasant language emphatically called "French" or the *Langue d'oc*, developed in various idioms, had ripened into consistency. The primitial specimens of the Norman *Langue d'oil*, eldest amongst the Romane modes of speech applied to literary purposes, are, as is almost invariable in similar examples, versions of the Holy Scriptures. The Cambridge Psalter, and the Parisian Codex of the Book of Kings,—both in the Norman dialect,—contend for antiquity. Textually, these curious relics cannot date before the eleventh century, but the regularity of their grammatical construction testifies a lengthened antecedent period of cultivation.

Cordiality between the Houses of Capet and of Rollo.

Very powerfully did this diffusion of the French ethos co-operate in consolidating Normandy with the other regions of Franco-Gallia. The new dynasties of Rollo and of the Beccajo had become thoroughly allied. The grudges of the Carlovingian era were sent to sleep, and the *entente cordiale* between the two Houses, which had subsisted since the day when the young Richard "commended" himself to Hugh le-Grand, and submitted to his marriage with Emma, continued undisturbed.

<small>987—996</small>

Richard Sans-peur, the prosperous Sovereign of a prosperous land, was the first among the Norman Dukes who struck money; and the "Sol Rouennois," ranks amongst the rarest of the tiny treasures coveted by the French Numismatist. Rapidly did the hammered coin circulate.—No rigid Raoul Torta stood by the Duke's side to check the expenditure. Each of Richard's Esquires received, day by day, nine of these sweetly ringing pieces of silver.

<small>Richard Sans-peur first amongst the Norman Dukes who coined money.</small>

§ 11. Richard Sans-peur being profuse in all ways, he bestowed a large portion of his wealth in re-endowing the decayed and dilapidated Monastic foundations, which, for the most part, had sunk into a miserable state of degradation, poverty, and dissoluteness. But a healthier spirit was reviving, and Fecamp, Richard's birthplace, became peculiarly the object of his care.

It chanced, that when standing on the lofty perron of the tall Ducal Palace, he looked down upon the mean, decayed, and neglected Church, the memorial of his poor father's pitiful vacillations: and it seemed to him a scandal, that the proud Mansion which Guillaume Longue-épée had reared, should affront the lowly House of Prayer. And he bethought himself

<small>Fecamp rebuilt by Richard Sans-peur.</small>

that he would rebuild the Church with decent magnificence. The details of the transaction are reported by Dudo de Saint Quentin with much particularity. The terms employed in the original text are remarkable, as shewing the distinctness of the Masonic calling, and the talent and skill which the Craft demanded. The diligent inquiry for a competent architect, made by the Duke's directions, proves that qualified masters of the science were rare.—The selected Brother carefully surveyed the surrounding country; nor did he commence his work until he had ascertained that the hills furnished quarries of gypsum and good limestone also.

Precious are these first explicit notices elucidating Neustrian architecture in Norman times. The only information we possess concerning the raising of a building in Normandy before the Normans came there, relates to Saint Ouen, in the old, old days of the Merovingian Clothaire. We are told that the edifice was constructed of well squared masonry, and by a Gothic hand —"*miro opere, quadris lapidibus, Gothica manu*" —the "Goth" being unquestionably a Master mason from Lombardy or the Exarchate.

The existing Abbatial Church of Fecamp, erected subsequently to Richard's age, still stands conspicuous as the most extensive in Normandy; and, towards the east end, the fabric probably retraces the lines of the original structure. The costly new Basilica was splendid; adorned by lofty towers, beautifully finished without, and richly ornamented within. But the moral re-edification was far more important than the material. The regular Canons, who had sadly degenerated into sloth and sin, were ejected, —and a Colony of Benedictines from Clugny, under the guidance of Saint Mayolus, rendered the renovated Fecamp pre-eminent for sanctity and learning.

967—996

Moral renovation of Fecamp.

There was one object however, which excited much speculation. It was a large block of stone, placed right across the path which led to the transept door-way, so close to the portal, as to be beneath the drip of the eaves; or, at all events, within the splash of the stream gushing on rainy days from the queer wide mouth of the projecting gurgoil, stretching out his long neck. Fashioned and located by Duke Richard's order, the stone was hollowed out so as to form a huge, strong, chest; which might be used either as a coffin or a sarcophagus. Its present employment, however, was for the living, not the dead. On the eve of every Lord's day, the chest, or whatever it might be called, was filled to the brim with the finest wheat-corn; then a cate, or luxury, as it is now considered in many parts of France. To this receptacle, the poor resorted, and each filled his measure of grain, and into each open hand were dropped five dulcet-chinking pennies: whilst the lame and the bed-ridden were visited by the Almoner as he made his rounds through Fecamp town, and by each was the dole received.

The chest of stone across the pathway.

§ 12. Some few years subsequent to this re-foundation of Fecamp, Richard's health declined. His constitution broke up. Painful disease ensued: he retired to a Ducal residence in the neighbourhood of Bayeux,—according to tradition in the pleasant village of Noron,—a neighbourhood consecrated by the reminiscences of early youth.—Worse and worse did the sinking old man become. More pain, more debility; and he requested to be conveyed to Fecamp Palace, close to the Abbey, he suggesting this removal for the purpose of avoiding, as he declared, the agitation which would be occasioned in a populous town, by the Sovereign's demise, and the trouble and disturbance attending the funeral. Yet these reasons are scarcely adequate, and we suspect he was actuated by a political motive; namely, to guard against the possibility that the important proceedings for effecting the settlement of the Ducal succession might be troubled by any factious party gathered in the Capital of the Danishry.

At Fecamp, Richard's strength failed rapidly, and his brother Raoul of Ivri, and his other Nobles assembled.—No parallel case had yet occurred.—When Rollo was dying, there could be no doubt who should succeed him, Guillaume Longue-épée was his only son.—When Guillaume Longue-épée departed, he left no other heir except the fearless boy, between whose tender hands, the three Chief Nobles had performed the act of fealty—but many were the sons by more than one mother, who might contest all or part of Richard Sans-peur's Duchy. The order of succession was considered as depending upon the father's will and pleasure: the right of primogeniture not being acknowledged as indefeasible.

987—996

The Nobles, therefore, sought that the departing Prince should declare his will. Counsellors and friends congregated round the bed-side. Raoul of Ivri spake for the rest, and humbly and kindly supplicated that Richard would be pleased to nominate the one amongst his sons who should inherit the "Monarchy?"—"He who bears my name, let him be your Duke—your Ruler."

He appoints his eldest son and namesake, Richard II., his successor.

Another question ensued—and, as to the brothers?—Richard having fully considered this delicate point and determined how he could provide for them without dismembering the Duchy, was prepared to answer the question.

The doctrine of "Commendation," so impressively taught by Hugh le-Grand, was fully accepted in his son-in-law's great Province, destined to become the thorn in the side of the Capets.—Let them take the oaths of fealty, said the dying man, addressing Count Raoul,—acknowledge Richard as their superior: and, placing their hands in their brother's hands, receive from him those domains which I shall name to thee.

Richard's worldly affairs thus settled, his sufferings became sharper, yet he rose from his bed, and clothing himself in sackcloth, crept to the Church, and kneeling before the Altar, placed his gifts thereon: and then Count Raoul instanced him to give directions for his funeral.

Richard takes order for his interment.

Richard had long bethought himself concerning the deposit of his corpse. In many of the ecclesiastical provinces of Western Christendom, the very antient canons—still generally enforced among the Eastern Churches,—forbidding that the House of God should be defiled by decay and foulness—a law dictated equally by good sense and reverence—were not obsolete. The awful cemetery of "*Arli sul Rodano,*" the Aliscamps, that solemn field of the dead, manifests at the present day, though defaced and degraded, how strictly the prohibition was obeyed in Southern Gaul. Cospatrick's tomb, lying without the walls of Saint Cuthbert's Minster, dimmed by the humid atmosphere, embedded in the damp lush turf, and curtained by the grey sky's canopy, attests the same feeling. But the practice of rendering a mistaken honour to mouldering bones and corruption was rapidly becoming prevalent. Prelates were interred within the walls—Sovereigns as frequently.—Geoffrey Plantagenet is deposited in his Cathedral.—Rollo rests in Rouen Choir, Guillaume Longueépée, nigh his father,—not so Guillaume's son.

Inter-mural interment not practised in the early ages of the Church.

People might have perhaps already formed shrewd conjectures concerning the ultimate destination of that huge monolith, the receptacle of the weekly dole, standing so strangely athwart the lichgate; and now all doubts were solved. Richard's last instructions were that the chest should contain his corpse, lying where the foot should tread and the dew should descend, and the waters of heaven should fall.—He died on the feast of Saint Maxentia.

996—1003

20 Nov. 996— Death of Richard Sans-peur.

§ 13. RICHARD LE-BON came to the Duchy with a good name, inherited from his popular father. With him, commences a new era, of which he was equally the fashioner and the fashioned, signalized by the thorough assimilation of Normandy to the French community.

Robert reigning in France, Richard performed homage by "Parage," of which more hereafter. —First amongst the lay Peers, his precedency was never contested, and he welcomed the King of France, not simply as a Suzerain, but as an ally and friend. The influences were operating which produced a new state of society;—new constitutional doctrines, new institutions, and new social feelings, and peculiarly so with respect to the civil hierarchy.—No one who possesses the distinction of antient descent, a pre-eminence beyond the power of man to grant, imparted alone by the Creator, can forget the inherent prerogative given by the ancestral blood which flows in his veins. Yet, hitherto, the Danish conquerors or their offspring, do not seem to have insisted stringently or offensively upon the political or social privileges of nobility. The deck is a great leveller of distinctions:—they are in abeyance amidst the howling of the wind and the

Assimilation of Normandy and France commenced during the reign of Richard II., or "le-Bon."

28 ACCESSION OF RICHARD LE-BON.

<small>996—1003</small> tossing of the waves:—and, to a great extent, the Danes continued seamen upon the land.

<small>Rise of the Norman nobility.</small> During the twenty years that Richard le-Bon ruled Rollo's sovereignty, a new combination of elements ensued. Henceforward, the Norman annals abound with those historical Names, rendered illustrious by the illusions of time, and the blazonry which imagination imparts. With few exceptions, the principal Baronial families of Normandy arose during this reign. The fading reminiscences of Scandinavia became fainter. And, in the next generation, those relationships were established between young Normandy and decrepid England, destined to accomplish the renovation of the latter community, through the accession of Richard's conquering grandson to the Anglo-Saxon throne.

<small>Apanages of Richard Sans-peur's children.</small> Richard fully and fairly executed or conformed to his father's testamentary dispensations in favour of his brothers, nay encreased their endowments by his bounty. We find them all <small>Geoffrey, Count of Eu.</small> in high estate. Geoffrey acquired the County of Eu, the Marchland between Ponthieu and the Rouennois, and the noble Seigneurie of Brionne, which afterwards was reckoned amongst the strongest fortresses of this northern frontier.

Mauger, much distinguished by his policy and valour, was invested with the extensive County of Mortaigne as an inheritance, whilst, through marriage, he obtained Corbeil.

William, whose course was much chequered,

was in the first instance guerdoned with the opulent territory of Hiesmes; that lost, he received another endowment from Richard's liberality.

996—1003

Robert, the clever Archbishop of Rouen, had already a good provision: He espoused, according to the Danish fashion,—for assuredly no priest would give the benediction,—a damsel named Herleva, by whom he had many children. It is not clearly ascertained whether he obtained the County of Evreux during the lifetime of Richard Sans-peur his father, or whether his brother, Richard le-Bon, bestowed this endowment, causing him to be styled the Count Archbishop. A great-grandaughter ultimately brought this County into the Montfort Family.

Robert, Archbishop of Rouen and Count of Evreux.

Three sons had Archbishop Robert.—Richard, the eldest, became Count of Evreux, and was enrolled amongst the Conqueror's followers; from him originated the baronial branch of Devreux.

Sons of the Count Archbishop Robert, viz., Robert Devreux, Ralph Gace or Tête-d'âne, and Guillaume.

Ralph Wace or Gace, the Count Archbishop's second son, colloquially designated Tête-d'étoupe, or Tête-d'âne, was invested with the high hereditary dignity of Grand Connétable, and became the ancestor of a very powerful and truculent family.

The third son of the Archbishop was Guillaume, the companion of Robert Guiscard,—whose veritable portrait should display him as armed with bowie knife and revolver:—he is prominent amongst the Apulian Baronage.

996—1003

Guenora's kindred were much favoured by open-hearted Richard le-Bon.—Richard's uncle, Herfastus, Guenora's brother, was enriched with those ample possessions, which, through his son, established the renowned family of Fitz Osborne.

Adelina and Gueva sisters of Guenora.

§ 14. Adelina and Gueva, Richard le-Bon's maternal aunts, respectively espoused Osmond de Bolbec, and Thorold the son of Torf, grandson of Bernard the Dane; but the lineage was now thoroughly Romanized. Thorold became Baron of Pont-audemer. Employing the Herald's scientific phraseology, his descendants "gave" a very clever "canting coat," a bridge, crossing a conventional similitude of water, which we must accept as suggesting the sea, over which same bridge a bold Lion is pacing; and there is some other clench about the local name.

These "canting coats," phonographic hieroglyphics as they may be called, are excellent aids to the memory: and the historical student, bewildered in the labyrinths of genealogy, might wish that the fancy had been more prevalent.—The Beaumonts, Counts of Mellent, and numerous other illustrious branches started from this ramification of old Bernard's progeny.

Prosperity of the families descending from the Guenora connexion.

Guenora should be pourtrayed in full length by the side of the branching stem, whence sprung the best families in noble Normandy. All the Houses founded by her own progeny, or her father's progeny, or her mother's progeny. Brothers and sisters, Brothers-in-law and sisters-in-law; Sons-in-law and daughters-in-law;

Uncles genuine and uncles *à la mode de Bretagne,* or as we should say "Welsh uncles;" asked and got, and spread themselves over the lands at the Duke's disposal.—Giffords and Tankervilles, Gourneys and Baskervilles, Limesay and Lindsay, Saint Sidoine and Centvilles, Warrene and Tillieres, Moubray and Mortimer, were branches, or suckers, or seedlings, who sprung or were raised from the Forest of Arques. _{996—1003}

Indeed, all the principal Baronial families, originated, or made themselves, or put themselves in evidence, during the reign of Richard le-Bon. Never was any region more peopled with men of known names, known deeds, known passions, known crimes, than antient Normandy. You can hardly meet a man whom you do not recognize as an acquaintance when he mentions his name.—He needs no other introduction. You are constantly *en päis de connoissance,* constantly at home, and this knowledge of the dramatis personæ compensates in a very considerable degree for the scantness of information concerning the early Norman laws and institutions, a scantness contrasting singularly with the abundance of our English constitutional knowledge. _{Rise of the Baronial families—abundance of information concerning them.}

§ 15. From Ethelbert's days, Dooms and Documents, Laws and Land books exist, enabling us to recognize distinctly the main features of the English Commonwealth, and the ranks, attributes, and duties appertaining to the various ranks and orders of Anglo-Saxon society. High or low, laic or cleric, churl or earl, who they were and what they were, and their relations towards each other, and towards their Sovereign. The very apices of our antient laws can be deduced from the old times, notwithstanding all their mutations and expansions, whether by positive legislation, or influential custom. If we ascribe Trial by jury to Alfred's wisdom, and derive the Constitution of the Commons from the Witenagemot, we are fairly correct in our general reasoning, though we begin by accepting ideal representations and apocryphal traditions.

Quite otherwise in the antient Terra Normannorum. There we know nothing concerning the laws of the land, the Courts of justice, or the mode of procedure,—save an Oriental tradition—a Horror,—and a Hurrah.—The three legal Legends concerning Rollo, the lawgiver, contain all the information transmitted relating the primeval legislation of Normandy. Yet naught have we seen or heard besides the bracelets glittering in the sun, suspended from the branches of the trees on the brink of the Roumare,—and the gallows forks between which the thievish Churl of Longpaon and his vicious wife are hung,—whilst the "Clameur de Haro" alone breaks the silence.

The Norman antiquary delves for the records of his country anterior to the reign of Philip Augustus, but none are found in the Trésor des Chartes of Paris, or the Hotel de Ville at Rouen, whilst the English Custos stumbles upon the earliest muniments of the *996—1008* Duchy, in the days of Henry-Fitz-Empress: the dusty, musty, cobwebed membranes—the Rolls preserved in the antient English Treasury of the Exchequer at Westminster, though recording the Norman revenue.

Strange and singular indeed is the fact, that, save and except some very trivial breathings, we scarcely possess any knowledge of Norman jurisprudence, until Normandy is lost to the Anglo-Norman line. The proverbially litigious Province cannot produce any substantive evidence of her laws until she becomes a portion of France, when a popular belief arises that the elements of her Code have been previously supplied from vanquished England.

No distinct information concerning the laws or customs of Normandy until after the reign of Philippe-Auguste.

The "*très ancienne Coûtume de Normandie,*" is venerated by the monks of Saint Evroul as dictated by the Confessor's wisdom.—Ask the Norman archæologist for the muniments of his Constitution, and he might proffer, as their foundation,—not the *Charte Normande* of Louis Hutin,—but a Norman exemplar of Magna Charta: an exemplar, *mutatis mutandis,* word for word with our own, securing to the Church of Normandy the liberties of the Church of England, and adapted to the Rouen meridian, by substituting the name of Rollo's Capital for London.

At length, in the age of Montesquieu and Mably, a learned advocate of the Norman Parliament, he who rejoices in the noble name of "Howard," proclaims the recovery of the long lost national legislation in the venerable volumes which we inherit from Bracton, and Britton, and Fleta, and Littleton.—He dreams that he discovers the Northman's code in our English standard authorities—in the forms of English procedure—in the decisions of English Judges and Justiciaries,—in the relics of the Anglo-Saxon laws,—and in the tenures, purely English, as the forms and practices were settled and altered by the English Parliament, or the doctrines matured by the wisdom of Westminster Hall.

§ 16. The engulfment of all legal memorials, nay, of all information, during a period comparatively so recent as the reigns of the natural and kindly Norman Dukes, from Rollo to John Lackland, is an unparalleled historical phenomenon. Yet the history of Normandy offers a living revelation of her institutions as they worked in real Norman times. Textually, the laws have disappeared, but we can attain to their general character by social and moral induction. The atmosphere refracts the image of the objects which are below the horizon. The general state of the Country comes to our aid, and discloses the constitutional principles—employing the term constitutional in the widest sense—which then were ruling. The Hotel de Ville charter-chest is empty, but the traditions of the Municipalities sufficiently declare, that the Roman organization was impressed upon these communities, and guided their internal government.—The existence of the opulence, which, displayed by the Rouen

Burghers, tantalized Louis d'Outremer's greedy soldiery, and teazed them the more when he denied them the licence of plunder, enables us to pronounce that the machinery which promoted such an acquisition of wealth, must have been wisely planned, and effectually worked. Lastly, the military strength acquired by the Burghers, whilst cultivating the industrial arts, affords full evidence of the freedom they enjoyed.—Stout their grateful hearts, and earnest the affection for their Fatherland, which strengthened the warriors who manned the ramparts, when Flanders, France, and Germany combined against the Norman Commonwealth. *996—1003*

Annual Mercantile Fairs were accustomed in Normandy. Established by usage and utility, ere recognised by the law, their origin bespake a healthy energy. Foreign manufacturers were welcomed as settlers in the Burghs,—the richer the better.—No grudge entertained against the Fleming; and the material prosperity of the country and the briskness of commerce carried on in all the great towns, proves that the pack horses could tramp along the old Roman roads with facility. Indeed, amongst the Normans, commercial spirit was indigenous. The Danes and the folk of Danish blood were diligent traders. The greed of gain unites readily with desperate bravery. When occasion served, gallant Drake would deal like a Dutchman.—Any mode of making money enters into facile combination with the bold rapacity of the Flibusteer. *Commercial prosperity of Normandy.*

996—1003

Norman peasantry.

§ 17. No direct information has been transmitted concerning the customs regulating the occupation of the glebe. Yet, pursuing this deduction of the unknown from the known, we may assert that the tenures and usages under which the successors of the Roman *Coloni* enjoyed their lands, were easy and unoppressive. Well to do, and thriving, were the Norman peasantry, bearing themselves as freemen in all which constitutes the Freeman's pride. No other condition could have created those bold and stalwart rustics, sturdy and loyal, who swung their flails, and flashed their scythe blades, and wielded their clubs, when they hacked and mashed and battered the Germans, in the green lanes of Bihorel and Maromme; or, joyfully obeying their Sovereign's call, plunging with him into the splashing fords of the Dieppe water, and conducting him triumphantly to his Palace at Rouen.

Character of Richard le-Bon.

§ 18. Such was the state of the population over whom Richard was called to reign. Fair was the good report inherited by Richard from his father, and he encreased it.—As evidence of character royal epithets do not stand for much, but if "Sans-peur" sounds heroic, "le-Bon" is sweeter.—He suited his people, and pleased their taste. A merry Duke; a liberal Duke; and who did not in any wise make himself a disagreeable example. *Vive Henri quatre! Vive ce roi galant!* The darling hero of France won his subjects' good-will quite as much by his failings as by his bravery;

and between him, and the Norman Dukes generally, there was much in common. In one respect, however, Richard le-Bon departed widely from the doctrines by which his ancestors had been guided. Hitherto, whilst the principles of aristocracy were accepted as the foundation of politic society, yet, in no part of Western Christendom, had these principles degenerated into any invidious distinctions between free-man and free-man, more worrying and teasing than absolute tyranny.—All were *"hof-fæhig,"*—thank you Vienna, thank you Berlin, for the term, no English tongue could have compounded it!

996—1003

Hereditary aristocracy not necessarily exclusive.

Nobility did not yet constitute a closed Caste, requiring to be bred in and in: and the determined repudiation of such a doctrine, has been the most influential amongst the moral causes of British prosperity. That the father should ennoble, and the mother enfranchise, is an intelligible dogma, not involving any degradation. Assuredly, low birth and coarse manners might combine to render a favourite unpopular, as in Hagano's case: and when can such favouritism be otherwise? Yet, the necessity of absolute purity of blood—an aristocracy of the aristocracy—was not admitted as a normal principle in Normandy. No one had been excluded from the Ducal presence or from the Ducal favour by the absence of this qualification, nor can we trace any approximation to its existence, until this period, when the landscape begins to be rendered gay by the bursting blossoms of chivalry.

§ 19. Richard le-Bon, however, departing from ancestorial precedents, would admit none but pure Gentlemen into the Court circle.—No office was to be enjoyed otherwise than by a Gentleman.—About the Duke's person, none but gentlemen must figure; not some gentlemen, but none other than gentlemen.—A gentleman, the Chaplain who mumbles the early morning mass;—a gentleman, the clerk, who drives the pen in the Chancery;—a gentleman, the High Seneschal, who bears the first dish;—a gentleman, the chief Butler, who fills the Duke's mazer;—a gentleman, the Marshal, who rules kennel and stable;—a gentleman the Chamberlain, who stands by the Duke's bed-side;—and a gentleman, the Usher, who holds the latch of the door, and kicks away every intruder. Every member of the Household was fed and clad by the Duke, drawing his rations, receiving his robes. And, at every great Feast, the garments (the "Livery," *par excellence*) were delivered out; their materials of the best quality.

The workings of this ungracious principle were neutralized amongst the higher and more substantial ranks, by the general institutions of the country.—The Clergy possessed an indefeasible position; nor had the rights of Christian equality been affronted by that miserable jealousy which became embodied in the heraldic doctrine of the "sixteen quarters;" the absence of which condition incapacitated Louis Quatorze from becoming a Canon of Strasbourg, by reason of the defilement his blood had received 996—1003 through his plebeian grandmother, Marie de Medicis, and her mercantile ancestry.

The Bourgeois had a pride of his own, which enabled him to snub the Courtier's morgue. He clapped his hands upon his well filled pouch, and was clad with the importance appertaining to the member of a powerful community; but the bad feelings generated by this exclusiveness operated with unmitigated potency upon the tillers of the land. *(This new aristocratical principle falls peculiarly oppressively on the peasantry.)*

§ 20. At this era, the larger portion of the *Terra Normannorum* may be mapped as Bush and Back-wood; so wide and broad were the Forests which covered the face of the country. Forest-land either under your feet, or included within your horizon: though you would not always recognize it as such, according to the conversational notions conveyed by the familiar term of Forest-land.

Amongst the infinite varieties of word-delusion, rendering speech so often the means of confusing our ideas, perhaps there is none more extensive, or detrimental to clearness of conception than when the connotation of thought, denoted by a written word, remaining unaltered, is either contracted or expanded through usage, so as no longer to fit the original meaning. Such is the term "Forest:"—a Forest, during the mediæval era implied, not simply wood-land, but marsh and moor, and rough land *(Forest—application of the term according to mediæval phraseology.)*

and heath, excluded from the speeding of the plough.

Forests and Forest law.

For the most part, the Norman Forests were Ducal domains. Previously to the Danish settlement, the forests were probably communal lands; the Roman legislation having combined with the agricultural systems of the Gauls.

But, even amongst the heathens, no attempt had ever yet been made to restrain the enjoyment of the gifts of God, which no human law can really invest with the attributes of individual property. Rights must be defined by law, yet all human legislation should be consonant to the great truth, that the Earth, and the fulness of the Earth, is the Lord's. Man is never otherwise than an accountable usufructuary. In this high sense, no human being whatever has a right to do what he will with his own. And, whenever human laws are such as to provoke our fellow creatures to sin, that sin lies at the Legislator's door.

Limitation of the rights of property by principle.

Game laws.

Hard indeed is it to establish the proposition that the wild Deer, which flees from the face of man, can be any man's property, like the Ox who knows his master's crib. Or that the possessors of the soil can exclusively demand as theirs, the fowls of the air, who are fed by their and our Father; or the fishes in the teeming stream, the creatures who never hear man's voice, who dwell in an element where man cannot dwell, and are yet bestowed by Providence for the sustenance of mankind. But the claims of property had recently become more stringent, 996—1008 more encroaching upon man's natural rights; the water ways were closed, the vert and venison appropriated, pecuniary impositions exacted, and unprecedented services imposed.

From Rollo downwards, to the reign of Richard le-Bon, the Forests seem to have been principally crown lands. Latterly, the numerous apanages, newly created, and the copious grants made to the great families who were winning the Sovereign's favour, multiplied the number of Landlords, and brought them into closer contact with the peasantry. Tolls and dues and corvées, were exacted with harshness previously unknown, and the yoke became more galling under the influence of the new notions of gentility. Oppressions sustained by the Peasantry, under the influence of the new opinions.

The people often accept the prestige of being ruled immediately by the Sovereign, as an adequate compensation for harshness, scarcely distinguishable from tyranny. The more exalted the Despot, the more bearable the slavery. The Baron's clenched fist may hit harder, but his open hand feels softer. In Normandy, the personal loyalty excited by the Dukes is a certain test that as yet they never had abused their power.

§ 21. A lingering recollection of the Roman administration still subsisted. Under the Empire, the Duumvirs were chosen in each Pagus, who, when convened, constituted a municipal assembly. Possibly, the institution was not wholly 990—1000 Organized communal confederacy amongst the peasantry.

996—1008 obsolete. Such elections and meetings were now secretly revived by the Norman peasantry. Oaths sworn; and, as we are informed by the Trouveur, who speaks the sentiments, which, traditional in France, were logically deduced from the doctrine of the "gros vilain," they began to enquire, why and wherefore did they allow themselves to be thus oppressed. They told their numbers, they reckoned their strength;—to every one of the gentlefolk, a score or more of churls.

The Duke obtains knowledge thereof.

Whether through incautious boasting, or enthusiastic confidence, the crafty spy, or the treacherous confederate, the burst of anger, or the hilarity of drunkenness, some angry retort or heedless jeer, the secret became known to Duke Richard; and soon did he learn that the villains were erecting themselves into a "Commune," a word of fear, even in those days.

    Par cels ditz è par cels paroles,
    E par autres, encor plus foles,
    Ont tuit cel conseil graanté
    E sont entreserementé
    Ke tuit ensemble se tiendront
    E ensemble se defendront.
    Esluz ont ne sai quels ne kanz
    Des plus habiles e mieux parlanz,
    Ki par tut li päiz iront
    E li sermenz recevront.
    *   *   *   *   *
    Assez tost oï Richard dire,
    Ke vilains commune feseient,
    E ses droitures lui toldreient,
    A li et as altres Seigneurs
    Ki vilains ont Vavasseurs.

A revolution now commenced, which, considered either with reference to manner or object, or to origination and character, commencement or termination, retraces the events and plots, and hopes and fears, which ever and anon are re-appearing in the civilized commonwealth, as though propagated by secret tradition. Under this great strait, Richard had but one confidant whom he could trust, Raoul, the Count of Ivri. No man better fitted for the task of vengeance. Acute, well-taught, born and bred amongst the country folk, his father only an opulent churl, whilst he, Raoul, was accepted as Premier in the land, ranking immediately below the Sovereign. Raoul was imbued with all the sympathies, and had absorbed all the prejudices and antipathies, of a born Noble. Rarely is the Parvenu blessed with the Grace enabling him to resist the temptations inseparable from an exaltation often so honourable, and sometimes so degrading. Raoul stipulated that, supported by the Ducal cavalry, the expedition should be trusted solely to him. Thus we have so far the satisfaction of ascertaining that Richard is practically exonerated from active complicity in the atrocities which ensued.

The Count of Ivri enjoyed the sport of dogging the Villainage. He fell upon the Communists;—caught them in the very fact,—holding a Lodge,—swearing-in new members. Terrible was the catastrophe. No trial vouchsafed. No judge called in. Happy the wretch whose weight stretched the halter. The country was visited by fire and flame; the rebels were scourged, their eyes plucked out, their limbs chopped off, they were burnt alive; whilst the rich were impoverished and ruined by confiscations and fines.

<small>But the ultimate result not unfavourable to the Villainage.</small>

In the days of the Eidgennossenschaft, club and blade and morgenstern, ultimately gained the mastery over the shield and lance of the Suabian chivalry. This Norman rebellion was put down; yet, in the long run, it fructified, both parties learnt their lesson, and a fairly good time was looming. Within the Federation of Franco-Gallia, no Province or "Gouvernement" continued so free or became so free as Normandy. When we reach the era of written evidence, all absolute servitude has become obsolete. The very Charter which designates the *Terre-tenant* as a *Servus* guarantees his personal freedom.

<small>Freedom of the Channel Island tenures.</small>

The territorial tenures in the island gems of Normandy, which still continue set in the British Crown, exhibit the holdings as they subsisted, when the continental portion of the Duchy was wrenched from the race of Rollo; and the villains of Guernsey and Jersey, their custumal unaltered, were as free as any yeoman could have been in the brightest ages of old English history.

<small>Position of Richard's brothers and nephews.</small>

§ 22. The testamentary directions given by Richard Sans-peur, for the establishment of his numerous progeny, may have been partially effected during his life-time, but so as to require the confirmation of his successor. — Various doubts have been raised by genealogists and local historians. In some cases the names of the sons seem to be confounded, and other discrepancies may have originated by territorial exchanges; but we are able to ascertain with sufficient accuracy what position each individual held, when he becomes prominent in history.

996—1008

Geoffrey, who does not seem to have been a child of Guenora, received the endowment of Eu and Brionne, during his father's lifetime. He died early in the reign of Richard le-Bon, leaving Gilbert, his son and heir. A dispute had arisen between him and his uncle, the young Duke. They were probably about the same age. The gallants quarrelled. Richard resumed the apanage. Possibly Gilbert had either refused to perform fealty or had defied him; for arbitrary as a Norman Duke might be, it is difficult to suppose that such a resumption, of which there are other examples, could be exercised without some colourable reason. The young Gilbert, turbulent amongst the turbulent, quarrelled with his ugly-named cousin Ralph Wacé or Gacé, otherwise Tête-d'âne or Tête-d'étoupe, the sobriquet possibly acquired by his shaggy head, and Ralph slew him. Gilbert left two sons, Richard and Baldwin, who took refuge in Flanders until they returned to Normandy, under the protection of the Conqueror.

Geoffrey, Count of Eu and Brionne, succeeded by his son Gilbert.

William, "the Bastard of Normandy," as he is termed, like his future name-sake, by the most industrious of genealogists, Père Anselme,

William much favoured by Richard le-Bon, from whom he receives the Hiesmois.

the son of an unknown mother, received from his brother Richard, the Hiesmois, otherwise the County of Exmes.

<small>996—1008</small>

Three very important towns were included in this dotation. Exmes, Argentan, and, preeminent in every sense, the rock-crowned and rock-crowning Falaise, at this period a most flourishing manufacturing town, and soon destined to exhibit the noblest example in Normandy of stern architectural grandeur.

<small>Falaise, its antiquity and importance.</small>

Falaise boasted of high antiquity; but we may excuse ourselves from discussing the questions raised by the Celtic antiquaries as to the honours there rendered to shadowy Belinus. —The Roman camp, very considerable vestiges whereof still exist, was undoubtedly raised during the reign of some Cæsar, and, therefore, the popular tradition which ascribes this and every monument of the same nature to the Cæsar of the Cæsars, is at least excusable. Within the grass grown mounds of the Legions, arises the famous Castle, the earliest specimen in Normandy of the huge square donjon tower, borrowed from Maine, but which has become the very type, so to speak, of Norman feudality. Various outworks were added at subsequent times, existing now only as rough, massy fragments.

<small>Castle of Falaise, the type of Norman feudality.</small>

Finely is the structure's outline varied by Talbot's tall round Tower, which still continues firm, unscathed, and unharmed, and either the pattern or the model of the cognate edifice, still

surviving though dilapidated in the English 996—1008
warrior's Norfolk lordship of Caistor.

The country about Falaise is rich and flourishing; the pastures, abounding with flocks and herds; and the Flemings, then ever diligent in seeking new fields of industry, had settled in and about the bourg and its spreading suburbs.

Falaise drove a flourishing trade in leather, *Commercial opulence of Falaise.* and the rushing stream laving the rock and over-looked by the great Palatial Tower, had invited the establishment of numerous Tanneries. Moreover, there were extensive manufactories of serge and other woollen stuffs, probably introduced by Belgic industry. If tradition be correct, the accidental discovery of a statue in the suburb called Guibray, supposed to represent the Virgin, had, in the Carlovingian age, suggested the establishment in that faubourg, on the festival of the Assumption, of an annual mercantile Fair: *The fair of Guibray.* whilst those devout antiquaries who profess the Druidical persuasion, derive the name of this locality from a Gaulish term for misletoe, and suppose that the Fair succeeded to some Pagan Festival.

Any how, Guibray grew into importance, and the Fair became, in Normandy, what Stourbridge was to England. The Dukes patronized and encouraged this mart. Charters were granted by Richard, and by Robert, the Conqueror's father. The Conqueror himself, whose name is so intimately associated with

996—1002

these vicinities, continued to encourage the mart, and Guibray-Falaise held a conspicuous station in the map of commercial France, even till the commencement of the present century.

1002— Count William revolts against his brother the Duke.

§ 23. Whether confirmed by Richard le-Bon, or granted by him, such an apanage as the Hiesmois was a boon well deserving Count William's gratitude; but his riches and power encreased his pride and haughtiness. Summoned repeatedly to render his services due for his fief, he as repeatedly made default. Woe betide him! Raoul, Count of Ivri, was at hand, and he advised the Duke to proceed against the rebel by military execution.

Unrestrained either by tenderness of heart or connexion in blood, the sturdy Bear-hunter went forth: and in proportion to the offence, and the quality of the offender, the chastisement was as rough as the punishment he had inflicted on the peasantry.

William imprisoned at Rouen.

William was cast into prison.—Rollo's tall Tower at Rouen detained his descendant in penal captivity; but the prisoner's partizans were numerous and annoying, and the disturbances continued flickering until put down by Raoul d'Ivri's resolution; and many were the adherents of William who escaped the gallows only by fleeing the country. Hard was his captivity, bolts and fetters bound him, till at length he escaped by swarming down a long rope, supplied, as it was reported, by a fair and compassionate hand.

A break-neck exploit, successfully accomplished.—But William's streights recommenced with his liberation. The Ivri hounds were always close at his heels, until, weary of his hunted life, he determined to implore mercy. He guessed where of all places his brother could best be addressed, most pleased and most placable; not in the Palace,—not at Church,—but plaguing the beasts, as he William, was plagued,—disporting amongst the merry green wood shades: and William sought him in the Forest of Verneuil.

He cast himself at Richard's feet, telling the tale of his trials and sufferings. The somewhat frequent recurrence of such a dramatic situation—as in the case of Otho and Liudolph, —may perhaps lead to the supposition that the encounter was concerted, to save the honour of both parties.

William obtained an unconditional pardon; and more than pardon, grace and favour. The Hiesmois was not restored,—but, in full compensation, his brother Richard granted him, as a guerdon, the lapsed County of Eu. Our old English authorities spell the name "Owe" or "Ewe;"—and, with Eu,—William received the hand of Thurkettle's lovely daughter Elce, Alice, or Lescelina, who, as the story runs, helped him in his evasion. The descendants of this marriage became prominent in Anglo-Norman history.—Amongst them we find Hugh, the sagacious Bishop of Lisieux;—Robert, who

996—1003 commenced his career by affording important assistance to the appointed Conqueror of England, in the great Battle of Mortemer, and who was rewarded by those extensive domains in the County of Sussex, known as the Honour of Eu;—and Robert's son William, (in France called William Busac,) enriched, like his father, by the spoils of the Anglo-Saxon, and, who came to a fearful end.

Henceforward, we are constantly gaining nearer views of England.

Chapter II.

ROBERT KING OF FRANCE AND RICHARD LE-BON.

996—1024.

CLOSE ALLIANCE BETWEEN NORMANDY AND FRANCE—ROYAL AND DUCAL MARRIAGES—WARS AGAINST FLANDERS, BLOIS, CHARTRES, CHAMPAGNE, AND BURGUNDY.

§ 1. It is needful, in the first instance, to exhibit Robert of France, and Richard the Norman, in the respective relations of Suzerain and Vassal. Yet, not merely bound by formal oaths and legal covenants, but cordial friends, actuated by community of interest and sincere feeling. Richard, without renouncing in any wise that connexion with the Scandinavian nationalities which his father had maintained, nay, diligently cultivating their amity and alliance, was thoroughly a Frenchman; and though he did not entertain any serious apprehension either of his avowed or secret enemies, he needed that countenance which the King of France could alone bestow. Moreover, King Robert well deserved esteem and affection. *Entente cordiale between King Robert and Duke Richard.*

Hugh Capet's anxiety to accelerate Robert's Coronation within the year, was sagaciously motived, being evidently dictated by the con- *Hugh Capet's anxiety to associate Robert with him in the Royal dignity.*

sciousness that, though his mental powers continued undiminished, his bodily strength was waning away.

Robert's education and moral worth.

Very carefully had Robert been trained; Gerbert, his instructor. From such an intriguing Master of arts a royal Pupil might have learnt over-much; but Robert improved himself by his Preceptor's lore, without imbibing any of the Philosopher's political perversions. So long as Hugh Capet lived, Robert offered a character rare in history: an Heir of whom the Parent had no real reason to be jealous; a son in joint seizin of the Palace with his paternal Sovereign, against whom no well grounded suspicion ever arose; a father and a child between whom no grudge was permanent. Robert ruled as his father's co-equal, sat by his father's side. The Royal charters ran in their conjoint names. Hugh directed the councils of the Realm; Robert obeyed his father's voice when that father had descended to the abode of silence; and the course of government adopted by the primal Capets, enabled their lineage, from father to son, to possess the throne for a period approximating to a Chiliad,—nor has a male child of the loins of Robert le-Fort ever failed.

Hugh le-Grand's policy grounded upon centralization.

§ 2. Hugh Capet's policy was grounded upon unity. He did not proclaim any plan for the future, but provided for the future through the present. Having been raised to the throne by feuds and internal dissensions, he had felt their evil, and he guided himself by his father's doctrine and example. We have heard how (996—1024) Hugh le-Grand based the existence of the body politic upon the doctrine of mutual relationship, "Commendation," accepted as the bond of the Commonwealth; no man to be masterless; all dependant upon the Sovereign as the central orb: the theory which feudalized the Kingdom. The antient constitutional maxims of the Realm, enabled the son to effectuate the father's designs. The tranquillity of Hugh Capet's reign was the result of internal activity. The bright Lilies were growing in the darkness of the night;—the next reign exhibited their full budding beneath the azure sky.—*Nulle terre sanz Seigneur* became an incontrovertible legal position. Under Hugh Capet, arose the Court of Peers, before which tribunal any offending Peer was to answer the complaint or accusation of the Sovereign. Moreover, it was now accepted as a fundamental principle that no crown-vassal could lawfully carry on war, otherwise than immediately under his Sovereign, or by royal command. *(Tranquillity and contentment of Hugh Capet's reign. Feudal doctrines of Government established by Hugh Capet.)*

§ 3. The respect shewn to the Sovereign, the nation's choice; and the indomitable firmness of the Ruler, were so efficient, that, save and except the last struggles with the expiring Carlovingian dynasty, no attempt was made during Hugh Capet's reign, to raise a hand or wag the tongue against him: and the Historian scarcely finds an event to record.—A dull narrative, when the historian or biographer has next to nothing to say; neither to deplore the calamity nor exult in the glory, is, perhaps the most assured token of national as it is of individual happiness.—Rest, is promised to Man as the highest felicity.

<small>496—1024</small>

<small>Fortifications raised by him throughout the realm.</small>

Amongst the few incidents exhibiting Hugh Capet's ethos, one may be noticed as elucidating both the man and his times. Royal Strongholds or Castles were not yet numerous, but Hugh availed himself of the prevailing quiescence, for the purpose of adopting precautions against discontent, by raising fortifications throughout the country; and, in one instance, Hugh did so under circumstances which rendered the transaction peculiarly memorable.

<small>"Advocatio" or right of Advowson.</small>

Every Ecclesiastical Foundation, and every Ecclesiastical Person or Parson was consorted with a Protector or Patron under the name of "Advocatus," whose duty was to stand up for the Community or the Clerk, in the right or in the wrong, whether in peace or in war, in the Court of Justice or in the Field.—This obligation constituted the "Advocatio" or "Advowson," a lot so often put up for sale at the Auction mart, and cheered when it is announced that the income, "capable of considerable encrease," reaches four figures; the estimate accompanied by the smiling comment that the clerical duty is in the inverse proportion,—*corruptio optimi est pessima*,—and, with this old adage, nothing the worse for wear, our moralization begins and ends.

The "Advocatus" of the Bishop and of the

Bishopric was usually the Sovereign.—The "Advocatus" of the Monastery, the Sovereign or the Count, or some other tall nobleman.—The Baron or Lord of the Demesne or Manor was the natural Advocatus of the parochial Priest and Parsonage, for which arduous duty he was to be recompensed in prayers. But, from time immemorial we have traces, more or less distinct, that, either in meal or in malt, in pence or in power, the Advocatus generally contrived to gain some further advantage from the protection he bestowed.

996—1024

According to the established cast of French historical characters, there are eras, especially the mediæval, when the national Clio imperatively requires for her epos a "*Prêtre cafard*," and a *Roi superstitieux*, or some equivalent great puppet, whose strings are pulled by the Cafards, if a King cannot be found: just as the Gallic Melpomene comes to a standstill in her domestic drama, if she lacks a "*Père Noble*" and a "*Jeune ingénue.*"

We are therefore consistently taught by modern French Historians to contemplate Hugh Capet simply as the Sovereign of the Priests, and that his chief, if not only, business was to grant land to religious Houses, he being enslaved by bigoted devotion. But the attributes thus assigned to the Capet are consequential upon the conventional mode of delineating his portrait, which, however it may conform to popular, and therefore welcome, ideas, is merely an imagination, adopted in order that the Monarch may be painted in keeping with the theatrical background. A very curious contradiction to this ascribed fatuity is found in Hugh's dealings with the great Monastery of Saint Riquier, a house of Royal foundation and under his peculiar advowsonship.

The Ponthieu coast being dangerously open, equally to the invasion of the Danes and the hostile projects of Flanders, keen military discernment suggested to Hugh Capet, that, in or near the estuary of the Somme, not far above the too famous Saint Valeri, there were three farms or domains belonging to the Abbey, adjoining each other, which could be united as an excellent out-work against any enemies of the French Crown:—that is to say—" Encre," " Saint Medard," and a villa or township specially called the " Abbot's villa." The said three " Mansi " King Hugh seized for the good of the State ; and caused to be encircled with walls and towers ; and such was the origin of the flourishing town of Abbatis-villa, or Abbeville. The Monks groaned at the usurpation of their property ; but they could not resist ; and we are left to conjecture whether the Advocatus gave them any compensation.

Taken as a whole, the temporal policy, steadily and acutely pursued by the Founder of the Third race, is to be estimated by its effects : and Robert, conjoining the statesman's ability with the warrior's boldness and the monk's humility, was enabled to assume his right by survivorship, without disturbance or opposition. He came 996—1024 into sole possession of the Kingdom as though it were a private estate. So tranquil, indeed, was Robert's accession, that the event was scarcely noticed by the Chroniclers.

§ 4. Gerbert's scholar had profited thoroughly by his Preceptor's lessons; but Robert possessed an unteachable talent. Though the Troubadours might be preparing to raise their voices; no real genius had, as yet, been exhibited in poesy, save in the highest application which that transcendent gift can receive.—Many of Robert's compositions are extant, displaying equal harmony and feeling—some continued to be sung at Saint Denis till the Revolution; the *Veni Sancte Spiritus* for example, not to be confounded with the *Veni Creator Spiritus*, the last being ever pre-eminent amongst the magnificent Pentecostal Hymns. *Robert's talent as a poet.*

Robert's charity was unbounded; and, combined with all these loftier endowments, he was distinguished by the seductive faculty of drollery and whimsical humour. The anecdotes exemplifying this idiosyncracy, for which he loved himself, are numerous. One prank, played off at Rome, may be selected as an example. King Robert entered the Choir of Saint Peter's Basilica bearing a chalice, which he deposited reverently upon the High Altar; in it, a parchment scroll covered with writing, conspicuously peering above the rim. A grant without doubt of some important domain—may be a Duchy, and why not the *Robert's humouristic simplicity.*

Realm, thought (we may fancy) the expectant Pope and Cardinals hopefully rubbing their hands. Scarcely able to restrain their curiosity, they rushed up the gradients, as soon as Robert had descended, to peruse the deed of donation. Alas, for their disappointment! though the parchment was inscribed with what Robert valued more than house or land.—Could such a thing as copyright have existed in those days, the Pope and Cardinals would have acquired the property of Robert's famous chaunt, "*Cornelius Centurio.*"

Let us excuse the vanity of the Author, and view Robert as a Sovereign. Resolute, prudent, and cautious, he maintained good order, and strenuously and energetically defended the rights of the Crown. He had succeeded to a well governed and prosperous Kingdom; yet a Kingdom which could not be administered without continuous exertion; and Robert was well prepared to display his strength whenever occasion should require.

§ 5. Many and powerful were the Chieftains of France, but Robert's principal trust was placed in Normandy, and with reason.— Amongst the Nobles who raised Hugh Capet to the throne, none so potent and pre-eminent as the *Dux Piratarum.* Hence the spite with which the Carlovingians regarded him, their enmity pursuing his corpse to the grave.

Was not Richard of Normandy King Robert's feudatory? Weighty are the considerations upon this question—feudatory—but how far could France command his aid? From the pacification concluded on the island of the Epte, until the expiration of the Norman Sovereignty, we are unable to define satisfactorily the obligations subsisting, or which ought to have subsisted between the Duke and the anointed King. Had they originated from a treaty signed and sealed by Plenipotentiaries at a Congress, we could scarcely have been gratified with greater ambiguity.

996—1024. Uncertainty of the obligations resulting from the Carlovingian homages.

In the first place, not a single official document exists which can lead or mislead us. Rarely is the Ducal tenure noticed by the antient French historians. When the question is perfunctorily brought before us in narrative, the Duke is described as holding *en parage*.—Richard le-Bon held *en parage*.—The third Richard, his eldest son, held *en parage*. Robert, Richard le-Bon's second son, (who, whether he deserved either or neither of the two epithets, *le Diable* or *le Magnifique*, I will not debate,) held *en parage*. But there was one who is never recorded to have performed any homage; and that was Robert's son, William the Conqueror.

Sovereigns en parage.

We possess a general knowledge of the obligations arising from this same tenure *en parage*, yet not with sufficient clearness for our enquiries. We know nothing precisely of its legal construction, until the period when the subtle labours of the jurist imparted that technical development to the feudal laws, which has been accepted as their original character; the pen having become more efficacious than the sword.

In the days when the astute Sages of the Long robe were the masters of the Seigneur, and the echoing *Salle des pas perdus* had begun to be more dreaded than the Donjon Tower, this tenure was distinctly defined in the north-eastern provinces; Champagne for instance, where it prevailed. The usage is exemplified in those cases where a *fief noble* became partible amongst brothers. When a division ensued, the juniors performed homage to their one elder brother, rendering their respective shares of the services, not to him, but to the chief Lord of the fee, and yet acknowledging the Elder's superiority. As was the wont of these Legists, they discover a corresponding example in Holy Scripture. But the fact is, that the Tenure whereby Normandy was holden of France became a special and peculiar political relationship, existing singly in this one case; having much affinity nevertheless with the March tenure between the King of Scots, as Lord of Lothian, on the one part, and the Anglo-Norman Sovereigns, as successors of the Anglo-Saxon Basileus, on the other part. As far as we can construe the submission, it conferred a nominal, though jealous, priority of rank.

§ 6. Indeed, the antiquated transactions of the Carlovingian era had scarcely more than an indirect bearing upon the position which the Duke of Normandy filled subsequently to the accession of the Capetian Line. Old things—let alone grudges and enmities, sometimes dormant, but always liable to be roused—had passed away. The vicarious homage rendered by Rollo to Charles le-Simple on the island of the Epte was recollected only as a merry tale. All the oaths taken, all the declarations of fealty made by the kneeling Guillaume Longue-épée to Louis d'Outremer were merely testimonies of untruth; and by the transactions which ensued upon the liberation of that Louis from his captivity, nothing remained to the Carlovingian King of France except an honorary precedence:—the bond was snapped asunder.

996—1024
Feudal obligation of Normandy to the Capet anterior to the accession of King Hugh.—See Vol. II. p. 494.

Richard Sans-peur had been the Man of Hugh le-Grand, Duke of France and Burgundy; and, when Hugh le-Grand departed, Richard became the Man of Hugh Capet. The convulsions which accomplished the Capetian Revolution superseded all notions of subjection to the discarded family; and Richard, during the last eventful struggle, having renewed his homage to Hugh Capet, he came in with the Capet. The former relations between Normandy and France were superseded. All the homages rendered to the expelled Dynasty had vanished. Richard le-Bon held his Duchy by a new and higher title. He was a Capetian Peer created by the Revolution; Premier amongst the Lay Peers of the kingdom of the Fleur de Lis;—a prerogative which his progeny retained until John Lackland's forfeiture.

Richard's "Commendation" to Hugh le-Grand and to Hugh.

Richard brought in as a Peer by the new Dynasty.

The present alliance however, between Nor-

996—1024 mandy and France was stronger, warmer, heartier, than any connexion arising from legal forms or state reasons. Richard Sans-peur's timely co-operation had placed Hugh Capet upon the throne. There was a debt of gratitude due from the Capets to the House of Rollo. The Minstrel of Henry Plantagenet's Court delighted in reminding the Capets of their obligation, whilst Richard le-Bon, for his father's sake, persevered in steadily aiding the second Capet, as that father had aided the first.

Richard's personal feeling to the Capets.
Never was a Norman Duke so friendly towards the Capets as Richard le-Bon. Never, in after times, did any Duke of Normandy love a King of France. Warmer, in most cases, is the affection entertained by the individual who has done a kindness, than by the object of the kindness. On the one side, the pleasure of continuing to benefit those whom you or yours have aided, and, on the other, a sense of the weight of the obligation.— It is more blessed to give than to receive.

Such was the aspect presented by public affairs when the well-governed Franco-Gallia passed under Robert's sole authority: a Realm demanding uninterrupted vigilance on the part of the Ruler; and yet at the same time, not threatening any contingency for which the Sovereign was unprepared. His administration was vigorous, and he possessed the gifts and virtues most conducive to domestic happiness and public utility; yet they were unfortunately rendered fruitless. An error stigmatized as a sin, though unrebuked by conscience;—and a mistake which the wisest might commit, marred the comfort of his life and damaged his authority as a King.

906—1024

§ 7. The three original bad-neighbours of Normandy had all been gathered to their account.

The old "bad-neighbours" of Normandy.

First, as to Thibaut le-Tricheur. His flight from Hermondeville was his last exploit.— Chartres, flaming, gave him his quietus, and, tamed by age, he abode peacefully at home during the remainder of his days.

Thibaut le-Tricheur.

But, whether in amity or in enmity, in peace or in war, none of the great Feudatories were, at this juncture, so influential in the affairs of Normandy and France as Thibaut le-Tricheur's descendants. They continued waxing in power and influence, and their territories so opened upon the frontiers of the Duke and the demesne provinces of the King as to afford always the temptation and often the opportunity, of giving annoyance.

We know not when Thibaut's long life ended, for he passed away so gently that the time of his death can only be conjectured. This is one of the few instances in which the *Art de verifier les dates* does not fully satisfy the promise held out by the title page. But no negligence can be imputed to the most industrious compilers of this inestimable work.—They had not the wherewithal to give the information. The "*Pays Chartrain*," though rejoicing in famous Fulbert, is almost wholly destitute of Chronicles.

Thibaut le-Tricheur's eldest son by Liutgarda,

Eudes or Odo, first of the name, but second Count of Blois, succeeded to his father. Our knowledge concerning him politically and personally is scanty, considering his importance. He became very rich, and inherited, usurped, or conquered the six Counties of Blois, Chartres, Beauvais, Tours, Meaux and Provins,—Provins where in these our western climes, the Queen of flowers first blushed with oriental splendour.

Singularly candid in owning to the pride of wealth, Eudes the First assumed in his charters the style of *Comes Ditissimus*. His wife, Bertha, —daughter of Conrad the Pacific, King of Arles or Provence, and great grand-child of Henry the Fowler, first emperor of the Saxon line, whom Robert claimed also as a common ancestor,—was rendered illustrious by her exalted lineage, and equally,—it is said,—by her virtues. Great friendship subsisted between Robert and Eudes, the latter being distinguished as Count of the Palace. Robert, then married to a Princess Rosella, became sponsor at the font to one of Bertha's children. He and Bertha—who possibly then first became acquainted with each other—might also call themselves cousins,—but cousins related to each other in the fourth degree; a consanguinity so diluted, that it usually escapes recollection, except when our memory is refreshed by our kinsman's wealth or station.

Return we now to the Comes Ditissimus.— Much will always want more. The Ditissimus engaged in war with Fulke Nerra the Count of Anjou; but, in the midst of his warlike operations, the narrative is stayed by the notice of his death, which ensued at venerable Marmoutier. He left two sons, Thibaut, second of the name in Chartres and third in Blois; and Eudes le-Champenois, who, his elder brother dying without issue, succeeded to all their father's dominions, (that is to say his brother's share and his own,) with the addition of Champagne and Brie.

As for Bertha, the widow of the Comes Ditissimus, she did not mourn long in her weeds,—say a quarter of a year,—when she yielded to the wooing of her late husband's friend, King Robert;—Robert, who now in consequence of Queen Rosella's death, could present himself as a childless widower. Much loftier had been King Hugh Capet's aspirations: fain would he have matched his son with an Emperor's daughter.

§ 8. The results of this union between Robert and Bertha constitute a most important passage in French history.

Marriage between first cousins is discouraged by popular feeling;—the Physiologist may perhaps speak dubiously as to the expediency of such a connexion; but he does not venture further:—whilst the Church, actuated by an honest though exaggerated desire for the preservation of family purity, prohibited all intermarriages between parties related to each other, even in the remote degree of consanguinity existing between

996—1024 **Robert and Bertha.**—Dispensations might be given, but they were very rarely granted.

996—999 Gregory V. the first Transalpine Pope. For the first time since the martyrdom of Saint Peter, the Apostolic Chair was filled by a Transalpine Pope. Hitherto, none but Jews or Syrians, Greeks or Romans, had attained the dignity. Many amongst the supreme Pontiffs were individuals of mean birth; a circumstance redounding equally to their own honour, and the benefit of the Church. But Bruno the German, reigning as Gregory the Fifth, appointed by the interest, or rather upon the nomination, of Otho III., might boast of the most exalted ancestry in the Western Commonwealth, he, being the son of Otho, Duke of Carinthia, and grandchild of Liutgarda of the silver spindle.—We have already made acquaintance with her as the wife of the unhappy Conrad, who fell on the Lechfeld, fighting against the Magyars.

Much coolness, approximating to schism, subsisted between France and Rome. Arnoul, the Archbishop of Rheims, had been re-established by Papal authority, but Robert refused to liberate the Prelate from arrest. At length, the King gave way to the instances of the Legate Leo, in the expectation that the Pope would reciprocate by legitimating the irregular union:—not so, fresh difficulties arose. The Young Emperor, the third Otho, glowered against the Capetians. The soundest Divines denounced the marriage. Moreover, the spiritual affinity between Robert and Bertha,—created, as it was held, by their having joined in sponsorship,—presented an obstacle not less formidable than the natural affinity. A Council assembled at Rome, the Emperor being present. Terrible was the excommunication fulminated against the delinquents. Robert and Bertha, commanded to separate, were, in conformity to the canons of the Church, respectively enjoined to perform penance during seven years. At this era, the Pontiffs were no respecters of persons in judgment, hence the contumely cast upon them by the world. If guilty, they humbled the Sovereign, even as the meanest sinner,—"Thou art the man,"—was the sentence which condemned him.

Gregory acted cautiously, calmly, and considerately, and without displaying much partizanship; but Gerbert, who sat at the foot of the throne, that throne soon to be ascended by himself as the first Pope of the Romane tongue, exerted all his powerful influence against Bertha. An overwhelming majority of the French Clergy opposed the King and Queen, entering into the controversy so passionately, that the excellent Abbo of Fleury repaired to Rome for the purpose of supporting the Pontiff in his adverse decision.

Public opinion in France ran equally strong amongst the Laity against the Royal delinquents. The connexion was stigmatized as foully sinful, and the feeling excited thereby cannot be dis-

996—1024 tinguished in mental or moral nosology from the furor recently prevailing amongst us, when an endeavour was made to annul the prohibition of a marriage belonging to a class which we have termed incestuous, by reason of legal affinity: that is to say, an artificial affinity created by the municipal law, and not grounded upon nearness of blood; a doctrine accepted meekly by the Church of England from the Church of Rome—such prohibition being not merely wholly absent from the Holy Scriptures, but contrary to their spirit.—Whilst an apostolic injunction, forbidding Matrimony in one special and individual case, speaking as clearly as words can speak,—a prohibition which if the canonical impediment should be offered as a caveat upon the *si quis*, would,—unless, Parliament should grant a Privilegium,—absolutely, irremediably, and irrevocably, prevent episcopal consecration,—is always cast to the winds.

Confusion produced by the interdict.
At the same time that the interdict threw the whole kingdom into confusion, the People were so highly wrought up, that when the King or the Queen entered a City, divine service was wholly suspended. All Robert's domestic servants abandoned him, except two or three of the lowest degree. The meat which Robert touched was abhorred as polluted: and the menials flung to the dogs the food which the King's hand had left in his dish; or threw the fragments on the fire.

At length, the misery became so great, that

Robert was forced to repudiate Bertha. They were childless, for agitation of mind disappointed the expectations which Bertha's situation had raised.

Robert repudiates Bertha. 996—1024

§ 9. The royal issue having failed, Robert was compelled, by the ordinary reasons of State, to seek another Consort, and his choice fell upon, or was directed to Constance, generally considered as the daughter of William, Count of Arles or Provence; although there be genealogists who hold that she was the daughter of Guillaume Taillefer, Count of Toulouse. We continue to labour under a dearth of information in all matters connected with the *Langue d'oil.* To encrease our perplexity, the Princess is also denominated *Adela* or *Adelaide*, a popular name scarcely distinguishable from an epithet; whilst many historians speak of her as *Blanche*, or *Candida*, —denominations possibly bestowed by poetical fancy, but appropriate, since she was a brilliant beauty.

He marries Constance, a Princess from the Midi.

Borrowing the untranslatable idiom current amongst our neighbours, thoroughly did Constance deserve the epithet of a "*Mattresse femme*,"—meriting that designation in all its bearings, being qualified equally by her personal gifts and her commanding talent. This same shrewed Constance holds a prominent station in the category of the women who have guided the fates and fortunes of France, whether for good or evil. Witty, winning, attractive, bright and clever, she nevertheless exhibited all the ca-

Cultivation and talent of Constance counterbalanced by her bad temper.

996—1024 prices and artifices, libelously ascribed by the Satirists of olden time to the female sex,—obstinate, intriguing, peevish, avaricious and imperious.

Conduct of Robert towards Constance—His humorous disposition.

The husband, however, bore very patiently with his Vixen. The Queen's moral character was irreproachable, and her mental endowments inspired respect. As for Robert, when she annoyed his poor dependents, he exhibited himself to them as a fellow-sufferer. If Lazarus, crouching on the parquet, stripped the golden fringes from the hem of the royal robe, or his compeer cut off the bullion tassels which ornamented the royal lance, the King only warned the rogues to be wary, lest the Queen should detect the larceny.

Constance fully appreciated her husband's merits, she admired his poetical genius; but never had he rendered the due tribute of Lay or Sirvente to his splendid tormenter. Robert's Muse had not sung for her, and she urged the Poet

Trick practised by Robert upon his Queen.

to celebrate her praise. This was a measure which Robert could not tune his voice to; but having composed his celebrated hymn *O Constantia martyrum*,—he chaunted the stave before her; and the cross-grained enchantress, hearing the sound of her name, received the verses as a personal compliment. If we may quote one of Robert's commemorated facetiæ, he was accustomed to repeat, my hen pecks, but she gives me chickens enow; and indeed, they had a fair tale of children;—sons, Hugh, Henry, who succeeded to the Throne, Robert, afterwards Duke of

Burgundy, and Eudes;—daughters, Adelaide, Countess of Auxerre, and Adela. *996—1034*

§ 10. Robert's conduct, in following his humorous inclination was very natural, yet neither right nor wise. It may be a hard saying, but the words of an Apostle warn us, that "*Eutrapelia*," the expression which a faithful Parkhurst might, amongst its other meanings, render " wit," approximates to sin, or at least may be conducive to sin. Habitual facetiousness not unfrequently engenders substantial hardness of heart; since the admiring yourself as a joker, often generates the unkindness of neglecting or offending others' feelings. Have we not had Judges who punned upon the name of the criminal when they were dooming him to the gallows?

Trivial anecdotes are not always to be rejected as trifling. They act as a mordant upon our fleeting ideas, fixing the personages in our minds, by enveloping them in circumstances: and, if they are found in the sources of history, they must, upon fitting occasions, be employed as materials of history. No normal rules can be assigned for maintaining the Dignity of History, nor any particular mode of treatment prescribed. The Historian ought to fashion his garment out of the stuff which is prepared for him, or let the task alone. This submission to necessity becomes imperative in treating the era of French History upon which we are now engaged: for, concurrently with the extinction

<small>996—1024</small>

<small>Rise of a new school of chroniclers.</small>

of the Carlovingian line, we lose the fine old diligent monastic Chroniclers and Chronographers. Conscientious labourers were they, bearing witness as a duty, and performing that duty under a sense of responsibility, their pages redolent of the lamp; they are succeeded by a class of a different character. I mean those writers who think more of themselves than their works, and seek distinction from their literary acquirements; and, whilst they are singularly unheedful of chronology, they embroider their narrative with a useless display of learning. This is peculiarly the case with Rodolphus Glaber, the smooth headed Cluniac Monk, whose work becomes the main foundation of the history of this period, so far as France is concerned; but he, good man, is confused and diffuse, though not proportionally instructive.

<small>Peculiar richness of the Norman Chroniclers.</small>

The Norman Chroniclers, possessing a peculiar and richer character, are in advance of the French. Ordericus Vitalis, and Guillaume de Jumièges, may be particularized as the precursors of Monstrellet and Froissart.—The rough venerable Romanesque style is beginning, if we may employ such a comparison, to exhibit the modifications of the Ogival architecture which bloomed into the Renaissance.

§ 11. King Robert's matrimonial trials and vexations did not in any wise diminish his energy as a monarch: perhaps rather the contrary. Under his unhappy domestic circumstances, war must have been a distraction from care; and he had not to go far to find it.—At the period when he was most troubled, an opportunity arose for manifesting the King of France's alacrity, and displaying the Duke of Normandy's ready fidelity.

996—1024

Until the dissolution of the marriage between Robert and Bertha, Eudes le-Champenois was, in a manner, Robert's step-son; but, when the connexion ceased, there was not even the grimace of respect or mutual affection: and soon was a sufficient provocation given by the active and ambitious warrior.

Eudes, as Count of Champagne, had widened his dominions close up to France. The Duchy of France, on the French frontier towards Champagne, was nearly conterminous with the "gouvernement" afterwards emphatically denominated "l'Isle de France." And here were two strongly fortified French posts, by which Champagne was kept completely in check, Melun and Corbeil, both very defensible, but particularly the former.

999—1000 Eudes le-Champenois threatens France.

Seldom do we approach any commanding position, whether in France or in Great Britain, dropping down from the Pentland Firth to the Land's End, without discovering that we have been preceded by the Eagle. "Melodunum," is described by Cæsar, as being not far from Paris; and situated upon a river island. The capture of the Gaulish position offered some difficulties to Labienus, but Melun had now become more important than during the Roman era, for, under the Carlo-

Importance of Melun, as described by Cæsar.

vingians, the town had, like Paris, spread out upon both banks of the stream.

Aymon, the son of Osmond de Centvilles, and who had rendered good service to Richard at the siege of Rouen, held both Melun and Corbeil under the Crown.—Antiquarian whimsies accept this substantial Aymon as the mythic father of the renowned Four Sons, the heroes of the semi-black-letter romance entitled the *Quatre fils-Aymon*, which, slightly modernized in orthography, constituted one of the most vendible articles in the Colporteur's basket, even until our own age; when the prurient productions of the Paris press supplanted the old Gothic national fictions.

In the reign of Hugh Capet, much distinguished among the young Nobles of the Court, was young Burchard, the son of Fulke le-Bon, Count of Anjou, rendered so memorable by his favourite adage, *Rex illiteratus est Asinus Coronatus*. And truly, Fulke must have rejoiced in the training which Burchard was receiving. The custom of placing the young nobility under the Sovereign's care, was not only politic, but advantageous to both parties. The Tyro was, in some measure, a pledge for the loyalty of his father, and his father's men likewise.—King Hugh conscientiously and ably performed his trust: and, Burchard, until called into active life, was educated as befitted a Christian and a soldier.

§ 12. Early in Robert's reign, Aymon departed in pilgrimage to Rome, but ere he reached Saint Peter's threshold, he died in consequence of the fatigue attending the journey. This misfortune, by no means unfrequent during the mediæval era, suggests a clearer idea of the perils encountered in the Alpine Passes than can be afforded by any description.

996—1024. Death of Aymon; Burchard marries his widow.

Celibacy amongst the laity was not considered creditable. The Clergy viewed such conduct, if pursued without sufficient cause, as tending to sin, marriage being enjoined by revelation and by nature, unless conscience called the youth to enter the sacerdotal order, or seek seclusion in a monastery. Burchard, feeling a tendency to the latter course of life, delayed making his choice. King Hugh and his Nobles urged the young Beau-sire to take a wife, but not confining themselves to unpractical counsel, they gave him the means of following it, pointing out a congruous and fitting spouse, the noble widow Elizabeth, the childless relict of Count Aymon. The Matron was nothing loath, the young Esquire not unwilling, and the marriage ensued. It is worthy of remark, that in this transaction, the King did not claim any right of wardship over the widow, but the union was effected by the gentle persuasion and affectionate intervention of mutual friends. We cannot ascertain that the Countess Elizabeth had a right either to Corbeil or Melun, though she was in possession

Melun and Corbeil granted to Burchard.

of the towns, still less could she be accepted as military Commander of the antique Merovingian Castle on the island in the Seine; but Hugh bountifully granted to Elizabeth's young husband the two Grand-fiefs as well as the custody of the Palace Castle, the latter constituting the Caput Baroniæ of the Senechalship of France, an office previously held by Geoffrey Grisgonnelle.

§ 13. Grievous to Eudes Count of Blois and Chartres, of Champagne and Brie, were these acts of esteem and favour: but he restrained himself until after Robert's accession. He and his lineage had been very desirous to acquire a firmer position on the left bank of the Seine, where they already had obtained footing. Moreover, Eudes claimed to be Count Palatine. Burchard had placed the noble Gautier, the King's Liege-man, in command of Melun. Eudes, secretly negotiating with this Officer, spared neither gifts nor promises, and, having succeeded by the aid of Gautier's spouse, a lady of noble birth, they surrendered Melun to him. Eudes entered the Place during the dark midnight hour; assuredly not an unprecedented season, yet a species of stealthiness, which aggravated the treachery in public opinion.

This misdeed excited great surprise as well as indignation throughout France. Robert forthwith acted as beseemed a Sovereign, and issued his Precept enjoining Eudes to evacuate Melun, and give security for peace. But at the same time he was willing that Eudes should be allowed to support his claim before the proper tribunal. Eudes refused, and insolently.—He never would give up so long as he lived. Even had the enmity between Duke Richard and the mal-veisin family been less, Robert knew he could rely upon Richard's assistance. A Parliament, a Court of Peers, was forthwith convened: Richard entered heartily into the scheme; Normandy was overflowing with a warlike, restless, ambitious population, ready for the battle anywhere, combining the Berseker's desperate valour to the skill imparted by Romane cultivation, and Richard could not be otherwise than glad to give them employment. Richard headed the enterprise. It was not the Vassal following the Suzerain, but the Suzerain following the Vassal. The combined forces of France and Normandy surrounded Melun; the ambient stream encreased the difficulties of the attack, and the Normans being first and foremost in the assailing ranks, corresponding exertions were made by the besiegers.

Incessant were the discharges of artillery. Missiles darted by night and by day, until garrison and inhabitants conjoined in tendering their surrender: not to King Robert, though King Robert was there, but to Richard the Norman. Richard, indeed, had made the adventure his own. Gautier and his lady were sternly visited

996—1024
Robert's considerate conduct; Eudes obstinate and insolent.

Richard assists the King in recovering Melun.

996—1024

Melun surrenders. Gautier and his wife hanged.

by avenging justice; Gautier's treachery was the more odious, because when he betrayed the City to Eudes, Burchard was on duty at Paris attending the King. No compassion did the noble but forsworn vassals obtain. The hideous gallows was raised, and, when day was dawning, the quivering corpses of Gautier and his wife were seen suspended from the fatal tree. Such a degrading execution of a high-born woman has very few parallels: and yet, comparatively, the judgment was passed in mercy, for had the law taken its course, she would assuredly have been burnt alive. Burchard re-entered Melun, and resumed his authority there. Eudes marched up, and was thoroughly defeated, flying disgracefully. And thus was the pride of the House of Blois temporarily brought low.

§ 14. The recovery of Melun having been thus effected by Richard's sturdiness, a sharp but brief contest called him again into the field. War had broken out between Henry the Emperor,—Saint Henry, as he is termed—and the then reigning Count of Flanders, Baudouin-à-la-belle-barbe, great grandson of Arnold le-Vieux, whilom the worst of the three bad neighbours;

Lyderic, Count Forester of Flanders, Vol. I. 532.

but Lyderic's lineage may be presented to us under a more pleasant aspect—he, the said Baudouin, being grandfather of William the Conqueror's excellent wife Matilda: for he was the father of Baudouin de Lisle, or le-Pieux, of whom Matilda was the eldest child.—Baudouin obtained his popular epithet from the beauty and amplitude of his chesnut-coloured beard.

996—1024

A good and kindly prince was Baudouin, but, inheriting the ambition of his ancestors; he asserted claims to Valenciennes in Hainault, and the Emperor applied to King Robert for aid. Robert assenting, he summoned Richard le-Bon to his assistance, who gladly accepted the invitation.

1006 Baudouin-à-la-belle-barbe—Richard assists in the siege of Valenciennes.

Emperor, King, and Duke, beleaguered the city. A compromise ensued, and a change of opinions having taken place, a good understanding subsisted henceforward between Normandy and the country whose sturdy sons contributed so influentially to the Conquest of England, and also scarcely in a less degree to the reduction of Scotland under the Anglo-Saxon race—for what are the Lowland Scots but Danes or Flemings, or Anglo-Saxon Northumbrians?

§ 15 Bright visions of ambition floated before the mind of Richard; indistinct, yet sufficiently perceptible, inasmuch as they afford us some guidance whilst investigating a most perplexed history, in which any trace or track is acceptable in guiding us through the labyrinth. These schemes for the future enhancement of Norman glory, Richard could not forward otherwise than by a cordial alliance with King Robert, and circumstances were such as now enabled him to render most important help to that Sovereign. Normandy, tranquil, prosperous, and teeming with a military population, every serviceable man yearning to do service, ever rejoicing in siege, battle, inroad or plunder; whilst at the same time the restless Armoricans were not only unable to give him uneasiness or annoyance, but anxious to obtain his support and aid.

The history of this important territory, so intimately connected with Normandy, and through Normandy with England, must here be perfunctorily resumed.

Since the death of Alain Barbe Torte, six Counts had succeeded, either nominally or really, to his authority; or perhaps we should say more correctly, to contest that authority either amongst themselves or against the wily Blois and ambitious Anjou; and, whenever the latter house is named, the ancestors of the Plantagenets come before us, encreasing in power and magnificence. At length Geoffrey, Count of Rennes, prevailed over his competitors:—a bold and active Prince, the first who wrote himself Duke of Brittany. Under his authority, the Armorican Commonwealth assumed more consistency, but Blois menaced sullenly: Anjou, more formidably, proffered protection to Geoffrey; the Danes were threatening; and the renewal of the antient connexion with Normandy afforded the best expectation for political security,—which soon took place most cordially.

§ 16. Like Austria, Normandy owed much to marriage, and there was a plausible foundation for the merry saying, that Normandy's Daughters contributed to her singular aggrandizement no less than the valour and policy of her sons. Certainly,—according to the common colloquial expression, these Princesses had a right to be winning,—their witchery was in their blood.— They were handsome by inheritance.

§ 17. Again we are entangled amongst the complications of this family history. There are two arrays of damsels with whom we ought to deal—the daughters of Richard Sans-peur, and the daughters of Richard le-Bon; but the information we possess concerning Richard Sans-peur's female issue is neither consistent nor clear, —even their number is uncertain. Three or four of them present themselves, about whom the most critical Genealogists contend; and each has an alias, further perplexing us. No one amongst Richard Sans-peur's girls was married during her father's lifetime, and, therefore, upon his demise, Richard le-Bon became the natural guardian of his sisters. Hawisa, the third, is the first whom we are called upon to notice, and her marriage constitutes an important era in the conjoint annals of Normandy and of Brittany.

The lusty Males of Rollo's house appertained to a fine race; and if any potent Count or Baron from beyond the border sought a consort in the Ducal Palace, he was assuredly attracted equally by talent and by beauty. Happier far, however, were the *Normandes* in their position than

996—1024 they would have been, had they obtained such importance as is attached to Woman in the history of France: the Ladies connected with the Ducal circle rarely became influential otherwise than when presented in their proper sphere. It is as discreet wives and affectionate mothers that the Norman Athelizas are mainly known—we encounter only one exception. And,—despite of irregularities—the history of Normandy abounds with examples of decent and pleasant gallantry; no family record in which we find more sincere Wooers, the flame of love honestly kindled by the good report of the goodly damsels: real *bonâ fide* love-matches, the Suitor coming forward in person to make himself agreeable, like Tête-d'étoupe, when he was so disdainfully kicked by Guillaume Longue-épée.—Such a one was Godfrey, the son of Conan, now ruling in Armorica.—As a *Preud Chevalier* does the Briezad Chieftain now appear before us. The Trouveur delights in telling how the young Duke of Brittany put himself in thorough order for courting, having, as we infer, received encouragement from Richard le-Bon, when he solicited Hawisa's hand.—Nor did any bashfulness, real or conventional, delay her yea-word.

996. Duke Godfrey of Brittany marries Hawisa, Richard le-Bon's sister.

Some remarkable circumstances attend this marriage. It is expressly stated by the prose Chronicler, that Godfrey and his Bride were married *more Christiano*, implying, according to the emphasis laid upon the fact, that the sanction of Church ordinances was not always given as a matter of course amongst the Bretons. The Cymri were not scrupulously rigid in this matter; nor must it be forgotten that, according to the tenets of the Church, the essence of the contract consists in the free and mutual consent of the parties, though they incur the censure of irregularity by cohabiting until the ceremony be fully performed.

The good will between Normandy and Brittany, hitherto rivals, encreased. Some time after Hawisa's marriage, Richard le-Bon espoused Judith or Iuetta, Godfrey's sister, distinguished by her sagacity. Very splendid were their espousals, celebrated in the Abbey of the guarded Mount, where Celtic traditions combine with Christian legends; and whose architecture, imparting form and substance to the dreams of romance, testifies the mutual action and reaction of poetic art and fantastic Chivalry. In due time, five, or as some genealogists reckon, six, children were the fruits of the marriage. Three were the sons :—Richard, third of the name, his father's successor, but who flits before us like a shadow—Nicholas (some call him William), who ultimately sought refuge, shall we say safety? in a Monastery—and Robert, the second in the Norman dynastic sequence, if Rollo, under the name of Robert, be accepted as the first, Lord of the Exmois and Falaise, the father of the Conqueror: the Robert who received the epithets of Le Mag-

996—1024

Marriage between Judith, or Iuetta, of Brittany, and Richard le-Bon.

nifique or Le Diable, both, in the opinion of his age, being almost equally laudatory.

As for the daughters of Richard le-Bon, the eldest, denominated Alice, or perhaps emphatically described as the Atheliza, became the consort of Renaud Count of Burgundy, the Franche-Comté, the free County, a dominion which became weighty in the balance of power; whilst Eleanor, the youngest (as some say), captivated the Count of Flanders, Baudouin de Lisle; and amongst their children we may be proud to reckon the tender and excellent Matilda, the Conqueror's Queen.

Iuetta's death opened the way for Richard le-Bon's second marriage. He is said to have taken Estritha, the daughter of Sueno, the Danish king, of whom more hereafter. Estritha received the name of Margaret; but, like the persecuted Ingeburga, this Danish damsel did not find favour in her husband's eyes. Richard put her away: she then espoused Jarl Ulph, the Anglo-Dane: and, at a somewhat advanced age, our Richard le-Bon obtained a third wife, Papia. Concerning this Lady we possess scarcely any information beyond her name, perhaps not even that; the appellation given to her seeming to be one of those sobriquets of fondness which grow up in families; her sons were William, the unfortunate Count of Arques, and Mauger, the wretched Archbishop of Rouen.

§ 18. A threefold cord is a type of strength, but the antecedents of the Conquest, involving the histories of four Nations or four Realms, present a fourfold tangle. The various coloured skeins must be unravelled as we proceed.

996—1024

In the first place, and yet subordinately, we are concerned with the English and England. Even when we name England not, England is uppermost in our thoughts.—In the second place, and yet most prominently, the Normans and their community.—Thirdly, the Danes and the Northmen, who concern us vitally in relation to English affairs, though we must watch them in Scandinavia and the Baltic islands.—Lastly, yet ever in sight, whether in the foreground or in the background, France, and the Frenchmen, the French Provinces, the French Kings.

The only passage of European history, offering equivalent perplexity, is furnished by—

"*Il bel paese che il mar circonda e l'Alpe:*"

her annals overwhelm us with events, so interesting that we grudge to lose any one of them, whilst their multiplicity renders them unmanageable. Hence we cannot adopt any plan whereby the fortunes of Italy—that is to say, her misfortunes—are rendered intelligible, except an arrangement of the matter in parallel columns. This labour has been performed conscientiously and accurately; but the work, under which the Writer died, is unreadable.—Bear with me therefore in my present task, and tolerate the imperfections which the complicated theme renders inevitable.

§ 19. The several matrimonial alliances al-

996—1024.
Advantages resulting from the Norman Marriages.

ready detailed and recorded, tended greatly to enhance the splendour, the prestige, and the power of the Norman Duchy. Very substantial advantages, both social and political, were gained by these intermarriages:—frontiers widened, connexions strengthened, dominions acquired. They became accumulations of force: and, not the least amongst the benefits resulting to the Norman Sovereigns, was the opening afforded for their interference in the affairs of the States with whom they connected themselves, a position which they skilfully and politically improved. But the most important union remains to be told,—the unhappy marriage between the ill-starred Ethelred and Richard Sans-peur's Emma, effected, not by plan or forethought, by passion or policy, but by a combination of circumstances which no human devices could have disarranged, or human prescience have foreseen—the union through which the influence of our Anglo-Norman Empire has become œcumenical.

828—834. Partial conversion of the Danes—Christianity introduced by Saint Auscar.

§ 20. At this period, the Danes conjoined the energies of Heathendom with much of the cultivation accompanying Christianity. Nearly a Century had elapsed since the Gospel had been preached in their regions, mainly by the exertions of Saint Auscar,—Churches built, and Communities founded,—but conversion proceeded unequally. Much opposition had subsisted in the various classes of society. Many a "Herred" and many a "Syssel" retained the worship of

Thor and Odin; nay, human sacrifices belonged to the nation's yesterday. On the whole, however, the people at large were more ductile than the Rulers, and, for a while, Harold Blaatand was expelled by his subjects, faithful to their new Faith, but not to their antient Sovereign.

<small>996—1094</small>

<small>936—986. Harold Blacktooth's varied fortunes.</small>

The very essence of an Empire is aggression. *Augustus*, from "*augeo*," was the admitted etymology of the Imperial title. As in the human frame, so in human authority; the cessation of growth is the first symptom of death. Otho Augustus, *Mehrer des Reiches*, "Encreaser of the Empire," true to his vocation, laboured to render free Denmark a Feud of Charlemagne's crown: he pursued his military operations strenuously, even beyond the Danish border; and the *Ottensund*, between Sleswick and Hedeby, marks the extent of the Emperor's victorious advance.—The dim dark sea has disappeared.—Shoals and shallows have absorbed this gloomy Sound; but the name subsists, and commemorates the triumph of the Cæsar.

<small>966—973. Otho the Great—his expedition against the Danes.</small>

<small>The Ottensund.</small>

Otho, like Charlemagne, probably, or at least possibly, was not clearly conscious of the double motive rendering the Faith which he was diffusing ancillary to his schemes of conquest, the healing Cross employed as the hilt of the devouring sword. Through the exertion of his missionary Bishops, there now existed a recognized, nay a powerful Christian party.—Harold Blaatand submitted to Baptism, and Otho be-

<small>972. Sweyne baptised—Otho his sponsor.</small>

came the Sponsor of Harold's triply denominated son and heir.

Swend, the appellation which we Anglicise as *Sweyne*, was the proper name bestowed upon the wailing babe, when presented to his father immediately upon his birth; "*Svend-Otto*," the baptismal name imposed in honour of his Imperial Sponsor; and "*Svend-gabel-bart*," or *Svend-Tveskiœg*, "Svend with the forked beard," as he is often called in history, was the designation suggested by the appendage, conspicuous in his aspect as the second William's fiery hair.

These two Monarchs—son and sire—whose strenuousness first imparted consistency to the State of Denmark, must be particularly distinguished as the most bitter amongst the foes raised up for the chastisement of England. One third part of unhappy Ireland had been devoured, subdued, or overspread by the Ost-men.—They had acquired about the same proportion of Great Britain. The territories on the Anglo-Saxon main-land, from the Humber up to the Firth of Forth, and all the Britannic and Scoto-Pictish Islands East, North, and West, to the Isle of Man, were grasped by the Raven. The Norwegian Olave joined the Danes; and they, the appointed precursors of the Norman William, now resolved upon the complete subjugation of all the Tribes and Nations dwelling within the circuit of the Four Seas. The scourge wielded by Svend-Tveskiœg cut deeper into the flesh than any punishment which the English had hitherto sustained; whilst the disgraceful burden of the Danegelt exacerbated the misery. *(996—1024)*

More qualified than ever were the Danes for the dire task of destruction. The acceptance of Christianity familiarized them with the arts of Civilization, as inherited from the supremacy of old Rome;—and, most of all, the Art of Arts, the Art of War.—Denmark was now a Christian country;—large numbers of the population had accepted Christianity. Episcopacy flourished; the Clergy, poor, few, and energetic; the grosser abominations of heathenism had been suppressed. And the Scandinavians generally, so nearly akin to the Germans, and yet so antipathetic, preparing for complete incorporation in the Christian Commonwealth. But their lust for conquest,—the instinct of the natural man, uneffaced by the lessons of Peace and Good will,—glowed fiercely as ever. Nay, in our days, does it not rather seem as though the sabre acquires a keener edge when whetted upon the Bible? Indeed, may we not fear that our full knowledge of God's will and the ways of salvation, aggravates our national guilt?—Do we love our Enemies, when the yell of "Extermination" howls throughout the Hall as the antiphonal response to the hoarse Slogan of "Evangelization?" *(Advance of civilization amongst the Danes.)*

§ 21. Never can we discover any age or era when the vaunted Law of Nations recognized in public policy the teaching of the

Gospel, or the relations of a Christian people towards their brethren. Amongst the vulgated traditional anecdotes floating about the world, without any possibility of verification, is the facetious story, purporting, that when the Venetian gallies were aiding the Infidels, and some few of Saint Mark's gallant sons felt a creeping compunction, which made them uncomfortable at the notion of acting against fellow Christians, so that they hesitated—or were fancied to hesitate—whilst about to apply the match to the bombard—Fire away boys, we were Venetians before we were Christians,—cheered the Captain,—and off went the volley.

§ 22. Was there ever any Minister, Chieftain, or Sovereign, able or willing to define the boundary between natural self-defence and needful aggression, or who strove, whether in the Cabinet or during the Campaign, to regulate his conscience in public or practical action by the ethics of Christianity? As far as my knowledge extends, only one instance, approximating to an example, can be recollected in all history, and neither the personage nor his *entourage* are elegant. The example occurs in the case of an ugly black fellow, with a tattooed face, and a queer name, Heekee, the Maori.— The British troops besieged his Pah; the Lord's-day came on, and well-taught Heekee, who had sat at the feet of the Missionaries, abstained from even loading a musket, simply concluding, that, in conformity with Gospel teaching, the White man would also take his rest, and the sun set on the Lord's day in quietness and peace. Not so. The assailants were up and doing. Steady and sharp were the volleys discharged against the Pah; and Heekee came forth as a suppliant, weeping, and bearing the corpse of his wife, who had been slain.

§ 23. During the visitations of England by the dreadful Danes, what had her people to hope or fear from the Norman power? When the old Carlovingian Chronicler, standing by Richard Sans-peur's grave, speaks of the defunct as the *Dux Piratarum,* we take offence, because in our ears the title sounds as though spoken contemptuously. Richard Sans-peur has long been our favourite Hero. We have admired the fine boy, nursed on his father's knee, whilst the three old Danish warriors knelt and rendered their fealty. During Richard's youth, adolescence, and age, our interest in his varied, active, energetic character, has never flagged, and we go with him in Court and Camp till the day of his death.

In fact, it is we who are too sensitive as to the implied opprobrium: Richard himself would have construed the epithet as a compliment, and more, a distinction in which he placed his pride. He was indeed the Leader of the Pirates; he never cast off their amity, or disclaimed his origin, and it was with hearty affection that they followed him. The Danes had virtually accepted Sans-peur as

906—1024

Harold Blaatand's settlement in the Cotentin. (Vol. II., p. 464.)

their Leader, when his youthful perils summoned Sithric and Thormod to his aid. Most signally did he shine as *Dux Piratarum*, when Harold Blaatand, accepting the invitation, had settled himself in the Cotentin, the very Normandy of Normandy; the point from whence the Danes might have renewed their inroads upon France; and the extent of the peril was fully disclosed at Jeu Fosse. — Harold, then and there surrounded by the sturdy Cotentin men, landsmen and seamen, filled the whole Kingdom with consternation. Neither was there in the character of Richard's Danish kinsfolk, any feature which might alienate the cognate Norman, or excite distrust or fear in his mind.

§ 24. The English historians represent the Danes as monsters of rapacity, insolence, and ferocity; tossing up infants in the air, and receiving them on the points of their spears.

Unhappily there was much truth in these accusations. But the English estimation of the Danish character and savagery must be received with all the modifications required by the natural sentiments of an enemy. Man's conception of man never is, and never can be, otherwise than subjective.—" Handsome is who handsome does,"—homely as the phrase may sound, —involves the whole philosophy of Humanity.— My feelings, my likings, my dislikings, my principles, my loves, my hatreds, my fancies, my tastes, my politics, my creed, my graces, my vices, my failings, furnish the standards by which I judge of you.—Your feelings, your likings, your dislikings, your principles, your loves, your hatreds, your fancies, your tastes, your politics, your creed, your graces, your vices, your failings, are equally the standards by which you judge of me.—The cruel and bloody men, whom we anathematize on the thirtieth of January, with as many implied curses as Ernulphus could have cogitated, are honoured by Baxter as Saints in heaven.

996—1024

In their own country, the Danes were a rough folk, but possessing many social virtues. Stalwart warriors also were they, always ready for cut and thrust, yet no less diligent in pursuit of gain. The tendency of the Danskerman's character approximated closely to the Dutchman's coolness in the proud days of de Ruyter or Van Tromp, fighting men to the backbone, but always eager to turn a penny; selling spare powder to the enemy during the lull of a sea-fight.—"*Se non è vero è ben trovato.*" Highly as the chivalry and heroism of Hawkins and Drake may be honoured where the British Jack is flying, it was as fiends incarnate that our Elizabethan worthies were recollected all over the Spanish main.

Character of the Danes.

§ 25. All the feelings of Richard Sans-peur had descended to Richard le-Bon. He had pursued his father's policy both in peace and in war. Without sharing the danger, Normandy prospered upon the prey which the Danskerman made in England. The Normans were a thriving

The Normans a commercial people.

and money-getting people. The great fair of Guibray attests their national tendency. The liberal policy of the Dukes is also forcibly illustrated by the remarkable treaty of peace concluded between Richard le-Bon, and Olave, the Norskman; securing to the rovers the right of free trade in Normandy. No certificate of origin was required when the big bales of English stuffs were offered to the chapmen at the bridge-head of Rouen: and the perils of England were much enhanced by the *entente cordiale*—this expression has become technical, and therefore, untranslateable—subsisting between Romane Normandy, and the Northmen of the North.

Richard le-Bon's dubious neutrality during the Danish wars.

§ 26. If the conduct pursued by Richard could euphemistically be denominated neutrality, it was a neutrality scarcely differing from hostility. Always were the ports of "*Ricardes Rice*,"—as the English named Normandy,—open to the Northmen. The active mercantile Normans could not afford to close their waters to fellow-traders; and, when a black-sailed keel hove in, it was difficult to distinguish whether she was fitted out for trade or war. In the Norman harbours, therefore, the Danish vessels could always obtain shelter. Every movement which the Danes were making, was more or less threatening to England; and Ethelred, yielding to morbid activity, instead of concentrating his operations and bestowing his whole care upon the defence of his kingdom, was pestering the British natives, the antient tribes, who still were fighting for their existence in Cumbria, Reged, and fair Strath-Clyde. At this critical period Richard le-Bon welcomed the Danes in his dominions during a whole season: they were under his special protection. Indeed, they could occupy a position which they might call their own:—the antient Cotentin was Harold Blaatand's barony.

margin: 906—1094

§ 27. Much as we may regret the shock given to our historical reminiscences, when we employ a modern geographical nomenclature in the place of the antient appellations: yet, wise in their generation, and in duty bound to despise all such æsthetic considerations, were the Statesmen who severed the antient France of the Drapeau Blanc, into the eighty-three districts, constituting modern France of the Tricolor—the sagacious dissection which has guaranteed to France her unity and indivisibility. The indignant groan extorted from the British Orator, exclaiming that France had been treated like a conquered country, expresses an irrefragable truth; France was conquered,—conquered by the most despotic of all conquerors—new ideas. With the obliteration of the venerable names of Dukedoms and Marquisates, and Seigneuries, receding into the dim clouds of antiquity, disappeared all former privileges and immunities, as well as all political relationships which might disturb the practical working of revolutionary institutions. The whole

margin: Departmental division of France, necessitated by the Revolution.

machinery of the *ancien régime* was crushed into the ground.

Under a scientific aspect, also, the names of the Departments were well chosen by the Savans, to whom the task was assigned of framing the new chorography, which inscribed the Revolution on the face of the land. No example exemplifies their acuteness more pertinently than the appellation bestowed upon the antient Cotentin, which, with the Avranchin out of which it grows, is now known as the "Département de la Manche;" and a French Statesman might maintain that the English Channel appertains in a manner to this Department, whereby the entrance from the High Seas is completely commanded. Look on the Map.—You will be struck with the singularity of the features presented by the territory, stretching out as a mighty quadrangular bastion, watered on three sides by the waves. Amongst other peculiarities you will note, that it is one of the very few peninsulas ascending from the Equator to the Arctic Pole; none other taking a similar direction, with the single exception of Jutland. Moreover, anterior to the subsidence of the submerged isthmus, the bridge which enabled our few ophidians and our sufficiently numerous mammalia to pass over from the continent, extending from Cape Grisnez to Shakespeare's Cliff, the Cotentin performed the duty of Jutland, in constituting an inland Sea.

The Cotentin, for we must now revert to the

historical nomenclature, is not merely the physical bulwark of Normandy, but the very kernel of Norman nationality. During the lower Empire, the Cotentin was known as the "Littus Saxonicum," or the "Otlingua Saxonica;" either for the reason that some tribes of the Continental Saxons,—and the Saxones Baiocassini are particularly mentioned,—had settled there,—or by the rule of contrary, because the Saxon shore was garrisoned for the purpose of defending the country against the Saxon rovers: a difficult question, but upon which it is not needful I should here enter, having elsewhere discussed the same.

<small>996—1024. The "Otlingua Saxonica," see *Rise and Progress of the English Commonwealth*. (Vol. II., pp. 359—384.)</small>

§ 28. Furthermore, over and above the strength of the Cotentin, resulting from position, the materials of which the natural bulwark is composed, encrease the strategic importance of the district. The granite formation which here and there pierces through the humus of the interior, encircles the sea-board with jagged rocks, infamous to the navigator; and rarely do these rocks disappear, except when the marshy meadows on the coast melt into treacherous shoals, more dangerous than the rocks themselves.

<small>Natural strength of the Cotentin.</small>

The summit or northern face of the bluff, solid Peninsula constitutes a noble Bay, terminated by Cape Barfleur on the East, and the well-known Cape of the Hogue on the West, a sweeping segment of a circle, symmetrical as though the general outline had been traced by human hand. This shore exhibits a curious

<small>Geographical aspect of the Cotentin.</small>

correspondence with the adverse shore of the Channel; for, could the Isle of Wight be towed across the water, the southern moiety of the rhomboid would drop into the opposite roads.

All the layers of population, the successive occupants of this region, have endeavoured in their turn to render the advantageous locality more defensible. The earliest amongst these works, presenting a series commencing with the dawn of civilization, and prosecuted uninterruptedly until our times, is evidently the "Hogue Dyke," an entrenchment exhibiting the unskilled labour of the pre-historic age. The Dyke isolates the Cape of the Hogue, thereby converting the Head of the Promontory into a species of rude stronghold. Various examples of this device exist in Great Britain; and the Downs, all around the "Hogue Dyke," are dotted with sepulchral Tumuli, constituting the class which gladdens the merry heart of the Archæologist, when, as the Manager of the jovial desecration— the savoury contents of the basket spread on the elastic turf,—he startles the ladies by wielding the carious thigh bone, or bowling the grinning skull. As to the name of the "Hogue Dyke," transmitted by the enchorial tradition, it is clearly Teutonic; but nothing more can be predicated concerning the etymology.

§ 29. Only two harbours or waters of refuge are found in the Peninsula.—Barfleur, the one Port, though during the middle ages, the most accustomed, offers but a perilous entry or departure; haunted by the gloomy celebrity resulting from the shipwreck of the "Blanche nef," and the unhappy loss of that wayward child, not the less mourned by reason of his errors, the Atheling William, in whom the male line of the Conqueror became extinct, and after whose death the Royal father never smiled again.

996—1024
1120— Shipwreck of William the Atheling.

A most ample compensation however is afforded for Barfleur's disadvantages, in the excellence of the harbour and the magnificent roadstead for which Cherbourg, the other Port, lying, as nearly as possible, in the centre of the magnificent sweep of the northern bay, is renowned: and it was to this station that the Romans first directed their care. "Cæsaris Burgus" has continuously attracted the attention of the Rulers of the Gauls, of Normandy, and of France. The supposed etymon of the name may be a scholastic fancy, but it is very certain that Cherbourg's present defences replace the fortifications raised by the Masters of the World.

Danger of Barfleur as a port compensated by the excellence of Cherbourg.

Cherbourg fortified by the Romans.

Subsequently to the Imperial age, the more antient muniments were included in, or concealed by, a mediæval fortress, the occasional residence of Harold Blaatand. The Norman Dukes, as English Kings, and the Capetian Kings of France, and the successors of the Capetian Kings, have constantly and steadily directed their vigilance to these quarters. The prudence of Louis Quatorze bestowed the additional strength which,

996—1024 in his time, was necessary for the security of a position threatened by the most formidable amongst his maritime enemies. When the bastions of Vauban arose, the relics of classic antiquity disclosed how sagaciously the Cæsars had anticipated the great teacher of modern strategy. Whilst I am writing these lines, the Statesmen of the Tuilleries are hastening the works considered as imperatively demanded for the safety of the State. And the cyclopean constructions battling with the waves, will, ere long, complete the pride of Maritime France.

Bravery of the inhabitants of the Cotentin. The inhabitants of the Cotentin were congenerous with the natural citadel, of which, so to speak, they composed the garrison. When the region and the people first come under our cognizance, we find a race descended from the purest Danishry, retaining all the vigour of their progenitors conjoined to the lessons derived from civilization; soldiers and sailors, the bravest on land, the most skilful on the seas. Who so prompt for service, who so clever, who so agile, and who so stalwart, as the Cotentin Butsekarls, ever ready to affront their foes or defend their land? They inherited all the boldness, and all the skill of the antient Vikings.

§ 30. The repartition of the country amongst Rollo's followers was prosecuted immediately after the conclusion of the treaty which recognized his domination. Here he fixed the brave and trusty Oslac, whom we have reverenced

Oslac settled in the Cotentin by Rollo.

as the grey-headed guardian of Richard Sans-peur. 996—1024

Another donee is known. Evidence concerning the process adopted in settling the primary allotment of the Neustrian land amongst the Northmen is exceedingly rare; but the Seigneurs of Saint Sauveur long treasured amongst their archives, a copy of the grant by which the territory had been bestowed upon their ancestor, Richard, one of Rollo's principal commanders. The domain is described as principally consisting of wood and waste land. Herbert, Bishop of Coutances, consecrated the domestic chapel, and the instrument attesting the performance of the rite rehabilitates the primal concession, which, the example being solitary, we might otherwise be apt to reject altogether. The barony of Saint Sauveur created by Rollo.

This circumstance, however, would not furnish an irrefragable reason for critical scepticism. It is certain that the donations made by the Conqueror in England required to be attested by his charter under seal, and yet, only one such charter, amongst the many hundreds that were granted, can now be found.

The Castle of Saint Sauveur still exists; and it is possible that some portions of the primitive structure may be incorporated in the picturesque ruin.

This same Barony of Saint Sauveur is of great importance in Norman history. The dotation in question, composing the premier Barony of

999—1024

Nigel, Vicomte of the Cotentin.

the Cotentin, descended to Richard's son Neel or Nigel, who was also appointed Vicomte of the Cotentin; and the dignity continued hereditary in the Saint Sauveur family, till forfeited by rebellion.

In Normandy, as in England, the Jurists held that the erection of a Castle, unless sanctioned by the Sovereign's licence, was an illegal act. But whether or no, the Cotentin Baronage freely assumed the power; and, within three generations and four, from the first settlement made by Rollo and his feres, the Cotentin bristled with the fortresses which the Baronage had raised.

The Cotentin Castles.

The massy quadrangular Keep, so impressive upon the imagination by its bulk and stately solidity, and commonly accepted as the normal type of a Norman Castle, was introduced into Normandy from Maine. Nevertheless, the Cotentin Castles, wide in their range, and richly varied in their architectural style, constitute the ornament of the landscape: and, after all the dilapidations, restorations, or destructions, which they sustained, whether occasioned by war, or consequent upon peace, effected by violence, or dictated by taste or necessity, more than one hundred of these structures still survive.—We read the history of the country on the face of the country

The Cotentin the peculiar nursery of the Conquerors of Apulia, Sicily, and England.

Each of these Castles proclaims the lineage to whom the stronghold whilom appertained. No Baronage in France more pure in race, more active, more sturdy, or more needy. The population was teeming, the sterile land could not feed them, but the roaring surges surrounded them. All loved the sea, and upon the waves, and beyond the waves they were ever seeking their fortunes. From Hauteville, nigh Coutances, came the Conquerors of Apulia and Sicily. And when we call over Battle-Abbey roll, or search the Doomsday record, or trace the lineage of our antient Aristocracy, we shall find that the Lords of these same Cotentin Castles, with scarcely an exception, served in the Conqueror's army, or settled in the Realm they won.

§ 31. The reception given to the Danes by Richard provoked Ethelred's anger, and justly; for such a neutrality was far more dangerous than avowed hostility. Ethelred was not unready, but ever ready at the wrong time.— More detrimental than sloth is misplaced diligence.

Ethelred declares war against Duke Richard.

In proportion to Ethelred's defective judgment was the intensity of his impotent ire. Summoning his fleets at Portsmouth, he proclaimed the extent equally of his vengeance and of his mercy. Richard, transported, was to be brought to England as a captive—his hands manacled behind his back—the whole country wasted with fire and flame; the guarded Mount, dedicated to the Archangel, alone exempted from devastation. The English fleet, obeying the King's hasty and injudicious instructions, made for the mouth of the Sarre, rising very near Cherbourg, and falling into the sea just above Barfleur, a streamlet scarcely to be called a river, useless to the invaders, but which would facilitate the movements of the inhabitants against them.

Soon as the English fleet hove in sight, Neel de Saint Sauveur, true to his trust, defending his Suzerain's rights and his own, hoisted the Vicontiel banner. The Knighthood flocked in, whilst the amphibious population of the Cotentin, skilled at sea and fierce on land, would have mustered without call or summons. Joyfully did all the peasantry rise *en masse*, just as their progenitors had done, when, during the wars of Sans-peur, fighting for their homes against the King of France, or the Teutonic Emperor, they had deployed themselves in the forest defiles of Maromme, or the banks of the Rougemare, or splashed across the Dieppe water, or stumbled with uncertain footing amidst the spongy salt marshes of Corbon. The like did they now.

Forth they came, as they were bound to do, with hook and with crook, with fork and with spike, with club and with flail; the women taking an efficient part in the conflict. The English were completely cut up. None escaped, save those who fled to the shore, where, crowding into the six largest vessels, all the remaining craft were abandoned to the victors.— Many a Knight, many a Squire, many a Vassal, many a Varlet, who fought on the field of the

Sang-lac, beneath William's consecrated banner, 999—1024 was invigorated by the tale his old father had told; how despitefully the English had ravaged their homes, and how he, the now grey-headed speaker, then young and strong, had helped to dispatch the English dastards.

§ 32. A pacification ensued between the English and Norman Sovereigns; a certain fact, but as to period, mode, and manner, perplexingly obscure. To both nations, the transactions seemed somewhat discreditable. Either party attempted to cast some disgrace upon the other. The Normans were insulted, the English worsted, but the Normans had no need to be ashamed of the insult. The Cotentin invasion was one of the links in the chain of causation, which led to their triumph and to England's subjugation.

A document is extant specially relating to this same pacification, possessing great interest, inasmuch as it is the earliest formal convention between two independent States appearing in European diplomacy. Whether original or transcript, a plausible text has been preserved. The instrument purports to be the result of a Congress at Rouen, held pursuant to the intervention of the supreme Pontiff, anxious to prevent the shedding of Christian blood. We read the articles *in extenso*, as transmitted to us by the most discriminating and trustworthy amongst our Historians; — perhaps the only writer who, during the mediæval era, combines

999—1024

*985. Peace between Normandy and England concluded by the intervention of a Pope, "John XV."
—See Art de Verifier les Dates.*

an intimate acquaintance with public affairs with classical taste and critical discernment.—Perpetual peace, a sorrowful illusive covenant, is stipulated:—and, as the best means of ensuring this condition, a paragraph is inserted, which, could the clause have been observed, would certainly have tended to promote international amity. Neither party was to receive the enemies of the other, not even his liege subjects, unless the latter should be furnished with a passport under his Sovereign's seal.

Such is the main substance of this remarkable compact, singular in every sense; consistent, clear, agreeing with the circumstances under which the parties were placed, yet nevertheless of highly dubious authenticity. The Pontiff, entitling himself *"Johannes XV., Sanctæ Romanæ Ecclesiæ Papa,"* is represented as employing a style utterly unknown in the Vatican. Never did the *"Servus servorum Dei"* narrow his œcumenical authority by writing himself "Pope of Rome"—or in any bull, brief, or rescript add a regnal numeral to his name. Indeed this practice did not obtain in the Court of any Prince or Sovereign until a comparatively recent era.—No mediæval Referendary or Chancellor would acknowledge the form. Were an English Patent produced, in which "Henricus filius Johannis Regis" is made to assume the style of "Henricus Tertius," the parchment would attest its own spuriousness. We do not discover any example of the present prevailing style in any public transaction of any country until far later times — never did Louis-Quatorze distinguish himself from his predecessors or successors by the number which has become the symbol of his glories. France knew not the usage until Napoleon proclaimed himself *le premier,* with the anxious intent of securing the omen that there should be a continuance of the Dynasty.

999—1024

But whilst we reject the Convention in the shape now presented, we accept its import.—The quarrel and the reconciliation are unquestionable verities. Ethelred, surrounded by a cloud of enemies, sought to expand the Norman neutrality into a close alliance. At this period Ethelred was the father of ten children: six sons, the eldest the heroic Ironside, who, had his exertions been permitted to prosper, would have averted the ruin of the falling kingdom; also, four daughters. Yet so fragmentary and failing are the sources of information relating to these troublous times, that our classical Historian, the member of an antient Community whose archives were peculiarly rich —he himself distinguished by acumen, knowledge and industry—informs us, that he knew nothing concerning the mother of this numerous family. The name of Ethelred's Queen, says William of Malmesbury, is lost in the shades of antiquity.

Ethelred's family by the daughter of Earl Thored.

Obscurity of this era in English history.

But a Chronicler in the distant North, Ailred of Rivaulx, affords us the information concealed from his brother in South Britain; for he testifies

Ethelred's Marriage.

999—1024 that Ethelred's first Consort was a noble lady, daughter of the Ealdor-man Thored.—Therefore, all the doubts which have been surdly raised concerning Ironside's legitimacy are dispelled.

§ 33. None of the Norman marriages contributed so potentially to the prosperity of Rollo's race as the matrimonial alliance contracted with the Ruler, who, in the midst of all his disasters, continued to style himself, "Ethelred, by the grace of God Basileus of Albion, King and Monarch of all the British nations; of the Orkneys and the surrounding Islands."

Deficiency of information. National antipathy,—deficiency or loss of information,—and worse than deficiency, perversion of information, have all conjoined to involve in great obscurity the history of the transactions relating to Emma. We have seen how the antient Historians themselves confess their ignorance. The disturbed chronology of the events betrays the confusion of the times; and we pick up our facts like counters cast upon the ground. But more generally the dates are wholly omitted. In the six books of the history which we owe to Guillaume de Jumièges, constituting the main basis of our narrative after Dudo's demise, only three quotations of the current year can be found to give us anchorage.

The order of narration which I have adopted throughout the whole length and breadth of these perplexing chapters is such as appears to me to afford the most plausible mode of presenting causes and consequences. Let the arrangement be accepted with allowance for its difficulties, as the best chronological hypothesis which I can form. *999—1024.*

The peace concluded, Ethelred sought to unite himself with Normandy by a closer bond. Could he become Richard's brother-in-law,—could he engraft the branch of Cerdic upon the stem of Rollo, would not England obtain a far greater power amongst the nations? And, over and above the political advantages promised by such a marriage, the personal attractions of the Adeliza Emma may have had some weight in this politic scheme.

Ethelred shewed himself in earnest. The English Monarch passed over into Normandy; urged his suit in person; and wooed successfully. *Ethelred crosses over to Normandy and pursues his suit in person.* The Lady's natural guardian assented; and, the preliminaries being settled, Ethelred, having quitted Rouen, was succeeded by the appearance of a noble cortège despatched from the English court, who returned to England with Emma as his affianced Bride.

Such was Ethelred's impatience, that the espousals took place, contrary to the ordinances of the Church, during the Lenten season. Ethelred bid high for Richard's sister. Very ample was the dowry the Lady of Normandy received; but testifying rather to the bridegroom's liberality than his judgment. The Atheliza received extensive domains in the maritime counties of Devon and Hants.—The whole circuit of *Ample dower bestowed upon Emma by Ethelred.*

999—1024 the "Rote-land" or "Redland," a bailiwick not yet brought into Shire-land—for the forest of Luffield then covered the whole,—Winchester, the capital of the Anglo-Saxon Empire,—and Exeter, the pride and fortress of South Britain. Placed in actual possession of these domains; Emma was gratified with the power of appointing her own officers; and she exercised authority by granting the command of the last-mentioned City, where the Cornubian Britons had lingered till the reign of Athelstane, Ethelred's grandsire, to her Chamberlain and Confidant, the Norman Hugh. No fear of the Natives now.—They had been "exterminated," that is to say, they had been cleared out: whether up to the Exe, or up to the Tamar, the effect was the same.—"*Ex-termino.*"—How singularly do we trace the logical sequence disclosed by etymology.—Hunt and herry the weaker races out of their houses and homes, and they dwindle away.

The English give to Emma the name of Elfgiva.

Emma was welcomed by her new subjects as the "Gem of Normandy." They could not gainsay her beauty, but her foreign manners told against her. Her "uncouth," or unknown appellation in particular, sounded unpleasantly upon the English ear.—Like the Russians, the English sought that their Sovereign's strange spouse should be at least apparently nationalized; and they bestowed upon her the name or epithet of Elfgiva, honoured or dishonoured by the widow of Charles le-Simple, and the mother of

Louis d'Outremer;—that wife so true, that mother so bold and tender, but of whom we have long since taken our leave, as the doating grey-haired widow running away with a big boy.

999—1024

The heavy misfortunes sustained by the English had impressed them with the feeling that their sins would bring on their punishment, and that they would be brought to confusion. Rowena's cup was a poisoned cup. The Anglo-Saxon domination was founded upon fraud and violence. Retribution was impending; and many of the faithful raised up for the warning of their fellow countrymen survived to witness the chastisement, which their profound belief in the eternal justice of the Living God visiting the sins of the fathers upon the children, had enabled them to foretell.

Presentiments of retribution.

§ 34. The union, commenced with simulated rejoicing and triumph, was speedily interrupted by calamity. Emma returned to her native home. More than one reason is assigned for this ill-omened flight of the Bride. According to some authorities, Ethelred disgusted her by his profligacy, incontinence, wine-bibbing, and gluttony. Other causes may be conjectured. The churl Hugh was accused of having betrayed his trust to the Danes, and Emma may have been suspected of conniving at her Chamberlain's treachery. In that same year also, or within the year, Ethelred perpetrated the Blood-bath or Massacre of Saint Brice, his day; and Elfgiva Emma took refuge

1001. Emma's discomfort—she returns to Normandy.

in her native land from the horror and confusion. But, whether guilty or innocent, the result was the same. The heart of Emma clung more and more to her native land. Her feelings were inherited by the children who were afterwards born to her — they imbibed them at their mother's breast. Their hearts were thoroughly alienated from England, and the Normans and Normandy became as their kindred and their home.

§ 35. We must now view Richard as the ally of France. Most memorably was young Normandy's encreasing strength manifested during the obstinate warfare waged by King Robert against Burgundy, constituting, equally in its immediate results, and remote consequences, the most memorable passage of his reign.—The Low Countries, Spain, Portugal, Italy, all came within the wide sphere of Burgundian influence, and the death of Philip le-Hardi upon the field of Granson, was the event, which, by liberating the Eidgenossen from his fear, decided the fate of the Empire.

Dignified by the reminiscences of antient Barbarian royalty, Burgundy had been retained as the peculiar apanage of Robert le-Fort's descendants, their firmest stronghold, supporting them during the contests with the Carlovingian dynasty: and, when Hugh le-Grand was preparing the way for his son's accession to the throne, the Style assumed by the wise politician marked the importance he attached to the constitutional distinction between the two Dominations, avoiding any confusion between the rights of the Duke of Burgundy and the rights of the Duke of France—the throne he sought, and the possessions which enabled his son to win the sceptre.

999—1024

Since Charles le-Chauve's reign, Burgundy had been divided into the "Duchy of Burgundy" and the "County of Burgundy," afterwards emphatically denominated the "Franche Compté," such appellation testifying that the fief was not held of the Counts of Burgundy, but of the Sovereign.

Division of Burgundy, Cisjurane, and Transjurane, into the Duchy and the Franche Compté.

This interesting country, so picturesquely covered by the roots of the Jura, and including various territories wrested from the Duke in later times by the formidable and fraudulent Switzers, was dependant upon the Crown of France. But the political relations subsisting between the Dukes or Counts of Burgundy and the Fleur de lis, rank amongst the vexed questions of French constitutional history.

Burgundy was distinguished by the sanctity, the opulence, and the numbers of her religious institutions. Her ecclesiastical annals are therefore sufficiently ample; but no Historian of any note was nurtured in the Abbeys, consequently, her secular annals are defective and imperfect, and the wide discrepancies between the authorities, concerning the dates of events, when they ought to run parallel with the occurrences in France and Normandy, frequently perplex the narrative.

Deficiency of Burgundian Historians, and consequent obscurity of her History.

VOL. III. I

999—1024.
965—1002.
Henri le-Grand first Duke of Burgundy of the Capetian line.

At the period when Hugh Capet acquired the throne, the Duchy was held by Henry, his brother, distinguished in history as Henri le-Grand, though, according to the ordinary sense in which this much abused and often mischievous epithet is employed, we cannot discover any appropriateness in the application thereof to him.—Henry was really a good man, a quiet man; never did he give the slightest disturbance to his neighbours, never did he perform a warlike deed, never did he engage in any intrigues political or amatory, his time and mind being completely engrossed by higher objects. A Charter, however, can be quoted in which Hugh Capet bestows upon his brother the title of "Grand Duke," but the original is not extant. Possibly, the expression intended to bestow upon Henry a superior constitutional dignity, became colloquially attached to his name.

Adalbert, son of Berenger, King of Italy, (see Vol. II., 671—672,) marries Gerberga of Chalons—Otho Guillaume their son.

By a strange concurrence of circumstances, the legitimate representative of the Lombard Kings of Italy had settled in Burgundy. The romantic adventures of the Prince and Pirate, Adalbert, or Albert, the son of King Berenger and bold Guilla, have been elsewhere told. Strenuous and astute, Adalbert sobered as he grew older, and, wandering beyond the Alps, he espoused Gerberga, daughter of the much honoured Lambert, Count of Chalons, by whom he had one child, Otho Guillaume.

Adalbert gathered to his fathers, Gerberga

effected the conquest of worthy old Duke Henry. May we not suppose that she possessed her namesake's energetic qualities: at all events her son was distinguished by valour and talent; and, such was the influence which they both gained over the venerable Duke, that he adopted the youth, declaring him his successor and heir. Duke Henry did not possess any legal power to make such a grant; and, upon his demise, the Duchy reverted to the Crown. But Otho Guillaume fully deserved the authority, and, one individual alone foreprized, he obtained the general support of the Burgundian Clergy and Nobility.

965—1024. Gerberga, upon Adalbert's death, marries Duke Henry, who adopts Otho Guillaume.

King Robert, albeit entranced by his poetry, diligent in works of charity and piety, and perplexed and plagued by his cross-grained Beauty, had fully prepared for the contingency of his dear Uncle's death, and forthwith applied to Richard of Normandy for aid. Equally on the alert was the Duke; and a large army, amounting or magnified to the number of thirty thousand men, mustered under the Norman standard, which was borne aloft by Roger de Toesny. Very powerful did the united families of Toesny and Conches become in England, and the Standard bearer's grandson married the Adeliza Judith, the widow of the unfortunate Waltheoff, Earl of Huntingdon.

1003. The great invasion of Burgundy—Powerful assistance rendered to Robert by Richard le-Bon.

Round numbers are necessarily incorrect: making, however, in this case, the fullest allowance for any exaggeration, far did the force brought up by Richard exceed any contingent which King Robert could claim as a right from the Duke of Normandy, Rollo's heir. Richard, in fact, acted in the character of an ally rather than as a feudatory. Nor can we doubt but that a large portion of his troops were mercenaries serving for their solde or pay; and they cared not against whom they drew the sword. Normandy was overflowing with a military population, anxious for employment, and for plunder. It was the universal feeling that the land was not wide enough for them.

<small>1003—1004. Auxerre besieged by the French and Normans.</small>

Rapid was the march of the combined armies. —Duke Henry had scarcely been gathered to his fathers, when the assailants presented themselves before Auxerre, the frontier City between Champagne and Burgundy. Secured against an enemy by the broad Saone and the encircling walls and towers, popular belief imparted a greater power of defence to "Autissiodurum" than could be bestowed merely by lime and stone. The inhabitants were persuaded that the protection given by Saint Germain to the locality where his corpse was deposited, rendered the Place impregnable.

Landric, Count of Nevers, commanded the city. The Abbey had been fortified. Abbot Adalric interceded on behalf of the citizens, but fruitlessly; and Richard and his Normans commenced the blockade.

This was a season of remarkable atmospheric and cosmical phenomena. A fiery dragon shot quivering across the heavens, rising in the north and setting in the south. A portentous mist then came on, shrouding earth and sky. Auxerre was involved in darkness. The Arbalisters could not aim their bolts,—those weapons so destructive when sighted by the Norman eye and supported by the Norman arm,—whilst all the missiles told upon the besiegers. King Robert, however, contending against every difficulty, continued his operations steadily; and the charters dated from his Camp, pending the siege, exemplified the vigour of his royal authority at the very time he was most stoutly opposed: but the perseverance of the Auxerrois was rewarded; the invading forces, abandoning the Leaguer, struck their tents and moved on.

999—1024. Atmospheric phenomena —meteors— extraordinary omens —raising of the Siege.

An obstinate warfare ensued. Otho Guillaume, able and active, had won the people's hearts, and the Burgundians availed themselves of the natural defences afforded by their mountainous regions. Only one single Noble adhered to King Robert, Hugh, Bishop of Auxerre as well as Count of Chalons,—who will ultimately appear in a ludicrous as well as humiliating position. What think ye of a Count-Bishop, literally saddled and figuratively bridled?

Support given by the Burgundians to Otho Guillaume.

Normans and French advanced up the country. Avalon,—whose Celtic name strangely interests us by the recollections which the sound suggests of the mythic Arthur's sepulture,—Avalon, dreary Avalon—was invested by the enemy,

Siege of Avalon.

_{994—1024} but in vain; for the bleak and rocky hills of that remarkable region, where every stone exhibits the mysterious seals testifying the evolution of life, and the infliction of death, in time, but before time, at the Almighty's behest, constituted a series of natural fortifications which greatly impeded the besiegers; the inhabitants however, not having been enabled to provision their town, they were starved out, and surrendered.

The country was ravaged, but the talent of the Lombard Statesman and Warrior had won the hearts of the Clergy and Nobility. Otho Guillaume commanded the suffrages of all ranks. King Robert had not gained an adherent, save and except that one Count-Bishop, he of Auxerre and Chalons. During nearly twelve years the war continued obstinately, until, at length, a _{1015—1032. Henry eldest son of King Robert, first Duke of Burgundy, of the Royal House of France.} compromise was effected. Henry, second Duke of the name, King Robert's eldest son, was appointed Duke of this much contested land. But the government was nevertheless carried on by King Robert, until his son, King Henry, ascended the throne, when he bestowed the Duchy upon his father's homonym, Robert the younger, though denominated Robert le-Vieux, and he must be accepted as the founder of the Capetian line of Dukes, so active, so influential, so splendid, but so troublesome to the dynasty from which they sprung.

As to Otho Guillaume, he was ultimately compensated by receiving the Franche Compté.

His son Renauld succeeded to his authority; his marriage with Alice, otherwise Judith, the daughter of our Duke Richard, connected him with Normandy. In the next generation we shall find his descendants asserting a claim to Normandy, and giving trouble to the Conqueror; and from Otho Guillaume was the royal house of Portugal also descended.

904—1024

995. Otho Guillaume succeeded, 1027, by his son Renauld.

Chapter III.

RICHARD LE-BON AND HIS SUCCESSORS, RICHARD III—ROBERT LE-MAGNIFIQUE OR LE-DIABLE—EARLY INFANCY OF WILLIAM THE BASTARD.

1024—1035.

§ 1. RICHARD, called again to Burgundy, had enjoyed sufficient opportunity for keeping his eager Normans in training; and, towards the conclusion of his reign, he was again roused by Eudes le-Champenois.

County of Dreux, between the Pays Chartrain and Normandy, occupied by Richard Sans-peur.

Between the Pays Chartrain and Normandy there was a debatable land, a territory originally included, as the old historiographers maintain, in the cession made to Rollo; but lost and won. We are speaking of Dreux, the County of Dreux, which County in subsequent times became a splendid illustration of our baronial history, when Pierre de Dreux, Count of Brittany, acquired the noble Honour of Richmond. You may see his bearings in the Chancel window there; "chequey, or, and azure, a Canton of Brittany," but you may search in vain for any such heraldic memorial of him in his own land. Originally the *Pagus Drocensium* constituted a portion of Rollo's dominions, but at a subsequent era more clearly within our ken, Dreux had been held by a line of Counts whose last representative disappears in Richard Sans-peur's reign. Richard seems to have treated the County as a Fief which had devolved upon him by escheat, inasmuch as we find the great Seigneurie in his possession without any war, at least no war is noticed, and he annexed the same to his dominions.

1024—1035

The territory is bounded towards the north by the streamlet Aure, which falls into the Eure. The acquisition was important. The country was open to inimical Chartres: and a Roman road connecting Dreux and Chartres, extensive remains of which may yet be discovered, must have been at least as passable in the eleventh century as our Watling Street in old Norman times. But if the Romans multiplied communications between the various parts of their dominions, they were equally careful to provide the means of defence; and a station, the *Castrum Tegulense*, was raised, adjoining the banks of the river—a memorial of their vigilant strategy; just as Aldershot affords a living testimony, so to speak, of their acuteness and military judgment. Subsequently a town was erected there, which obtained the name of *Tillieres*. The original name of the station, the *Tile-Kiln*, bespeaks the nature of the soil; Tillieres is in fact the original *Thuilleries*, and, building materials being close at hand, Richard le-Bon had very considerately founded a castle upon the Roman site. It is always more than an even

1007. Tillieres— Castle erected there by Richard le-Bon upon Roman foundations.

chance that the mediæval engineers selected for their fortresses the positions where the Cæsars had been before them.

Eudes le-Champenois had been thoroughly baffled by Richard at Melun, but a pacific feeling arose, or, at all events, both parties concurred in desiring peace; Eudes sued for, and obtained the hand of Maude or Matilda, a daughter of Richard Sans-peur. Her brother Richard le-Bon testified his approbation by granting to her a very handsome dowry, inasmuch as he settled all differences by guerdoning the bride with one moiety of the County of Dreux. Whether this was an actual partition by metes and bounds, or whether made by ceding particular and specific towns, seigneuries, or domains, cannot be ascertained; and it was a reasonable condition imposed by Richard le-Bon, that, in the event of Maude's death without issue, the gift should revert to the Donor.

§ 2. All promised fair, but to Maude was denied the usual fertility of Normandy's daughters. Year after year ran round; no jolly cheerful messenger appeared at Rouen respectfully summoning Richard to stand godfather to any children of hers; no little nephews or nieces presented to him; no babe to rejoice the heart of the father—she died childless. And now Eudes acted in conformity to the spirit of his lineage. The Pays de Dreux constituted a very important border-land. In possession, Eudes determined to keep possession, and refused to surrender the dowry lands. Tillieres was in a good state of defence. Very probably the anticipation of such a demur had previously suggested to Richard the expediency of encreasing the fortifications; anyhow, he profited by these precautions, and the war began. {1094—1095}

§ 3. Harrying the Chartrain territory, Richard victualled the Castle at the expense of the plundered enemy, and he forthwith summoned his baronage. Distinguished among them was Neel de Saint Sauveur, commanding the Cotentin warriors, fretting within their narrow boundaries, the men of Northern descent, amongst whom the Danske dialect was worn out, but who nevertheless were fully animated with the Danish spirit. With him, Ralph de Toesny, and Roger, yclept the Spaniard, Ralph's bold son. Roger appears as Standard-bearer of Normandy, equalling that father in valour, and rivalling him in ferocity. {Angry war between Richard le-Bon and Count Eudes. Richard le-Bon assembles his baronage—at their head Neel de Saint Sauveur, Ralph de Toesny, and Roger his son.}

Richard commenced operations by insulting Dreux.—Eudes held hard and fast; and, confident in his strength, he resolved to retain his acquisitions, and secure them, by destroying the wasp's nest at Tillieres. Large forces had been levied or obtained from his own subjects, as well as from his allies. In particular, he was powerfully supported by Waleran de Mellent and Hugh Count of Maine, the district which became often so troublesome to the Normans, {Eudes determines to destroy Tillieres—Waleran of Mellent and Hugh Count of Maine join him.}

1024—1035 until the Conqueror annexed that antient domination to his territories.

A forced march during the night brought the Lords of Mellent and Maine before the walls of Tillieres. Richard was ready, and forth he sallied. Three were the Champions appointed Constables of the Host, Neel de Saint Sauveur, and Ralph and Roger de Toesny, the formidable sire and son. Ample reinforcements also; Frenchmen, described as such. The national appellation of "Français" had already become attached to all the Romane populations; and the Normans themselves did not repudiate the term, so influential amongst the causes, and so important as the consequence, of that feeling which has imparted an indomitable vitality to the Capetian Realm.—Republic, Kingdom, or Empire, France, centuries before the Tricolor was unfurled or the Eagle raised, felt herself one and indivisible.

The sally from the Castle — Richard heads his men. Eudes defeated, and he and his troops put to flight.

Richard did not wait to be attacked. The three gonfanons floating in the air distinguished the three squadrons which sallied forth; whilst, pre-eminent amidst them, was the Ducal standard, marking the spot where Richard was wielding his sword, spreading dismay amongst the enemy: Saint Michael's banner inspired as much terror as the Danish Raven. A desperate sortie, made by the besieged, produced a sudden rout of the besiegers. Eudes, himself, scoured the field as a fugitive, rapidly as his father had done after the defeat of Hermondeville. He would have been captured had he not been rescued by Waleran de Mellent's aid, who conducted him home in safety. All fled for their lives, or next to it. Men had much to fight for;— a fearful fate threatened the captive. Courtesy to the vanquished, even in the days of chivalry, was very capricious; the more distinguished, and therefore the more valuable, the prize, the more jealous the custody. Had Eudes been caught, he might have pined for months, nay, for years, dropped in the dungeon pit, loaded with chains, or sometimes, as an alleviation, exchanging those chains for a link clinking on his right leg, dragging a clog.—You may see a brace of these clogs in the old Norman Keep of Castle Rising: the biggest is called "roaring Meg;" her sister, somewhat smaller, "pretty Bessy."

Hugh Count of Maine galloped away till his horse stood stock still, the animal being completely winded: he also fell into a ditch, and sustained other mischances, as the Trouveur tells. The Normans were tracking him, and he was fully aware that they were on the scent. Off he cast his hauberk, and flung away his spurs. A Shepherd sheltered him, and he tended the sheep. The Normans continued hunting the enemy, they bore a grudge against him. He fled from the sheep-cote and concealed himself in the woods, skulking till he reached.

margin: 1024—1035

margin: Narrow escape of the Count of Maine.

1024—1035 — Le Mans, his naked limbs all torn by the thorny bushes and the flinty ways.

Richard invites the Northmen under the Kings of Norway and Sweden.

§ 4. But the power of Chartres was not affected by such a defeat, the discomfiture was a graze, not a wound. Richard was in a great strait, and we are in a manner startled by the appearance in the field of Olave the Norwegian King, and another King who was denominated King of the Swedes. English chronicles identify him with the King Olave, who was subsequently canonized. A Church is dedicated to the memory of this King Olave in the "South-work," now emphatically called *the* Borough; and, in "Tooley Street," we may be interested by the homely, nay, almost vulgar fusion of the Scandinavian name.

The Northmen land on the Coast of Brittany.

§ 5. Again the Northmen are pursuing their devastations. The Danes having assembled their armies, and probably sailing from England, their fleet, so terrible to the miserable English, assailed the shores of Brittany.

It seems they were driven in by a storm; and they immediately turned the mischance to account. All along this northern coast considerable changes have taken place,—the land gaining upon the sea. The vicinity now presents many features susceptible of strategic improvement,—here available to the inhabitants, there to an invader; but the Bretons were not a match for the amphibious Northmen, whether on land or water. The doleful bridale of Dôle had not taught them caution, and they allowed

The Bridale of Dôle.

the enemy to make the most of their opportunities.

The story is reported to us amply though confusedly. The city of Dôle is commanded by the Mount Dôle, boldly rising from the plain, between the city and the sea; and here an examination of the locality induces us to place the Danish encampment. The Bretons, whose local chieftain was a certain Count Solomon, a name which is tolerably familiar in the Armorican genealogies, rallied their forces, and summoned all absentees to return and aid in the defence of their homes. Their strength mainly consisted in their cavalry; the Northmen knew it, and slow and cautious were the operations on either side. Preparing for an attack upon their entrenchments, to be made from the level below, they dressed the field for the fight, by adopting a stratagem not unfrequently employed. They scored the ground with pit-falls, and planted them with stakes: the artifice was stale and rude, and yet it usually succeeded. The Pirates soon afterwards practised the same device in Acquitaine, to the great discomfiture of the inhabitants, and we find it repeated upon English ground in the battle of Hastings, and also in the famous battle of the Standard, between the representative of Blois and the Plantagenet, so celebrated in Northumbrian history. The Bretons, unsuspicious of the contrivance, were thrown into confusion. Solomon took refuge in Dôle; the Danes fired

128   TREATY OF COUDRES.

1024—1035 the town; Solomon was slain, the country plun-
Danes sail dered, and the Northmen now set to work upon
up the Seine. the business for which they had been called. They
hoisted their sails: favourable winds facilitated
their voyage through the Channel, they entered
the Seine, and their keels, pulling up to the
Norman capital, they were hailed by their friend
Richard.

Alarm created in France by their appearance.—King Robert's sagacity and firmness. This transaction was simply a perseverance in the policy which Richard had notoriously adopted for consolidating his alliance with the Northmen; but the re-appearance on this occasion of these plunderers by nature and breeding, rendered his predilections more patent and more alarming to the French than any previous act. All the apprehensions excited by the black Danish blood were revived; and not unreasonably: King Robert felt the full extent of the impending danger. No one of his predecessors or progenitors could have displayed more resolution, nor a truer sense of his royal duties and prerogatives, than this henpecked King.

1020 The treaty of Coudres— Peace restored by the intervention of King Robert. Forthwith he assembled his Peers, and having advised with them, he summoned the two warlike litigants to appear before him, at Coudres in the Evreçin. Thanks to the Roman road, the locality was convenient to all parties, and the place, now obscure, may then have been rendered more important by the remains and relics of antient grandeur. Traditions of the old times continue to be rife at Coudres. There is a field there, which has been always known to the peasantry, as the "*Champ d'argent*," though no token appeared above ground justifying the appellation.—But the tradition told truth.—Scarcely thirty years have elapsed since the plough turned up a vase, filled with plenty of "*argent*," in the monetary, though not in the metallic sense,—large Roman brass—six or seven hundred coins.

[1024—1035]

Here King Robert, as Conservator of the public peace, arbitrated between the contending parties—not by any means an easy task.—He had to snatch the bone from the jaws of two angry hungry mastiffs. However, the litigants obeyed his award.—Dreux, thenceforward, became annexed to the County of Blois and Chartres; the town of Dreux, the ample forest, and the noble Castle towering above the plain, whose chapel now exhibits, vainly or prophetically, according to the political opinions of the observer, as he may be guided by hope or fear, the thirty-two cenotaphs constructed by an exiled Monarch, and destined by that Exile to receive the mortal remains of his rejected Dynasty. Henceforward, the antipathy between Blois and Chartres, and Normandy, diminished. Anjou was becoming more formidable to both parties. Stephen of Blois, the son of Eudes by Hermengarda of Auvergne, contracted a marriage with a Norman Adeliza, Duke Richard's daughter. And the fear of Normandy encreased all around.

[Dreux—Castle and Chapel.]

§ 6. At the commencement of Richard's

1024—1085

The great Burgundian wars.

Count of Burgundy courts and marries the daughter of Richard le-Bon.

military career, Burgundy, and Burgundy's Sovereigns had afforded the most exciting motives, and the most ample field, for the exertion of his prowess: and now, in connection with Burgundy, was that career concluded. Renaud, the son of Otho William, who obtained possession of the much coveted *Franche Compté*, was a worthy and renowned Prince, and he sought the hand of a Norman Atheliza. I shall not attempt to open the oft recurring question, whether this denomination, bestowed by historians upon damsels of Regal or Sovereign race, be an epithet or a name. The reputation of her virtues and beauty extended far and wide: and, instead of wooing through the medium of an ambassador, Renaud, conforming to Normandy's gallant etiquette, the bright dawn of ideal chivalry, repaired to Rouen in person, won her heart, gained her hand, and triumphantly brought her home.

Hugh the uxorate Bishop of Auxerre and Count of Chalons.

§ 7. The Bishopric of Chalons continued to be the scandal of all France. Lambert, the son of Robert the Count of Autun and Bishop of Chalons, married Adelaide the daughter of Count Robert his predecessor; and their son Hugh, inheriting his father's temporal preferment, became Bishop of Auxerre, and took a wife, the daughter of Geoffrey Grisgonnelle. This disgraceful breach of his vows may in some degree be palliated, inasmuch as Hugh Capet had coerced him either into the marriage or into the dignity, we can hardly tell which.

Some time afterwards, a quarrel broke out between the Count Bishop and Count Renaud. Defeated and captured by the clerical warrior, Renaud was treated with great severity, loaded with chains and cast into a dungeon. Duke Richard despatched ambassadors to the Count Bishop, earnestly beseeching that, for his sake, he would be pleased to liberate his daughter's husband. Renaud's Countess also interceded. All supplications were fruitless. Hugh not only augmented the duresse of the prison-house, but he turned away money; refusing the large proffered ransom. Duke Richard forthwith determined to revenge the affront by carrying the war into the Bishop's dominions. A numerous Norman army was mustered against the ambiguous Lord of Chalons. Richard's eldest son and namesake was now a full-grown youth, prudent and bold, though he had not yet attained his majority; but, young as he was, his father was well contented to conjoin him in the enterprise.

1024—1035. Renaud taken prisoner by the Count Bishop, and treated with much severity.

Richard's eldest son—his good qualities.

If, as some authorities state, Robert, Duke Richard's second son, (so well known as Robert le-Diable,) accompanied his brother, they parted before the termination of the war.

King Robert facilitated the operations: and, it is important to remark, that the Norman army could not have marched through France otherwise than with the Sovereign's permission; a circumstance testifying the extent of the royal prerogative, as well as King Robert's vigilance

Norman army sent against the Bishop of Chalons under the command of Richard's sons.

K 2

in guarding his rights. Furthermore, Duke Richard purchased the alliance of the Count of Peronne by granting to him certain fiefs in the Hiesmois. The Normans and their allies fiercely ravaged the enemies' territory as they advanced, and invested Mirmande, a locality named without comment, as being familiarly known; but the incidents, like all connected with the Burgundian affairs, are told so confusedly, that even the laborious and learned Benedictines, whose history of the country fills four folio volumes, are unable to fix the date of these transactions, or discover any such town in Burgundy. No "Mirmande" is noted on the map, save and except Mirmande near Valence, which never had belonged to the Count Bishop; so distant also from the field of operations, that it could not have been in the route of the belligerents at any period during the war we are now detailing. Nor are we assisted in our inquiries by the knowledge that the fortress was also denominated *La Merveille.*

The massacre at Mirmande.
Mirmande, however, was certainly in Burgundy, and very defensible; probably a position somewhere amongst the hills. The garrison resisted most sturdily, until the Normans gained the Place by storm. All the inhabitants were massacred, man, woman, and child; and the Normans, having burnt the town to the ground, continued their march, perpetrating all the mischief in their power. The Count Bishop fleeing for his life, took refuge in Chalons, but dreading an as-

sault from the combined forces, and fearing also lest the tonsure, concealed by a helmet, might fail to ensure ecclesiastical immunity, he did not shrink from seeking pardon in the most humiliating guise.

Ludicrous humiliation of the Count Bishop.

Chalons' gate opened.—Out trudged our Bishop with a shabby old saddle slung round his neck, and hanging down his back; and, as the Trouveur intimates, he offered Richard a ride. Some authorities add, that he cast himself at the young Duke's feet, rolling upon the ground.

1026. Death of Richard le-Bon.—Richard III. his successor.

§ 8. Very joyful was the conclusion of this campaign. Renaud, being delivered from captivity, the young and victorious Richard returned home in triumph: and greatly was Richard le-Bon delighted by his son's good fortune and valour. But the Duke's time was come. He sickened; and knew that he was dying; and, like his father, he chose to end his days at Fécamp. There, according to the constitutional usage, he summoned his Nobles, spiritual as well as temporal peers, his children being by his bedside also.—Having confessed to the Bishops, he called in the Barons, and declared his last will and testament.

He designated Richard as his successor; and, perhaps with some presentiment of evil, he expressed an earnest hope that the Normans would be faithful to him. He is a good youth, said the expiring father. To Robert, his second son, he appointed the County of Hiesmes, otherwise the Exmois; and upon the express trust that he should be helpful to his brother. Concerning Mauger, an unfrocked monk,—a character amongst the vilest the most despicable,—no directions are recorded: he ultimately became Archbishop of Rouen.

Richard departed quietly; and Fécamp Abbey received his body. But, in a subsequent generation, Henry Beauclerc caused the remains of Richard Sans-peur to be removed from the sarcophagus under the spouting gargoyle, and deposited in the adjoining Basilica. A new tomb was provided for father and son, near the High Altar; and Master Wace informs us, that, when the translation took place, he had the opportunity of contemplating both the corpses.

Foundations of early Norman history.

§ 9. The early history of Normandy, constituting the period anterior to the Conqueror's reign,—Normandy with all her specialities, Normandy self contained,—rests mainly upon two authorities; the conscientious and laborious

The prose authorities.

Dean of Saint Quentin, and the much perplexed and perplexing Guillaume de Jumièges, whose abounding information must be accepted as a compensation for his deficiency in historical skill.

The Trouveurs, Wace, and Benoit de Saint More.

Important adjuncts to these memorials, and grounded upon them, are those bequeathed to us by the Trouveurs, Master Wace, and Benoit de Saint More; the metrical form which their productions assume, not to be considered as detracting from their trustworthiness.

With respect to the prose writers, honest and

hard working though they be, they lack the method and solidity which distinguish the Carlovingian Monastic Chronicles properly so called. The style of the Capetian compositions is uniform. Dates most scanty.—Recollections recollected, constitute their basis, not the collections resulting from research or study. Narratives of this class bear a strong affinity to the later French memoires, of which they are the mediæval precursors; *Sagas:—sayings*, tolerably veracious so far as they extend, and always more animated than desk work, grounded upon the muniments or volumes before you.

<small>1024—1035</small>

The subject would widen upon us were we to discuss it in all its length and breadth. Sternly and acutely has the general credibility of antient history been investigated, sifted, criticised, and assailed in our times. Even Brutus and Tarquin are elided from the schoolboy's manual, and classed with the grand-dame's tale; majestic Clio crouches in the hearth-nook beside the garrulous Crone.

<small>Traditional history.</small>

It is a mortifying example of unconscious reasoning, that, in the English language one and the same word has become equivalent to truth and to fiction—a *History* is a *Story*; as though untruthfulness were an inherent element. The discussion of the moral or mental causes leading to this amphibology, must be left to that cotemporary expositor who has so ably demonstrated how the study of words involves the most valuable moral lessons, and the most transcendental philosophy. Without pursuing the investigation, it is sufficient to observe, that the Tale-teller will frequently omit matters peculiarly prominent in his mind, upon the supposition, that the Hearer is already acquainted with them. The silence of the multiplicity of authorities in cases where you might expect the record of a particular fact, should not necessarily cast doubt upon the incident or event recorded by one competent authority. Ample as may be the information we possess concerning Richard le-Bon, we scarcely know anything relating to his sons Richard the Third and Robert, (their births being merely noticed parenthetically,) until we reach the concluding Burgundian Campaign; when, depending upon French sources, we collect that the third Richard was sufficiently qualified to warrant his being trusted by his father with the command of the Norman forces. Differences subsequently arising between him and his brother, the latter took affront, and returned home during the campaign, at the very crisis when hearty co-operation was most needed.

Be this as it may, Richard le-Bon's appointment of the elder brother as his heir was accepted without cavil or difficulty, and the third Richard, hailed by the Baronage, who became his Men, was inaugurated at Rouen, and we may view him as invested with the Coronal of the Duchy.

MARRIAGE OF RICHARD III. 137

Thus, having received the submission due from his own vassals, Richard forthwith fulfilled the obligations which he on his part owed to his Suzerain for the Dukedom; he repaired to Paris and performed homage "*en parage*," — the acknowledgment of personal superiority to the equal in degree.

margin: 1024—1035. 1026— Richard III. performs homage as parage to King Robert.

§ 10. Further consequences arose from this State visit. Duke Richard became affianced to his Sovereign's daughter, then a baby in the cradle. Unnoticed by historians, whether French or Norman, the engagement is proved by very satisfactory evidence. The transcript of the original settlement is extant, whereby "*Richardus Normannorum Dux*" bestows upon "*Domina Adela*" a noble dowry, the Seigneurie of the whole Peninsula of the Cotentin, besides various communes and baronies in demesne; — Cherbourg, whilom Harold Blaatand's Castle; Bruot or Bruis and the neighbouring Château d'Adam, the real cradle of Scotland's royal line, of which only one fragment subsists, scarcely discernible in the tangled copse, and shapeless as the rock upon which the wall is founded; pleasant Caen, and all members thereunto appertaining; Valognes and Cerisy; and the Pagus of the Hogue. —Egglandes or Oglandes also; Moion or Mohun; and "Piercei," a name grotesquely construed in England as signifying "Pierce-eye," and commemorating the deed whereby Hotspur's mythic ancestor, having more regard to success

margin: Richard III. espouses a daughter of France. Settlement made upon the marriage consisting of the Cotentin.

than good faith, is fabled to have rid himself of an imaginary enemy.

It may appear singular that amongst the domains selected by Richard for the purpose of affording a secure and adequate provision for his future spouse, many should respectively have sent forth families to either side of the Tweed. But they are for the most part situated in the Cotentin or its vicinity; a district from which the nobles and gentlefolk may be said to have turned out bodily, when the Conqueror's great expedition was proclaimed.

So far, well. But the clouds gathered simultaneously with the rising sun. Robert became savagely discontented, and Richard was not without blame. The fine County of Hiesmes was regarded as an important apanage; but Falaise, a separate Bailiwick, though a portion of the Hiesmois, was withheld. Robert resented the loss. His dissatisfaction, not entirely causeless, was fomented by a certain Ermenoldus, a Breton, who appears and vanishes, veiled in a species of mystery. To the epithet "Theosophist," assigned to him in the dubious account of his treasons, no definite meaning can be ascribed. The obscure denomination of "Philosopher," also applied to him, is rendered more intelligible by the charge of dealings with the Fiend, which would lead to the supposition, that, like Gerbert, he excelled in physical science.

Ermenoldus was a doughty champion. Having

impeached certain Norman nobles of conspiracy against the Sovereign, they severally challenged him to the ordeal combat. All the Appellors were defeated; but he himself succumbed in a duel with a Forester, whom he had accused. The death of the mischief-maker did not allay the bad feeling. Robert had many instigators, who urged him to do justice to himself by the strength of his own arm, and vindicate his rights and his reputation. Ready enough were those who gave the counsel to aid him in executing such counsel. Robert was very popular amongst the class whom Napoleon termed *chair à canon*. The distinctive energy of the Scandinavian Races has continued in full vigour amongst us, and still continues unexhausted. No country testifies to the potent influence of Scandinavia's blood more than our own. However mingled our Populations, each emigrant ship steaming from our shores bears away a large proportion of passengers who may claim real Danish ancestry. Many are the Danish Havelocks in our ranks, undistinguished by that heroic name, renowned of old in the Trouveur's lay.

margin: 1024—1085; Ermenoldus slain in the ordeal combat.

> HAVELOC tint en sa baillie
> Nicole et tote Lindesie;
> Vingt anz regna, si en fu rois
> Assez conquist par ses Danois;
> Moult fu de lui grand parlance.
> Qi aunciẹn par remenbrance
> Firent un lai de sa victoire
> Qe touz jours en soit la memoire.

1024—1035

Norman population encreasing beyond the means of subsistence.

§ 11. As in frozen Iceland, so in fertile Neustria, the land everywhere unable to house her children. Normandy was overflowing with the unemployed, encreasing—according to the formula which has now become technical in the science of political economy—beyond the means of subsistence. Large families gathered round the hearth, for whose keep the father could not *Anglo-Saxon Commonwealth, vol. II. p. ccvii.* provide. The land cut up into quillets; not a *mete-home*, a feeding farm, as it was called in old English, to be had, upon which a man and his family could live,—universal unease therefore prevailing. The great Norman military emigrations were now commencing,—not differing in essential character from those which appalled the Empire, in the ages when the epithet of *Vagina gentium* was first applied to the teeming North. Fair Apulia yielding to the Flibustier pilgrims, unrestrained by faith or truth, but whose robberies, enhauncing the renown of the Norman name, afforded relief to the burdened mother country. Crowds of young soldiers came flocking to Falaise, opening their ready hands for the tinkling sous Rouennois, offering their aid; and Robert, casting off his allegiance, appeared in open rebellion.

Robert's rebellion— Richard besieges Falaise.

§ 12. No lingering on Duke Richard's part. Summoning his forces, Richard invested Falaise. Besiegers and besieged were equally inflamed by the malignity inseparable from civil war,—brother always fiercest against brother. The ducal

ordnance was brought to bear upon the out- *1024—1035*
works, whilst Robert's soldiers were cleared off
from the walls by the bolts which the arbalests
discharged.

Richard became exasperated; Falaise, more *Pacification between the brothers, who agree upon a partition of the Duchy.*
and more straitened. Robert might dread to be
dropped into the dungeon pit if the Castle were
stormed. He was advised to sue for peace. The
competitors agreed upon a partition. The Hiesmois was conferred on Robert; but Falaise was
reserved to the elder. Merrily did they return
to Rouen. Great rejoicings ensued. A banquet,
in Rollo's palatial Castle, imparted splendour to
the reconciliation. But the young and flourishing
Richard was suddenly stricken; and he passed
from the hall to the death-bed. Many of the
party shared the same fate. Whilst the exhila-
ration of the feast was at its height, the funeral
bells were knelling. No one doubted but that *1027 Sudden death of Richard attributed to poison.*
poison had been in the cup. Never was Robert
exonerated from the imputation of fratricide;
never was the dark stain effaced; never was the
obscure suspicion dispelled.

§ 13. Robert's accession did not experience *Accession of Robert II.*
any opposition, but the event is related without
emphasis.—No expression of sentiment recorded.
—No prayer or benediction in the Cathedral. At *Illegitimate children of Richard III.*
the time when Richard's marriage contract was ex-
ecuted, the young Duke had already three children
—chance children as they would be euphemized
amongst our country folk—a son Nicholas, and

1094—1095 two daughters. Nothing is said or hinted concerning their mother or mothers, yet Robert acted as though he had some reasons to apprehend rivalry from the boy Nicholas; and he was tranquilly put out of the way. The stripling, placed as an Oblate in the Abbey of Fécamp, took very kindly to his clerical vocation. He grew up to be a learned and a good man, in due time Abbot of Saint Ouen. He rebuilt the Abbey Church; and, if the opinion of some architectural antiquaries be correct, the apse, so well known as the "*tour des clercs,*" is the memorial of Nicholas, who, living through three generations, attended the Conqueror's funeral.

988—1086
Baudouin
à-la-belle-
barbe, and
Baudouin de
Lisle, his son.

Adela
married to
Baudouin
de Lisle.

§ 14. Baby Adela, the poor little ducal widow, obtained, in due time, a suitor without any coquetry. Baudouin à-la-belle-barbe, Baldwin Bushy-beard, sued for the infant daughter of France on behalf of his son Baudouin, (afterwards Count of Flanders,) Baudouin de Lisle. She became the mother of Matilda,—our Matilda,— the Conqueror's Queen.

Robert's
epithets or
sobriquets,
"le-Diable,"
or "le-Mag-
nifique."

§ 15. Historians and archæologists have bestowed much unprofitable pains upon the legends, in which they discover grounds for a vague conjecture, that the solid sturdy Robert became identified with a certain imaginary or legendary hero, and in such manner as to earn the ugly epithet of *le-Diable*. Other archæologists seem to enlist our Duke in the *meisné* or train of Hellekin, or Hurlekin, the Gallic *Wilde jæger*, or Wild huntsman. Yet, whatever may have been

Robert's secret crimes, he never manifested any 1024—1035 open tendency to outrage or cruelty. Courteous, joyous, debonnaire and benign, was the son of Richard le-Bon before the world; and his life and conversation consistent. The poor and diseased ever commanded his sympathies, and particularly did he labour to relieve the sufferings of the miserable mesel. This Robert, second of the name in the opinion of those genealogists who accept Rollo-Robert as the first, was truly *Robert le-Magnifique*, as well as *Robert le-Diable*. Fully did he deserve the epithet earned by his abounding munificence.

The *Magnifico* commenced his reign by increasing the salaries of his retainers, and duplicating their liveries,—the Court allowances for back and belly. According to popular exaggerations, which may in some degree be accepted as expansions of truth, Robert's gifts were so liberal, that those whom he benefitted died of joy. He never could satisfy himself that his bounties were adequate to the claims of the receivers: and, endued with a virtue far more rare than liberality, his heart never grudged what his hand bestowed. Yet, despite his generosity and joyous munificence, Robert's general conduct was unsatisfactory, and in the last year of his life he displayed all that wild, exuberant hilarity which saddens the thoughtful observer more than grief: an unseasonable joke may be more melancholy than the darkest despondency.

Once settled in his authority;—at least as

much settled as his flighty hilarious character would allow him to be, Falaise became his favourite residence. Site, air, water, hunting grounds, copses, shaws, all pleased him; and the various anecdotes concerning Robert's demeanour, trivial in themselves, but which acquire value by accumulation, are evidences that the young Duke mixed pleasantly with his inferiors.

The peltry manufacture, and all the branches of the leather trade flourished in Falaise. Buckskin and doe-skin, calf-skin, and sheep-skin, and the bullock's tough hide, were supplied cheaply and abundantly from the glade and the pasture. Foreigners resorted to the thriving bourgade and were welcomed as denizens. Thus, in the time of Richard le-Bon, a certain Herbert, or Robert, or Fulbert, three names which may be easily confounded the one with the other by the careless transcriber, established himself there.

"Robertus Belliparius," as Alberic of Troisfontaines writes the word Pelliparius, following the thick German pronunciation, was born at Chaumont, in the Walloon country, near the Abbey of Florines, in the Diocese of Liège, but he and his wife, Doda, removed to "Hoie," where, as it is noted, they dwelt in the Market Place, near the old Exchange.—"*Manentes ad veteras cambias in foro Hoiense.*" And Alberic also furnishes some particulars (not relevant to our history) concerning the courtship and marriage of the "Belliparius," with the said Doda, otherwise Duida. *1024—1085*

Considered in themselves, these circumstances are somewhat trifling, but they were traditional in the localities. Alberic, who collected the information on the spot, informs us that he had heard old folks tell the story of the fortunate Currier's family; and the minuteness of these details testifies that Fulbert continued a "celebrity" in his former neighbourhood more than a century after his grandchild the Conqueror's death, and imparts identity to the personage. One daughter had the Belliparius and Doda, the Arletta, or Herleva, of the Norman chroniclers. Fulbert was wealthy; a currier or tanner by trade, he also carried on the business of a beer brewer.

§ 16. A strong prejudice exists in Germany against the artificers who furnish the currier with the raw material needful for his manufacture. Those who pursued the useful, albeit disgusting, trade of skinning beasts, were stigmatized as a distinct and degraded caste— ranked amongst the *races maudites* of France, holding a place somewhat between a *mesel* and a gypsey, cohabiting or marrying only amongst themselves. It was the ever present and intolerable burning brand of unmerited and unremoveable ignominy, which drove the famous Rhine robber, Schinderhans, to desperation. *The Skinners antiently a degraded caste.*

The opinion concerning the foulness of the

vocation seems to have been very general. The antient Hebrew gnome:—Let the learned man skin dogs, or break the Sabbath, rather than abase his talent by employing the gift as the means of making money, affords equally a curious exemplification of the honour rendered to intellect by the fine old Rabbins, and their detestation of the disgusting business which, employing an excusable exaggeration, they paralleled with so great a transgression as the violation of the Seventh day's rest.

All analogous avocations—all employments dealing with the raw hide—participated in the same obloquy. Prosperous as Fulbert was, he could not merge the Tanner in the Brewer. It is probable that the union of these trades encreased his unpopularity. In England, Tanners were prohibited from brewing, as though the junction of these callings might be injurious to the public health, or productive of some other inconveniences. There are queer—and, to ale drinkers, —rather disagreeable stories current, concerning the smoothness imparted to the good liquor by animal matter. And whoever sought to tease or scoff at Fulbert or his, led you into the tan-yard. Such being the state of the public mind, we may easily imagine the sensation created in Falaise, when, adopting the expression so familiar among our lower classes, it was talked and gossiped all round the town how the Duke "kept company" with the Tanner's daughter. The Chroniclers detail these amours with much gusto. Some say Robert became acquainted with the damsel at a dance: others, that he was first attracted by seeing her delicate little feet gleaming through the translucent streamlet, still rippling round the base of the rock upon which the huge Donjon stands. The window is shewn through which as the Cicerone now tells you, the Duke first beheld her.

<small>1024—1035 Arletta, the Tanner's daughter, and the Duke's concubine.</small>

Arletta did not affect coyness; but Fulbert, who desired she should be married honestly in her own station, opposed the Duke's haunting the house. The Duke, however, neither could nor would be warned or driven away from the premises. One son, one only son, was acknowledged as their offspring. Robert bestowed upon the boy the ancestral name of William, and he was nursed in the house of his Grandfather, the Tanner.

§ 17. Such a connexion as Robert had formed with the ultra-plebeian Arletta, could not fail to be resented by her aristocratic betters as a personal affront; but her inferiors, whether male or female, were far more offended;— would it not have been more than could fairly be demanded from poor human nature, that such an insult to respectability should be condoned.— Arletta's pretty feet had taken the shine out of all the other pretty feet in Falaise.—We may picture to ourselves how the Burgess wives, who prided themselves in character and decorum, avenged themselves by scorn; the like, their husbands, who would be equally provoked by the hybrid Tanner's good fortune. And it was with the dear delight of mortifying a flourishing neighbour, that a worthy Burgess, residing near the Tannery, observing Guillaume, old Guillaume Talvas, (so called, as it is said, from the hardness of his disposition, popularly compared to the toughest of bucklers,) — Lord of Belesme and proud Alençon, sauntering along the street, he, the said Burgess, merrily, and with malice prepense, invited the noble Baron to walk in and admire his Suzerain's son.

This Talvas was very distinguished by his ancestry; he, the representative of one of the three greatest Duchy families, the three leading lineages of the land. When Richard Sanspeur established feudality in his dominions, Osmond de Centvilles, the trusty friend who had rescued the young Duke from captivity or death, was acknowledged as Premier among the nobility; —Bernard, the Dane, the bulwark of the Terra Normannorum, from whom sprung the Harcourts and their wide ramifications, the second;—and Ivo de Belesme, the faithful vassal of Guillaume Longue-épée, the third; and of this Ivo, the Guillaume now before us was either the son or the grandson. The Belesme family appear inferior in nominal precedence to the two others, but equal, perhaps more than equal, in prepotence and power.

Earnestly did the austere Chieftain, burning 1024—1035
with indignation, gaze upon the babe, who, as
we collect from the lively tale-teller, Master Wace,
behaved very much like ordinary babies.

"Shame!—shame!—shame!" exclaimed the Talevas curses the baby.
Baron; "for by thee and thine, shall I and
mine be brought to loss and dishonour."

>Guilleaume fu varlet petit
>A Falaise fu nurri;
>Le viel Guilleaume Talevaz
>Ki tint Seez, Belesme, e Vignaz
>Par Falaise un jour trespassout,
>Ne sai dire quel part alout.
>Un des Burgeis l'ad apelé
>En riant ad lui a parlé.
>Sire, dit il, ci vous tournez,
>En cest ostel céauns entrez.
>Veez le fils vostre seigneur
>Si semblera bien a ennur!
>Ou est? dist-il, montrez le moi.
>Aporter le fist devant soi.
>Je ne sai ke l'enfanz fist
>Ne s'il pleura, ne se il rist,
>Quant Talevaz l'out esgardé
>De pres véu, et avisé
>Honte soit dist-il, honte soit!
>E par tierce foiz dist, Honte soit
>Car par toi e par ta ligné
>Iert la mienne moult abaissé
>E par toi e par ton lignage
>Oront mes hoirs grant damage
>Volentiers empeirie l'eust
>De la parole, se il peust
>Talevaz ainsi s'en tourna
>De grant pose mot ne sonna.
>
>* * * * * *

<small>1024—1035</small>

The imprecation bespake the bitterness of the old man's heart, seeking to blast the infant by the Evil eye, and smite him by the curse. Nor were the words idle. As far as belonged to the unconscious infant they prognosticated the troubles which would fall upon his head, the malediction the cause of its own fulfilment; and they become peculiarly significant when we listen to Guillaume Talvas as speaking the sentiments pervading the country.

<small>Robert gives more public offence.</small>

§ 18. Further offence was speedily given by Duke Robert. He continued defying and despising popular feeling—a line of conduct bespeaking either conscientious courage or egregious folly. Fulbert, having doffed his blouse, struts in peacock-pride, invested with the office of Court Chamberlain; whilst Arletta, coming forward from behind the half-drawn curtain, stands before the world in her ambiguous station of honour and shame; less than a wife, and more than a concubine.

It is a consistent contradiction in the human character, that any strong point on which we value ourselves is likely to exhibit our most desperate failure. The Dukes of Normandy had prudently attended to the advantages resulting from the matrimonial alliances contracted by their daughters: but, with respect to their own personal conduct they blindly obeyed the unbridled impulses of their lusts. From Rollo downwards, Richard Sans-peur was the only one who had a lawful wife absolutely exempted from cavillation; and he was unfaithful to her. In a licentious age, the Dukes of Normandy, casting off all yoke, were distinguished by their contempt of all moral restraint; sons of Belial: and, to the small degree that the viciousness of private character damages the influence of public men, the profligacy of the Norman Dukes diminished Normandy's importance in the eyes of foreign Powers. — How often had Richard Sans-peur been flouted in high places as the son of a concubine.

[1024—1085]

Whilst the debonnaire Robert conciliated the community on his own behalf, all the liberality of the Magnifico could not purchase favour for his child. In previous cases, the illegitimacy had either been removed by a mantle marriage, or, if that ceremony had not been performed, condonated; and the Norman people hugged themselves in every delusion whereby the opprobium could be extenuated or concealed. Look to Guenora, the daughter of a very humble functionary, but who could boast, (as the world affirmed,) of her antient Danish descent — how cordially was she received. Far otherwise with respect to Arletta; her elevation was intolerable. From first to last, wherever William her bastard moved, whether in Court or in Camp, he was always more or less in bad odour, surrounded, so to speak, by his native air, the fetid atmosphere of the unsavoury tan-yard. Had the laws of heraldry been then settled, as

[Stigma attached to William by reason of his mother's plebeianism.]

1024—1035 they subsequently were, by the snip and the clip of the Tailor, we may fancy that, upon his *cotte d'armes*, the abatement of bastardy, the bende sinister, (which, according to the modern indulgent Code of the Lord Lion beyond the Tweed, assumes the more elegant shape of an orle wavy,) whether Or or Argent, Azure or Gules, would have always looked like a strip of raw leather.

The bastardy of the Conqueror never forgotten. William the Conqueror, the founder of the most noble Empire in the civilized world, could never rid himself of the contumelious appellation which bore indelible record of his father's sin.

In all history, William is the only individual to whom such an epithet has adhered throughout his life and fortunes. Was the word of affront ever applied to Alphonso, the stern father of the noble house of Braganza, by any one except a Castilian? Not so, William—a Bastard was William at the hour of his birth;—a Bastard in prosperity;—a Bastard in adversity;—a Bastard in sorrow;—a Bastard in triumph;—a Bastard in the maternal bosom;—a Bastard when borne to his horror-inspiring grave. "William the Conqueror," relatively, but "William the Bastard," positively; and a Bastard he will continue so long as the memory of man shall endure.

§ 19. Discontent was leavening broad Normandy. All the numerous and powerful collateral descendants of Guillaume Longue-épée, nay, of Rollo, were collectively and individually insulted through the Tanner's grandchild. He would cut them off from every chance of the succession. Each resented the exclusion from the inheritance as an unpardonable injury; and Belesme-Talvas had spoken out for them all. Amongst the disappointed kindred, the most formidable was Robert, the married clerk, Archbishop of Rouen, and Count of Evreux, Duke Robert's uncle, the legitimated son of Guenora, the marriage subsequent to cohabitation being fully satisfactory to the Norman mind; and he was also the lawful heir. Had Robert died at this juncture, leaving only Arletta's stigmatized issue, then, if law was law, the rights of the Count Bishop were incontestable.

There were not those wanting, especially, as we may collect, amongst the nobles, who roused Duke Robert's suspicions against his relations; and, wisely preparing to prevent the danger, he laid siege to Evreux. In this position the Archbishop assembled large forces. Reduced to great straits, he attempted to support himself by his spiritual authority; and he fulminated an excommunication against his nephew, at the same time, placing Normandy under a general interdict. The Archbishop then withdrew to the court of King Robert, who received him hospitably. Duke Robert relented. Some say that he discovered he had acted on false suggestions, and he recalled the Archbishop, who thenceforth avoided giving occasion of offence.

§ 20. This annoying contest concluded, another of a similar character emerged. Hugh, Bishop of Bayeux, was the son of Ralph, Count of Ivri, the half-brother of Richard Sans-peur, the queller of rebels, who had crushed the insurgent peasantry; and, whether by right or by wrong, the Bishop took possession of Ivri. He caused the awe-inspiring dungeon tower to be well prepared for defence. But Duke Robert, according to his accustomed tactics, was enabled to reduce this important possession without bloodshed. He blockaded the castle so straitly, that Bishop Hugh, like his cousin the Archbishop, was obliged to sue for mercy. It was granted, but upon the hardest terms. He went forth, and wandered many years in exile. The too celebrated Odo, Arletta's son by Herlouin de Conteville, the husband taken by her after Duke Robert's death, and who figures at full length in the acts and transactions of the Conquest, was Hugh's congenial successor.

Robert proceeding boldly onwards, now assailed a far more dangerous enemy. Fully was he conscious of the spite which the Talvas entertained towards him. But he had the great feudatory in his grip, and he knew how to work his ducal prerogatives. Alençon, where, as we collect from subsequent events, the Duke's connexion with the loathed Tanner's daughter had excited great and permanent disgust, was held by Talvas, *jure beneficii;* or, in more modern constitutional terminology, a Feud. Robert's _{1024—1035} purse commanded Robert's soldiery; and, raising his troops, he besieged the town.

§ 21. The Ducal forces were so vigilant that Talvas could not discover any means of escape; he was now paying the cost of the imprecations he had fulminated before the cradle. Haughty Talvas was compelled to seek pardon—pardon was granted,—but, painful the pinch sustained by the Premier baron. He submitted to the chastisement, which was now becoming a species of established law. Unshod and half stripped he came forth, the saddle girt upon his old gibbous shoulders. Robert was satisfied; and Talvas, having rivetted his broken oath, prepared for mischief, when the good time for turbulence should really come.

Talvas surrenders.

§ 22. Robert le-Magnifique's position, geographical, political, and social, enabled him to exercise considerable influence over his neighbours' affairs. Normandy presents herself as one of the great powers composing the Capetian Confederacy —perhaps the greatest. France and England beheld in the Norman Duke, a Potentate who could support or menace either kingdom. Emma's husband had jarred against Richard le-Bon; and the matrimonial connexion had failed to extinguish the smouldering enmity. Ethelred's unhappy expedition against the Cotentin testified the anxiety created in England by the possibility of an invasion from the warrior-teeming, iron-bound

Political importance of Robert le-Magnifique.

1024—1035 — coast; which, culminating at Cherbourg, always threatened the Channel shores. Moreover, the smiling countenance which the Norman Sovereigns turned towards their Danish kinsmen, was a suspicious feature in their policy.

Baudouin à-la-belle-barbe takes refuge under Robert's protection.

§ 23. Flanders, at this juncture, afforded to Duke Robert a favourable opportunity of manifesting his own political importance. The younger Baudouin, known in history as Baudouin de Lisle,—he who had espoused the Adela,—rose against his father, Baudouin-à-la-belle-barbe. The venerable parent, expelled by the valiant, sagacious, but undutiful son, sought refuge in the Castle of Falaise,—Falaise—for it was in this stronghold that Robert resided and held his court, whilst he deserted the antient palace of Rouen.—Did any harassing reminiscences haunt Rollo's banquet hall?

Flemish revolt suppressed—Robert pacifies the country.

Duke Robert willingly afforded his aid to the suppliant Count; he brought up his army into Flanders, perpetrating devastations so germane with the character of a Robert le-Diable, that some suppose it was by reason of the ferocity displayed during this foray, that he acquired his mythic name. Yet we may half condone the delight which must have been felt by a great grandson of Longue-épée, when he could punish the land of Old Arnold the murderer.

The insurgent nobles who headed the revolt abandoned the insurgent son; and, soliciting peace, they besought Robert to act as mediator.

Tranquillity being restored, the pacification between Normandy and Flanders expanded into that amicable intercourse, which, old grudges forgotten, placed Baudouin de Lisle's excellent daughter, the affectionate Matilda, on the English throne—she,—who humanly speaking,—became the only source of real happiness which the weary Conqueror enjoyed.

1024—1035

§ 24. About this time good King Robert was gathered to his fathers, a sexagenarian. His death marked a great crisis. Two generations only of the royal Capetian line had reigned. Time is the essential element of regal authority. Never can the right of succession be firmly established in any Dynasty, until three generations and four have been permitted to occupy the throne.

1031. Death of King Robert—right of regal succession not yet entirely settled in France.

Hereditary right, so far as politic society is concerned, involves two conditions—primogeniture or seniority,—and the principle of representation from heir to heir. But whether,—employing the antient Anglo-Saxon formula,—this right subsists only on the "*Sword side*," or male line, and fails altogether on the "*Spindle side*," or female line, as in France and most of the German Sovereignties; or whether it may subsist on the spindle side, but pass to the daughter's male heir, ascending to and descending from the *stirps* however distant, is a question which each nation's ethos and traditions must determine. Capetian France was still a kingdom of the first

1024—1035 impression, and therefore comparatively feeble. Monarchy lives upon recollections, and, until they have accrued by effluxion of time, her path is staggering—the irrevocable past is the gift of God's Eternal Providence; nor can any human contrivance compensate for the irrevocable.

Canon of descent as yet uncertain in the French Monarchy. Constitutional principles were as yet unmatured in the Capetian Monarchy. The exclusion of females, and of all heirs claiming through a female, was the only French canon of descent which we can consider entirely free from cavil. Primogeniture or seniority was not indefeasible; the will of the reigning Sovereign determined whether, as amongst the sons, an elder or a younger should be his successor.

1026 -1037 Dissensions in France by reason of the succession. Exerting, therefore, his prerogative of selection, King Robert had caused his son Hugh, who does not appear to have been the eldest, though there is some obscurity on this point, to be accepted as King, and crowned. The confusion of early Capetian history comes out in strong contrast with the comparative lucidity of the Carlovingian era. Hugh's disposition was excellent; but cankered Constance crossed him: and, provoked by his mother's harshness, he revolted against *Henry succeeds, against the wishes of his Mother.* authority. He died prematurely; and Henry, his brother's *puisné*, was by the father's appointment also crowned as the associate King. But Constance hated Henry, and laboured incessantly that Robert of Burgundy, the Cadet next in order, should be preferred. Henry inherited his amiable father's character, Robert took after his mother; Constance, therefore, insisted that Henry was a poor creature, incompetent to exercise the royal functions. His spirited brother was the one entitled to the preference.

1024—1035

Upon King Robert's demise, the Realm devolved upon Henry, who had been already installed. Forthwith, a most bitter civil war arose; and a powerful faction amongst the baronage, including Eudes le-Champenois, and Fulk of Anjou, sided with the Queen. Thus supported, the Virago's party prospered. The principal Places in the very heart of the kingdom, comprising the Duchy of France Proper, the antient Capetian patrimony—Senlis and Sens—Sens then so strong in her Roman walls,—alas! most recently eradicated by modern vandalism—much contested Melun, Dammartin, Poissi, honoured Couci, and Puiseaux, opened their gates to Constance, and closed them in the face of the unfortunate Henry, who fled the country; and, on the eve of the joyful Paschal feast,—*Pascha florida—Pâques fleurie,*—so unfortunately disguised amongst us by its Heathen name, he presented himself as a suppliant before Duke Robert at Fécamp: small and mean was his Royal train—*Duodecim clientuli*—Twelve Vavasours.

1026—1027. Constance and her party obtain much success.

Henry compelled to fly the country craves Robert's support.

Henri fu moult epouvanté
Que il ne fait désérité,

1024—1035

> A Robert vint en Normandie
> Un jour devant Pasches fleurie,
> O douze Serjants seulement
> Vint le Roi chetivement.

Mournfully, by this transaction, was France humiliated before Normandy. The circumstances attending the receipt of the parage-homage were sufficiently mortifying. Grievous must have been the vexation on those occasions, when the King of France was compelled, for the purpose of receiving the jealous submission due to the successor of Charlemagne, from the successor of Rollo, to go forth, and meet his inferior, half way down the border: but harder that he should now, as a suppliant, be seen a suitor of the Norman Duke, beseeching the great Vassal by his faith and fealty, to grant protection against his own mother and his own brother.

Duke Robert supports the King effectually. Duke Robert enhaunced his own consequence, by receiving the illustrious petitioner with great respect and honour; and he worked effectually for his Suzerain's restoration. In the first place, Eudes le-Champenois had to be brought over or bought over. Eudes knew his own price, and stipulated that one moiety of splendid Sens, the key of Champagne on the royal frontier, should be surrendered to him. Heartily did Duke Robert support King Henry's rightful cause against his unnatural mother, pouring in troops, burning, destroying, no mercy shewn, no quarter granted to the insurgents;

they were dealt with, not as enemies, but as rebels. Well, too well, are we taught by the old thrummed proverbs and popular saws,—the outspeakings equally of human depravity and of human sagacity,—that success constitutes the sole distinction between patriotism and rebellion. "Treason doth never prosper.—What is the reason?—That when it prospers, none dare call it treason."

1024—1035

Under our chivalrous Edward, Scotland's Champion was vituperated as an infamous thief. —*Ille famosus Latro, Willielmus Wayleys*, quoth our true born Englishman.—Surely, it was a gaudy day for the burly London Citizens, when, crowding to enjoy the delicious spectacle, they beheld the Scottish Hero dragged on a hurdle through their filthy flinty streets, hanged and cut down, all quick and breathing, his writhing bowels plucked out from the quivering carcass by the Executioner, whose infernal skill prolongs all the powers of action, intellect, and sensation, during a paroxysm of inconceivable agony;—and then—that ghastly head and those mangled limbs, rotting upon the Gate-towers!

Wallace, the traitor.

Was there ever any consistent justice in the sentiments entertained against a Rebel?—How many a swarthy Zemindar, whose parched skeleton, picked clean by kites and vultures, and now swinging from the gallows, may, in the eyes of posterity, earn an historic reputation proud as that enjoyed by William Tell and the

Confederates of Grutli.—Nay, were the Novelist of Certaldo living amongst us to publish a sixteenth edition of his once popular essay, *De Claris Mulieribus*, would not the devoted Rannee of Jansee rank with Boadicea?

<small>1031—1033 Duke Robert continues his exertions on behalf of Henry.</small>

Robert's campaign on behalf of royalty was judiciously conducted: he placed large detachments in all the strongholds and frontier positions. Mauger, Count of Corbeil, fierce and crafty, acted as his nephew's Lieutenant, and displayed an energy corresponding with the confidence he had earned. Fully does King Henry appear self-vindicated from the stigma of inertness, the failing assigned by his vixen Mother as justifying her schemes for aggrandizing her darling at the expence of her warling. Eudes le-Champenois, under the stress of the Norman power, was compelled to restore the domains he had usurped. Constance's schemes being no longer favoured by fortune, public opinion ceased to favour her. Fulk of Anjou objurgated the dowager Queen, rebuking her harshness towards her children; she fell ill and died, and was buried at Saint Denis, beside her husband.

§ 25. The services rendered by Robert to King Henry, were so valuable, that he might have made heavy demands upon his Sovereign's gratitude, but Henry anticipated any such request.

Interposed between Normandy, as ceded to Rollo, and the *Regnum Francorum*, was a portion of the *Pagus Veliocassinus*, the *Vexin Français*, constituting a species of abnormal sovereignty under the Capets and their predecessors; held by a line of Counts who trace their descent from Charlemagne, whilst a rival genealogical scheme deduces their stem from the Merovingian Childebert. The name of "Nivelong," he who appears as the first of these Counts, connects us with the mythic age. No Child of the Mist, however, no cloudy Niebelung was Nivelong, but a venerable off-shoot from the Merovingian race; son of the second Childebrand; and satisfactory evidence exists, affording full proof of his solid personality.

<small>1024—1085</small>
<small>875 The Vexin. Nivelong the first known Count thereof.</small>

The dominion having escheated to Hugh le-Grand, passed into another line; we know not how; but in the same year that Robert le-Magnifique became Duke of Normandy, Drogo, the son of Gautier le-Blanc, had succeeded to the Vexin. He was Duke Robert's intimate, and their dispositions harmonized.

<small>1027 Drogo or Dreux Count of the Vexin.</small>

The Counts of the Vexin held a unique station between the Baronage and the Hierarchy; equally Vassals and Patrons of Saint Denis. The Advowson or Advocatio of that regal Abbey belonged to them. The Count of the Vexin was privileged to bear the Auriflamme. When War arose, he raised the consecrated banner from the Altar of the Martyrs: and, after the County had lapsed to the Crown, the Standard displaying the bright incarnadine commingled

1024—1035 with the glistening Orfray, became the Sacred insignia of the Monarchy. In his style, the Count of the Vexin asserted complete independence; repudiating every earthly superior,— *Superni Regis nutu Comes . . . nutu solummodo Dominorum Creatoris Comes*. Despite this outbreak of magniloquence, which might almost lead to the supposition that he was crazed by vanity, Count Drogo was wise and strenuous, the true friend of Duke Robert, who, in consequence of a cession made by Henry, became his Suzerain. He was also Lord of precipitous Mantes and the Mantois, either a dismemberment or an enclavure of the Vexin.

Drogo's marriage with Ethelred's daughter. We include this same Drogo in our English historical gallery by reason of the matrimonial connexion he contracted with Goda, Ethelred's daughter, and the Confessor's sister; and who, after his decease, espoused Eustace, Count of Boulogne. A second Goda, and perhaps a third, is noticed in the Chronicles, which multiplicity may lead to the supposition that *Goda* was an epithet equivalent to " *Good wife*," or " *Goody*." Normandy gained by this transaction all the Border country, heretofore a debatable country. Trie became absolutely a part of Normandy. The celebrated Oak of tryst now grew on Norman soil, and the Norman frontier was extended as far as Versailles and Saint Germains; in fact, to the very gates of Paris. But, had Robert been cursed by an insight into futurity, how deeply would he have deployed an acquisition which, through the mysterious links of causation, brought his conquering Son to an untimely and inglorious death.

1024—1035

§ 29. Brittany, the source to Normandy equally of peril and of power; a bulwark of strength, a breach in the wall, was now acquiring encreasing influence and importance in and over Norman affairs. Armorica had hitherto been ruled by Chieftains, Counts as they were denominated according to the Carlovingian usage. From Conan Meriadec, Prince of Albania, established in this region, as it is supposed, by the Emperor Maximin, a continued dynastic series is extant, truth and fable blended; but the spectral forms of these " Mactierns,"—Erech, Daniel, Budic, Hoel, Judicael, Rivod, Jarnithan, Morvan, Viomarch,—flit before us merely as shadows. Their mutual jealousies, the snare and bane of Gomer's descendants, consumed the country's resources, and, attracting the persecution of the Danes, wasted the energies and power of the Race. And yet the fiery valour of the antient Bretons enabled them to assert and re-assert their national individuality against their numerous foes.

Brittany—its great importance in Norman history.

383 Conan Meriadec said to have been established by the Emperor Maximin.

After the death of Solomon, the son of Rivalon, of whom we have heard in the preceding era, all these districts or territories merged in the three dominations of Nantes, Rennes, and Cornouaille. Amongst the Celts concord was im-

857—874 Solomon, Son of Rivalon.

Brittany settled into the three Counties of Rennes, Nantes, and Cornouaille.

possible. In early times Nomenoe, the Ruler of Cornouaille, had assumed, by Papal authority, the royal style, but the Counts of Rennes acquired the pre-eminence over the other Chieftains. Regality vanished. Geoffrey, son of Conan, with whom we made acquaintance when he sued for and won the wise Hawisa, Normandy's daughter, must be distinguished as the first Duke of Brittany. He constituted himself Duke simply by taking the title. This assumption may possibly have been sanctioned by the successor of Saint Peter; and, by degrees, his rank in the civil hierarchy became ultimately recognized.

Let Geoffrey, therefore, be honoured as the Founder of the Duchy, symbolized by her ermine, even as France by her fleur-de-lis, a crowned Duke, reigning with regal pretensions and almost regal power. The Counts of Brittany, and the Dukes in like manner, in later times, rendered homage *en parage* to Normandy in the first instance, and that same homage was afterwards demanded by the Crown of France. But the Capetian monarchs refused to acknowledge the "Duke," until the time of Peter Mauclerc, son of Robert, Count of Dreux, Earl of Richmond. An interesting memorial of this powerful vassal still exists in the Borough. Mauclerc's chequered shield, Or and Azure, floats before our eyes as when we beheld it in the east window of Richmond Chancel. But this title did not confer any additional power upon the feudal Sovereign of Brittany. *1024—1035*

§ 27. Armorica no longer included the full length and breadth of territory which she had possessed in the brilliant days of Nomenoe and Herispoe, and Solomon, when Brittany expanded even unto the centre arch of the bridge of Angers. Geoffrey, however, claimed to exercise his supremacy, from the tall rugged monolith of Ingrande, the *Petra de Ingrand*,—a monument, which, according to the spurious nomenclature whereby all Celtic history has been mystified, would be termed Druidical,—as far as the Archangel's guarded mount, St. Michael in the peril of the sea. *Extent of Brittany under Duke Geoffrey.*

First among the Armorican Sovereigns who struck white money was Geoffrey: sols of silver did Geoffrey coin — rarest of the rare in the numismatic cabinet of France; small black money also in greater plenty, base enough without question. *Geoffroi the first Armorican Duke who coined money.*

Many and brilliant were the battles which Geoffrey fought against the recalcitrating Count of Nantes, Judicael; but the memorials preserved concerning these Princes are meagre and confused, and shrink into a narrow compass. Two children were born to Geoffrey by faithful Hawisa, the sister of Richard le-Bon, that is to say, Alain, third or fifth of the name, who succeeded Geoffrey—and Eudes Count of Penthievre.

§ 28. About ten years after Geoffrey's marriage, he visited Rome, rather as a pleasure traveller than a Pilgrim, leaving his wife Hawisa under Duke Richard's fraternal protection. Merrily did Geoffrey make his journey, and in such guise as beseemed his quality; hawk on fist and sword by side. But a mean misadventure shortened his days. On his returning route, safe and sound, his unhooded bird flew at ignoble game,—at a hen belonging to the good wife who kept the hostelry where the Duke—pilgrim we can scarcely call him,—had been lodging. The angry Crone flung a potsherd at his head which fractured his skull.—Thus did the doughty warrior die at the hands of a crabbed old woman.

Alain, Geoffrey's son, commenced his reign under the guardianship of his energetic mother Hawisa, and her tutelage and guidance enabled the young man to vindicate his authority. Well did he need sound counsel, for now ensued a perilous period. The revolutionary example of the Norman peasantry became contagious. In Normandy, the discontent may have been embittered by the effects of the Scandinavian occupation or conquest. But the Breizad cultivators were oppressed by Lords of their own blood; and the fire continued smouldering for nearly twenty years, until, at last, the conflagration blazed out with direful fury. The accounts of the Breton insurrection remind us of the German Baurenkrieg.—If the ferocity exhibited by the revolters may be construed as affording any measure of the hardships they avenged, galling indeed must have been the yoke they endeavoured to cast off.

_{1024—1085}

§ 29. The Nobles were appalled. Not so brave Hawisa. Obeying her advice, the Boy leapt into his saddle. Forth he rode, leading on his Nobles, and the insurgents were completely subdued.

Time wore away; Duke Alain grew up from boyhood to manhood, when dissensions arose between him and another Alain.—Alain Caignard, Count of Rennes. Many Alains recur in Armorican history. The Breton onomasticon was singularly scanty, a circumstance adding to the confusion of their perplexed annals. Their examination becomes a puzzling task; and, whilst endeavouring to harmonize these records, I may have nodded now and then.

Alain Caignard's grudges were not without justification, inasmuch as, during his nonage, a considerable portion of his inheritance had been usurped by Duke Geoffrey. The gallants were congenial spirits. Duke Alain had wooed Bertha, daughter of Eudes le-Champenois, the son of the Comes Ditissimus, who succeeded to the noble territories of Champagne and Brie. Eudes refused. This denial was a personal affront, as well as a cross in love.—Was there ever a rejection of a matrimonial offer which did not partake more or less of this double character?

<small>Alain Caignard, Count of Rennes.</small>

<small>Duke Alain's courtship of the daughter of Eudes le-Champenois.</small>

1024—1085

Alain was a fine young man, fully the equal of the Champenois, whether in power or in station; but, however courteous the terms in which the French nay-say was conveyed, he could discern a sneer. Indeed the Celts were unwillingly admitted by their fellow Christians into the civilized commonwealth. An equivalent antipathy was entertained by the Teutonic races; equally the crime and curse of both populations.—*Spurcitia Britonum*—was the popular dictum throughout the *Langue d'oil*, one of those national floutings which contribute so detrimentally to the exaltation of national vanity, and the perpetuation of envy, malice, and all uncharitableness; and yet, nothing like so poisonous as the correlative,—national self-praise;—each individual gulping the flattery for which he credits himself on his private account, through the agency of the Community whereunto he appertains. How many of the faults, the defects, the sins, which stain the English character, have been fostered by the self-laudations of "John Bull."—You and I, and every one of us, appropriating to myself or ourselves the whole tribute of our own self-bestowed encomiums.

§ 30. In early times, abduction, nay all the natural consequences of abduction, must, rude as the process may appear, be regarded as a phase of Chivalry. This feeling is not wholly extinct, even in our age. Assuredly a plea put in by the

Traverser in the dock, that, when carrying off the coy object of his affections, he has merely followed the brilliant example afforded by Amadis of Gaul, would scarcely be received by the Judge of Assize in County Tipperary: although, on the other hand, the Jury might be much inclined to overrule his Lordship's ruling, that the offence is a grievous misdemeanour, approaching to a felony.

1024—1085

Such was the state of feeling in Armorica when Alain Caignard, anxious to serve his Liege-Lord, and probably not sorry to spite the French, made a forcible seizure of the Damsel, and conducted his prize triumphantly to Rennes, where she was espoused to young Duke Alain, "*more Britannico.*" This expression is somewhat ambiguous. We cannot doubt, however, but that the young couple duly received the benediction of the altar.

By the help of Alain Caignard, Duke Alain obtains the Lady.

All the Nobles were convened; rich gifts and guerdons copiously bestowed by Alain's own hand. Gauds or garments however could not satisfy Alain Caignard, the disappointed Count of Cornouaille; he claimed his inheritance. Alain promised the restoration of the usurped territory, all the Nobles assenting and applauding this act, certainly of grace, and possibly of justice. The chief parcel consisted of well known Belle Isle, also called Guedel, a Celtic name, which became obsolete at an early period. Belle Isle, lying just over against Quiberon, is the largest amongst

Duke Alain restores to Alain Caignard the island of Belle Isle.

the islands appertaining to the Continent of France. The English reader will recollect the locality as figuring, though not very gloriously, in our naval annals.

Jealousies between Normandy and Brittany. Hawisa's son and the Norman Duke were mutually jealous; the former assumed a proud position, the like of which was scarcely paralleled by the traditions floating concerning his semi-mythic ancestors. Alain acquired the name of *Ruivriz*, signifying, as we collect from master Wace's interpretation, the *Roi Bret*, the Breton King.

Thanks to the fervid fancy of the Celtic littérateurs, a morbid enthusiasm has infested the romantic French writers of the modern picturesque school, teaching them to gild and illuminate their historical delineations in the style of a mediæval missal; and in consequence of this affection or affectation, the traditions of Brittany have acquired an Ossianic character, compelling distrust where the enquirer would gladly yield credence. But the ascription of regal state to the earlier Breton Dynasts was probably not entirely groundless, and Duke Alain chafed against the Norman superiority.

> Le Duc Robert tint bien sa terre,
> Par tout vouloit son droit conquerre.
> Entrer veult par force en Bretagne,
> Ne veult k'Alain en paiz remaigne,
> Ki a sa Cort ne veult venir
> Ne a lui ne deigne obeir

> Comme ses ancessurs feseient,
> Cil qui Bretaigne anceiz tenerent.
> Cosins esteient moult prochein,
> Chescun filz de uncle et d'antein ;
> Pur ceo k'il erent d'un parage,
> D'une hautesse e d'un lignage,
> Alain, Robert servir ne deigne
> Ainsi monta entre eux l'engaigne,
> Alain ne se deigne abaisser
> Et Robert ne lui en voult laisser.

The Respondent Alain, when repudiating the homage claimed by Rollo's representative, conducted his argument with a Special Pleader's astuteness. Tacitly admitting the antient submission, he argued, that he and duke Robert were of equal rank, by reason of their consanguinity, Sword-side and Spindle-side counterchanged; one the son of an Aunt, the other the son of an Uncle. Hostilities arose. The war was popular in Normandy, being waged against a near neighbour; and joyfully did the fretting fighting men of the crowded Cotentin, now let loose, expand over the enemy's territory. Vicinity and kindred, as usual, encreased mutual animosity, and the quarrel was envenomed by the very circumstances that ought to have dictated friendship and goodwill. Only a streamlet separates the countries, and again the moral philosophy of words is illustrated by the disputes which "rivality" engenders.

§ 31. The two dominions are separated by the river Coesnon, meandering amongst the rich

1024—1035 pasturages, source of Armorica's agricultural wealth. Niel de Saint Sauveur came forward at the Duke's summons. His terror-inspiring standard floated in the breeze; and, with him, fought the renowned Warrior, who rejoiced in the name of *Auvrai le-Gigant*, or Alfred the Giant. Under these two Chieftains a large division of the army was placed, but the picked troops, marshalled under Robert's own command, constituted the central battalion. Robert's movements bespake or threatened a permanent occupation of the country. He constructed a Castle, denominated "*ad Carrucas*," nigh the frontier river, possibly encroaching upon the Breton territory. To Niel de Saint Sauveur and the Giant the fortress was confided. Fierce was Robert's rage. Dôl suffered again severely; the memorable bridale seems to have brought bad luck upon the ill-starred City.

Provoked, though not alarmed, Alain, hardy and bold, summoned his lieges far and wide, and spiritedly did the Armoricans obey the call. But Celtic valour has always lacked the balance of discretion. Niel and the Giant were well served by their spies. The whole strength of the Avranchin was roused—Nobles and peasantry, horse and foot.—Hit away, cut away, was Saint Sauveur's exhortation to his men; stab horse and rider.

The chosen men of the Norman forces had dropped down into a dell, where, though close to the Bretons, they were completely concealed. *1094—1035* Forth they rushed, their banners waving. Prudently had Niel taken the precaution of planting the Ducal Standard as a rallying point, in case of discomfiture. The war cry was raised.—*Dex aie!* the Norman slogan;—*Maslon!* (not interpreted by the French authorities) shouted the Bretons. The Bretons gave way. Alain *Victory of the Normans.* had mustered a noble band; all Chieftains of high degree, a splendid display of wasted bravery. But now came up, rushing from the hollow, Alfred the Giant, leading on his troops. The Bretons fled for their lives, and nevertheless, the corpses lying on the field exceeded the number of fugitives. The Avranchin peasantry hunted the enemy, conducting their chase cleverly. Here, lying in wait,—there, joining in pursuit; and so many Bretons perished, that as the Trouveurs sang, it would seem a fable to tell how terrible the slaughter.

§ 32. Robert le-Magnifique, Robert of Normandy, had been for some years past the Protector,—sole protector, of Cerdic's fated line. The Athelings, his cousins, our hallowed Edward *The English Athelings, Edward and Alfred, in Normandy, under the protection of Duke Robert.* and his brother Alfred, sheltered by their kinsman's power, had sought and found a refuge in Normandy; profiting by Normandy's civility, acquiring the language, adopting the manners, and imbibing the opinions of the people amongst whom they sojourned; and Robert's affection or policy now induced him to attempt their restoration.

1024—1035

Canute was reigning, and not merely reigning, but the heartless Emma enthroned by his side. She, "gem of Normandy;" she the pest of England; she the source of England's degradation and ruin. Warily and discreetly Robert opened the negotiations. An amicable compromise was suggested; an equitable division between the representatives of the two Dynasties—Cerdic's line and the line of truculent Rollo; and a precedent was familiar in the partition between Canute and Ironside.

Canute's defiance—Robert prepares for the invasion of England.

Canute's reply was a defiance. Let them hold what they can win; and Robert le-Magnifique accepted the challenge on his kinsfolk's behalf. Tancred de Hauteville, the subjugator of Apulia, had given the example of such inroads, and gladly they prepared themselves for the Conquest of England. All the Baillages and Ports in Normandy furnished their contingent, ready for service by sea or land, and none more alert, none more robust, than the adventurous population of the amphibious Cotentin. Skiffs and crews, pilots and mariners, sturdy knights, active squires, weather-beaten butsecarles, and keen-sighted arbalisters, assembled at Fécamp. Brightly shone the cloudless sky, the fleets preparing to hoist sail, when suddenly did the weather change, clouds gathered, a tempestuous

The expedition frustrated by a storm.

night ensued. The North wind blew furiously, the fleet was dispersed; many of the vessels driven into Jersey, the first time, as far as I recollect, that Cæsarea receives a notice in mediæval history. *(1094—1095)*

A flotilla of keels having entered the Seine, sailed up the Channel; and, long afterwards, were the decayed hulks to be seen rotting at Rouen. But the main body of the Armament escaped damage. The Athelings continued on board, lingering for the opportunity of presenting themselves; whether as English Sovereigns, or as foreign enemies. No opening ensued. The scheme became abortive, and the Normans afterwards laboured to believe that the expedition had been providentially frustrated, to the end, that, unpolluted by bloodshed, England should devolve upon the Confessor, he, through whose bequest the Conqueror claimed. How happy are we to discover any pretence of right, whilst doing wrong—clever in cheating the Devil, or rather cheating our own souls. The Propagation of the Gospel urged in conjunction with the violation of the Gospel precepts; the Divine sanction claimed for the breach of the Divine law;—"Give no quarter," our authorized version of "Love your enemies."

§ 33. Strangely is the sequence of events confused, equally by the Normans and by the English historians. Either, during the same season, or afterwards, Robert again directed an expedition against Alain: "Rabel," was the Armada's Commander: his name is remarkable, rarely occurring elsewhere than in the Tankerville genealogies. This family enjoyed the confi-

(Robert's second expedition.)

dence of the Norman Dukes, and the individual, whom we are now called upon to notice, was probably a Tankerville. The office of High Chamberlain became hereditary in the family.

Plunder, herry, burn, were the instructions which Robert's troops received. Alain, the Breton Prince, could not withstand the Norman attack, and he entreated his uncle, Mauger, Archbishop of Rouen, to mediate on his behalf. The hybrid Prelate, Soldier and Priest, a species of ecclesiastical centaur, entered heartily into his nephew's pacific policy, and interposed between the angry cousins. A family meeting was held in the sea-girt Abbey of the Guarded mount; a cordial meeting. Alain solicited peace, and performed homage.—This, for the Duke, a great but joyless triumph.

§ 34. Robert was victorious; but, in despite of his successes, he continued sad at heart. Well, too well, did Robert know, that the child upon whom his affections were concentrated, the boy William, hated throughout Normandy, was the object of universal contempt: Talvas, cursing the babe, had spoken as the mouthpiece of the whole Community. Heavily was the father's sin, that sin, so readily condoned by the world;—now, the theme of a luscious ballad; now, the subject of a merry tale—visited upon the child, clothing him with a garment of ignominy, even until the shroud enwrapped his corpse.

Not merely was William base born, but,

in the eyes of the world, even worse — he was low born. No lineage could be more blemished than the house of Rollo, yet ingredients had been found imparting a fancied good odour on the inherent contamination. Guenora was fondly considered to be of an antient race. Was not her father a ducal officer — her brother also, Herfastus? — her sisters, Gueva and Adelina, married into the noblest families?—she, rendered an honest woman, and her children all unbastardized by the mantle marriage. But, in the present case, no extenuation could be suggested.

1024—1035

That foul Tan-yard and its sickening pools! The place stunk in everybody's nostrils, not merely figuratively, but literally; and the prospect of being ruled by the filthy Tanner's grandson, was abhorrent to the Norman aristocracy. Who, could kiss the hand of such an imp? who, tolerate the shame? who, endure the degradation? Talvas had spoken for them all.

Antipathy entertained against the boy William.

§ 35. Such was the temperature of public feeling when Robert, having withheld any intimation of the intentions fermenting in his mind, suddenly convened his Prelates and Nobles —Bishops, Abbots, and Barons, and announced to them his determination of proceeding as a Pilgrim to the Holy Land. Go forth would he— poorest of the poor—bare-footed,—bare-headed, destitute even of any upper garment which

Robert suddenly announces his intention of proceeding to the Holy Land.

could protect his poor chapped flesh from the cutting winds.

Direful the consternation excited in the *Cour plénière*, when the Duke communicated this project to his Lieges. If Robert died childless, and he was worse than childless, all men foresaw the certainty of discord and confusion.

Robert's wasteful munificence failed to command respect or gratitude: a gift that costs you nothing, is as nothing in the valuation of the receiver. The theory of rank and station was well understood by the Normans. Arletta's conduct was gross, even for those days; no single trait of character is recorded which redeems the fornicatress. The only anecdote we possess concerning her, shews that she was denied the instinct of natural modesty. But Arletta was well-matched: Robert did not deserve a better consort; and he would have been provoked at the suggestion of a more decent union.

The Count Bishop of Evreux, Mauger of Corbeil, Guy of Burgundy, the Breton lineages, all the male descendants of Rollo, even all the male descendants of females, would assuredly contest the right of the low-born, base-born Mamzer. Pitiful was Robert's earnestness when extolling the Child's promising disposition, so fitting to render him a competent Sovereign. All the virtues, which the Courtier's glozing flattery attributes to an heir-apparent, were truths in the conception of the uneasy adulterer, wrestling against the consequences of his vice. All the nausea, all the remorse, all the prickings of conscience, all the stings of worldly shame, spread over the life of a putative father: all the feelings of love and loathing, which chastise his sin, were concentrated in that miserable hour. Earnestly did Prelates and Barons repeat their remonstrances, expatiating upon the impending dangers. Robert on his part persevered, obstinately, vehemently; until the Assembly, yielding to his urgency and moved by his misery, assented to the demand.

1024—1035

§ 36. If words convey any meaning, if legal forms possess any stringency, no Act of State could be more binding than the confirmation which the child's title now received.

Solemn confirmation of the Bastard's title.

In the first place, the proud and vexed Baronage performed homage and fealty. Whatever duties or services a Vassal owes to his Suzerain, would the Lieges render to the Heir, rising seven years of age.

This very important engagement imparted to William a valid or constitutional title as between him and his Vassals; but the Duke himself would grow up a Vassal, and the assent of his Superior was needed. Robert therefore brought the child, his child of dishonour, before King Henry, surrendering the Duchy in the boy's favour; and the lad, duly performing homage, became the liegeman of the Monarch.

§ 37. This important transaction completed,

1024—1035

Regency appointed by Robert.

Robert proceeded to provide for the government during his absence; and here, he had to grapple with the great difficulty. At this era, Robert's various collateral kinsmen, the descendants of his father, and the descendants of his grandfather, and the descendants of his great grandfather, and up to Rollo—nay, beyond Rollo unto Malahulc, the uncle of Rollo, constituted the Baronage of Normandy; and amongst these was to be sought Rollo's right heir, the young William being in every sense illegitimate, and barred from every lawful claim.

Great the jeopardy in which the title of the Bastard was placed. But there was one who came to the rescue.—Chief amongst the kindred, nearest and most powerful, was Alain, the child's cousin, Duke of Brittany, and he, with equal honour and truth, accepted the duty and the charge. Alain, appointed Regent, was empowered to exercise all the duties and functions of government and justice; and the Archbishop of Rouen, associated in the Regency, promised to render all the aid in his power.

Injudicious conduct of Robert.

Could the Normans have forgotten that William was the son of a concubine, and she a Tanner's daughter, Robert would not let them; and if they did entertain suspicions that the child was supposititious, he could not have adopted a more certain mode of raising a prejudice against the boy, than by labouring, as he did, to bully or to argue his Lieges into the conviction, that, although William was the Concubine's child, he was 1024—1035 his putative father's truly begotten son. Robert seemed possessed with a morbid determination to cast doubts upon the child whom he declared to be his own. It was entirely within the plenitude of his power to legitimate the Mamzer in the same manner as his own father had been legitimated, that is to say, by espousing the mother.— Take her therefore as your wife, my Lord Duke, —would any truth-speaking, sincere friend, have urged upon him,—take her, and all will be well.

The maxim, *hæres legitimus est quem nuptiæ demonstrant*, is fully accepted by Roman and Canon law, and consonant to natural feeling. —Marry her, therefore, my Lord Duke! The retrospective action of your nuptials will, at any time, nay at the last hour, legitimate your dear boy.—Marry her, my Lord Duke! and all your troubles will be dispelled.—But Robert did not marry her,—would not marry her,— could not marry her. He could not abide the Tanner's daughter sitting as his equal by his side. — A Bastard, William is born; a Bastard, William reigns; and a Bastard, William dies.

§ 38. And now Robert commenced his pilgrimage, making his way very consistently; abundant were the alms he bestowed; the stream of his bounty never ceased to flow. If the Normans, when he first announced his intention of departing as a Palmer to the Holy Land, really apprehended that his health might suffer

Robert commences his pilgrimage.

from the severity of his self-inflicted macerations when crossing the snows and glaciers of the Mons Jovis, or that he might perish through the tenuity of his garments and never descend the perilous pass to Aosta, these prophecies were soon forgotten. Yet we may excuse such fears in the minds of those who had never galloped up a hill bolder than the *Dunes* or *Downs*, imparting their name to the celebrated battle field, which rendered William truly Duke of Normandy; or listened to any cataract more precipitous than the twenty toises of silver streamlets constituting the only cascade in France—the fall of Mortagne.

Speedily were the lieges reassured, and satisfied that there was not any reason for anticipating disaster; Drogo, Count of the Vexin, accompanied his friend to share the pleasurable excitement of the perils attendant upon the journey; and Toustain le-Blanc, afterwards so distinguished in the field of Hastings, slept in his liege lord's chamber.

Harbingers went forward to prepare the splendid lodgings; and, lengthened were the trains of grooms and stable folk, leading the sumpters of burden, the coursers of state and pleasure, and the snorting steeds of war. One adventure only occurred, offering any incident approaching to trouble or danger; a scuffle at Besançon with a drowsy, perhaps drunken, Warder. The gate was narrow, the street, long, and the Porter, doing his duty and something more, cudgelled the pilgrim Duke, to make him move on. The Duke's followers and companions would have brained the rascal with their bourdons, but Robert restrained their indignation. It was needful,—according to his pious exposition,—that they should exhibit themselves as patterns of patience and humility, and suffer for the good of their souls.

§ 39. *Tutte le strade vanno a Roma*—all roads lead to Rome,—and thither, in due time, arrived our Pilgrim. It is intimated, rather than asserted, that Robert received the Pilgrim's insignia from the Holy father, but no record is extant of any donation to St. Peter's shrine.

Robert proceeded merrily; exhibiting his munificence, in a manner consistent with his own natural character, and equally inconsistent with the penitential part which he was acting before the world.

The earliest mediæval guide-book existing, is the little treatise entitled *Mirabilia Romæ*; and, amongst these marvels, ranked very highly that noble equestrian statue, now ascribed to Marcus Aurelius, but then commanding greater veneration as the supposed memorial of the first Christian Emperor.

It was a standing joke amongst the Citizens,—one of those local facetiæ which descend by inheritance—that Constantine never moved for sunshine or frost, for wind or for rain; and this proverbial whimsy suggested to Robert a corresponding grave drollery. It is a characteristic of the mediæval ethos, that, although the lighter compositions abound with jests, they are for the most part flat, coarse, licentious, or dull. A bale was unpacked and a rich mantle taken out, which Robert cast upon the effigy.—Shame befal you Romans,—quoth he,—you who allow your Emperor to remain scorched by the heat and pinched by the cold, exposed to wind and rain.

Robert's conduct throughout the journey was reckless, strange, and as a man unhinged. Wild his display of wealth, neither encreasing his comfort nor really enhauncing his dignity. He caused his mules to be shod with shoon of gilded silver, fastened to the hoofs by a single nail; enjoining his men not to pick up these adornments, when cast by the ambling beast upon the road, but to let them lie.

Robert at Constantinople.

§ 40. We now encounter our pilgrims at Constantinople. Here Robert attempted a clumsy display of wealth, or rather of wealth's insolence; whilst, at the same time, he enjoyed the dear delight of wounding the feelings of those whom he despised. The contempt wherewith we drench the Orientals, is an antient Latin inheritance. The barbarity of Frank or Lombard, is the pride of civilization. To make an insulting mock at matters in themselves indifferent, is only a degree less reprehensible than the making a mock at sin. When Robert entered the By-

The Normans exhibit the pride of civilization.

zantine Audience Hall, followed by his cortége, he, grimly, and without salutation or other shew of deference, flung his splendid mantle upon the pavement; and, bundling up the garment, sat down thereon. The like, his suite; but the Imperial attendants sagaciously avoided coming in collision with the barbarians.

In fact, the Duke and his Normans assumed that they were privileged to be rude, and they were permitted to be rude; much according to the toleration we should extend to a Feejee, exhibited at an evening assembly.

Therefore, when Robert rose up and was about to depart, the Imperial ushers prepared to re-invest him. "It is not the fashion in our country," exclaimed Robert, "to carry our seats with us," as the incident is described in the passage which learned Ducange has quoted, for the purpose of affording a lively view of the scene. The Emperor on his part, displayed that appreciation of refinement and politeness which provoked the scorn of Frank and Lombard, who regarded all Orientals with that ignorant contempt which disgraced themselves; whereas the Emperor Michael did honour to his own self, by displaying all the courtesy in his power; possibly however not without some degree of apprehension, lest his guests should visit him again, with arbalist and spear!

Michael defrayed all the travelling expenses of the Normans, an act equally prudent and courteous, as he thereby lessened the chance of quarrels between the Norman swash-bucklers and his citizens. It is said, that the Emperor prohibited the sale of fire-wood to the pilgrims, whereupon Robert and his folks warmed themselves before a crackling blaze of pistachios.

§ 41. Robert journeyed onward, and we may discern the symptoms indicating that his overworked mind was failing: the decline of his bodily health was manifest, he became worse and worse, day by day. No longer able to walk or to ride, he hired a gang of Negro Palanquin bearers, and the novelty of this mode of conveyance amused him in his misery. Toustain officiated as his Chamberlain. The intermediate stages of Robert's progress are not detailed, but his friends at home were sufficiently supplied with intelligence.

§ 42. The Levant abounded with Latin travellers, pilgrims, or vagabonds passing for such: the majority from Normandy, but no bailliage or seigneurie supplied so large a proportionate number as the maritime Bessin, the Avranchin, and the Cotentin, then teeming with the sturdy unemployed, seeking for sustentation wherever it could be found, and who founded so many good families in England. Usurped Apulia constituted a station on the journey, greed and fraud attracting a never failing supply of devout Flibusteers; cadets of noble families, bearing the Cross of salvation embroidered on the gowns which concealed the murderous sword.

The stricken Robert proceeded, and, with mournful merriment, described himself as borne like a corpse on a bier. He encountered a Norman, and more than a Norman, a *Normand et demi*, a blade doubly sharpened, a Cotentin man, from the Bailliage of Pirou, a locality very notable, even now, by reason of the Castle near Coutances.—Monseigneur, enquired the doleful Pilgrim, what shall I say concerning you when I shall have reached home? Robert replied with affected jocularity: but grim and doleful was the unseasonable joke.—" Say you saw the devils bearing me to Paradise."

The Mahommedans luxuriated in the full pride of domination. Robert travelled incognito, according to the fashion which kings and princes adopt, when they wish to enjoy the ease of privacy, concurrently with the privileges of station, yet not suppressing the *gratus risus ab angulo*, which betrays them — ill content would they be were their dignity quite eclipsed! But Robert's concealment was incompatible with Robert's profusion. A pilgrim tax was levied at the gate of Jerusalem—one bezaunt per head—the same for the rich man as for the poor, and very numerous were those, who, destitute of the needful viaticum, congregated outside the walls.

Robert lightened his heavy purse by paying the toll for them all. The Saracen Admiral, or Emir, the governor of the city, would not be out-

Robert and Drogo poisoned at Nicea.

done by the Magnifico; and, therefore, when Robert quitted Jerusalem, he restored all the bounty his visitor had bestowed. But the Duke and his companion were sinking under the effects of the poison which had been administered to them; and, dying at Nicea, they were entombed in the Cathedral.

> Sun repaire fust tresk à Niche,
> Iluec fu mort par un toxiche;
> Ke li duna par felonie,
> Un Pautonier ke Dieu maldie.

Judging by the name of the *Pautonier*, or Vagabond, the rascal who had envenomed the cup was a Frenchman or a Norman, not a Greek or a Saracen. At this period the Southern settlements founded by the Northmen were encreasing in magnitude and importance; and a suspicion floats before our mind, that either Tancred de Hauteville, or Guiscard, or some other of the adventurers, whose only virtue was their valour, dreading lest a Norman Duke might claim supremacy over them, thus delivered themselves from their apprehensions of Rollo's son. Toustain brought over to Normandy the relics Robert had collected for his abbey of Cerisy. The name, Toustain, is still common, both in Normandy and Brittany. This fortunate Adventurer bore the Conqueror's standard on the field of Hastings, and obtained a large endowment in England.

Chapter IV.

Part I.

WILLIAM THE BASTARD, DUKE OF NORMANDY.

1035—1047.
1047—1066.

§ 1. CONTEMPLATED by any enquiring stranger, the Norman Ducal family would, at this era, have presented a singular example of regular irregularity. Every child, from Guillaume Longue-épée downwards, had been born out of lawful matrimony, and subsequently brought within the pale of legitimacy by a mantle marriage; or some other traditional mode of wedding, plighting faith, or pledging, equivalent to a marriage in the Norman mind: some ceremony imparting a legal and moral sanction to these unblessed nuptials, and received as equivalent to the sacerdotal benediction, being, in fact, the law as now subsisting beyond the Tweed. *Troubles consequent upon Robert's death. Irregularity, under a Christian aspect of the marriage ceremony amongst the Normans.*

Elsewhere have I stated how the venerable Anglo-Saxon formula still subsists as the kernel of the solemnity, according to the Anglican ritual. Each mother, honoured or dishonoured in her turn by the Duke's affection or protection, appears primarily in the character of a concu-

1035—1047
1047—1066

bine, whilst, each in her turn is accepted by the Northmen's progeny, and the child's disgrace condoned. From Rollo downwards, only one exception can be discovered in the Neustrian annals—the case of the Bastard *par excellence*, the most illustrious of them all. The curse imprecated by ferocious Talvas, as he bent over the sleeping babe, is ever ringing in our ears. Yet in Talvas himself was the Conqueror's adage exemplified—Curses, like chickens, come home to roost.—None more chastised than the cankered veteran, who sought to blast the cradled infant's fortunes.

Summary.

§ 2. So fruitful had been the stock of Rollo's sturdy race, that the individuals included therein constituted a ducal clan; each branch expanding over the genealogist's rolls. But William was repudiated and discarded.

Guido the Burgundian lawful heir of Rollo.

Pre-eminently formidable amongst the swarming foes was Guido the Burgundian. It is somewhat remarkable, that when Robert sought to shield his child from future evil, Arletta had not been appointed or invited to join or concur in the guardianship of her son. Possibly Robert had seen enough in that light-hearted damsel to determine him, that, though, by the laws of nature, entitled to exercise the personal guardianship of her boy, she should be excluded from the regency. Be that as it may, the young Duke

The young Duke placed in the Castle of Vaudreuil.

was placed in the strong border Castle of Vaudreuil, in the Evrecin, under the personal charge

Chapter IV.

WILLIAM THE BASTARD, FROM HIS ACCESSION TO THE BATTLE OF MORTEMER.

1035—1054.
1054—1066.

§ 1. Toiling, moyling, we at length attain the era, equally interesting and perplexing, so long looming in our horizon; that era when the adverse fortunes of Normandy and of England are about to conjoin. Albion's white cliffs rise before us, whilst we are crossing the narrow sea. The roll of Time unfolding, we become dimly enabled to discern how all events, though, to us successive, are contemporaneous in the foredoomed chain of Causation; decreed when Time was not, and vanishing in Eternity. Past, Present, Future, inscrutable and inseparable. *1035—1054*

William's reign, as Duke of Normandy, commencing about the tenth year of his age, assumes the form of a three-act drama, each act concentrated upon a battle. When we record the history of our fallen race, we dip our pen in gore; and the three verdant fields of Val des *The three victories marking the three eras of William's Ducal reign.*

1035—1054. Dunes, Mortemer, and Hastings, respectively define the three decisive epochs of the Ducal domination;—that domination predestined to create the British Empire. In the annals of the Human race, no one crisis more influential than William's Conquest; for it was the combination of the Norman's astuteness and the Englishman's sturdiness, whereby their descendants have been enabled to girdle the terraqueous globe; diffusing the good and the evil, the blessing and the bane, each and all alike the results of civilization.

William's guardian appointed by his father.

§ 2. Wild, rash, thoughtless, as Duke Robert, when determining on his pilgrimage, appears to us, he had previously taken one important practical step, manifesting much sagacious forethought and pertinent wisdom; namely, the appointment of Alain, Count of Brittany, Hawisa's son,—and, consequently William's near kinsman,—to exercise the powers of government in Normandy during the father's absence and the young Duke's minority.

The selection was judicious. Alain's affinity might inspire him with some small share of natural affection. Next of kin by blood, yet not legally entitled to claim the succession, and, therefore, somewhat less tempted to rivalry, he commenced his Regency wisely and energetically; and, so long as he lived, he restrained the malicious hostility of young William's swarming enemies.

Messenger after messenger dropping in from Palestine, severally and successively repeating and confirming the mournful intelligence, how Robert's strength was failing, much in body, more in mind, had virtually anticipated the last fatal tidings. The Tocsin tolling; the news spread amongst the Lieges, rapidly as though the Fiery Cross was circling round the land; and the Ducal dominions forthwith, lapsed into direful anarchy.

§ 3. According to the principles of mediæval jurisprudence, the French forensic axiom, *le mort saisit le vif*, was not admitted simply: nor did the Ancestor's *demise*, a technical expression, than which, none more significant amongst the pregnant "*Termes de la Ley*," forthwith vest the inchoate title in the Heir. The right required realization.

The Sovereign was the Fountain of Justice; therefore the stream ceased to flow when the well-spring was covered by the tomb. The judicial Bench vacant; all Tribunals closed. Such was the antient doctrine—a doctrine still recognized in Anglo-Norman England. Consequently, according to our constitutional law, all Commissions and other delegations of power emanating from the departed Ruler, become null and void upon his death. But, in the present day, we avoid the inconvenience which would result from such a collapse of national vitality, partly by Statute, and partly by a Royal Declaration authorizing the various Functionaries so circumstanced, to continue in the exercise of their offices until otherwise provided. This procedure was not adopted during the period with which we are now concerned; therefore, the land was lawless, until the "King's Peace" (that most significant designation) was proclaimed. The sword of Themis dropped from her unnerved hand. The Norman Duke was the sole Judge to whom the Baronage were amenable. From him, all superior criminal justice emanated. And, therefore, until the recognition of the Sovereign, an interregnum ensued. Such was the condition of Normandy at the juncture we are now describing. Each man acted as seemed right in his own eyes: *Faust-recht,* or *Fist law,* according to the emphatic term which the Germans employ, superseded all other remedies against wrong. Riot and robbery prevailed throughout the land, with increased exacerbation.— Thorns strewed the path prepared for the glorious Conqueror; his destiny, a life of agony, a death of sorrow.

During the latter declining years of Robert's slothful government, the due enforcement of the laws had been neglected. The erection of a Castle, unless with Ducal licence, was illegal. Such a Castle was termed "adulterine"—an appropriate form of speech, designating the structure's vitiated origin. Numerous were these strongholds, each a centre of rebellious violence, (*Raubschlosser,* "Robber's nests," as they are termed by an expressive German idiom,) which had arisen during Robert's reign,—tokens of his culpable indifference,—whose picturesque ruins now adorn the landscape, particularly in the Avranchin, the Bessin, and the stern Cotentin, where at this very moment, whilst I am writing, the Titanic Cherbourg appals our shores,—these three Baillages, or Viscounties, being the districts which contributed the largest contingent to the Conqueror's army; and within whose boundaries, one hundred and thirty-two of these edifices are still subsisting, in greater or lesser stages of decay. 1035—1054

Every child of Rollo's race, from Guillaume Longue-épée downwards, had been born out of lawful matrimony, but all had become subsequently legitimated by a mantle marriage, or some other traditional mode of plighting faith, pledging, or wedding; some archaic rite or ceremony accepted, from time beyond memory, as imparting a legal sanction to these unblessed nuptials; being in fact analogous to the law as now subsisting beyond the Tweed. Each mother in her turn, honoured or dishonoured by the Duke's affection or protection, appears primarily in the character of a concubine; whilst the progeny of each favourite was treated as lawful, and the child's disgrace condoned. One exception only can be found in the Norman annals—the case of the Bastard *par excellence.*—The malediction imprecated by ferocious Talvas is ever ringing in our Ethnic form of marriage. The curse of Talvas.

1035—1054 ears; yet it is in Talvas himself that the Conqueror's adage, "Curses, like chickens, come home to roost," received its full exemplification. No actor in the great drama was punished more severely than the cankered veteran who sought to blast the smiling infant's fortunes.

§ 4. Upon whose brows ought the Ducal Coronal to descend? Alice, Richard le-Bon's daughter, herself spurious, had espoused Otho William, "Count of Burgundy," this style distinguishing transjurane Burgundy,—Burgundy beyond the Jura, from the splendid "Duchy of Burgundy," that Dukedom ranking as a kingdom; and by him she had one son.

Guido of Burgundy— his claim to the duchy of Normandy.
This son, named Guido, was, therefore, William's cousin,—a relationship constituted by elastic bonds of affinity, closer or nearer as measured by the length of the purse; the object magnified or diminished, brought nearer to your eye, or driven further from your view, according to the end of the spy-glass which you turn towards the party, or the unequal heights of the social level respectively appertaining to, or claimed by, the Observed or the Observer.

The Burgundian Prince is much vituperated by the Norman writers: so far, however, as we can collect his character from their own testimony, we do not discover any other reason for their censure save antipathy. But Guido did not stand alone; he lacked not Competitors.

So numerous had been the offspring of the

Norman Dukes, that the family constituted a species of Clan or Sept; but, assuming the existence of any definite right of hereditary succession, Guido,— if we choose to overlook the rotten spot at the fork of the branch from which he sprung,—would have possessed a very strong ancestorial claim; enhanced by the splendour of his position, and his family power. At all events, the arguments which Guido might employ to support his pretensions were sounder than any could be alleged on behalf of the baseborn William; he who came in merely by the disposition which his putative father had made.

§ 5. It is a painful token of the sentiments brooding in Robert's mind, that the Mother had not been named as the guardian of her Child. Even rigid Casuists may be quoted, who argue that the degraded parent does not forfeit her natural prerogative. But, stern was the rebuke conveyed by the neglect; hence arose the fitting retribution following the sin; for although illicit love may be accompanied by affection, confidence is rarely inspired. The sweetness of the philtre palls on the palate, or turns sour. A wardship was indispensable. Arletta was silently elided from the list; and Gilbert Crespon, Count of Brionne, Châtelain of Tilliers, and Thorkettil, also called Thorold, were appointed to the trust. Gilbert, a wise and influential officer, acted pursuant to Robert's testamentary directions; and William, severed from his mother, was placed, as well for education as security, in the stronghold of Vaudreuil. The Castle, standing in the valley formed by the confluence of the Seine and the tributary stream, the Reuil,—a situation imparting to the locality the name of the "Vallis Rodolii,"—was familiar to the Conqueror's family; inasmuch as there whilom had dwelt the good man Sperling, the rich Miller, whom Espriota had condescendingly taken as her husband.

Strength and position combined to recommend Vaudreuil as a neighbourhood pre-eminently calculated for the orphan's safety. Yet that knowledge of human nature which the Statesman ought to possess, might have taught Robert to shun a bad omen. It is a fanciful, and yet a natural feeling, that a structure should inherit a moral character from its Founder. Sanctity suggests sanctity; crime, crime; and this grim edifice was haunted by the memory of the Fury Fredegunda, pursuant to whose behest the frowning towers first arose.

Ambiguous, therefore, was the aspect according to which the Castle might be viewed,—a palace, and a prison; a building not destitute of amenity, and yet inspiring awe, shading into horror. The nucleus of the building had been raised by Roman hands. We can guess its general outline; for in the very heart of Paris, the vaulted halls traditionally associated with the name of Julian, may, without any strained conjecture, be regarded as displaying the distinguishing features exhibited by the apartment assigned to the boy. *1035—1154*

§ 6. Castle or Palace,—this edifice, sheltering the young Duke, he being about twelve years of age, was assailed and stormed by his foes,—their leader the turbulent William, son of Roger de Montgomery; whose name, the token of subjugation, is still stamped upon the Cymric soil. The chamber door was forced open by the insurgents. Osborne, the young Duke's kinsman, son of Herfast, brother of Guenora, who slept in the boy's bed, was stabbed by his side. So sudden the blow, that the victim passed from sleep to death. Thorold, the Duke's Preceptor or Governor, was also butchered. Rescued by his uncle Gautier, the boy found refuge in a peasant's cottage, till the first storm had passed away. *Vaudreuil attacked by the insurgents against William's authority.*

§ 7. We shall hereafter contemplate the glorious Conqueror upon his death-bed, labouring under that mysterious conflict of feeling, symbolized in the antient paintings, the productions bringing before our eyes the inward mind of past generations; the Good Angel and the Evil Demon respectively awaiting the departure of the Soul. Fallen nature clinging to earthly things, though tortured with the entire consciousness of their worthlessness. Penitence and obduracy; self-condemnation, and self-justification; the scales of the balance trembling between Heaven and Hell—then, during that awful agony did William recapitulate his life of trial and sorrow: and, *William's death-bed.*

1035—1054 — from his own lips do we learn the dangers and tribulations he had sustained. None more bitter than those occasioned by the enmity and treachery of his kinsfolk, who, constantly combining against him, sought to deprive him of his dominions—nay, of his life. The whole of William's memorable reign constitutes a perpetual commentary upon that night of terror.

Private wars.

§ 8. A moral insanity desolated the land, reeking with gore. It seemed as though, according to the Hellenic myth, the glebe had been sown with the teeth of the dragon—the whole territory, marsh, and hill, and plain, teeming with the young Duke's enemies. A general insurrection ensued—crime, contagious. The abusive usage of private warfare was pursued with merciless inveteracy, and degraded into foul and horrorful murder. During such moral epidemics, generated by the combined influence of mental and physical causes, man, like beast, becomes maddened by the sight and stench of blood and carnage. Warring against each other, the weak became the prey of the strong. The villains were despoiled, the open towns and thorps burnt and plundered: and, sorrow upon sorrow, the rebel-roll recorded the names of the most illustrious in the land.

Truce or Peace of God proclaimed in the council of Caen.

§ 9. And thus did Normandy endure with few exceptions until, in the Council of Caen, the Norman Church adopted the "Truce of God," or "Peace of God;" (it is difficult to distinguish between these most humane institutions;) and, during twelve years, or thereabouts, the land enjoyed rest—a rare, and all but solitary historical example of national violence being practically restrained by the influence of the Gospel. It was enjoined by the Fathers that, from the fourth day of the week at sunset, until the rising morn of the second day in the following week, no attack should be made upon any enemy; no stroke stricken; no sword unsheathed; no bolt darted from the arbalest; no battle-axe wielded; no bullet shot from the mangonel; no assault made upon any Castle, or any Town, or any Borough, or any Village, or any habitation of man, during the space of the period thus hallowed. Thirty years' hard penance in exile, to be accepted by the transgressor seeking pardon. Moreover, ere commencing his self-imposed banishment, he must make reparation for all the evil he had committed; and for all the spoil, restitution was to be made. All who abetted the offender participated in the doom. If, whilst abiding in contumacy, he was stricken by death, Christian burial was denied to him as an obdurate sinner, and his carrion corpse abandoned to the fowls of the air.

1035—1054

The whole season intervening between the first day of Advent, and the Octave of the Epiphany, and from the Rogation day, until the Octave of Pentecost, received the protection of the Truce. But such injunctions were too burthensome for unconverted man; and, though more than once repeated, and at Rouen commemorated by the Church of "Sainte Paix," the usage wore out, and became, what it is now, a curiosity of history.

§ 10. Numerous and formidable the factions headed by Mauger, the turbulent Archbishop of Rouen; and his brother, William d'Arques; William's kinsmen. The Montgomery party also. Fierce Roger had then retreated into France, banished, or self-banished thither. With him his five sturdy sons—emulating their father in all wickedness. Conspicuous also among the Bastard's enemies rose Hugh de Montfort; but the most precocious of the rebels was Walcheline, Baron of Ferrers; this Walcheline being the first who actually kindled the torch of rebellion. He erected his fortifications on the banks of the Coesnon, and conjured his friends to aid him in avenging the grievous affront he had received from Hugh with the Bushy-beard, Count of Montfort, and son of Thurstan de Bastenborg. The latter, confiding in his fortalice, and, in order to prevent the enmity of that Baron, so well known in subsequent time from his canting bearing, the Horse-shoes, sallied forth as in desperation. So fierce the fight, that both the doughty combatants were slain. The arms given by Ferrers, that antient title suggesting such lamentable recollections, commemorate the tenure of Walcheline's Barony, as being the Ducal farrier; and he dug the ore on his own lands.

But none amongst the rebel host inspired greater apprehensions, whether by birth or possessions, talent or cruelty, than the famous, or infamous Roger de Toeni.

Roger de Toeni—his bad reputation.

Like the Scots, the Normans entertained a firm belief in the opinion, that disposition of mind, whether for good or evil, crime or talent, was stubbornly inheritable in families. In our age, such a tendency is diminished or concealed by civilization; but the innate idiosyncrasy occasionally crops out—the very consciousness of the imputation occasioning its realization. Now, in Normandy, the *mauvaise engeance* of Eric, Hirc, or Hulc, to which family Toeni belonged, was famed for ferocity. Hulc bore Rollo's standard, and, according to the family traditions, valiantly assisted him in subjugating Neustria. From him came the proud and powerful Roger—this pedigree affording one of the very few instances in which the ancestry of a Norman is deduced from a genuine Northman.—Fully did he assert the imputed character of his race, inasmuch as when he passed over into Spain, he distinguished himself by valour and savageness, preventing Richard Cœur de Lion in his atrocities.

Roger de Toeni in Spain.

It is a sorrow that traditional adulation should teach us to admire this last mentioned sanguinary and licentious Anglo-Norman Monarch—affording one of the innumerable instances of the false judgments, whereby history becomes corrupted into a constant source of erroneous feeling. As for our Norman Baron, the day he landed was a day of battle. He caused a Saracen prisoner to be quartered as though he were an ox: and, the quivering limbs cast into the seething cauldron, he smacked his lips when, in the presence of his congenial followers, he partook of the horrible viand. Whether the anecdote be true or false, the circumstance is equally characteristic of both eras; that one and the same act of ostentatious brutality should be assigned to two diverse national heroes. Some time afterwards Toeni returned to Normandy, and found the Bastard ruling in the land. He was direfully offended; and none more competent to do mischief than he. He arrived at the juncture when the revolt against the Child William was raging. Most of the old and trusty friends placed about William by his father, had been assassinated; and the wide-spread antipathy entertained against the boy produced the effect of a regularly organized conspiracy.

William's character—bodily and mental gifts.

§ 11. As for William, his character received full developement at an early age. He conducted himself wisely and discreetly, and the sagacity distinguishing the man, had previously been conspicuous in the boy. To varied talents of a high order, William conjoined athletic vigour and a noble form. It was talked of as a truth, or accepted as a truth, that none but Duke William could bend Duke William's bow. His natural 1035—1054 gifts, whether bodily or mental, marked him for a Conqueror; and the hard discipline he sustained in his youth trained him to become a Chastiser of nations, a minister of punishment and of vengeance. But his greatest victory was over his own natural passions:—in an age of gross and unbridled licentiousness, the Conqueror of Carthage was not more distinguished for continence and chastity than William. He soon acquired importance beyond his years. A powerful and brilliant Court assembled around him. So splendid, so influential, was the youth, as to excite King Henry's jealousy; and the monarch, secretly alarmed at his vassal's rising reputation, was obliged, even then, to treat him with a degree of deference beyond what his years could claim. In no one point of character did William display his aptitude for government more satisfactorily than by his readiness to follow counsel. And, submitting to the advice of those about him, he appointed Robert de Gacé to assist him in political, as well as in military affairs, until he himself should attain full age.

§ 12. The perplexities attending the investigation of Norman history continue to press upon us during the early years of William's reign. An era of confusion has bequeathed to us an inheritance of confusion. The enmity which the boy encountered constitutes the leading and prominent feature of the period, until we find him

1035—1054 firmly settled in his authority. But, though considerable difficulty may be experienced in determining the sequence of events, there is none whatever as to the main course and flow of William's fortunes. It does not appear that any precise age of majority was defined by the legal constitution: we know it was not so in England; and Henry the Sixth, the child, scarcely more than an infant, affords a very signal example of the mischief occasioned thereby. The like in France; indeed, we may say, throughout Christendom.

The Baronial conspiracy.

§ 13. William may have been cruel, but never obstinate. His reign, if, at such an early age, his exercise of sovereignty may be termed a reign, opened with misfortunes: the dissatisfaction of the Barons increased and matured into a combination against him; and, seeking the tranquil Henry, they roused him to action against the rising rival.

There was reason for apprehension. The Norman settlement cuts into the French territory, and the descendants of the Danes were always within a short march of the gates of Paris. We do not possess any particulars concerning the Baronial conspiracy. Guillaume de Jumiéges is our solitary informant, and he whispers in our ears: "That these are the very men who yet live and now make profession of being the most faithful, and upon whom our Duke has conferred the greatest distinctions and favours."

§ 14. Normandy's perennial opponent and implacable enemy, Henry of France, had, as we have seen, fully and solemnly confirmed the young Duke's reversionary right and title, which acknowledgment, he, upon Robert's request, and in Robert's life-time, had ratified by all the solemnities of law ; but the transaction was construed by the French Court to be void *ab initio;* still were the Normans despised as barbarians, and dreaded as Pirates. The waters of Jordan could not wash out the black blood stain, and Henry, partaking in the general feeling, determined to unsheathe the sword, and extirpate the odious usurpers of the land.

1035—1054
1040—1047

§ 15. It is not always easy to determine satisfactorily the line of demarcation severing historical biography from biographical history. Ought the Hero to rise before us, as the system's centre, around whom all the events circumvolve, or should the unity be constituted by the Epos ? Are we not compelled to elect between Napoleon's achievements, and the foundation of the French Empire ?—Between Achilles' anger and Ilium's conflagration ?—Between the conquest of Gaul, and the laurels of Cæsar ?—In our present task, no such difficulty perplexes us. Hero and Epos are one. Either of the epithets bestowed by history or by tradition upon Arletta's son, equally pourtrays William's complete mission, from his joyless cradle to his miserable death-bed. Whether you designate him as the Bastard,

Historical biography contrasted with biographical history.

Unity of action in the present subject.

1035—1054
1040—1047

or as the Conqueror, the effect upon the mind is complete: the whole history of the Man, and of his times, unfolds before us.

Magnificence of William's mission.

Magnificent was William's destiny. Can we avoid accepting him as the Founder of the predominating empire now existing in the civilized world? Never does the sun set upon the regions where the British banner is unfurled. Nay, the stripes and stars of the Transatlantic Republic would never have been hoisted, nor the Ganges flow as a British stream, but for the Norman's gauntleted hand.

Elsewhere have I spoken of the Saga-like character of the Norman historiographers, resulting from the general absence of dates, whether in text or margin, so that, for the most part, we can only guide ourselves by the synchronisms which we gather from the Capetian annals or the English authorities; as to the case, immediately before us, we can, with respect to William, roughly calculate that, whether influenced by policy, or restrained by apprehension, the young Duke's swarming enemies, domestic or foreign, had, after the first hostile explosion, allowed him to

Tranquillity of the first twelve years of William's reign.

continue unmolested, whilst about twelve circling years were rolling away; during which period the young Sovereign, attaining man's estate, settled into pacific tranquillity. Sedulously did he attend to his affairs, though his time was fully as much employed in his recreations and amusements. It is related with much zest by the tonsured Chronicler, how the young Duke disturbed the sweet refreshing solitude of the damp and cool forest glades, by setting apart Preserves or Parks for sport; that is to say, for the purpose of enjoying the anguish and misery inflicted upon the Creatures whom their and our Creator has placed under man's supremacy. But the political calm was deceptive. Whatever apparent respect Henry may have rendered to his Vassal, it was always accompanied by the mental reservation that the pact was binding only so long as convenient,—a principle silently pervading most diplomatic arrangements: and many domestic ones also.

§ 16. William, as yet only a youth, was tolerated rather than acknowledged by his Suzerain; and, when the good time of doing evil arrived, Henry poured his forces into the young Duke's territory. No courtesy displayed, or feigned; no, not even fair warning. No message delivered; no gauntlet thrown down; no challenge given; no defiance proclaimed; no trumpet sounded. Henry invaded the Evreçin, accompanying his aggression by demanding the immediate demolition of the much-contested *Castrum Tegulense*, or Tilliers:—Tilliers must be razed to the ground. A harassing warfare was now waged by both parties;—desultory skirmishes;—assaults, obscure, inglorious, indecisive, yet nevertheless possessing much political importance, for the quarrel fretted the

1085—1054
1040—1047

Tilliers surrendered to Henry.

half-healed sores ; keeping alive all the old grudges between the Frenchman and the Northman, so that the two Nations relapsed naturally, so to speak, into the normal relations of rivals and of enemies.

The fortress had been placed under the charge of sturdy Guillaume Crespon, whom we may designate as Guillaume Crespon the First, thus distinguishing him from a namesake. A message was despatched, instructing him to surrender the charge of the stronghold; but he acted as though he could not comprehend the order, and held out. The young Duke besought his sturdy guardian to comply; and the fortress was given up. Henry repaired to Tilliers, placed a garrison therein, contrary to his engagement, and having obtained this grip upon Normandy, he suspended hostilities, and a pause ensued.

Guido of Burgundy: how educated at the Norman Court; his revolt.

§ 17. Guido of Burgundy now suddenly asserted his claims, or pretensions. Kindly and confidentially had the Donzell been reared at the Norman Court. From the time he could cross a horse, he was treated almost as an heir presumptive. The Youth had been received in the Halls of Falaise as an *enfant de la maison;* and, when he attained the canonical age, the degree of knighthood was conferred upon him by his Liege Lord. Moreover, several important Baronies were granted to him; and Alice of Normandy's son occupied a station scarcely less prominent before the world than the son of Arletta. He was courted in accordance with his station and pretensions. To him resorted the discontented and the scorner, the ambitious and the covetous, and all who hated or despised the Bastard: and the scarcely concealed enmity soon exploded.

The instigators of rebellion were found in the very Danishry of Normandy;—in the Bessin, where the speech of Scandinavia had been so long cherished; and in the frowning Cotentin, crowned by the massy bulwarks whose threatening image is ever rising before our eyes.

The chief fomenter of discontent was Neel, or Nigel de Saint Sauveur, the premier Baron of Normandy, descended from the most distinguished amongst Rollo's followers. Neel, whose progenitor stood as first individual amongst the Pirates who had received their domains from the great Northman's grant; Neel, pre-eminent by position, wealth, and talent; Neel, whose possessions commanded sea-bord and inland; Neel, rendered equally formidable by the extent of his dominions, and the sturdiness of his vassals, —they who won such fair possessions in England, and who now combined the Frenchman's cultivation with the Berserker's savage valour. —Hamo Dentatus, or "Rattle Jaw," also joined the insurgents; he, the founder in England of the Durdent family: and Grimoald de Plessis, owning the Barony which, at the present day, still bears his name, and commemorates his mis-

1035—1054
1040—1047

William at Valognes.

fortunes. And all the Confederates bound themselves by a great oath to work the intruder's destruction.

But, where are we to seek young William, who now rises before us as Chief of the Norman Commonwealth? Not in powerful Bayeux, where the speech of the Northmen still lingers as a living tongue. Not in proud, opulent, rebellious Rouen. Not at towering Falaise, where his infant wailings were first heard. But at pleasant Valognes, where temple and hypocaust, theatre and amphitheatre, testified how, in the luxurious Roman days, the locality had been prized. Here William had established himself, holding his Court. Amongst his guests none more important than Golet, the fool. Half demented, though acute withal, this Merry-man becomes conspicuous in the history of Court-jesters; and he had gained cognizance of the conspiracy. In the midst of the night he presented himself at William's door, in full official costume, his bauble slung round his neck; and, knocking violently, he shrieked out, "Up, up, my lord Duke! open! open! flee! flee! or you are a lost man! Delay is death. All are armed; all marshalled; and, if they capture thee, never, never wilt thou again see the light of day!"

Golet, the fool.

William's flight by night.

William obeyed the warning without even a thought of hesitation. No questions asked. No companions to support him. No groom aiding. Half clad, starting from his couch he rushed into the stable, saddled his beast, and made for the ford of Vire. Hard by the river's mouth stood, and still stands, the Church of Saint Clement, close upon Isigny.—Here, he tarried; may be, prayed. Bayeux he dared not enter; therefore, he edged his track between the Saxon city and the sea, skirting a neighbourhood, whose name is echoed on our shore of the channel, the bourgade of "Rye." Doubting the loyalty of the inhabitants, he sought for the "Manoir," the dwelling-place *par excellence*, a term which, amongst us, is extended to the whole demesne. But this signification first obtained in comparatively modern times: and so recently, that I cannot recollect a single example of the word's occurrence in an antient English Court roll. Day was dawning; but, ere the sun had cleared the horizon, William had arrived at Hubert's door. William's horse, white with foam, bespoke the urgency of the danger which had driven his rider thither. The road through which William escaped still retains the name of *la voie du Duc*. The local traditions and the Trouveur's lay agree with singular accuracy, and the whole of this narrative abounds with particulars so minutely descriptive, that none but the illustrious fugitive could have told the tale.

North lies Cherbourg, that adamantine, stern, threatening arsenal, where, instead of the wooden mallet's dead thud, thud, thud, we are now startled by the harmonious clink, clank, clink, of the hammer striking upon the sides of the iron-clad vessels, whose terrors are summoning the willing warriors from their homes to defend our shores.

Hubert's sons conducted the Duke to palatial Falaise, where he bided his time; his flight the signal for the baronial rebellion. The "Vicecomites," the governing nobility of the land, who appear in England as the "*Sciregerefas*," seized the Ducal dominions. A hard trial now had William to sustain. He sought refuge at his Suzerain's court. At Poissi, the royal residence, it was in the character of a Vassal that the future Conqueror craved his Liege Lord's aid. Gladly the King welcomed the illustrious applicant, whose submission purchased protection. Intent upon vengeance, William told over the chief rebels, man by man. It was a proud duty which Henry was required to fulfil, that he should be invoked as William's protector, the heir of Rollo being as yet only dubiously invested with the ducal dignity.

§ 18. William summoned his Lieges from those Baillages in which his authority had been most cordially acknowledged. Rouen manifested unusual loyalty, and the whole Roumois assembled in defence of Rollo's descendant. Caux, and the sturdy and opulent Cauchois, co-operated cheerfully and powerfully. Princely Eu and the Lieuvin poured forth their chivalry: also antique Evreux and the Evreçin; and the combined forces assembled on the wide-spreading undulating hills, which impart their name to Val des Dunes,—a region whose conformation displays the original conjunction of these continental downs with the corresponding tract in our island; the elastic turf, clear of trees, inclining towards the rising sun. The topographical details are given so picturesquely as to convince us that the Trouveur had studied the scenery which his verse describes.

1035—1054
1040—1047
1047 Val des Dunes, nigh Caen.

Amongst the Barons, there was one who, adopting the phrase employed during our civil wars, sometimes seriously—sometimes sarcastically—was distinguished as a "waiter upon Providence." This individual was Ralph Tesson or Tasson of the Cinglais, Tesson the Badger, so skilful in burrowing his way; equally qualified by cunning and by power.

Cunning Ralph Tesson. His importance in the war.

Tesson's men were stationed apart, and their bannerols, waving bright from their lances, rendered them conspicuous.—"Friends or enemies?" enquired the King. The doubt was immediately removed. The stubborn, wily chieftain presents himself first and foremost in the Baronial ranks, whom the chances of civil war would entitle to be honoured as liberators of their father-land from the Bastard's degrading yoke, or branded as rebels. As for Tesson, he had sworn on the shrine at Bayeux, that he would open the fight by striking the first blow upon the helm of the base-born Pretender. But the Barons were divided in opinion; many saw in William the rightful heir, and

Tesson takes the lead in the Baronial army.

Tesson's vow.

Tesson fought for his life. Well had he deserved the vengeance due for treason.

1035—1054
1040—1047

Now ensued the shock of battle; and loud the rallying cry of the Harcourts, who were the most intent in the cause. "Thury!" was their slogan, still heard in the local name of "Harcourt Thury."—Was it here that they chose the pleasant and comforting motto which they bear in the conquered land, "*le bon temps viendra?*"—And they expected the good time in this present conflict. But the Scandinavian enthusiasm of the modern Normans, tempts them to hear in this war-cry the invocation of Thor, the thunderbolt's wielder.

The charge of the Barons.

Dauntless William headed the Normans, whilst from the hostile ranks "Montjoie Saint Denis!" resounded through the air, to which the rallying cry "Saint Sauveur," shouted by the Bessin troops, headed by Ranulph of the Briquessart, responded. He, ready to risk his purse, his treasure, nay, his very life, for the purpose of crushing the enemy. Fierce the fight; Henry and his squadron faced the Cotentin men. The King of the French was dismounted, but through great exertion, his life was preserved; whilst the glory of the Cotentin was commemorated by the popular rhyme which, transmitted to subsequent generations, attested the monarch's discomfiture.

The Ducal troops charge the enemy.

King Henry's dangers.

De Costentin sortit la lance,
Qui abati le Roi de France.

Another war-horse brought up!—Henry vaults into the saddle, and the conflict is renewed with increased desperation. Neel de Saint Sauveur maintained the fight until the rebels fled in dire confusion; and, so thick fell they, that the narrow, foaming mill-race of Bourbillon, which you look down upon as you hang over the shattered parapet of the one-arched bridge, was choked with bloody corpses. Hamo slain, and, borne away upon his shield, the vanquished rebel was entombed nigh the border of the stream. Discomfited, dispirited, shamed, the insurgents sought mercy. William was prudently gracious. Gifts and promises were followed by pardon. The forfeitures which the Barons had incurred were remitted; but Neel, who did not humble himself by "seeking grace at a graceless face," found a refuge in his castle of Brionne-sur-Rille.

1035—1054
1040—1047
The rebels resisting desperately, are completely defeated.

Henry continued to aid the Norman Duke, despatching further reinforcements. But so strong was Neel's position, or so imperfect and desultory the means of attack, that three years elapsed ere the fortress surrendered. Merciful were the terms extended to all the Captives, save one. Grimoald de Plessis was dropped into the dungeon-pit, manacled and fettered, the cankering iron eating into his ulcerated flesh; and, in this misery, protracted during three years, he expired: —the victor's spite pursued the traitor to the grave—for he was buried in his bonds; so that

Siege of Brionne-sur-Rille.

Miserable death of Grimoald.

the sad tale of his fate might prove an awful warning. As for the other delinquents, William made a bridge for the flying enemy. Guido's renunciation of allegiance was accepted; and, retreating to Burgundy, he disappears ignominiously from history. This trial of strength settled all disputes between William and the recalcitrating Normans. All who had rebelled against the Bastard made full acknowledgment of his authority.—Fealty and homage rendered,—hostages given to secure the plighted troth,—the adulterine castles razed to the ground,—a new field of exertion opens for the Conqueror.

§ 19. Hitherto, though considerable jealousy had subsisted between the powerful lines of Anjou and Normandy, no hostile collision had yet ensued; but much rivalry, fair or unfair, had been mutually cherished between William and Geoffrey Martel, Count of Anjou, the famous son of Fulk Nerra, whose *sobriquet* (distinguishing him from his namesake Geoffrey Grisgonelle) so well designates his heavy hand. In both these Princes the mental talents and moral failings of their respective lineages were signally exemplified. One cause of offence arose from the conduct pursued by Geoffrey towards the House of Champagne and Blois, whose possessions were at this period divided between Stephen the son of Eudes, and his brother Thibaut. Fiercely were the passions of all parties roused. Martel warred steadily and sturdily against both these princes. Stephen was defeated and expelled. Nevertheless the balance of fortune was fairly counterpoised. Thibaut was captured and kept in duresse, until he surrendered Tours and Chinon—Chinon, afterwards so gay under Plantagenet ascendency.

<small>1035—1054
1047—1055</small>

The contagious ill-will amongst these nobles excited much enmity against Martel in particular. Other causes were abundantly found in the clannish feuds which rise so prominently before us during this era of Norman history.

§ 20. Geoffrey Martel's conduct was tortious; employing bribery and corruption, he obtained possession of Alençon, defended by the site and by the people's valour, and constituting with Domfront the basis of a line of operations, which could be equally employed, whether for the assault or the defence of the Duchy.

<small>Alençon. Importance of the position.</small>

From this position, Geoffrey, true to his epithet, incessantly made Normandy feel the full weight of his crushing hand, driving all before him, affronting the Norman pride. Merely to stand up against an enemy, is, under certain circumstances, considered an act of boldness; whilst William may be said to have advanced, bearding his foes; another expression grounded upon the same idea.

<small>William continues his campaigns.</small>

A very powerful partisan, who occupies a special position, was William Fitz-Osborne, son of honest Osborne; he who sheltered William in his earliest childhood, and who had con-

<small>Fitz-Osborne. His truthfulness.</small>

tinued so true and affectionate in the midst of the treacherous crowd.

These men of might were destined to become Doomsday Barons, and to rule respectively in England, as Earls of Hereford and Shrewsbury.

William's spirit.

William continued to prosecute the campaign with insulting unconcern, savouring of affectation, hawk on fist, or following the hound, as though the country did not remain to be acquired, but had been already gained. Well nigh had the commencement cost him dear. His own people grudged the vailing of their caps to the Tanner's grandson. The disgust which turned their stomachs against the Bastard, was contagious amongst all the revolters, and all their party: the very horses shyed at the stench of the tanyard; and one individual, "the traitor of traitors," whose name is concealed by Guillaume de Jumièges, nearly succeeded in betraying our Duke to captivity or death. Indeed, there could not have been any other alternative for such a captive,—his prison doors could not have opened except for the grave.

1048. William besieges Alençon.

Such were the feelings actuating all Belesme's peculiar seigneurie. To fall under the domination of the Tanner's grandson,—the contemptible Bastard,—was intolerable. He was loathed and detested. William made straight towards

Alençon. He found the inhabitants all ready to greet him:—calthrops sown,—fosses deepened,—walls heightened,—palissades bristling all around; whilst the town-folk accumulated insult upon disloyalty. To spite the Tanner's grandson, the walls were tapestried with raw hides—the filthy gore-besmeared skins hung out, and as he drew nigh, they whacked them, and they thwacked them; "Plenty of work for the Tanner—plenty of work for the Tanner,"—they sang out, shouting and hooting, mocking their enemies.

They sought to sting William to the quick, and did. He swore his great oath, that dearly should they pay for their insolent bravado. They acted advisedly; they knew their peril and had prepared themselves for it, yet scarcely realizing the extent of their danger. The bridge was barricadoed, and they made a bold—a desperate sortie. The outwork was stormed. The stakes stuck in the ooze were plucked up. Many of the Alençon men fell into William's power, and atrocious his triumph. The prisoners were brought before the walls and there endured the most infernal tortures; their fellow-townsmen crowding the battlements, agonized by the appalling spectacle. Eyes spiked out, hands and feet chopped off, and the mangled members and limbs shot into the town, earnests of the Duke's vengeance. These horrors were intolerable: the Alençon men, pitifully craving mercy, were permitted to capitulate; and William, having entered on the proper Angevine territory, erected a castle at Ambières, and returned triumphantly to Rouen.

§ 21. William's renown spread far and near. The clerks' glozing erudition assured him that he might appropriate to himself Cæsar's alliterative boast. His Barons renewed their homages; the aspect of his affairs became brilliant; and a grand alliance with the Kaizar encreased his influence. No real addition of authority did William obtain by this measure; nevertheless, the connection was politically advantageous. Though frayed and faded, the Imperial purple still triumphed supreme, as the most dignified symbol of human power. Moreover, it was possible that, through the prerogative ascribed to the Imperial head of the Christian Commonwealth, Normandy's Ruler might assume the royal style, and his dominions acquire the title of a kingdom. Hungary and Poland offer examples of such a recognition. Hence we obtain an explanation of the jealousy excited amongst William's neighbours; and, therefore, his enemies.

§ 22. William's whole position was fraught with danger, and he knew it. Swarming were the foes who grudged the pre-eminence acquired by the bastard brat of the unsavoury Tanner's daughter. William's stern and sagacious energy commanded external submission, and excited internal exasperation. But the stigma imparted by William's illegitimacy was indelible. The blemish was a permanent ulcer which no Leech could heal. Enmity may be subdued by Christian feeling, but contempt arising from birth, is not to be washed away by the waters of the font; nay, not even by the consecrated oil. Do not we Septuagenarians, retain a living recollection of the least respected in the category of our Sovereigns, who sneered at Napoleon because he was not a gentleman? An equivalent feeling was contagious amongst the Rulers of all the States by which Normandy was surrounded. William might be admitted to their consultations, but not cordially received *ad eundem*. Grudgingly would William have been invited by the tabarded Herald to enter the lists, had it not been for his well weighted purse; nor could he expect to establish his position, until he should have obtained unquestionable superiority.

§ 23. The apanages and baronages held by William's kinsfolk, on the right hand or on the left, comprehended some of the broadest and most tempting Seigneuries of Normandy—none more important than the noble barony of Mortaigne, so attractive to the Traveller, impressed by the feeling peculiarly the creation of our times, the sense of the picturesque—a sentiment scarcely older than ourselves, even Anna's golden reign was strange to the sensation—inasmuch as the locality contains the only waterfall in Normandy.

<small>1085—1054</small>

<small>William the Warling.</small> Now started up as a newly declared enemy, William, the son of Mauger, nicknamed the Werling, or the Warling. He, like his father at Corbeil, secluded himself in his rock fortress, apparently disconnecting himself from public affairs. Rarely is he noticed by the Chroniclers; but secret activity compensated for outward apathy. A plot had been concerted by the Bastard's enemies, for raising the Warling to the Ducal Dignity; and the conspiracy was on the point of exploding, when an imprudent confidence reposed in Roger Bigot, the great Earl of East Anglia—(antiquaries please themselves by showing you the model tower which they bestow upon him)—revealed the treacherous confederacy. Arraigned by his angry Suzerain, the Felon dared not deny the charge, and was thankful for a decree which permitted, or compelled him, to seek his fortune in opulent Apulia.

<small>Bigot's tower.</small>

<small>The Warling banished.</small>

§ 24. Mortaigne, which belonged to the Warling, was dealt with as an escheat. William bestowed the fine domain upon his half-brother Robert de Conteville, the son of Arletta and Herlouin, who subsequently becomes conspicuous as a most energetic and adventurous supporter of William's power. Yet the leaven of discontent continued fermenting. William, surnamed Busac, second son of William, Count of

Arques, now revolted against the Duke, relying *1035—1054* upon the support he expected from France. But France favoured him not. Busac quailed before the Bastard, whose good fortune encreased with accelerated rapidity.

§ 25. During the early incursions of the North- *Ponthieu. Importance of the territory.* men, the greater portion of Ponthieu had been occupied by the Danes. According to the course of argument, so convenient, like all diplomatic arguments to the strongest, the geographical position of this Pagus would be employed to prove that the district naturally appertained to Normandy. But what the shaggy Northmen won, the shrewd Norman lost; and "Centulla of the hundred towers," together with the Abbey of Saint Riquier, had been rased to the ground by the Pirates. The Abbey Church was subsequently rebuilt, and the structure exhibits a most elegant example of the florid ornamentation characterising the profligate but tasteful era in the renaissance.

When the Scandinavian storms were lulled, a *Nithardus, the paramour of Bertha, abbot of St. Riquier.* Bourgade of some extent had nestled beneath the Abbey's shade. The line of ruined walls and flanking towers, still discernible in the pleasant fields, marks out the extent of the antient settlement, and the graceful Beffroi indicates that the civic community had acquired, or re-acquired, some municipal privileges. The opulent foundation continued to prosper, and her annals exhibit a long series of jolly prelates, amongst whom Nithardus is distinguished in literature by his very valuable chronicle; whilst his furtive amours with Bertha, Charlemagne's daughter, render him conspicuous in the romance of history.

Abbeville, originally a dependance upon St. Riquier.

§ 26. Abbeville, "Abbatis Villa," in Ponthieu, originally a grange depending upon the Abbey of Saint Riquier, became the Capital of the Seigneurie, and sometime imparted a title to the Suzerain who owned it. This Pagus included the Boulonnais; and the tract constituted a very important position, commanding the Channel waters, from whence the Norman Duke could, were he to renew the menaces which his father fulminated in the days of Ethelred, terrify, or even assail, distracted England, whose unsettled condition invited the enemy.

Prerogatives of the Seigneur of Ponthieu.

It was upon these shores that the Seigneur of Ponthieu was accustomed to put in use the odious privilege of attaching the person as well as the property of the tempest-tost Mariner. The inhuman prerogatives expressed in English legal phraseology by terms appropriately uncouth, "laggan, flotsam and jetsam," subsisted to the fullest extent upon the Ponthieu shores. And the Counts, when exercising their inhospitable rights, displayed such exorbitancy, that even in a barbarous age, the conduct was stigmatized as atrocious. Besides their violent seizure of stranded goods, it was their custom to treat the shipwrecked crew and passengers as captives, nay, as criminals; casting them into prison, and extorting a ransom, not merely by the *squalor carceris*—that legal term which conveys such a fearful idea of Scottish cruelty in those good old times when mercy to man or humanity to beast were sentiments unknown—but even by torture.

§ 27. During Richard Sans-peur's domination, the Normans made an attempt to recover the fertile district between Ponthieu and the Somme, the Vimeux as it was subsequently denominated; and which, according to the ratiocination so convenient to the stronger, he considered as included within the natural boundary of Normandy, and therefore to belong to the stronger. Here was the port of Saint Valeri, commanding the estuary of the Somme, a most convenient point for embarkation; and within the opulent Pagus were included the dominions which rendered the matrimonial alliance with the "She-wolf of France," so important in English history; whilst the illustrious field of Agincourt, also situated in Ponthieu, imparts historical splendour to the territory. Now, under these circumstances, facility tempted and crafty policy suggested to Guillaume of Arques, how advantageous it would be to connect himself with Ingleram, the Count of Ponthieu, distinguished equally by ability and ferocity. A dangerous foe was Guillaume Lord of Arques. The Count preferred his claims as Rollo's legitimate heir. It is doubtful whether Civilian or Canonist would give an opinion that his title was made out. But all the inhabitants of the surrounding country were in his favour, even up to the very walls of Rouen. His castle, now frowning in ruin and desolation, towering over the breezy downs, apparently furnished the model for that great fortress which first greets the mariner approaching the opposite shore, the memorial equally of England's subjugation and renovation.

Rebellion of the Count of Arques.

From this position the Count defied the spurious superior. Away with bastards! Duke William at this juncture was occupied in the Cotentin, that focus of insurgency, that fertile source of trouble. He marched up from this position, and attacked the rebel, proclaiming that he was warring to vindicate his legitimate title to the Ducal power. The Count of Arques he compelled to take refuge in his own stronghold. Any attempt to storm the Castle would be useless. William, therefore, established a strict blockade; and having directed the construction of certain fortified posts, by which the communication with France could be cut of, he departed. Arques was well garrisoned, and the garrison apportioned to the extent of the fortress, but this strength was weakness,—so many men —so many mouths requiring to be fed. The most important element was wanting. The emphatic employment of one word, *provision*, one and the same word designating the highest power of mind, and our food, is a curious example of instinctive ratiocination. The supply of victual was not adequate to the number of the occupants. Strict the blockade. King Henry became troubled at the danger which threatened his ally, and summoning the Ponthieu forces, awaited farther help in the enterprise. Hugh Bardulph's name appears in the muster roll of the Insurgents, and the ultimate result decided the question who were the true men and who the traitors. [Arques meantime was captured, and the Count fled to Eustace of Boulogne. Ingelram was killed in arms before the completion of the siege.]

margin: 1085—1054

margin: 1053

§ 28. A threatening power was gaining strength on the west. William was menaced by the young, the intrepid Conan, who, being a kinsman, was naturally the more envenomed against him. Was not Conan entitled to assert his father's rights; nay, more, bound to avenge his father's murder?

margin: Enmity of Duke Conan.

Again, [looking back a few years, we see in Brittany] kinsmen bristling against kinsmen. Eudes, Conan's [uncle], who held Penthièvre, together with other large apanages, assumed the title of Count [on the death of Alain], claiming supreme dominion over the whole Armorican land. The Child, then scarcely three years old, was seized by his kinsman, and detained in

margin: 1040—1047

close custody at Rheims; and some doubted, others feared, whether or no he would ever enjoy liberty again. During seven years he was detained in respectful captivity. And now arose the perplexing question, whether representation or proximity should prevail.

A large proportion of the baronage supported the lineal heir; Conan, rescued from his uncle's grip and restored to his dominions, comported himself as though he claimed, like his father, to be reckoned the *Rui-Breizad*—the British King, who, according to Bardic prophecies, was destined to restore the honours of his antient race, renewing their glories.

§ 29. Five sons had been born to Eudes, the Count of [Penthièvre]. Four amongst the five are subsequently distinguished as potent amongst the English Baronage. William gained ground rapidly. Events wing their way before us, and, even now, through the sea mists, we begin to discern the banners looming in the distance, on the opposite shore. Doomsday names, Battle-Abbey names, begin to sound in our ears. Geoffrey Botterel; Bryan Fitz-Count; Alain the Black; Alain the Red, or Alain Fergant, the Earl of proud Richmond, whose shield we have shewn you; Rivalon, the Breton of the Bretons, Lord of Dôl, Castle of Dôl, City of Dôl, and Barony of Dôl, all devoted to his cause. The French glowered at William, and scarcely knew how to keep sword in scabbard. But he scorned his competitors, and though unable to tranquillize his mind, he disdained manifesting any anxiety.

1085—1054

Guy [of Ponthieu] proclaimed that his brother's blood must be avenged. A universal jealousy raged against William amongst the baronage of Northern France, dwelling in the adjoining parts, and many of them brought nearer by family affinity. So much the worse,— a little more than kin, and less than kind.

Jealousy entertained against William by the Norman Barons.

The language of Normandy, was, in fact, to be identified with the cultivated or literary dialect of the *Langue d'oil.* Normandy produced, probably, the earliest, but assuredly, the best and most interesting poetry of the age. Normans and French wore the same garb, adopted the same manners, and were connected by family and territorial alliances. Notwithstanding the admixture of Danish blood, superadded to the old Franco-Roman hybrid, the elements had been thoroughly assimilated; and yet neither party could completely dispel the recollection of old grudges and grievances. No nation is clean from the mark of Cain; the inheritance of glory is the inheritance of crime and misery. Many of the Norman barons, who, during the troubles, had found refuge at the French Court, fomented the enmity; and Henry, being thus instigated and supported by his advisers, all accomplices, he issued his general summons, not for a mere frontier inroad,

French and Normans virtually one nation.

1054 Henry prepares operations against Normandy.

but with a declared intention of subjugating Normandy, and expelling the Pirates. Happy the day, could such a day ever dawn, when the Norman steersman should be compelled to turn the Norman keel away from the Northman's shore.

Muster of Henry's troops.

Henry's summons was readily obeyed by those who assembled beneath his banner, much more in the character of allies than of vassals: or rather as expectant partners and participators in the anticipated gains. How they poured in. They poured in from Burgundy; they poured in from Aquitain; they poured in from Brittany; they poured in from Anjou; they poured in from Maine; they poured in from Ponthieu; they poured in from all adjoining parts; all combining with one intent against the hated enemy. "Would not Julius Cæsar himself," quoth our chronicler, "have been appalled by such an invasion?" a pedantic and affected comparison, but evidencing the hopes and the apprehensions respectively entertained by either party.

Henry's campaign against Normandy.

§ 30. Henry schemed his campaign judiciously. Assailing the Norman frontier at the most vulnerable points, he determined to effect the complete expulsion or extermination of the hated Pirates; those Pirates so detested by the French, and yet essentially French, French to the marrow of their bones; Rouen as thoroughly French, as Paris higher up upon the Seine. Henry planned to gain Rouen by a *coup de main.* Lackland never lacks logic. When did an enemy, conscious of his own strength, fail in finding a reason for striking the first blow? Henry probably reckoned on receiving support from the discontented Citizens. The Tanner's grandson could not be made sweet—he stunk in their nostrils as strongly as ever. Now came up the enemy. The royal banner waved, as the Chroniclers tell us, at the head of the levies of Gallia Celtica. This expression must not be read as a pedantic tag brought in for the display of book learning; but as testifying the enduring reminiscence of the great Fourth Empire. Eudes, King Henry's brother, was the Commander.

§ 31. William, on his part, acted warily—caution is the surest element of conquest; and he hovered about King Henry's camp, taking good care to avoid crossing his royal opponent's path, shunning personal conflict, lance pointed against lance, sword clashing with sword. He might be arraigned as a felon if he struck his liege Lord. But, if his liege Lord struck first,—then, blow for blow. William had greatly annoyed the royal army, cutting off the supplies. Henry could not victual his troops otherwise than by actual pillage. A commissariat was unknown, and irregular plunder enhanced the miseries of war.

The French streamed in like a rushing flood; the conflict against the Pirates' progeny was a national enterprise; every Norman slain, helped to pay off old scores.

§ 32. The French troops began by directing their line of march through the Beauvoisin, a route which struck into the heart of the Pays de Caux, whose breezy, fragrant, undulating downs, offer such noble battle-fields.

Operations of the French and their allies.

A second division of the army being entrusted to Eudes, the *Enfant de France*, he directed his course warily, having full knowledge of the people and the region, and won praise and profit by spoiling the country. A third invading flood came down from Mantes, whose "*grande rue*" presents that precipitous descent, which sadly, sorrowfully, and ignobly, terminated the Conqueror's earthly career. Touraine and Blois also did their duty to the King. Robert, Count of Eu, for once acting faithfully. Hugh Gournay, grim old Gournay, fierce old Gournay, the pre-potent power in that region; and William Crispin and the Giffords; and the Montforts. William was seeking to perplex the invaders, and the French were allowed to enter the Norman territory without opposition.

The Pays de Bray.

A large and important portion of the rebellious Baronage who have been mentioned, held extensive domains in the Pays de Bray; a rich and fertile district, which never acquired any feudal denomination. A large portion had been won by the Gournays, and old Hugh Gournay led them on. This same Pays de Bray was, in fact, an essart from the antient forest of Lyons, 1035—1054 and the fertile soil was richly tilled, but, at the present juncture, taking the grazing shift as rich and productive pasture.

Many were the flourishing Towns and Bourgades, rising therein. The Capital, so to speak, was the antient Driencourt. Those sturdy archæologists who still adhere to the Druidical faith, find in the name's first syllable indubitable proof of Celtic traditions ;—Could any etymological acumen be so dulled, as not to discern the oak in the first syllable of that name? But a Castle, erected in comparatively modern times by Henry Beauclerc, subsequently caused Driencourt to obtain the denomination of Neufchatel, which it still retains, like its Helvetic congener. You smell the cheese in every room of your inn. This region is the dairy of Paris.

§ 33. Not apprehending danger, the French abandoned themselves to excess, pillage, and plunder, rapine and rape, and murder. The bourgade of Mortemer they occupied as head quarters. The local appellation seemed to indicate that a marshy pool had been the origin of the name, deduced by antiquarian acuteness from the Dead Sea. The castle rises above the surrounding country; the tall dungeon tower whose walls still crown the rock became the head station of the French troops, and they filled the fortress with the booty they had gained. The field of Mortemer, and the scattered farmhouses representing Mortemer, are standing immediately beneath that grim grey Donjon tower. The Normans diligently dogged the enemy, and when the day emerged from the night, which the French had passed in drunken debauchery, so often euphemized as merriment, they assailed the fortalice and fired the town. The dark, cavernous, antient church exists, in good repair; a score of straggling farmhouses are dotted in the surrounding pastures, and the charred timbers, turned up by the ploughshare, still testify the original extent of the town. Fierce was the conflict commencing with early dawn, "boot and saddle" pealing before the rising of the sun, whilst strife and clangour and clamour resounded throughout the day. The French, thoroughly routed, fled from the field bestrewed with corpses, every pit and dungeon was crowded with captives, and amongst them, the Count of Burgundy, his ransom worth a King's.

§ 34. William, however, could not take any personal share in this important conflict. He was employed in blockading King Henry, and the news was fantastically announced to his opponent. During the darkness of the night, bold old Roger de Toeny repaired to the rising ground which commanded the French encampment; there he clomb up a tree, and grimly proclaimed to the French their shame and misfortune. And during many generations were the

tidings he conveyed, commemorated in song *1035—1054*
and lay.

> "Franceiz Franceiz, levez levez,
> Tenez vos veies, trop dormez;
> Allez vos amis enterrer,
> Ki sunt occiz à Mortemer."

The suddenness of the spectral warning ter- *Retreat of the French.*
rified King Henry, and he purchased a shuffling
retreat, by concluding a discreditable pacification. Special negociations ensued, relating to
the liberation of prisoners, whose persons constituted a valuable portion of the plunder. The
French King moreover conceded that William
should retain whatever profit he could extract
or extort from Geoffrey Martel.

§ 35. With the Count of Ponthieu, Guy, *1054—5 Guido submits to William as his vassal.*
or Guido, whose ancestry and pertinacity rendered him the most formidable amongst William's
foes, William also made his own terms. His
keen conception and prophetic judgment had
disclosed to him the advantages which would
result to a Duke of Normandy, by obtaining the
superiority of that shore, so ample and commanding in its tidal stream.

Guido was now kept hard and fast in the
filthy dungeon pit, so often the facile descent
into the grave. Here he pined in duresse until
he consented to become William's vassal; and,
surrendering his County to Normandy's Coronal,
was content to receive his territory from the
Suzerain's hand.

1035—1054 The service of a hundred knights must Guido render to the Norman Victor. An enormous burden, ten times the tale claimed from the Norman Duchy by the Capetian Monarchy. High renown resulted to William,—already William the Conqueror. His success was rendered very important by the positive acquisition of the territory, but far more as displaying, to the world, the power which the predestined Lord and Master of England had obtained.

William's war with Anjou. § 36. William, nevertheless, continued to prepare against further perils from Anjou; folks might already have said that William was born to cut thongs out of other men's hides; but would any man living have jeopardized his own by such unsavory jocularity? King Henry, however, gladly availed himself of the opportunity, by playing off Rollo's descendant against the descendant of Tortulfus. It is worthy of notice, that William did not assert any litigious claim to the Angevine possessions or dependencies. He did not condescend to employ the conventional form of giving his reasons, or lamenting the sad necessity of drawing the sword against Anjou, but he went to war because he wanted Anjou to win that which was not his own; the acquisition he made was an unmitigated Conquest.

William was trying his hand at his trade— very slack and expansive was the feudal bond at this era, the feudal law about as stringent as the *jus gentium* at the present day; enough to ground a demand and justify the thing when done. This quarrel eventuated into a guerilla of varied fortunes, whereby William made that acquisition scarcely less prized in after times by the Norman Sovereigns, than the English realm,—the County of Maine.

1035—1054

Glorious was the ancestry of the Manceaux, and they prided themselves upon their antient deeds. Triumphant in the Capitol, Rome herself had quailed before them. Were not their achievements prominent in the history of the world? It was the Cenomanenses who had subjugated Cisalpine Gaul—it was the Cenomanenses who founded Trent, where the Teutonic dialect comes in collision with the Roman tongue. — It was the Cenomanenses whose circling ploughshare traced the ramparts of Crema.—It was the Cenomanenses who had founded desponding Mantua, and fated Cremona.—It was the Cenomanenses who had triumphed over the towering Bergamo, —the Pergamus of Cisalpine Gaul. It was the Cenomanenses who re-peopled Brescia of mystic mythology, and torrent-divided Verona. Nay, had not Cæsar himself quailed before these energetic conquerors?

County of Maine; ancient celebrity thereof.

Maine became distinguished in ecclesiastical history at a very early period of the Church. Hence came Clement, the successor of St. Peter, and sent forth by him to visit Saint Dionysius, who was the Apostle of that region, and the first Bishop of the Mans. Clinging to the Roman institutions, Maine retained her civic identity, and constituted a member of the Armorican Commonwealth. In the subsequent era, Maine, according to the traditional pride of her people, asserted her independence and identity, though locked in—may we say *enclaved*—by the kingdom of Clovis. A Count of Maine, bearing the title of "Defensor," succeeded to the antient Magistrate, continuing to exercise his authority under the supremacy of the Masters of the world.

The defensor of Maine.

An elective functionary was he indeed, prior to the domination of the Franks: an elective Magistrate he continued until a comparatively recent period, and the privileges guaranteed by the grim old Merovingian Sovereigns Childebert and Clothaire, confirmed the antient right, grounded upon the immemorial usage which had prevailed.

Towards the decline of the Carlovingian Empire, the increasing ascendency of the system conventionally denominated feudality, effaced the more archaic jurisdictions, and we hear of a Count David, whom local historians claim as the great Emperor's descendant. His reign, which, if faith be placed in the enchorial chronicles, endured more than half a century, enabled him to consolidate his authority.

Herbert Eveille-Chien.

§ 37. A son of this ruler was our old acquaintance Herbert Eveille-Chien, or, adopting the expression for which even the Monkish Chronicler apologises, *Evigilans Canem*. In many

a conflict did his activity animate the Man- *1035—1054*
ceaux, wedged in, as they were between Normandy and Anjou, and having to struggle hard for independence, crushed by these rival powers, but fully conjoined in their animosities against their foes. According to the Angevine pretensions, the Capets had granted to Grisgonnelle the County, the Country, and the People, or, in other words, all the elements of supremacy. But the Normans counter-claimed this independence, asserting that it was their Dukes to whom the Suzerainty appertained. Anjou was formidable; Herbert bold, open, and sincere, gifted with a fine and liberal mind, his kindred were as conspicuous for these qualities as the Angevine Counts, or their representatives, the proud Plantagenets, were by their fraud and cunning. Honest Herbert was unequally matched against such foemen, and acting somewhat incautiously he placed himself within the grip of his enemy, whom he visited in the Castle of Xaintes. Both were accompanied by their congenial Consorts. Her- *Herbert made*
mengarda of Anjou, beguiling her companion,— *prisoner by the treacherous device of Hermengarda.*
diamond cut diamond,—by a friendly greeting, and acting the part of innocent sportiveness, enabled her husband to seize and secure the generous Herbert. He might wake the dogs, but no less bold and incautious than his father, the watchman yielded to slumber.

Brutal was the treatment which the captive sustained from Fulco; and he might have rotted

1035—1054 in the deep, damp dungeon-pit had he not been rescued by his spirited Consort. She raising the Manceaux against Fulco, the latter was constrained to release his prisoner, rejoicing, nevertheless, in the receipt of an exorbitant ransom. [Unmoved by the treachery practised upon Herbert, his son Hugh], no less bold and incautious than his father, equally allowed himself to be taken prisoner. A misfortune, increased by close captivity,—incarceration enduring, as it is said, seven years—a quasi mythical number, often employed vaguely to signify a considerable space of time. It is doubtful whether [Hugh] ever re-entered his Capital; he continued under Angevine protection, much after the fashion, which in more civilized and happier times, we kindly extend towards a Maha Rajah. Nothing he can call his own, and to keep himself at his own cost and charges.

Hugh under the protection of Anjou.

[1051] Upon Hugh's death, an event which, no doubt, had been anticipated not long before the battle of Mortemer, Martel had possessed himself of the domain; he entering Le Mans by the one gate, whilst the widow Bertha and her three children dolefully departed through the other.

Geoffrey Martel treats Maine as his own.

So long as Martel lived, he treated Maine entirely as an inheritance. The second Herbert, son of the deceased Count, lived so peaceably or so sluggishly, that we do not know any thing concerning him beyond his name, and his mark subscribed to certain charters. Such the position of affairs relating to Maine, when the Mortemer treaty, sanctioned so far as Norman authority and Norman prepotence extended, the widening of Normandy's borders. Now in the blooming spring-tide, the bright days lengthening, the yellow iris gleaming on the margins of the waters, up and doing was William, as the Trouveurs sung; not a moment did he waste. His troops victorious,—his people animated with the flush of anticipated victory, he issued his command that his forces should muster, for the purpose of occupying the contested territory, and he entrenched himself in the position, whence he had observed that the fortress could be most easily assailed. Geoffrey Martel repaired to Anjou, bitterly complaining of the insult and the danger. A fierce spirit of hostility, embittered by disgust, was now raised against the Normans; they stunk in the nostrils of their enemies worse than ever. A traditional, undefined apprehension of their crafty cunning excited great apprehensions, rendering them more formidable even than their military power. An alliance was formed against the common enemy, the jealousy being enhanced by the rumour that William had declared he should one day become a crowned King.

Martel died four years before the Conquest. [Herbert's] one daughter Margaret [was] espoused to Robert of Normandy; but she dying childless, Herbert, on his death-bed, bequeathed his dominions to William, exhorting the Manceaux to acknowledge him as their Lord if they wished to live in peace; and the style he assumed, *Dux Normannorum et Cenomannorum*, proclaims the pretensions of England's victor.

[margin: 1035—1054 [See after, p. 269.]]

[margin: Anjou.]

§ 38. The two nations, Norman and French, were rapidly assimilating. Severed by political jealousies, they nevertheless constituted one nation. Manners, customs, and above all, language made them as one people. Nay, Normandy became the classical land of the Langue d'Oil. Yet the Roman speaking race nevertheless became black in the sight of the Frenchmen as the most benighted Pagan Dane. The Anti-Norman coalition assumed a formidable aspect. Poitou and Brittany impatient for the fight; nor could Henry settle upon the lees. They took down the spears from the racks, furbished the coats of mail, and sharpened their swords. Without challenge or defiance, no glove thrown down, no stroke stricken; not even a word before the blow, the Angevine broke the peace for which he had sued, and again invaded Normandy more savagely than ever. William, on his part, raised all the Norman forces. The whole arrière-ban, gentle and simple, the villainage being included in the national summons, answered to the call right heartily. Hatchetmen and hammermen, bowmen, clubmen, swordsmen, and spearmen, all up and doing. King Henry penetrated into the very heart of Nor-

[margin: The French and the French population invade Normandy.]

mandy. Caen, as yet unfortified, the dykes dug and stockades planted in haste, aided the inhabitants, and they rose as one man in defending the country against the invader.

1035—1054. Animated defence made by the Normans.

But, as before, the Frenchmen damaged their own cause. William prepared an ambush. There was a bridge crossing the river [Dive], also a ford called the Gué Berenger. William and his Normans assailed the enemy, who were marching out for the defence. The bridge broke down, the enemy fled from the assault. William won his spurs ten times over. King Henry escaped, and new terrors were roused by the Norman name.

[1058] Defeat of the French at the Gué Berenger.

§ 39. King Henry had mistaken his vocation in seeking military renown. Age and vexation subdued his vigour. He had been sinking under anxieties, and a peace eagerly sought, was concluded at Fécamp. King Henry had at this time a heavy burden upon his mind. Most earnest was he to secure the succession to his young son Philip, now seven years of age. Never before had that name, uncouth in the strict sense of the term, appeared in the genealogies of Latin Christendom. His mother was Anne, daughter of the Czar Jaroslaus. The Sclavonians were inspired by their antient recollections and traditions. It was their vaunt, that when the Macedonian Conqueror, whom history, poetry, and prophecy conjoined, had contributed to exalt into a mythic hero, espoused Roxolana,

Henry secures the succession of France to his son Philip.

1035—1054 he had bequeathed to his descendants, a universal empire. Henry had espoused Anne, the daughter of Jaroslaus, the only alliance which the Sovereigns of Western Europe had ever contracted with such an alien race. Philip, at the age of seven years, was raised to the throne of France by his father's appointment, and during his father's lifetime.

1059

Splendid coronation of Philip in his father's lifetime.

Splendid was the Coronation of the young Sovereign designate, at Saint Remy's Basilica. Never within the memory of man, had such an august assembly been held for such a purpose. There were convened, the Prelates, the Abbots, and the Nobles. Guienne and Burgundy, pre-eminent as representing, *par excellence*, the Franco-Gallic Commonwealth. The Papal Legates, Hugh, Archbishop of Besançon, and Hermenfrid, Bishop of Sion, were there. Hugh, son of Robert, Duke of Burgundy, and Geoffrey, Duke of Guienne, and Count of Gascony; Raoul, Count of Valois, Herbert, Count of Vermandois, William, Count of Soissons, Reginald, Count of Nevers; Guy, Count of Ponthieu, William, Count of Auvergne; Fulk, Count of Angoulême; and the Count of Limoges. The young King designate took the oaths, placing his hands between the hands of the Archbishop,—loud rose the voices proclaiming him their King.—Vive le Roi!

Chapter V.

PREPARATIONS FOR THE CONQUEST.

1054—1066.

§ 1. No event was so influential upon William's fortunes, whether as a man or as a Sovereign, as his union with Matilda, daughter of Baudouin de Lisle, the magnificent Count of Flanders, which ensued about this time. William seems, at an early period of life, to have determined that no child of his should sustain the ignominy which clung to him to his dying day, a portion of that mysterious dispensation, that the sins of the fathers are visited upon the children: and in an age marked by laxity of principle, no charge of the violation of the rules of morality was ever brought against him. But his situation was very anxious. According to the strict principle of law, a bastard has no heirs, and in the event of his death without lawful issue, the Normans would have had to seek their ruler amongst any of the descendants of Rollo, if there were any, who could connect themselves with that great parentage. Sanctioned by the advice of his baronage, this marriage was politic and wise under every aspect, encreasing his power, and contributing most influentially to the fitful gleams of happiness which he was permitted to enjoy during his dark and troubled career. Curious merry anecdotes, more grotesque than credible, were current concerning the process, somewhat violent, by which the sturdy wooer compelled the reluctant maiden to grant her hand. The laurel was interwoven with the bridal garland, and the marriage was celebrated with congruous splendour. Matilda, distinguished by her beauty and opulence, was rendered still more illustrious by those virtues which she displayed when seated on the English throne. We may dismiss as a merry invention of the Trouveur, the story that her hand and heart had been won by the rough process which, in the dark age of travellers' wonders, was believed to be adopted by the Russian wooer.

§ 2. According to the traditions of the Fleur-de-Lis, first and foremost amongst the lay peers arose the Counts of Flanders, the proud descendants of Lyderic the Forester. I have already spoken of Flanders, not a kingdom, but dignified as a kingdom, and a territory which subsequently acquired encreasing importance in English affairs, or rather, the affairs of Great Britain. The territories occupied by the Flemish race, employing that term in its widest sense, extended from Normandy's borders almost up to the Rhine stream. When you land at Calais, (originally *Vlæmskeland,*) the cheerful, chirping, chiming Carillon announces to the Englishman that he has planted his foot upon a land whilom of transcendent importance to his own. The Low Countries, including the County of Flanders, constituted one of the most influential elements of Latin Christendom,—they were the counterparts of those energetic Communities, who flourished under a brighter sky, the sources to Italy of her strength and her debility, her glories, her misfortunes, her private virtues and her national crimes. In the spirit of Liberty, the Belgians vied with Italy. Lille resisted against the violation of her "*Keuren*," rivalling the boldness and perseverance displayed by Milano la Grassa, or Firenze la Bella, when contending for their franchises. But very diverse were the fates and fortunes attending the respective populations. Whilst Fleming and Frison fought for liberty to the death, the Italians, traitors to themselves, succumbed to the most degrading tyranny.

1054—1066

National prowess of the Flemings.

Strenuous in arms, equally did the Belgians excel in the arts of peace; and the looms of Arras wove the tapestries which constitute the Vatican's splendour. The colours spread on the pallet of John of Bruges taught Titian to produce his bright groups. But, unlike him of Cadore, the Flemings never pandered to the basest vices of mankind. Their commerce enriched and adorned the realms of Latin Christendom. The Dames of Seville exhibited with

Their cultivation of the Fine Arts.

1054—1066 pride the delicate textures of Mechlin, and Antwerp's heavy keels crossed the track of the treasure-laden Argosies. The language of the Flemings does not yield, whether in richness or energy, to any of the Teutonic dialects, and surpasses them all in harmony, but the attractions of literature are wanting. No poets did they possess, beckoning us into the Stadthouse; whilst Dante and Petrarch live as our contemporaries, and are hailed as companions and friends. The very feuds and dissensions of Italy captivate our imagination.— The names of "Neri" and "Bianchi" are harmonious to our ears, and enrol us under their Standards;—they persuade us to adopt their politics and participate in their feelings. But never shall we be warmed with any enthusiasm by the scuffles between the salt cod fish and the hooks, the "Kabel-jauers" and the "Hœkjens."

Flandre-Flamingante and Flandre-Gallicante.

At an early period, a large proportion of the Belgic tribes had adopted the colloquial Latin or Roman language in various dialects, shading off from those spoken in Gaul. Hence the division of the country into "Flandre-Flamingante" and "Flandre-Gallicante." These dialects were very numerous, and their intermixture without confusion is singularly remarkable, broken up into spots and streams, like the colouring of marble-paper.

Throughout the northern regions of our island, the Flemings became very influential.

Swarms of their stout, sturdy, burly, fighting-men settled in the territories of the Scoto-Saxon Sovereigns, and broke the power of the Gael. The Celts could not stand against the well-tempered blades and keen lances of Flanders; and the ploughshare conquered more from the natives than the sword. They established themselves in every district between Tweed and Solway, and the Forth and Clyde.

1054—1066. Flemish Settlements under the Scoto-Saxon Sovereigns.

The most diligent amongst modern investigators of Scottish history, the victim of a sneer, whose ponderous volumes, slumbering on the shelf, have been abandoned to unmerited oblivion —has pointed out the lineages who inherited the regions won by the shuttle and the weaver's beam. From them came the Douglases—from them came the Leslies—from them came the Burgons—from them came the Flemings—all the Flemings here, there, and everywhere—the Flemings of Aberdeen, the Flemings of Seaton, the Flemings of Lanark, the Flemings of Dumbarton, and others of the same signification; flourishing families, whose origin is testified by patronymic and sirname. But above all, Freskin the Fleming, founder of the proudest and most patrician amongst the Earldoms, Honours, and Titles which dignify the Scottish land.

Nobility and gentry of Scotland descended from the Flemings.

§ 3. In a political point of view, the Imperial Eagle and the Fleur-de-Lis divided the supremacy of Flanders. To the east of the Scheldt the land was Imperial, whilst the re-

French Flanders and Imperial Flanders.

_{1054—1066} maining territory constituted a Fief of France, thus rendering the Count a Liegeman of two powers, but acknowledging practically only a scant obedience for either master.

Physical changes sustained by Belgium. § 4. Whatever divisions or severances subsisted, whether in dialect or policy, the character of these Belgic tribes was essentially uniform. Physical convulsions and catastrophes, the inundations which submerged and swept away so large a portion of the Batavian Islands—those tremendous floods, recorded by shoal and shallow, where the plough once traced the furrow, but now grated by the keel, the mutations, of which the vestiges upon the soil transmit their story, before that story was recorded by the pen of man; the migrations consequent upon these changes, or occasioned by political revolutions, perplex the ethnographical enquirer who labours to identify the races now swarming in the Belgic provinces, with the populations enumerated by their first Conqueror and Historian.

§ 5. But the valour which the victor of the Gauls ascribes to the Nervians and Batavians, must be received as the general attribute of the rough, tough, muscular, Flemish race. The commercial opulence, the abounding wealth, and the splendid prosperity enjoyed by this people, were equally the instigation and the result of their unwearied activity; and the sagacious and steady industry which enabled the inhabitants to transform their marshes and sands into the orchards and flower-gardens of modern Europe, was compatible with the most strenuous valour, or rather was the same valour guiding the ploughshare instead of wielding the sword. The most industrious amongst the races of the Scottish Lowlands and the proudest of their nobility, equally deduce their ancestry from these stalwart stems. Bruce and Baliol themselves find their origin in the regions of the Belgic race. It is amongst these Flemish lineages we must seek the stem-fathers of the Scottish feudal nobility. The Flemish element expanded with the Conqueror, in creating the national character of Scotland: nay, scarcely in a [greater] degree was the Norman himself the *causa causans* of the nationality of northern England.

The connexions of our Norman monarchs in tending towards Flanders, combining with the geographical vicinity, filled the English land with Flemish adventurers; kinsmen, though removed, and whether in peace or in war, their influence is prominently discerned. Moreover, our Anglo-Norman literature was forwarded and improved by the influence of the Romane-speaking, or Walloon population.——

§ 6. As for Matilda, a true woman, her goodness, her virtues may be frequently traced in history—her interference, never. Her patience under trouble and tribulation constitutes the main feature of her biography. The tapestry, which bears record of her husband's achievements, is a unique memorial both of his prowess and her industry; and the needles plied by herself and her damsels, have assisted as much as the historian's pen in commemorating his victories.

William's children.

Four sons had William by his faithful consort. Upon Robert the eldest he bestowed Normandy, the antient inheritance of the family, and therefore deemed the most honourable dominion which could be bestowed. To William, the second son, the father devised his *acquets*—England which he had won. The third, Henry, received a most munificent allowance; fabulously quoted as amounting to a hundred thousand pounds.

In this division we trace the foresight of the Sovereign avoiding the dismemberment of the Empire he had founded. The fourth son vanishes mysteriously from history;—his statue, adorning the magnificent portal of Wells, is the only memorial we possess of his earthly existence. Moreover, three daughters did William and Matilda leave. Adela, who espoused Stephen Earl of Blois, our King; Gundreda, espoused to William de Warren, Earl of Surrey, whose tomb has recently and unexpectedly been brought to light; lastly, Agatha, the virgin widow of Alfonso, King of Galicia.

* * * *

Lanfranc: his contemporary fame.

§ 7. The trying perplexity of Anglo-Norman history, is indicated by the very name; it is bilingual—appertaining to two countries. We must always keep in view both sides of the Channel. Lanfranc, friar of Bec, and Lanfranc, Archbishop of Canterbury, constitute but one individual. A Lombard, born in Pavia, the city of the hundred towers, he there acquired the learning which rendered him so pre-eminent in Normandy. In Normandy, Lanfranc won the confidence of the future Conqueror, whilst in England he became the patriarch of the race, whom the sword placed beneath the pastoral staff. No individual in that era, more influential in the fortunes of England. Learning, sound in the highest sense, now began to flourish in Normandy, and the providential consilience of events conducts to Rollo's dominions a stranger destined to breathe a new spirit in the Norman Church, and through that Church to impart a new vitality to the drooping hierarchy of England. It was through Lanfranc's exertions, more than by any other human agency, that the Church of the English was redeemed from the sloth and oscitancy into which she had fallen. Amongst his contemporaries, Lanfranc was honoured as one of the great renovators of sound learning throughout Western Christendom. "Fuit quidam vir magnus Italiâ ortus, quem latinitas in antiquum scientiæ statum ab eo restituta tota, supremum debito cum amore et honore agnoscit Magistrum, nomine Lanfrancus."—Expressions which have led the

<small>1054—1066</small> learned Dom Lucas d'Achery to suppose, that Lanfranc restored the study of the Latin language, his marginal note being to the following effect:—"Lanfrancus Latinæ linguæ restitutor et Græcæ non ignarus," and this curious misconception has been echoed and adopted by all subsequent authorities.

<small>His birth and family.</small> § 8. The future patriarch of the Anglo-Norman Church, was born at Pavia, the city of the hundred towers. Three only of these civil fortalices are now standing; and your Cicerone tells you that these structures, which in fact are monuments of domestic contentions, were raised by the great families whenever a son took his Doctor's degree. Lanfranc's name has a Teutonic sound, but this circumstance does not afford any proof that he was of Teutonic descent—the appellation, common in the city, was introduced by a popular Saint, under whose invocation a Church is still subsisting. This example is not without significance as explaining the manner in which barbarous names became engrafted upon families of Roman descent—and such probably were the ancestors of Lanfranc, who appertained to the Senatorial Order, the principle of hereditary judges being involved in the principle of hereditary Kings.

<small>Lanfranc's Italian education.</small> Lanfranc passed through the whole curriculum of the liberal arts, then usually comprehended under the denomination of Grammatica, as distinguished from Divinity. Great his quali-

fications, brilliant his talents; his speech, flowing like a torrent; his legal learning commensurate with his natural gifts; and the same abilities which enabled him to perplex his adversaries in debate, caused the sages of the municipal Republic to rejoice when they could profit by the opinions he gave. Secular learning, therefore, in all the branches of intellectual knowledge, constituted his main object; and quitting Pavia to profit himself, he returned thoroughly imbued with science. Lanfranc commenced his professional or public career in his own city, but he had no rest in his bones, and crossing the St. Bernard with a large following of Scholars,—then the only pass connecting Italy with the Northern "Latinitas,"—he settled at Avranches, where he taught School, or rather founded a College. It was or is the Oxford tradition, that any Master of Arts may do the like if he chooses. He acquired celebrity unexampled in that region, an early proof of the precocity of the Norman mind.

margin: 1054—1066

Never was learning more honoured than at this era, and peculiarly by the Normans; possibly a reflex of the benefit the Norsemen had derived from the cultivation in previous generations of their own vernacular tongue.

§ 9. But a deeper sentiment was now influencing Lanfranc's mind. He felt that his success might lead him astray, and he sought to renounce, not merely the social honour of his reputation, but the very fame he had acquired. Lanfranc

margin: Determines to quit the world; goes to Bec.

1054—1066 reasoned erroneously—you may disgrace your reputation, but you cannot renounce it; you may misemploy your talents, but you cannot discharge yourself from the responsibility they impose. But Lanfranc yielded to the impulse. Quitting Avranches, he tramped on the road to Rouen. His track conducted him through the forest, of which the essarts still constitute the prominent features of the pleasant region. Robbers attacked him. No use raising the *clameur de haro*—no one to hear. Stripped, and bound to a tree, he waited for the opening dawn, and attempted to repeat the service appertaining to the circling hours—the three Hallelujah Psalms, concluding the cycle of each day's prayer and praise. But he could not. He had never committed them to memory—and deeply was he stung by the sense of his neglect of holy things; and the preponderating worth he had attached to secular learning. The silent hours continued, and he endeavoured again to repeat the opening services—still he could not. Struck with compunction, he poured forth his mind in prayer; deploring the time he had given to human learning, the labour he had bestowed on literary studies; and now, when he ought to pray, he was unable to perform his duty to the Church; and he would henceforth devote himself body and soul to the Donor of all blessing. In the early twilight morning he heard footsteps approaching him—some peasants released him. During the darkness of the dreary night, his mind suddenly received a new impulse, and suggested to him the enquiry, whether there might not be some humble and sequestered monastery in the vicinity. What he sought he found, and he was conducted to a mean and humble structure then rising from the banks of a rivulet—the Bec, whence the Monastery derived its honoured name, Bec Herlouin, by which it was afterwards known. Herlouin, the founder, was of noble birth; the real old northern blood flowed in his veins, a knight until he renounced the world. Learning he had none.—When he first professed, he could not read a letter, and he subjected himself to all the austerities and privations enjoined by St. Benedict's rule. Manual labour was the employment of the brethren, and much was Herlouin derided by his former companions when they saw his coarse garments, and unkempt beard. Hard and fast Herlouin worked, aiding the building of the Monastery, however coarse or hard; except when chaunting in the choir, or partaking of the one daily scanty meal which he grudged himself, you would always find him digging and delving, or his hand grasping the spade, or with hod on shoulder, as Lanfranc found him, all begrimed with mortar, engaged in vaulting an oven. Lanfranc humbly made his obeisance to the Abbot. His aspect, or perhaps his accent, bespoke his country. "Art thou a Lombard?" said Herlouin, probably actuated by some secret presentiment as to the intentions of the stranger. Lanfranc replied that he sought the cowl. Herlouin, trowel in hand, desired a Monk to bring the volume, containing the rigid rule imposed by their founder; the preface was read, giving the postulant the summary of his duties, expressed with epigrammatic terseness. Faith and works; charity and humility; patience not alloyed by grudging; zeal deprived of asperity; and so on throughout the seventy-three chapters composing the code. Lanfranc disclosed his name, and Herlouin then certified of the stranger's eminence, cast himself at his feet; and Lanfranc was duly admitted into the community. Lanfranc's conduct in this matter was not wise, perhaps scarcely right—for of that which God has given us, it is false modesty to be ashamed. During his novitiate, Lanfranc strove to abdicate his pre-eminence; but the light shone too brightly to be concealed. Bec became proud of her inmate. He felt it his duty to employ his talent. Every member of the Benedictine Order was enjoined to earn his daily bread, by daily labour. But Lanfranc's time had been wasted, had he followed the plough, or trenched in the field; and he performed the duty for which he was so well fitted, that of being an instructor. Bec expanded into a College. He was a recognised professor, but under no pretence would he receive the proffered fees. All the higher talents of the mind were considered gifts of the Holy

Spirit; and it was deemed simony to employ them for money. The honorarium fell into the common fund. Scholars resorted to him from all parts of Christendom. Latin Europe, says Milo Crispin, the Monastic Biographer, acknowledged him as the great restorer of knowledge. Greece, the antient teacher of nations, did not disdain the lessons she received. Men of all condition and age, rich and poor, gentle and simple, smitten with this glorious contagion, came to Bec in frequent resort, bestowing their bounty upon the Monastery; whether in testimony of their respect towards Lanfranc, or in token of the instructions they received. Or, according to that peculiar refinement of feeling, [which we find in early times,] it was considered in those days that learning was too precious an article to be bought or sold, and the gift was received as an honorarium; or according to another view, that receiving money for a God-given talent, was simony. The principle exists in our law—Thus a Physician cannot recover his fees; nor a Barrister, the accompaniment, promised by the marked Brief. Nay, it was simony, at least in theory, for a champion to receive hire. Was not his strength and skill given to him by his Maker?

§ 10. Bec now flourished as an academy. Scholars encreased rapidly; and with success, emulation; and with emulation, envy, hatred, malice, and all uncharitableness. Parties arose in

1054—1066

Cabals against Lanfranc.

Bec. No brightness of spirit can extirpate the jealousies which spring up like ill-odoured weeds, in the damp corners and shady sides of any close community. Many the cabals of which Lanfranc became the object. But he heeded not the strife. He would not vex his spirit by striving against them; and he proposed to quit Bec, and seek his fortune elsewhere. Herlouin prohibited him, and appointed him to the office of Prior. Lanfranc,—he, destined to become so eminent a statesman,—was actively employed in literary, that is to say theological labour. The codices of the Scriptures had become much vitiated by the oscitancies of the transcribers, and manuscripts with his autograph corrections are still subsisting. Upon some portions of Holy Scripture he composed commentaries, but in his own day, the greatest worth was attached to the treatise by which he opposed the formidable Berengarian heresy. His many enemies,—for his reputation, and still more his virtues, had raised a host of critics, who maintained, that in opposing heresy, he himself was heretical,—[were roused against him]. Summoned to appear before the Pope, his vindication of his treatise was unanswerable. But the future Archbishop of Canterbury continued the object of much enmity and envy, which he provoked by his ready tongue. He possessed the true Italian love for fun, drollery, or jocularity. His simplicity was mingled with oddity and humility. A friend met him with a bundle tied behind him on his saddle: the bundle contained a cat, which he was conveying to make war against the mice by whom he was plagued. Bec now chanced to be visited by Herfastus, a clerk belonging to the ducal court, and whom we shall meet again in England. He arrived pending a concursus, a grand day of exciting disputation, and dialectic strategy. The Duke's chaplain, for such was the office held by Herfastus, was accompanied by a splendid train. Hoofs clattering, attendants clamouring, announced his approach to the monastery. Lanfranc, whether by some overt act, or possibly by some unguarded expression, had contributed to the difficulties (so it was reported) which had troubled William's marriage with Matilda. The reproof or remonstrance dictated by the Duke Herfastus conveyed disrespectfully. Herfastus was notoriously illiterate,—his whole language and conversation betrayed general ignorance. Lanfranc, pious as he was, had an innate tendency to sarcasm and drollery, according to the general ethos of his countrymen. Many other enemies did Lanfranc make by his ready tongue. Those whom he provoked, laboured, and successfully, to procure the scholar's expulsion from Normandy. William, in the plenitude of his power, issued his decree, and Lanfranc was banished; and at the same time, the angry Duke com-

1054—1066

Accused of abetting the canonical impediments to William's marriage.

William banishes Lanfranc.

manded that the granges of the Abbey should be fired.—A petty act of revenge, but testifying how entirely church-men and church-property were at the mercy of secular authority; and that, unless ecclesiastical privileges were protected by the consciences of the laity, the clerk had small security against wrong or injustice. Lanfranc departed from Bec with sorry attendants, mounted on a stumbling jade, the worst in the stable. It chanced, that when on his way, he crossed the road on which William was riding. He humbly saluted the Duke. His firmness of conduct, and hilarity of temper, enabled him to reinstate himself in the favour he had previously enjoyed. His influence at Rome, induced William to employ him as his ambassador, and solicit the revocation of the Papal censure passed upon his marriage, on the ground of the connection between the families. Adela of France, Matilda's mother, had been married, or may be, betrothed first to Richard le-Bon Duke of Normandy, the uncle of William. Lanfranc pleaded his master's cause learnedly and conscientiously. The Pope annulled the prohibition, and granted the dispensation by which the marriage was legitimated. The Pontiff imposed, as a penance, that husband and wife should each erect a monastery as a token of repentance. They gladly complied; and the two great foundations were determined upon, which still constitute the noblest monuments at Caen. At the one extremity of the city, hard by the castle, arose, and arises, Matilda's monastery of the Holy Trinity; and at the other, William's monastery of Saint Etienne. Of this monastery Lanfranc became the first Abbot, whilst Cecilia, Matilda's daughter, ruled as the first Abbess of the twin foundation. Lanfranc continued to pursue, with unabated zeal, the studies whereby he was raised to eminence, and which now gave him the enduring gratification of conscious utility;—training up others to pursue his steps in the good path he had opened. And when, upon the death of Maurilius, Archbishop of Rouen, that opulent See was offered to him, he demurred to quit the place where his lot had been cast.

*   *   *   *

§ 11. Had William, at this juncture of his life, been required to declare his feelings, he would have spoken nearly in the words of the great poet:

> "Nel mezzo del cammin di nostra vita
> Mi ritrovai per una selva oscura,
> Che la dritta via era smarrita.
> Hai! quanto a dir qual era è cosa dura."

He had toiled and troubled, sinned and sorrowed, but he had obtained but few of the objects he had coveted. His life had been engrossed by unwearied toil, exertion, and anxiety. He had conquered in many battles, he had widened his borders, the Trouveurs chanted his deeds, his fame was widely spread, the courtly monk had eloquently descanted upon his glories, and now fortune seemed to turn. Maine still grudged his supremacy. The countenance of France was stern; and though Henry had not attempted to regain the Vexin, still he was restrained from hostility only by the influence of Baudouin de Lisle; and the extorted homage of Ponthieu was more than counterbalanced in the scale of political influence, by the loss of the important acquisition which Robert le-Magnifique had made. The land of the Oriflamme had escaped the Norman grasp. Gautier, who had succeeded the friendly Drogo, entirely repudiated Normandy's suzerainty; and not contented with liberating himself from that dependence, he endeavoured to regain the Norman Vexin, and reunite it to his own territory. In this attempt Gautier had failed. But he delighted in the sport of war, and having espoused Biota, the daughter of Herbert Wake-the-Dog, had plausible pretensions to the county of Maine. Over and above being pestered by his enemies, much internal discomfort prevailed in Normandy. Want of occupation in the junior branches of the great families was a growing evil: Normandy continued to swarm with young nobles seeking service, competing, intriguing, fighting like people in a crowd, each provoked by the pressure he sustained from his neighbour, and which he returned with equal push and cram. Employment scarce amongst the more ambitious classes of society. Hostile parties and factions swarmed, and William, with less prudence than usual, had been won over by the wily, restless, Talvas; and Roger de Montgomery gaining his confidence, had excited him against all whom they delated as his enemies.

§ 12. Yielding to the machinations of this unscrupulous pair, William was induced to expel from his dominions fierce Ralph de Toeny, Hugh de Grantesmenil, and Arnould [d'Echaufour], the son of Guillaume [and nephew of Robert] de Giroi. He seems to have acted simply upon his own prerogative,—no hearing, no trial. This despotic proceeding provoked great discontent. A revolt ensued. Giroi's barony bordered on the Anjevine frontier, and, therefore, he had the means of becoming a dangerous neighbour. Fortifying his Castles of Saint Ceneri and La Roche Guyon against the Duke, [Robert had lately] prepared to give him much trouble. But from this anxiety William was speedily delivered. Whilst sitting by the wide chimney pleasantly talking with his wife, Robert de Giroi playfully snatched an apple from the hand of [Adelaide.] He ate the fruit, sickened, and died; and the symptoms disclosed the ministration of poison. Arnould, his heir, sought peace. William received him graciously, and obtained a favourable answer, much to the vexation of Mabel [daughter to William Talvas, and wife of Roger Montgomery], who plotted to rid herself of the young man by the same atrocious means. But he either apprehended the treachery, or had received

1060—1066 — due warning, and, therefore, escaped for this time. Mabel continued to dog him, with equal diligence and malevolence, under the roof or under the sky, till, his chamberlain conniving with her, she succeeded. Arnould, and two other knights whom the wicked woman sought to involve in the same fate, partook of the deadly beverage. The lives of these two knights were saved by timely antidotes, but Arnould fell a victim. When the Normans were under Italy's dazzling sky, they had become familiarized with this foul crime, and they bore the wickedness with them to their own land.

Death of Geoffrey. Maine plagued by Anjou.

§ 13. But Geoffrey Martel, worn out prematurely by the toils of government, sought retirement and peace in the convent of Saint Nicholas, at Angers, where he died childless. His next heirs had to be found amongst the progeny of Hermengarda,—Hermengarda, daughter of Fulke Nerra, Count of the Gatinois, and who represented the sturdy stock of Tortulf the Woodman. The worst features which tarnished or characterized the brilliancy of the Plantagenet, were developing themselves, to the fullest extent, in the person of Fulke, so well known by his epithet of *Le Rechin*, or the Shark. But Fulke's talents had been diligently cultivated, and some of the best characteristics of his gifted race were exhibited in him. He ought to hold a conspicuous station in the rank of noble and royal authors. To him we owe a spirited and valuable history of his ancestors; but neither

in this case, nor in any other, do we find that 1060—1066
literature, mere literature, ever softened or improved
the heart. The Rechin quarrelled with
his brother Geoffrey; the quarrel inflamed into
a wicked and desperate feud, and as the traveller
came in view of Chinon's noble castle, Anjou's
Windsor, he might hear how Geoffrey pined to
death in a miserable cell.

The Anjevine oppression in Maine became
intolerable; Herbert, [grandson to] our old friend
Wake-the-dog, most gladly sought any protector
he could find. Masters for masters, the Manceaux,
if driven to a choice, would have preferred the
Anjevines. But Herbert needed allies, and, to
obtain this advantage, he, so far as he lawfully
could, terminated the vexed question of suzerainty.
He fled to William, and surrendering his [See before, p. 243.]
County of Maine by the delivery of the rod or
staff, he accepted it again from William's hands,
as the symbol of investiture. Very remarkable
has been the longevity possessed by portions
of our old English common law; until our
own age this ceremony is observed upon every
transfer of copyhold or customary tenure in the
realm.

The Herbert with whom we are now dealing,
the grandson of Wake-the-dog, had but one
child, the little Margaret, who, according to
the usual fate of princesses, was destined to
be matched for political purposes. A marriage
might bring on a union between the lineages of
Rollo and of Tortulfus. The boy Robert and

the damsel were betrothed, and she was placed under the guardianship of her father-in-law, to be educated in his court. And Herbert, who, thanks to William, had recovered a competent portion of his dominions, died shortly afterwards, earnestly exhorting the Manceaux to accept the Northman as their sovereign. Herbert had acquired much popularity amongst the Manceaux, but any acknowledgment of Margaret's right might have given them a hated ruler. Consequently a revulsion of opinion ensued, and Geoffrey of Mayenne, and Hubert de Saint Sauveur, supported the claims asserted by Walter, Count of the Vexin. William invaded the country. Maine consisted of an Acropolis; the city, properly so called, was situated on the heights, and surrounded by very strong Roman walls. Wherever Rome trod, her footsteps became permanent in the soil. Some pacification or compromise ensued. Walter and his spouse, [Biota,] accepted an invitation to Falaise: they entered the gates cheerfully, but they never came out alive; the way opened for the conquerors by their death. But the sudden and appalling event excited suspicions, which always cast a shade upon William's name and fame. Indeed, so prominent were these misdeeds, that William is said to have had possession of the "transparent secret" of what has been called in modern times "the powder of succession."

William entered Maine triumphantly, pursuing his plans for bridling his subjects or his enemies, words then often synonymous. He erected two fortresses within the city. The cathedral was itself a stronghold, a massy and imposing monument, apparently dating from the Carlovingian age.

Now there was residing at Mantes, the widow of an English engineer, she herself well skilled in military mechanics, and she was employed by William in planning the needful defences. Most important amongst these was an outwork or tower, called La Ribaudelle, a name which, if we construe it correctly, was not peculiarly complimentary to the lady. The obedience of the Manceaux thus being enforced, they took the oath of fealty. The Mayenne party supported the claims of Herbert Wake-the-Dog's daughters, Gersenda and Paula. The damsels thus came into William's power. Margaret, [Herbert's child,] was tenderly and carefully educated, honoured as Countess of Maine, and was betrothed to young Robert, who received from his father the dignity of Count of Maine, in right of his nominal consort; but before the marriage was really solemnized she died and was buried at Fécamp.

* * * *

[The three fragments preceding are printed as left by the Author. They were intended to be worked up into the fifth chapter; but as, in their existing form, they do not present a consecutive history of the period following the peace of Fécamp, the Editor has thought it best to add here a short summary of events from that date:—mostly printed from a Chronological Abstract found amongst the Author's MSS. A few facts noticed before will be here repeated, and it is possible that some inaccuracies or incompleteness may exist in the summary, which was intended only as a guide to the Author: but it appears best that the story should be continued in his own words.]

§ 14. Five years follow the peace of Fécamp, an interval of comparative peace in Normandy, although the scanty records of the time display a state of lawless depravity.

Robert Giroi, encouraged by the hostile feeling of Anjou, fortifies his castles and makes war on William. The Duke is delivered from his enemy by a crime which occurs with terrible frequency in the Norman annals. Robert receives poisoned fruit from his wife Adelaide, William's relation. Arnould d'Echaufour, Robert's nephew, succeeds him.

The arm of Geoffrey Martel is unnerved; he dies; but his nephew, Geoffrey à-la-belle-barbe, rivals his kinsman. Was this amplitude of beard a rare feature, or a rare fashion amongst these populations? The razor and the barber's bason are not without importance in man's history. Our judges receive a character from their wigs, and the heroic Wolfe, in our conception of him, owes something to his *solitaire* and his pig-tail.

William takes possession of Neuf-Marché-en-Lyons, a name indicating that the Bourgade was a recent foundation in the essarts. Disputes arise between William and his baronage. He holds his court at Lillebonne, and perhaps he already begins to plan how he can best employ those turbulent servants who are attempting to become his masters. May not this meeting be confounded with the meeting at the same place on the eve of the Conquest? Here it is expressly said that he was reconciled with *some* of his Barons.

§ 15. [William, encouraged by Roger Montgomery and his wife Mabel, the wicked daughter of the wicked William Talvas], sought to increase his own power by disinheriting his Baronage. Of course this must mean, that he sought to resume the grants which he or his ancestors had made, resuming the loans which, according to the old German phraseology, he had made. Ralph de Toeny is noted emphatically as being one of the sufferers, together with Hugh de Grantesmenil; and Arnould Echaufour is also named amongst them, by an act which may have been legal, but certainly was ungracious. Arnould was not a man to settle on the lees, but invades the Lieuvin. It should seem that the

1060—1066 Castle of Echaufour had been resumed by William, and now it was no longer in Arnould's possession; but he went to work resolutely, and burnt the Abbey of Saint Evroul. William, defying the principle of election, imposes Osberne on the unlucky monastery; probably this is the reason why the Abbot departs to Rome.

See p. 268.
[The rest of Arnould's story—his flight, return to Normandy, and death by poison—has been already given.]

1062
Council of Caen.
§ 16. A great council or convention of the Estates of Normandy—Bishops, Abbots, Peers and Proceres—held at Caen, and a memorable law is enacted by the Sovereign. The curfew bell, so constantly represented as a badge of slavery, imposed upon conquered England, was neither more nor less than a salutary police regulation. It was rung in the city of London within my recollection.

[It was not only towards his men-at-arms that William showed his severity. Ecclesiastics were not exempt from the same high hand.] About this period some ecclesiastical changes were taking or had taken place, which, as usual, had much influence upon civil policy. According to the homely proverb, "the nearer the bone the sweeter the flesh," a dictum not always verified when applied with respect to consanguinity;

Mauger.
Mauger, [Archbishop of Rouen,] was not very closely connected with William, though an important member of the ducal family—the son

of Richard le-Bon, by his third wife, Papia. Amongst William's enemies none more pertinacious and teasing than Archbishop Mauger. Courtier, soldier, warrior, prelate, the mitre decked his head, and his mailed hand clutched the crosier: but he was so wild and ill-conditioned that we can scarcely think of him in his clerical character. If you looked at the episcopal officiant when he turned towards the altar, you would see that he lacked the Pallium, the snow-white Pallium, woven by virgin hands, and which heraldically figures in the bearings assigned to our primatial sees; for his incompetence, or worse impediments, were so notorious that the supreme pontiff refused to confirm him by its delivery. But this made no practical difference, for having been placed in his see by the Duke's prerogative, that prerogative kept him there, notwithstanding the breach of all ecclesiastical discipline. In an age distinguished by ecclesiastical corruption, Mauger was conspicuous for his depravity. He wasted and dilapidated the endowments of the See, and in him were combined the vices of the priest and soldier. His influence was enhanced rather than damaged by the popular belief that he commanded the aid of a household demon. The familiar answered to the name of Thoreit. The German scholar will be amused by this appellation: the French antiquaries, who luxuriate in detecting, not without the aid of a vivid imagination, vestiges of the

Scandinavian faith, discover in the name Thoreit, the exclamation Thor-aie, an invocation of Thor the Hammerer; but the vocable is pure *hoch deutsch*, and, however gained or bestowed, simply signifies Folly. Mauger supported his brother, the Count of Arques, with all his influence. [By the failure of that rebellion,] Mauger's power to excite trouble was diminished, but he might yet be dangerous. William, careful not to offend the Church, watched his opportunity. Force could not decently be employed. At a convenient season of tranquillity a synod was held at Rouen, and Mauger was deprived of his See. The gross licentiousness in which he had indulged was now found to afford a sufficient reason. Mauger was banished to Jersey, or perhaps fled there. Freed from every restraint, whether of authority or example, here he lived wildly and riotously, every now and then sailing over to the mainland in a fishing-boat, and shewing himself at Coutances;—visits which could not be other than annoying to Duke William. In one of these undignified trips the boat turned over and the Archbishop was drowned: fortunately for Duke William; for everything that tended to break down the old ducal family—a kinsman, a foeman—was good luck to the Bastard. Fortune continued to favour him; but no ease of mind did William enjoy on this side the grave; the up-heaved stone was ever rolling down again.

Mauger deposed, Maurillus succeeded him. Born of noble parents, at Roman Rheims, and soundly indoctrinated, first at Rheims and subsequently at Halverstadt, he was as remarkable for his good qualities as his predecessor had been for his vices and rebellion.

[William now expels Robert of Grandmenil from the Abbey of Ouches, on suspicion of rebellious language. The Abbot flies to Rome, obtains the support of Pope Nicholas II., and returns to Normandy with letters from him and two Cardinals. When William learns this, he exclaims, with fury, that he will hang any one of his monks who utters a word against him. Robert, hearing of this, returns to Italy and takes shelter with Guiscard.

§ 17. Now follows the conquest of Maine by William, already told.] War breaks out between Geoffrey, son of Eudes, and his cousin Conan. The Basilica of Rouen is completed, and Maurillus consecrates the splendid structure. William and his Barons, [during the war against Maine,] are reconciled, in order to have his hands clear. Perhaps the Palace of Westminster is looming in the distance, through the seamists. A stranger from England visits Normandy. It is Harold. Harold's oath: and bound by this oath, famous or infamous, he accompanies his new liege-lord in his expedition against Conan of Brittany, who, when William was preparing to pass into England and vindicate his rights by the sword, interposed and attempted to deter him. The shame of his illegitimacy was not sufficient. Conan denied that William was entitled to assert even this title; he was not even a Bastard. "And when Robert was about to depart for Jerusalem, he conveyed all his inheritance to Alan, my father and his cousin, but you and your accomplices invaded his land, I being too young to defend my rights, and against all justice. What right could or can you, as a bastard, claim? Return to me that Normandy which thou owest. Delay will ensure thee condign vengeance."

Brittany teemed with a wild and martial population; but Conan, though ruling ably and strenuously, had not yet been able to bring his troops into the field; whilst the border forces which William raised, and was raising, contributed to repel the Breton invasion.

Amongst the Bretons there was one who was an ambidexter, owing fealty to both Counts and not faithful to either, bearing messages between them. Conan was his master, and he acted as his valet. Conan, at this period, was quarrelling with Anjou, and was besieging Chateau Gonthier in Anjou, of which a detachment of knights constituted the garrison. In these wretched times, to repose confidence was to suggest treachery; and the recreants surrendered the fortress, or, if you choose, sold their services to William. Conan's valet poisoned the inside of his master's horn, and whilst the young and ardent prince was preparing for triumph, he suddenly sickened and died. The Bretons raged: William was vituperated as a robber and a murderer; no son of the late Magnifico, he,—not so much as a bastard—a changeling! and no one doubted the popular report that Conan had been poisoned by William's agency,—rumour accumulating crime upon injustice.

§ 18. [The thread which links the history of Normandy and England must now be again taken up. The last event noted, was the abortive attempt of Duke Robert against Canute. After Canute's death, and during the contested succession which closed in the assumption of sovereignty by Harold Harefoot, Edward and Alfred, the children of Ethelred and Emma, by the assistance of their friends, fitted out a fleet and sailed to England. Edward approached the port of Southampton,] where he found the inhabitants in arms, not to aid him in his enterprise, but prepared for the most strenuous resistance. Either they were really hostile to the son of the unpopular Ethelred, or they feared to draw down upon themselves the vengeance of the brutal Harold. Edward, therefore, had no choice; and abandoning the inhospitable shore, he returned to his place of refuge in Normandy.

Soon afterwards, an affectionate letter was addressed, in the name of Emma, to Alfred and

1036—1066 Edward, urging one of them, at least, to return to England for the purpose of recovering the kingdom from the tyrant. Alfred obeyed the summons; and with a few trusty followers, whom he retained in Flanders, he proceeded to England, where he was favourably received by Earl Godwin, at London, and thence conducted to Guildford. The plot was now revealed. Alfred was seized by the accomplices and satellites of the tyrant, blinded, and conducted as a captive to Ely, where death soon closed his sufferings. Godwin was very generally accused of the murder. The epistle had perhaps been forged by the direction of Harold. Rumour is always busy in these foul transactions; and Emma herself does not escape vehement suspicion; but nothing is known for certain, except the fate of the miserable victim and of his companions, who suffered an agonizing death.

Death of Alfred.

Death of Harefoot.

Harold expired after a short and inglorious reign. Upon his death, the Proceres or nobles, Danes as well as English, invited Hardicanute, [son to Canute, by Emma, after Ethelred's death,] to return to Britain, and receive the sceptre of the kingdom, [which he held for two years.]

1042 § 19. Edward the Atheling, the only surviving son of Ethelred, had been invited to England by Hardicanute, from whom he received great kindness. Hardicanute had no children, and the easy and quiet disposition of his half-brother averted all suspicion or anxiety.

[With some difficulty he was persuaded by Godwin to claim the throne.] Within a few days after the body of Hardicanute had been consigned to the earth, the prelates and great men of the Anglo-Saxon realms assembled at London, and accepted Edward as their king. William, Duke of Normandy, aided Edward by his influence; and it was intimated to the English, that if they refused to recognize the son of Emma, they would experience the weight of the Norman power. Yet the act of recognition was mainly owing to the exertions of the Earl of Wessex, and to the consequence which he possessed in the assembly. As soon as Edward was settled upon the throne, he invited over from Normandy many of those who had been his friends during his exile.

[This divided the English chieftains. The prepotent Godwin family took the lead against the Norman courtiers; Leofric of Coventry and Siward of Northumbria supported them.]

It is certain that the Norman party began to conduct themselves in such a manner as to occasion much disgust amongst the nation at large. Edward, during his residence in Normandy, had become partial to the customs of that country, and introduced many such usages into England. The Norman hand-writing was thought handsomer, by Edward, than the Anglo-Saxon; and he established the mode of testifying his assent to official documents by adding an impression of his great

1060—1066 seal, which was appended to the parchment, in addition to the mark of the cross, according to the Anglo-Saxon custom which I have before noticed.

Norman customs introduced. Hitherto the Anglo-Saxon kings never used a seal for the purpose of authenticating their charters. But the custom had been long established in France. And from the Frankish Monarchs Edward borrowed the practice, though the seal itself, exhibiting his effigy, surrounded by the legend '*Sigillum Eaduuardi Anglorum Basilei*,' seems rather to have been copied from the patterns afforded by the Greek Emperors.

Growth of the Chancery. It may appear that this innovation was no great grievance; but, upon examining the matter, it will be found connected with more important consequences. The adoption of these forms gave the king an additional reason for retaining about his person the 'Clerks,' whom he had brought from France, and by whom all his writing business was performed. They were his domestic chaplains, and the keepers of his conscience; and, in addition to these influential functions, they were his law advisers and also his Secretaries of State; and as such they seem to have formed a bench in the Witenagemot. The chief of these was his Arch-Chaplain or Chancellor; and through them, judging from the practice both of the French and English courts, it was the custom to prefer all petitions and requests to the king. One suitor was desirous of obtaining a grant of land—another, mayhap, required a 'writ' to enable him to recover amends for an injury; since no person could sue in the King's Court without a special permission—a third wished to ask for leave to quarter himself and his hounds and his horses on one of the king's manors—and, in such cases, we cannot doubt but that Robert, the Norman Monk of Jumièges, or Giso the Fleming, or Ernaldus the Frenchman, would have many means of serving their own party and disappointing their adversaries;—and many an honest Englishman was turned away, with a hard word and a heavy heart, by these Norman courtiers. The Chaplains or Clerks of the Chancery, were particularly obnoxious: many of them obtained the best pieces of preferment in the king's gift. The Bishoprics were filled by Prelates who might be good stout soldiers or clever lawyers, but who were therefore eminently disqualified for the stations in the church, which they had obtained merely by favour or importunity.

The Normans had, by this time, adopted the use of the French language, or, as it was then called, 'Romance.' Edward had acquired a partiality for this dialect, which had become familiar to him during his stay in Normandy, and by his example it was becoming fashionable amongst the higher classes, at least amongst the favourites of Edward; and we cannot doubt but that this circumstance tended to raise up a further cause of discontent. A nation which loses its own speech, is half conquered.

§ 20. [Meanwhile, as we have seen,] William had fully established himself in the Duchy, after encountering many difficulties. He now arrived from beyond the sea with a large and splendid train of Frenchmen, on a visit to his good cousin, Edward, King of England: cousins they certainly were; for Edward's mother, Emma, was own sister to Robert, the father of William; and even if the kindred had been more remote, it would still have afforded a ground for attention and civility. Prosperity acts like a telescope, and often enables folks to bring distant relations much nearer than they would be without its aid. And we shall not be guilty of any great breach of charity if we suppose that William, young, ambitious, and enterprising, did not undertake this journey purely out of natural love and affection towards his old aunt and kinsman. Did he begin to form any plans for the invasion of England? Did he contemplate the possibility of wearing his kinsman's crown? In our modern days it is not at all an unfrequent thing for a man to sit down and write his own memoirs; in which, with great ingenuity and accuracy, he tells you everything concerning his actions and intentions, or at least everything which he wishes you to believe. In the eleventh century, however, these *asides* were not so common. William the Conqueror neither wrote his autobiography, nor hinted to

any good and serviceable friend that he had no 1000—1066
objection to have his opinions reported for the
amusement and instruction of the world;—and
his "correspondence" is not extant,—therefore
I cannot exactly tell you what he *thought*.
However, I *can* tell you what he *saw*, and then
you may judge for yourself as to the sentiments
which possibly floated in the mind of the Norman
warrior.

King Edward was surrounded by Frenchmen State of England before the Conquest.
and foreigners, who filled his court, and were
spread over England. Of the few castles and
strongholds which were in the realm, some,
the most important, those towards the Welsh
marches, were garrisoned by French and Norman
soldiers, under the command of leaders of their
own nation. In the great towns and cities, no
inconsiderable number of Frenchmen were to be
found, who, having settled there, enjoyed what
we should now call the freedom of the corpora-
tion, living in houses of their own, and paying
scot and lot, or taxes, like the English burgesses. The country itself invited the attacks
of an enemy; the great towns, with few exceptions, were either quite open, or fortified only
by stoccades and banks, or, perhaps by a
ruinous Roman wall; and the Englishmen themselves, though very brave, were much inferior
to the continental nations in the art of war.
As soldiers, they laboured under a still greater
deficiency than any which can result from the

1060—1066 want of weapons or of armour. Stout, well-fed, and hale, the Anglo-Saxon, when sober, was fully a match for any adversary who might be brought from the banks of the Seine or the Loire. But the old English were shamefully addicted to debauchery, and the wine-cup unnerves the stoutest arm. The monkish chroniclers, as you will recollect, tell us that we learnt this vice from the Danes—a sorry excuse; and it is little to the credit of Englishmen, that drunkenness still continues to stain our national character.

Omens of the Conquest.   The empire was distracted by factions. The members of a very powerful family, whose conduct had excited the suspicions of the sovereign, had been deprived of their possessions, but certainly not according to equity, so that they and their adherents had a double cause of hostility—disaffection,—and the sense of the injury which they had sustained.

Edward was advancing in years, childless, and without hope of children. Upon his death, the royal line of Cerdic would be represented solely by Edward the "Outlaw," the only surviving son of Edmund Ironside, then a fugitive in a distant realm, far away in Hungary. Hardly did it seem probable that this Prince, so estranged from England, could possibly assert his right to the succession; and, therefore, as soon as Edward should be stretched on the bier, the vacant throne might be ascended by any one, who, whether by force or favour, could obtain the concurrence of any powerful partisans, or the sanction of the legislature. *1060—1066*

Such then was the state of affairs, when William, Duke of Normandy, afterwards the Conqueror, repaired to England. We have no positive evidence concerning what was said or done; and I am not prepared to relate the conversations between King Edward and his cousin, as if I had listened behind the tapestry. But the matters narrated by chroniclers I can repeat, and from their testimony we do know, that William was honourably received. He conducted himself with so much address as to acquire the confidence and good-will of Edward, who, by the expulsion of Godwin and his family, had obtained a temporary respite from uneasiness and disquietude.

This calm did not last long—[Godwin and Harold appeared in arms, and to avoid a battle, the quarrel was laid before the Witenagemot.] *1052*

The Great Council not only agreed that Godwin and his sons were innocent, but decreed the restoration of their earldoms; and such was the influence of the Earl of Wessex, that the Witan adopted all the views of his party. All the French were declared outlaws, because it was said that they had given bad advice to the king, and brought unrighteous judgments into the land; a very few only, whose ignoble names have been preserved — Robert, the Deacon, *Triumph of the Godwins.*

1060—1066 Richard, the son of Scrub, Humphrey Cock's-foot, and the Groom of the stirrup, — were excepted from this proscription: obscure, mean men, whom Godwin could not fear. Robert, the monk of Jumièges, who had been promoted to the Archbishopric of Canterbury, was just able to escape with his life, so highly were the people incensed against him. He and Ulf, Bishop of Dorchester, after scouring the country, broke out through the East-gate of Canterbury, and killing and wounding those who attempted to stop them, they betook themselves to the coast, and got out to sea. Other of the Frenchmen retired to the Castles of their countrymen. And the restoration of the Queen to her former rank, completed the triumph of the Godwin family.

Edward tries to settle the Crown in the Saxon family

§ 21. Old age was now rapidly advancing upon Edward. He was childless. He saw the increasing power of Harold, and that the kingdom which he had been called to govern would be exposed to the greatest confusion. He recalled "Edward the Outlaw," [sole surviving descendant to Edmund Ironside,] from Hungary, with the intention of proclaiming him as heir to the crown.

1057 Edmund Ironside had been much beloved, and greatly did England rejoice when Edward, no longer the Outlaw, but the Atheling, arrived here, accompanied by his wife Agatha, the emperor's kinswoman, and his three fair children, —Edgar, Christina, and Margaret. But the people's gladness was speedily turned to sorrow. Very shortly after the Atheling arrived in London, he sickened and died. He was buried in St. Paul's Cathedral; and sad and ruthful were the forebodings of the English, when they saw him borne to his grave.—Harold gained exceedingly by this event. Did the Atheling die a natural death?—the lamentations of the chroniclers seem to imply more than meets the ear.

1060—1066. Death of Edward the Outlaw.

Edward's design having thus been frustrated, he determined that William of Normandy should succeed him on the throne of England, and he executed, or, perhaps, re-executed a will to that effect, bequeathing the crown to his good cousin. This choice, disastrous as it afterwards appeared to be from its consequences, was not devoid of foresight and prudence. Edward, without doubt, viewed the nomination of the Norman as the surest mode of averting from his subjects the evils of foreign servitude or domestic war. The Danish Kings, the pirates of the north, were yearning to regain the realm, which their great Canute had ruled. At the very outset of Edward's reign, Magnus, the successor of Hardicanute, had claimed the English crown. A competitor at home had diverted Magnus from this enterprise; but it might at any time be resumed. And how much better would the wise and valiant William be able to resist the Danish invasions, than the infant Edgar? Harold was brave and experienced in war, but

1058—1066. The Confessor reverts to William.

his elevation to the throne might be productive of the greatest evil. The grandsons of Leofric, who ruled half England, would scarcely submit to the dominion of an equal; the obstacle arising from Harold's ancestry was, indeed, insuperable. No individual, who was not of an antient royal house, had ever been able to maintain himself upon an Anglo-Saxon throne.

William's claims.

William himself asserted that Edward had acted with the advice and consent of the great Earls, Siward, Leofric, and Godwin himself; consequently the bequest was made *before* the arrival of Edward the Outlaw. The son and nephew of Godwin, who were then in Normandy, had also been sent to him, as he maintained, in the characters of pledges or hostages, that the will should be carried into effect; or, as is most probable, that no opposition should be raised by the powerful earl. The three earls thus vouched were not living when William made this assertion; but if we do not distrust his veracity and honour, we may suppose that Edward, in the first instance, appointed William as his heir. As the king grew older, his affection for his own kindred awakened, and he recalled the Atheling; revoking his devise to the stranger; to which, however, he seems to have returned again, when his kinsman died.

The messenger by whom the intelligence of the bequest, thus made by Edward, reached William, was no other than Harold. There is much contradiction as to the immediate cause of Harold's journey; nor are we less in doubt concerning the minor incidents. [He is said to have been tempest-thrown on Ponthieu, seized in pursuance of local custom by the Count Guido, and liberated from him at William's order. The dramatic circumstances of Harold's oath on concealed relics, are totally unknown to the earlier and only trustworthy annalists.] Whether accident or design conducted him to the court of the Duke of Normandy, is uncertain; and the preceding account of the *two* wills in favour of William, is an hypothesis collected only from the general bearing of the narrations. William, well aware of Harold's influence, used every endeavour to ensure his future aid; and, in return, William agreed to bestow upon Harold the hand of his daughter, the fair Adela. The English earl promised that he would give up to the Norman duke the castle of Dover, a fortress belonging to him as part of the inheritance of Godwin, and considered as the key of England. He confirmed the engagement by oath, and became the "man," or vassal, of William, whom he acknowledged as his future sovereign.

§ 22. In the meanwhile Harold was rising in repute. He invaded Wales, and desolated the country. Griffith opposed him valiantly, but he was slain by the treachery of his own countrymen. His gory head was sent to the Confessor as a trophy of victory; his dominions were bestowed upon his brothers Blethyn and Rhiwallon, who were accessary to the murder. And these princes became the vassals, not only of King Edward, but of Earl Harold, to whom they performed fealty and homage. As Earl of Wessex, Harold could have no claim to this obedience, and if enforced by him, the act can only be construed as an attempt to establish a sovereign power.

Edward was now rapidly declining in health; he had rebuilt the ancient Abbey of Westminster, founded, as you will recollect, by Sebert, but which had been ruined during the Danish wars. And, holding his court, according to the antient custom, at Christmas, he caused the new fabric to be consecrated, in the presence of the nobles assembled during that solemn festival.

Edward felt that the hand of death was upon him. A little while before he expired, Harold and his kinsmen forced their way into the chamber of the Monarch, and exhorted him to name a successor, by whom the realm might be ruled in peace and security.—"Ye know full well, my lords," said Edward, "that I have bequeathed my kingdom to the Duke of Normandy, and are there not those *here* whose oaths have been given to secure his succession?"— Harold stepped nearer, and interrupting the King, he asked of Edward, upon whom the crown should be bestowed.—"Harold! take it, if such be thy wish; but the gift will be thy ruin. Against the duke and his baronage, no power of thine can avail thee." Harold replied that he did not fear the Norman, or any other enemy. The dying king, wearied with importunity, turned himself upon his couch, and faintly intimated that the English nation might name as king, Harold, or whom they liked; and shortly afterwards he breathed his last.

1060—1066

Harold afterwards founded his title upon Edward's *last* will; many of our historians favour his claim, and the different statements are difficult to be reconciled; yet taken altogether, the circumstances are exactly such as we meet with in private life. The childless owner of a large estate, at first leaves his property to his Cousin on the mother's side, from whose connexions he has received much kindness. He advances in age, and alters his intentions in favour of a Nephew on his father's side—an amiable young man, living abroad,— and from whom he had been estranged in consequence of a family quarrel of long standing. The young Heir comes to the Testator's house —is received with great affection—and is suddenly cut off by illness. The Testator then returns to his will in favour of his Cousin, who resides abroad. His acute and active brother-in-law has taken the management of his affairs, is well informed of this will; and, when the Testator is on his death-bed, he contrives to tease and persuade the dying man to alter the

Harold's claim to succeed.

1060—1066 will again in his favour. This is exactly the state of the case; and though considerable doubts have been raised relating to the contradictory bequests of the Confessor, there can be no difficulty in admitting that the conflicting pretensions of William and Harold were grounded upon the acts emanating from a wavering and feeble mind. If such disputes take place between private individuals, they are decided by a court of justice; but if they concern a kingdom, they can only be settled by the sword.

Chapter VI.

THE INVASION.

1066.

§ 1. Upon the death of Edward the Confessor, there were three claimants to the crown —his good Cousin, William of Normandy—and his good Brother-in-law, Harold—each of whom respectively founded their pretensions upon the real or supposed devise of the late king—and Edgar Atheling, the son of Edward the Outlaw, who ought to have stood on firmer ground. If kindred had any weight, he was the real heir— the lineal descendant of Ironside—and the only male now left of the house of Cerdic; and he also is said to have been nominated by Edward, as the successor to the throne.

Each of these competitors had his partisans: but, whilst William was absent, and Edward young and poor, perhaps timid and hesitating, Harold was on the spot; a man of mature age, in full vigour of body and mind; possessing great influence and great wealth. And on the very day that Edward was laid in his grave, Harold prevailed upon, or compelled the prelates and nobles assembled at Westminster, to accept him as king. Some of our historians

Margin notes: 1066. Competitors for the English crown. Edgar. Harold.

say, that he obtained the diadem by force. This is not to be understood as implying actual violence; but simply, that the greater part of those who recognised him, acted against their wishes and will. And if our authorities are correct, Stigand, Archbishop of Canterbury, but who had been suspended by the Pope, was the only prelate who acknowledged his authority.

Harold not universally accepted.

Some portions of the Anglo-Saxon dominions never seem to have submitted to Harold. In others, a sullen obedience was extorted from the people, merely because they had not power enough to raise any other king to the throne. Certainly the realm was not Harold's by any legal title. The son of Godwin could have no inherent right whatever to the inheritance of Edward; nor had the Anglo-Saxon crown ever been worn by an elective monarch. The constitutional rights of the nation extended, at farthest, to the selection of a king from the royal family; and if any kind of sanction was given by the Witan to the intrusion of Harold, the act was as invalid as that by which they had renounced the children of Ethelred, and acknowledged the Danish line.

His government.

§ 2. Harold is stated to have shewn both prudence and courage in the government of the kingdom; and he has been praised for his just and due administration of justice. At the same time he is, by other writers, reprobated as a tyrant; and he is particularly blamed for his oppressive enforcement of the forest-laws. Towards his own partisans, Harold may have been ostentatiously just, while the ordinary exercise of the royal prerogative would appear tyrannical to those who deemed him to be an usurper.

<small>1066</small>

Harold, as the last Anglo-Saxon ruler, has often been viewed with peculiar partiality; but it is perhaps difficult to justify these feelings. He had no clear title to the crown in any way whatever. Harold was certainly not the heir; Edward's bequest in his favour was very dubious; and he failed to obtain that degree of universal consent to his accession, which, upon the ordinary principles of political expediency, can alone legalize a change of dynasty. The Anglo-Saxon power had been fast verging to decay. As against their common sovereign, the earls were rising into petty kings. North of the Humber, scarcely a shadow of regular government existed; and even if the Norman had never trod the soil of England, it would have been scarcely possible for the son of Godwin to have maintained himself in possession of the supreme authority. Any of the great nobles who divided the territory of the realm might have preferred as good a claim, and they probably would have been easily incited to risk such an attempt. Hitherto, the crown had been preserved from domestic invasion by the belief that royalty belonged exclusively to the children of Woden.—Fluctuating as the rules of succes-

<small>Distracted state of England.</small>

Flaw in Harold's title

sion had been, the political faith in the "right royal kindred" excluded all competition, except as amongst the members of a particular caste or family; but the charm was now broken— the mist which had hitherto enveloped the sovereign magistracy was dispelled—and the way to the throne was opened to any competitor.

William learns the news.

§ 3. William was hunting in the Park of Rouen, surrounded by a noble train of knights, esquires, and damsels, when a "Serjeant," just arrived from England, hastened into his presence, and related the events which had happened:— Edward's death, and Harold's assumption of the crown.—The bow dropped out of the hand of the Norman, and he was unnerved by anxiety and surprise. William fastened and loosened his mantle, spake not, and looked so fierce and fell, that no one ventured to address him. Entering a skiff, he crossed the Seine, still silent; stalked into the great hall of his palace, threw himself into a seat, wrapped his head in his mantle, and bent his body downwards, apparently overwhelmed.—" Sirs "—said William de Breteuil the Seneschal, to the enquiring crowd—" ye will soon know the cause of our lord's anxiety;"— and then, approaching his master, he roused the Duke by telling him that everybody in the streets of Rouen would soon hear of the death of Edward, and of his claims to the succession.

Claims the crown.

William instantly recovered from his reverie; and upon the advice of a Norman baron, Fitz-

Osbern the Bold, it was determined that he should forthwith require Harold, the sworn liegeman of William, to surrender the inheritance, and to perform the engagements which he had contracted with the Norman Sovereign. *1066*

Harold answered, that the kingdom was not his to bestow: implying, no doubt, that he could not make the transfer without the consent of the Witenagemot. He also alleged distinctly, that he could not marry Adela without the advice of the nobility of his realm. If this assertion be taken in its strict sense, we must suppose that, as the queen had some, though a very undefined share in the royal authority, she could not be raised to that rank without the assent of the legislature. But perhaps we must receive the expressions according to a more qualified construction; and suppose that Harold merely meant to say, that it was not expedient for an English king to choose a wife in such a manner as might render him unpopular. But these excuses need not be weighed very accurately. Other parts of Harold's reply were scurrilous and insulting; and the whole is only to be considered as an intimation that the son of Godwin defied the power of William, the Bastard of Normandy. *Harold refuses.*

§ 4. Harold did not feel his own weakness, and he scarcely knew the resources of his adversary. Normandy, at this period, was in the height of its prosperity. Under the prudent government

1066 — of the late Dukes, Richard and Robert, there had arisen a race of wise, active, and loyal nobility. The heads of the great houses of Beaumont, Montgomery, Fitz-Osbern, Mortimer, and Giffard, were stout of heart and strong of hand: they could give the best counsel, and execute the counsel which they gave; and in the great parliament assembled at Lillebonne, the barons determined to assist their Sovereign in his contest with the English usurper, the perjured Harold.

Barons meet at Lillebonne.

Fitz-Osbern's zeal for the invasion.

In this memorable meeting, there was at first much diversity of opinion. The Duke could not command his vassals to cross the sea; their tenures did not compel them to such a service. William could only request their aid, to fight his battles in England: many refused to engage in this dangerous expedition, and great debates arose. Fitz-Osbern exhorted his peers to obey the wishes of their liege lord. After some discussion they allowed the intrepid Baron to be their spokesman; and in their name did he engage that each feudatory should render double the service to which he was bound by his tenure; and, moreover, he, Fitz-Osbern, promised to fit out, at his own expense, sixty vessels, all filled with chosen warriors.

Fitz-Osbern might make any promise on his own part, to which he was stimulated by his loyalty. But the other barons had not empowered him to assent on their behalf to bind them to similar exertions; and whilst he was speaking, such an outcry of disapprobation arose that it seemed as if the very roof of the Hall would be rent asunder. William, who could not restore order, withdrew into another apartment: and calling the barons to him one by one, he argued and reasoned with each of these sturdy vassals separately, and apart from the others. He exhausted all the arts of persuasion;—their present courtesy—he engaged—should not be turned into a precedent; the troops now granted as a favour should never be demanded as a right by himself or his successors; and the fertile fields of England should be the recompense of their fidelity.—Upon this prospect of remuneration, the barons assented; and, that they might not retract, the ready clerk wrote down in his roll the number of knights and vassals which each prelate and baron would furnish to this expedition.

William persuades the barons.

William did not confine himself to his own subjects. All the adventurers and adventurous spirits of the neighbouring States were invited to join his standard. Armorica, now called Brittany, had become a fief of Normandy; and though the Duke could not compel the baronage of that country to serve in his army, still they willingly yielded to his influence. Alan Fergant, and Bryan, the two sons of Eudo, Count of Brittany, came with a numerous train of Breton knights, all ready for the conflict—

Calls adventurers to join.

perhaps eager to avenge the wrongs of Arthur upon the Saxons, who had usurped the land of their ancestors. Others poured in from Poitou and Maine; from Flanders and Anjou; and to all, such promises were made as should best incite them to the enterprise—lands,—liveries,—money,—according to their rank and degree; and the port of St. Pierre-sur-Dive was appointed as the place where all the forces should assemble.

William's grounds for his invasion.

§ 5. William had discovered four most valid reasons for the prosecution of his offensive warfare against a neighbouring people:—the bequest made by his Cousin;—the perjury of Harold;—the expulsion of the Normans, at the instigation, as he alleged, of Godwin;—and, lastly, the massacre of the Danes by Ethelred on St. Brice's day.—The alleged perjury of Harold enabled William to obtain the sanction of the Papal See. Alexander, the Roman *Supported at Rome.* Pontiff, allowed, nay, even urged him to punish the crime, provided England, when conquered, should be held as the fief of St. Peter. In this proceeding, His Holiness took upon himself to act judicially, and in solemn consistory; not, however, without opposition,—but the measure was carried: and Hildebrand, Archdeacon of the Church of Rome, afterwards the celebrated Pope Gregory VII., greatly assisted by the support which he gave to the decree.

As a visible token of protection, the Pope

transmitted to William the consecrated banner, the Gonfanon of St. Peter, and a precious ring, in which a relic of the Chief of the Apostles was enclosed. Nothing could be more futile than the pretext that the war was undertaken for the purpose of redressing the wrongs sustained by Archbishop Robert and his companions, or of avenging the slaughter committed by Ethelred; and the sanction given by the Pope was in itself an attack upon the temporal authority. Yet the colour of right, which William endeavoured to obtain, shows a degree of deference to public opinion; he was anxious to prove that his attempt was not prompted by mere ambition or avarice; and that at all events, supposing Edward's bequest might be disputed, he was justified in his attempt by good conscience and honour.

§ 6. There was little regular communication between England and the Continent; but it was impossible that the extensive preparations of William should remain unknown to Harold; and he immediately began to provide for defence. He mustered his forces at Sandwich, and then he took his station at the Isle of Wight, during the whole of the summer and part of the autumn. Such a navy as he could assemble guarded the coast, while his land forces were encamped on the shore. During this period he transmitted a spy, to procure further particulars of the forces which the Normans had raised. The agent was

1066 — discovered, and carried to William, by whom he was received without either harshness or affectation of concealment, and dismissed without harm. The spy was informed by the Duke, that Harold need not take any trouble or incur any expense for the purpose of ascertaining the Norman strength; for he would see it, aye, and feel it too, within the year.

Number of William's ships.

§ 7. The computation of the navy assembled by William has varied exceedingly. Master Wace, to whose Poetical Chronicle we are so largely indebted, relates, that he often heard his father say, that the number of vessels amounted to six hundred and ninety-six; but that he found it stated in writing, that upwards of three thousand had been assembled. This latter computation, probably, included all the smaller barks; but, be that as it may, the fleet was the largest which had ever been seen. William's own vessel, which had been given to him by his wife Matilda, was distinguished above the rest; at night by the cresset which flamed on the topmast; and in the day, by its resplendent ornaments and decorations. The crimson sails swelled to the wind, the gilded vanes glittered in the sun,—and at the head of the ship was the effigy of a child, armed with a bow and arrow, and ready to discharge his shaft against hostile land.

Fleet sails.

The gathering of the fleet at the mouth of the Dive had been delayed by contrary gales, and

other mischances. The ships sailed to the 1066
Somme, but the winds were still unfavourable.
The relics of St. Valery were brought forth from
their shrine. On the eve of St. Michael, the Sep. 28.
patron of Normandy, a prosperous gale arose,
and the whole armament was wafted in safety
across the waves. Want of provisions, and other
circumstances, had compelled Harold to draw
off his forces from the coast, which was entirely
unprotected; and when the Norman armada
approached the shore of England, between
Hastings and Pevensey, not the slightest opposi- Sep. 29.
tion could be offered to the invaders. As the
vessels approached, and as the masts rose higher
and higher on the horizon, the peasantry who
dwelt on the coast, and who had congregated
on the cliffs, gazed with the utmost alarm at
the hostile vessels, which, as they well knew,
were drawing near for the conquest of England; portended by the fearful comet blazing
in the sky. The alarm spread—and one of
the few Thanes who were left in the shire
of the South Saxons—for the greater part
were on duty in the north—galloped up to a
rising ground to survey the operations of the
enemy.

The Thane saw the boats pushing through William lands.
the surf, glistening with shields and spears; in
others, stood the war-horses, neighing and paw-
ing at the prospect of release from their irksome
captivity. Now followed the archers, closely

1066

shorn, arrayed in a light and unincumbering garb; each held his long bow, strung for the fight, in his hand, and by his side hung the quiver, filled with those cloth-yard shafts, which, in process of time, became the favourite and national weapon of the yeomanry of England.

The disembarcation,

The archers leap out of the boats, disperse themselves on the shore, and station themselves in the out-posts, so as to protect, if necessary, the heavy armed troops who are about to disembark. The knights are now seen, carefully and heavily treading along the planks, each covered with his hawbergeon of mail, his helmet laced, the shield well strengthened with radiating bars of iron, depending from his neck, his sword borne by his attendant esquire. The gleaming steel-clad multitude cover the shingly beach in apparent disorder, but they rapidly separate, and, in a few moments, each warrior is mounted upon his steed. Banners, pennons, and pennoncels are raised; the troops form into squadrons, and advance upon the land, which they already claim as their possession.

Boat after boat poured out the soldiery of the various nations and races assembled under the banner of William; and lastly, came the pioneers, with their sharp axes, well trained and taught, and prepared to labour for the defence of the army which they had accompanied.

And entrenchment.

The quick eye of the Leader selected the spot for the stockades and entrenchments. The timbers and pavoises, and other materials, were floated from the store-ships, and dragged to the position which had been pointed out. The work began with the utmost skill and energy, and the Thane plainly saw that, before night-fall, the Norman Chief would be entirely secured from surprise. He waited no more, but he instantly determined to bear the ill news to Harold. He turned his horse's head towards the north, and riding night and day, he neither tarried nor rested, until he reached the city of York, where, rushing into the hall, he found Harold, banqueting in festal triumph, with hands embrued in the blood of a brother. [He was triumphing over Tostig and his ally, Harfager, of Norway, defeated in the great battle of Stamford Bridge.] 1066 Oct. 7.

§ 8. It was on the morrow of this battle that the Thane of Sussex came to Harold, and apprised him of the arrival of his most dreaded enemy. Harold immediately marched south, and halted at London, where he prepared to attack the invader. The best part of his troops had fallen; few others joined him, either as volunteers, or by virtue of their tenures or of their allegiance. Edwin and Morcar stood aloof; they did not support their brother-in-law; Algitha, his wife, also quitted him, and abandoned him to his fate. Harold's army too plainly testified the danger of his cause; his ranks were imperfectly filled by hired soldiers, who served him merely for their pay; and whatever force he had, was raised from

Harold learns the news.

the south of the Humber; not a man came from the north. Githa, his mother, sad and weeping for the loss of her son Tostig, earnestly dissuaded Harold from attempting to give battle to William; his other friends and relations joined her in such intreaties, none so earnestly as Gurth, Earl of Suffolk, Harold's brother, praised for his singular merit and virtue. Gurth pointed out to him that his troops were wearied and exhausted, the Normans fresh and confident; and furthermore, the Earl of Suffolk represented to Harold that the violation of his oath would lie heavy upon his soul in the field of battle. If Harold would send his troops against William, Gurth solicited that he, who was unfettered by any such obligation, might take the command; for it appears that the oath was considered as binding merely upon the individual Harold, and that it did not restrain him from sanctioning hostility in others. But Harold was influenced by that obstinate, self-willed determination, which leads the sinner on to his fate; and he persevered, and prepared to encounter his enemy.

Near London, at Waltham, there was a monastery, founded for regular or conventual canons of the order of St. Augustine, and containing a crucifix, supposed to be endued with miraculous power. The Abbey of the "Holy Rood" had been richly endowed by Harold, and before he set out against the enemy, he offered up his orisons at the altar. Whilst Harold was in prayer, in the darkness and gloom of the choir, we are told that the crucifix bowed its head. The portent may have been fancied, but there was a presentiment of evil abroad. It was one of those periods when men's minds are oppressed by the lowering of impending danger, and the Brethren of Waltham determined that two members of the convent, Osgod and Ailric, should accompany their benefactor on his march. Harold having arrayed his forces to the best of his power, directed his course to the shore of Sussex. At *Senlac*, now better known as Battle, he halted. His camp was surrounded by entrenchments, and on the spot where the high altar of the Abbey was afterwards placed, he planted his royal standard.

<small>1066</small>

§ 9. William had been most actively employed. As a preliminary to further proceedings, he had caused all the vessels to be drawn on shore and rendered unserviceable. He told his men that they must prepare to conquer or to die—flight was impossible. He had occupied the Roman castle of Pevensey, whose walls are yet existing, flanked by Anglo-Norman towers, and he had personally surveyed all the adjoining country, for he never trusted this part of a general's duty to any eyes but his own. One Robert, a Norman Thane, who was settled in the neighbourhood, advised him to cast up entrenchments for the purpose of resisting Harold. William

<small>Norman arrangements.</small>

replied, that his best defence was in the valour of his army and the goodness of his cause; and throughout the whole of this expedition, the cool good sense by which he increased the moral courage of his followers is singularly remarkable.

In compliance with the opinions of the age, William had an astrologer in his train. An oriental monarch, at the present time, never engages in battle without a previous horoscope, and this superstition was universally adopted in Europe during the middle ages. But William's "Clerk" was not merely a star-gazer. He had graduated in all the occult sciences—he was a necromancer; or, as the word was often spelt, in order to accommodate it to the supposed etymology, a *nigro*mancer—a "Sortilegus"— and a soothsayer. These accomplishments in the sixteenth century, would have assuredly brought the "clerk" to the stake. But in the eleventh, although they were highly illegal according to the strict letter of the ecclesiastical law, yet they were studied as eagerly as any other branch of *metaphysics*, of which they were supposed to form a part. The *Sorcerer*, or "Sortilegus," by casting "*sortes*," or lots, had ascertained that the Duke would succeed, and that Harold would surrender without a battle, upon which assurance the Normans entirely relied. After the landing, William inquired for his conjurer—A pilot came forward, and told him that the unlucky wight had been drowned in the passage. William then immediately pointed out the folly of trusting to the predictions of one who was utterly unable to tell what would happen unto himself. When William first set foot on shore, he had shown the same spirit. He stumbled, and fell forwards on the palm of his hands. "*Mal signe est çi!*" exclaimed his troops, affrighted at the omen. "No," answered William, as he rose; "I have taken seizin of the country," showing the clod of earth which he had grasped. One of his soldiers, with the quickness of a modern Frenchman, instantly followed up the idea—he ran to a cottage, and pulled out a bundle of reeds from the thatch, telling him to receive that symbol also, as the seizin of the realm with which he was invested. These little anecdotes display the turn and temper of the Normans, and the alacrity by which the army was pervaded.

§ 10. Some fruitless attempts are said to have been made at negotiation. Harold despatched a monk to the enemy's camp, who was to exhort William to abandon his enterprise. The Duke insisted on his right; but, as some historians relate, he offered to submit his claim to a legal decision, to be pronounced by the Pope, either according to the law of Normandy, or according to the law of England; or, if this mode of adjustment did not please Harold, that the question should be decided by single combat, the crown becoming the meed of the victor. The propositions of William are stated, by other authorities, to have contained a proposition for a compromise, namely, that Harold should take Northumbria, and William the rest of the Anglo-Saxon dominions. All or any of these proposals are such as may very probably have been made. But they were not minuted down in formal protocols, or couched in diplomatic notes—they were verbal messages, sent to and fro on the eve of a bloody battle, whereof the particulars were not related by historians until many years had elapsed; and therefore we have no reason to be surprised at the diversity of such narratives, nor is it at all necessary to attempt to reconcile them. The general truth is easily understood. It was evident to each of the chieftains, that they had respectively ventured their whole fortunes on the cast of the die; and before engaging in a conflict which must prove fatal to one of them, they made an attempt to avoid the danger.

The English camp.

Fear prevailed in both camps. The English, in addition to the apprehensions which even the most stout-hearted feel on the eve of a morrow whose close they may never see, dreaded the papal excommunication, the curse encountered in support of the unlawful authority of a usurper. When they were informed that battle had been decided upon, they stormed and swore; and now the cowardice of conscience spurred them on to riot and revelry. The whole night was passed in debauch. "*Wæs-heal*" and "*Drink-heal*" resounded from the tents; the wine cups passed gaily round and round by the smoky blaze of the red watch-fires, while the ballad of ribald mirth was loudly sung by the carousers.

In the Norman Leaguer, far otherwise had the dread of the approaching morn affected the hearts of William's soldiery. No voice was heard excepting the solemn response of the Litany and the chaunt of the Psalm. The penitents confessed their sins—the masses were said —and the sense of the imminent peril of the morrow was tranquillized by penance and prayer. Each of the nations, as we are told by one of our most trustworthy English historians, acted according to their "national custom;" and severe is the censure which the English thus receive.

§ 11. The English were strongly fortified in their position by lines of trenches and palisadoes; and within these defences they were marshalled according to the Danish fashion, shield against shield, presenting an impenetrable front to the enemy. The men of Kent formed the van-guard, for it was their privilege to be the first in the strife. The burgesses of London, in like manner, claimed and obtained the honour of being the royal body-guard, and they were drawn up around the Standard. At the foot of this banner stood Harold, with his brothers, Leofwin and Gurth, and a chosen body of the bravest Thanes, all anxiously gazing on that quarter, from whence they expected the advance of the enemy.

Before the Normans began their march, and very early in the morning of the feast of St. Calixtus, William had assembled his barons around him, and exhorted them to maintain his righteous cause. As the invaders drew nigh, Harold saw a division advancing, composed of the volunteers from the County of Boulogne and from the Amiennois, under the command of William Fitz Osbern and Roger Montgomery. "It is the Duke"—exclaimed Harold—" and little shall I fear him. By *my* forces, will *his* be four times out-numbered!" Gurth shook his head, and expatiated on the strength of the Norman cavalry, as opposed to the foot soldiers of England; but their discourse was stopped by the appearance of the combined cohorts, under Aimeric, Viscount of Thouars, and Alan Fergant of Brittany. Harold's heart sunk at the sight, and he broke out into passionate exclamations of fear and dismay. But now the third and last division of the Norman army was drawing nigh. The consecrated Gonfanon floats amidst the forest of spears; and Harold is now too well aware that he beholds the ranks which are commanded in person by the Duke of Normandy.

§ 12. As the Normans were marshalled in three divisions, so they began the battle by simultaneous attacks upon three points of the

English forces. Immediately before the Duke, rode Taillefer, the Minstrel, singing, with a loud and clear voice, the lay of Charlemagne and Roland, and the emprizes of the Paladins who had fallen in the dolorous pass of Roncevaux. Taillefer, as his guerdon, had craved permission to strike the first blow, for he was a valiant warrior, emulating the deeds which he sung: his appellation, "*Taille-fer*," is probably to be considered not as his real name, but as an epithet derived from his strength and prowess; and he fully justified his demand, by transfixing the first Englishman whom he attacked, and by felling the second to the ground. The battle now became general, and raged with the greatest fury. The Normans advanced beyond the English lines, but they were driven back, and forced into a trench, where horses and riders fell upon each other in fearful confusion. More Normans were slain here, than in any other part of the field. The alarm spread; the light troops left in charge of the baggage and the stores thought that all was lost, and were about to take flight, but the fierce Odo, Bishop of Bayeux, the Duke's half-brother, and who was better fitted for the shield than for the mitre, succeeded in reassuring them, and then, returning to the field, and rushing into that part where the battle was hottest, he fought as the stoutest of the warriors engaged in the conflict, directing their movements and inciting them to slaughter.

From nine in the morning till three in the afternoon, the successes on either side were nearly balanced. The charges of the Norman cavalry gave them great advantage, but the English phalanx repelled their enemies; and the soldiers were so well protected by their targets, that the artillery of the Normans was long discharged in vain. The bowmen, seeing that they had failed to make any impression, altered the direction of their shafts, and, instead of shooting point-blank, the flights of arrows were directed upwards, so that the points came down upon the heads of the men of England, and the iron shower fell with murderous effect. The English ranks were exceedingly distressed by the vollies, yet they still stood firm; and the Normans now employed a stratagem to decoy their opponents out of their entrenchments. A feigned retreat on their part, induced the English to pursue them with great heat. The Normans suddenly wheeled about, and a new and fiercer battle was urged. The field was covered with separate bands of foemen, each engaged with one another. Here, the English yielded—there, they conquered. One English Thane, armed with a battleaxe, spread dismay amongst the Frenchmen. He was cut down by Roger de Montgomery. The Normans have preserved the name of the Norman baron, but that of the Englishman is lost in oblivion. Some other English Thanes are also praised, as having singly, and by their personal prowess, delayed the ruin of their countrymen and country.

At one period of the battle, the Normans were nearly routed. The cry was raised, that the Duke was slain, and they began to fly in every direction. William threw off his helmet, and galloping through the squadrons, rallied his barons, though not without great difficulty. Harold, on his part, used every possible exertion, and was distinguished as the most active and bravest amongst the soldiers in the Host which he led on to destruction. A Norman arrow wounded him in the left eye; he dropped from his steed in agony, and was borne to the foot of the standard. The English began to give way, or, rather, to retreat to the standard as their rallying point. The Normans encircled them, and fought desperately to reach this goal. Robert Fitz Ernest had almost seized the banner, but he was killed in the attempt. William led his troops on, with the intention, it is said, of measuring his sword with Harold. He did encounter an English horseman, from whom he received such a stroke upon his helmet that he was nearly brought to the ground. The Normans flew to the aid of their sovereign, and the bold Englishman was pierced by their lances. About the same time, the tide of battle took a momentary turn. The Kentish men and East Saxons rallied, and repelled the Norman barons;

1066

Normans nearly defeated.

The last attack.

but Harold was not amongst them; and William led on his troops with desperate intrepidity. In the thick crowd of the assailants and the assailed, the hoofs of the horses were plunged deep into the gore of the dead, and the dying. Gurth was at the foot of the standard, without hope, but without fear—he fell by the falchion of William.—The English banner was cast down, and the Gonfanon planted in its place, announced that William of Normandy was the Conqueror.——

The flight.

§ 13. It was now late in the evening. The English troops were entirely broken, yet no Englishman would surrender. The conflict continued in many parts of the bloody field, long after dark. The fugitives spread themselves over the adjoining country, then covered with wood and forest. Wherever the English could make a stand, they resisted; and the Normans confess that the great preponderance of their force, alone enabled them to obtain the victory.

William as conqueror.

By William's orders, a spot close to the Gonfanon was cleared, and he caused his pavilion to be pitched among the corpses which were heaped around. He there supped with his barons; and they feasted among the dead. But when he contemplated the fearful slaughter, a natural feeling of pity, perhaps allied to repentance, arose in his stern mind; and the Abbey of Battle, in which the prayer was to be offered up perpetually for the repose of the souls of all who had fallen in the conflict, was at once the monument of his triumph, and the token of his piety. The abbey was most richly endowed: and all the land, for one league round about, was annexed to the Battle franchise. The Abbot was freed from the authority of the Metropolitan of Canterbury, and invested with archiepiscopal jurisdiction. The high altar was erected on the very spot where Harold's standard had waved; and the Roll, deposited in the archives of the Monastery, recorded the names of those who had fought with the Conqueror, and amongst whom the lands of broad England were divided. But all this pomp and solemnity has passed away like a dream. The "perpetual prayer" has ceased for ever—the roll of Battle is rent.—The shields of the Norman lineages are trodden in the dust.—The abbey is levelled with the ground—and a dank and reedy pool fills the spot where the foundations of the quire have been uncovered, merely for the gaze of the idle visiter, or the instruction of the moping antiquary.

1066

Contrast of its present state.

§ 14. The victor is now installed; but what has become of the mortal spoils of his competitor? If we ask the monk of Malmesbury, we are told that William surrendered the body to Harold's mother, Githa, by whose directions the corpse of the last surviving of her children was buried in the Abbey of the Holy Cross. Those who lived nearer the time, however, relate in explicit terms

Harold's fate.

1066

That he was buried on the coast.

that William refused the rites of sepulture to his excommunicated enemy. Guillielmus Pictavensis, the chaplain of the Conqueror, a most trustworthy and competent witness, informs us that a body of which the features were undistinguishable, but *supposed*, from certain tokens, to be that of Harold, was found between the corpses of his brothers, Gurth and Leofwine, and that William caused this corpse to be interred in the sands of the sea-shore. "Let him guard the coast," said William, "which he so madly occupied;" and though Githa had offered to purchase the body by its weight in gold, yet William was not to be tempted by the gift of the sorrowing mother, or touched by her tears.

§ 15. In the Abbey of Waltham, they knew nothing of Githa. According to the annals of the Convent, the two Brethren who had accompanied Harold, hovered as nearly as possible to the scene of war, watching the event of the battle: and afterwards, when the strife was quiet in death, they humbly approached William, and solicited his permission to seek the corpse.

The Conqueror refused a purse, containing ten marks of gold, which they offered as the tribute of their gratitude; and permitted them to proceed to the field, and to bear away not only the remains of Harold, but of all who, when living, had chosen the Abbey of Waltham as their place of sepulture.

Amongst the loathsome heaps of the unburied,

they sought for Harold, but sought in vain,—
Harold could not possibly be discovered—no
trace of Harold was to be found; and as the last
hope of identifying his remains, they suggested
that possibly his beloved Editha might be able
to recognise the features so familiar to her affections. Algitha, the wife of Harold, was not to
be asked to perform this sorrowful duty. Osgood
went back to Waltham, and returned with Editha,
and the two canons and the weeping woman resumed their miserable task in the charnel field.
A ghastly, decomposing, and mutilated corpse
was selected by Editha, and conveyed to
Waltham as the body of Harold; and there
entombed at the east end of the choir, with
great honour and solemnity, many Norman nobles assisting in the requiem.

[margin: 1066. That he was buried at Waltham.]

§ 16. Years afterwards, when the Norman
yoke pressed heavily upon the English, and the
battle of Hastings had become a tale of sorrow,
which old men narrated by the light of the embers,
until warned to silence by the sullen tolling of
the curfew, there was a decrepit anchorite, who
inhabited a cell near the Abbey of St. John at
Chester, where Edgar celebrated his triumph.
This recluse, deeply scarred, and blinded in his
left eye, lived in strict penitence and seclusion.
Henry I. once visited the aged Hermit, and had
a long private discourse with him; and, on his

[margin: That he survived Hastings.]

death-bed, he declared to the attendant monks, that the recluse was Harold. As the story is transmitted to us, he had been secretly conveyed from the field to a castle, probably of Dover, where he continued concealed until he had the means of reaching the sanctuary where he expired.

This tale contradicted. The monks of Waltham loudly exclaimed against this rumour. They maintained most resolutely, that Harold was buried in their Abbey: they pointed to the tomb, sustaining his effigies, and inscribed with the simple and pathetic epitaph, "*Hic jacet Harold infelix;*" and they appealed to the mouldering skeleton, whose bones, as they declared, showed, when disinterred, the impress of the wounds which he had received. But may it not still be doubted whether Osgood and Ailric, who followed their benefactor to the fatal field, did not aid his escape?—They may have discovered him at the last gasp; restored him to animation by their care; and the artifice of declaring to William, that they had not been able to recover the object of their search, would readily suggest itself as the means of rescuing Harold from the power of the Conqueror. The demand of Editha's testimony would confirm their assertion, and enable them to gain time to arrange for Harold's security; and whilst the litter, which bore the corpse, was slowly advancing to the Abbey of Waltham, the living Harold, under the tender care of Editha, might be safely proceeding to the distant fane, his haven of refuge.

1066

§ 17. If we compare the different narratives concerning the inhumation of Harold, we shall find the most remarkable discrepancies. It is evident that the circumstances were not accurately known; and since those ancient writers who were best informed cannot be reconciled to each other, the escape of Harold, if admitted, would solve the difficulty. I am not prepared to maintain that the authenticity of this story cannot be impugned; but it may be remarked that the tale, though romantic, is not incredible, and that the circumstances may be easily reconciled to probability. There were no walls to be scaled, no fosse was to be crossed, no warder to be eluded; and the examples of those who have survived after encountering much greater perils, are so very numerous and familiar, that the incidents which I have narrated would hardly give rise to a doubt, if they referred to any other personage than a King.

But not improbable or impossible.

In this case we cannot find any reason for supposing that the belief in Harold's escape was connected with any political artifice or feeling. No hopes were fixed upon the usurping son of Godwin. No recollection dwelt upon his name, as the hero who would sally forth from his seclusion, the restorer of the Anglo-

Saxon power. That power had wholly fallen—and if the humbled Englishman, as he paced the aisles of Waltham, looked around, and, having assured himself that no Norman was near, whispered to his son, that the tomb which they saw before them was raised only in mockery, and that Harold still breathed the vital air—he yet knew too well, that the spot where Harold's standard had been cast down, was the grave of the pride and glory of England.

Chapter VII.

ENGLAND AT THE TIME OF THE CONQUEST.

§ 1. W<small>ILLIAM</small> and his army, when they spread themselves over this fertile and much-coveted realm, beheld a country whose aspect differed strangely from the prospects which hill and stream and plain offer at the present day. What did England possess? riches—yet not such as ours. Theirs was not the age of great cities: none of those centres of civilization and corruption, then existed in portentous magnitude; huge agglomerations, ramifying into the meads and pastures, where the green grass, and the sweet cowslip, and the bright ox-eyed daisy, shrink away from hard pavement and smoky sky. The landscape was not adorned and varied, as now, by the villa, the workhouse, the manufactory, the gaol: nor were there existing then any of the signs and wonders produced by modern science and art, the viaducts, the railroads, the canals, at once the causes and the effects of our activity and opulence. But were the differences confined to the works of man? Not so. They extended to the features and characters affecting the whole

Physical aspect of England.

climate and region of the land. We have remarkable evidence that, within such limits as are consistent with the fulfilment of the covenant made by the Creator, the face of the globe, in so far as it depends upon the distribution of moist and dry, heat and cold, nay, even hill and dale, and land and sea, has sustained extensive change.

Temperature has varied.

We are warranted in asserting, from various incidental notices, too minute to be suspected of inaccuracy, too simple to be the result of exaggeration, that, even as late as the twelfth century, the general temperature of the midland and southern parts of the island was not very unlike that of Canada at the present day.— Enter the vineyards flourishing at Glastonbury, whose fruit produces a sweet and grateful wine; ascend the mountains of Craig-Eyriri, covered with unmelting snows, which then might have been called perpetual, from whence they derive their English or Saxon name; and you thus may mark the extremes of temperature prevailing within a comparatively narrow zone.

Prevalence of uncultivated soil.

§ 2. Probably one-third of the face of the island was covered with wood; another third, uncultivated heath and moor. Marshlands were very extensive. Towards the German Ocean, East Anglia was almost separated from the Mercian shires by the fen country, extending more than an hundred miles in length, a waste of waters interspersed with sedgy shelves and islands, spreading its bleakness far around. On the same coast, the driftings of sand and accumulations of earth have since converted many an æstuary into fertile fields, and filled up many a channel, by which the *broads*, as they are aptly called, communicated with the salt sea waves. The iron rings have shown how the vessels were moored against the walls of the Roman Caister near Norwich; whilst, much further inland, the flint arrow-heads lying beneath the strata imbedding organic remains, may perplex, or perhaps confute, all calculations as to the age of the deposit in which they are contained.

In other places within the limits of the *Northfolk* and the *Southfolk*, the recession of the waters—which seems to have taken place much about the time that the ocean, bursting over the Belgian lowlands, formed the Zuyder Zee—though less extensive, is very remarkable. In the quiet village of Reedham, on the banks of the sluggish Yare, we could hardly recognise the coast where, in the tenth century, Bruern Brocard, the Scandinavian, was cast ashore by the tempest. Did we not possess the united testimony of charters and parliamentary proceedings, and of historians, we might doubt that, in the reign of Richard II., Lake Lothing was the Kirkley road—the haven in which the navies of England assembled in days of yore; and the ineffectual attempt which has been made to re-open the navigation from the Lowestoffe mouth to the capital of the county, is a remarkable proof of the continued existence of the agency which occasioned the change. More or less, the same oscillations of land and water have characterized the whole of this eastern side of the island. Thanet, which, when occupied by Hengist and Horsa, was separated from the mainland of Kent by a wide channel, is now entirely joined to the continent; but Ravensburgh, the landing-place of Henry IV., is submerged in the waves.

Changes of Flora and Fauna produced by man.

§ 3. Considering the globe as a whole, it cannot be doubted but that the great, though limited, powers which man possesses, do produce correspondent effects, both in organic and inorganic nature. Many plants indigenous to Britain have disappeared: some within the last quarter of a century. You find them in Gerard's Herbal, but not in the fields. Amongst animals there has been a more evident and more remarkable process of destruction. Like the Dodos in the Mauritius, whole races have become extinct within a recent historical period. The beaver built his house on the banks of the stream beneath that summit where the eagle reared her young; and the British names of stream and of rock still remain, the witnesses of the former existence of the inhabitants which have passed away; whilst the egret and the crane, the bittern and the bustard have been lost within living memory. The bear and the wild boar ranged the forests at the era of the Conquest, the latter in the immediate vicinity of London. The wolf continued to infest the fold long after the supposed extirpation of the foe by the tribute which the Basileus of Britain imposed upon his British vassals; but in the loose nomenclature of popular speech, it is very probable that the hyæna of Yorkshire may also have been included among the animals to which the name of "wolf" was assigned, thus bringing the ossuary of the Kirkdale cave within the period even of the last population of the wolds.

In connection with this subject, it is not unimportant to remark that other notices may be found of the existence, within our historical period, in Britain in particular, and in Europe in general, of other species either banished from our regions, or wholly lost, as far as we can ascertain, to animated nature. The elk reared his tall antlers in Ireland, and probably in Scotland, until after the invasion of the island by our Anglo-Normans. In the thick and damp forests of Gaul, the urus or buffalo ranged. We learn this fact by the relation of the cruel revenge with which Gunthrum punished the wretch, suspected as the slaughterer of the royal beast of chace. This was not far distant from the period, when, according to the testimony of Alcimus Avitus and Sidonius Apollinaris, the volcanoes of Central France were yet in activity.

The *sarris*, a fierce, gigantic, and now wholly extinct species of chamois, was commonly found in the forests of the Pyrenees as late as the fifteenth century, being minutely described by Gaston de Foix. And, since the tiger is even now in full vigour amidst the forests of Siberia, we may consider this fact as affording support to the narrative of the lion-hunts in the Niebelungen lay.

Possible truth in dragon legends. More perplexing are the numerous legends of huge dragons, inhabiting rivers and lakes. Fabulous as they may appear in some instances, and strange in all, they yet raise a suspicion that there might exist some few surviving gigantic reptiles of the Saurian class, such as those whose bones are now found embedded in the strata,—individuals, the last, in each locality, of their species, like the boa by which the army of Regulus was assailed. Unquestionably, such relations were deeply tinged with credulity. The human mind was open to every kind of evidence, without examining the different degrees of confidence which each ought to receive. Making, however, every degree of allowance for the absence of correct observation, as well as for involuntary inaccuracies, and the tendency to seek pleasure by the marvellous, yet there will always remain a residuum, which, if we honestly endeavour to ascertain the truth, cannot be rejected consistently with right reason.

Scepticism is as great a foe to profitable

knowledge as credulity; if investigation is troublesome or disagreeable, or goes against our received opinions, we then are very apt to take refuge in a flat denial, and thus to discharge ourselves from the responsibility of inquiry, and the still greater trouble of having our preconceived opinions disturbed.

§ 4. The period beginning with the partition —(we use this term, because the Roman Empire in the West did not *fall* by the extinction of the imperial authority in the person of Augustulus: —it was *placed in commission* under the Barbarians until Charlemagne arose)—of the Western Empire amongst the Barbaric kingdoms and powers, and ending about the twelfth century, exhibited peculiar meteoric and atmospheric activity. The glaring parhelion, the pallid sun doubly reflected in the snow-fraught cloud, now a phenomenon of rare occurrence, so that perhaps few persons living have seen it, was repeatedly beheld in portentous aspect. Flaming lances and fiery squadrons—the flickering streams of the aurora, which, so long intermitted, appeared as a novelty to Newton and to Halley—beamed across the welkin, blazing in blood-red gleams. Astral showers covered the heavens, as if the stars were driven like chaff before a furious wind; being evidently the same stream of wandering fires, now again intersecting our sphere, and watched or sought from the observatory: but then indicating, as

Extraordinary prevalence of celestial phenomena.

it was deemed, the changes and the going forth of nations—the immediate harbingers of the Crusades. But no appearance excited so much awe in England as the Great Comet of 1066, such as never had been seen before. Pilgrim and merchant, monk and layman, had brought the frequent and dread report that Duke William of Normandy, Edward's cousin and appointed heir, was mustering his forces to gain and divide the land. Night after night did the appalled multitude gaze at the messenger of evil, the "long-haired star," darting its awful splendour from horizon to zenith; crowds, young and old, watched the token far beyond the midnight hour; and when they retired to their broken rest, its bright image, floating before the eye, disturbed their slumbers. Even if this were but an idle opinion, yet it was an opinion which became a reality as the moral world was then constituted. The conviction that the phenomena of nature and the destiny of mankind were bound up in mystic unity, gave more boldness to the fortunate, increased the anxieties of the desponding. And the English, throughout the whole of the Anglo-Norman period, acknowledged their subjugation to be a national punishment.

§ 5. Had William never held his great council at Lillebonne, never been encouraged by the eager boldness and rapacity of his Norman barons, never been favoured by the wind, never landed in safety, never been assisted by the cowardice or treachery of the northern Thanes, never overthrown the whole force of England in the one decisive battle, still it is fully evident to us *now*, that the appointed time had arrived for the extinction of the Anglo-Saxon monarchy.

The Anglo-Saxon monarchy had reached its limit.

In our age—the old age of the world—we are privileged to discern, more clearly than those who lived in its youth, the evidence how each successive incident is induced and led on by that incomprehensible union of free will on the part of man, and the foreknowledge of the Almighty, which equally guides the actions of each individual, and the collective fortunes of mankind. The more the successive facts accumulate upon us, the more clearly we obtain a knowledge, imperfect and limited though it may be, of the certain tokens which precede the decline and fall of empires. In this sunset of the life of the world, we more than ever distinctly observe how coming events cast their shadows before. When the corpse is borne to the grave, we then know the secret progress of death in life, the inward extinction of the vital fire, the wasting of the organs, the irretrievable decays, the causes of the slight ailments, the transient pains, the momentary depression, the langour, unaccountable at the time, but now proving to us that the term never could have been prolonged. The gust blows down the tree: you examine the fallen trunk, and then discover that its roots were so rotted in the soil, that though the winds might have been hushed, the weight of its own boughs would have laid it low.

Buying and selling in the Temple.

§ 6. The English clergy were grievously corrupted. The reforms so zealously and honestly attempted by Popes and Councils in other portions of the Catholic Church in the west had not reached them. Very many of the bishops and abbots had obtained their dignities by simony. Sinful as this bartering of holy things is under any circumstances, we hardly feel its full import in the middle ages, nor understand why the church, collectively, was so exceedingly earnest in labouring to repress the evil, as existing in individual members. We are accustomed to view simony merely as a spiritual offence—and as a violation of the sacred functions of the priesthood; but, in the middle ages, it was also a grievous offence against the civil relations of society. It was introducing base motives into all the various functions which were attached to the prelatic character. What people buy, they sell: the bishop who *bought* his bishopric would *sell* any ecclesiastical preferment within his gift. He was a trustee for the poor; but he had *bought* his trusteeship, and therefore he would *sell* their rights for his own advantage. The bishop was a member of parliament, and he had *bought* his seat in the legislature from the king, and therefore he would *sell* his vote to the king, his *patron* in every sense of the term. Ecclesiastical historians have obscured the real bearing of the conflicts between crown and clergy, and exceedingly damaged their own cause, by using language which obliterates the most important truth, that the contest for the liberty of the Church was in the main a contest for the liberties of the people. The open and shameless barter and sale of ecclesiastical dignities, throughout this period, is scarcely conceivable to us, amongst whom this abuse at least has ceased. "*Give* you a nomination to a prebend!" exclaimed Philip I. to an applicant, "I have *sold* them all already." The bishop was a judge, bound to attend to the reformation of manners, but he had *bought* his office, and therefore would *sell* impunity to the opulent transgressor; hence the universal relaxation of all discipline, and the prevalence, throughout England, of the lowest immorality. In all these transactions the clergy were the most guilty. Every simoniacal promotion they obtained was accompanied by perjury; the higher the standard of morality which the priesthood were bound to assert, the greater was their guilt, the more deleterious their example upon the rest of the community. Never does any neglect of duty in one class fail to extend its evil influence to the other orders of society. The foul marsh beneath the palace walls will diffuse its contagion to the presence-

Vast evils of these abuses to national morality.

chamber. Vices fostered or tolerated by ruling powers in the subject classes, work out their retribution by including governors and governed in the avenging punishment. Lust, luxury, and sloth defiled and enervated the aristocracy. The lower orders were heavily oppressed. Slavery was exceedingly extended. Hard as the situation of the *Theowe* had been in earlier periods, it had now become infinitely worse. The provision, merciful to a certain extent, which prohibited the sale of the slave out of his native country, was entirely violated; and it was the common practice to sell these miserable creatures to the pagan Danes in Ireland; so that Bristol was the regular slave-market; and the English connected their slave-dealings with the same disgusting profligacy which is now exhibited amongst their descendants, so proud of claiming their connexion with the Anglo-Saxon race, on the opposite shores of the Atlantic. There were, of course, many to whom these censures did not apply: many holy men amongst the clergy, many servants of God amongst the laity, but not sufficient to avert the destiny of the people,—and in one common ruin they were involved.

Although the empire of Britain appeared to subsist under Edward the Confessor, it was really on the verge of dissolution. As an ancient building is kept together by the roughnesses of the surface, and the ivy which has eaten out the mortar, and yet binds the stones by its frail tendrils, and the iron clamps giving a temporary support to the walls which they have split and rifted, till the blow comes which beats them down:—so are ancient States sustained by dull habit, by usages which have lost their original principle, by institutions which have ceased to command respect, and by the convulsive energies of rash innovation, affording a temporary vigour, though they exhaust vitality, till the appointed season of destruction. In the case of Britain, some additional duration had perhaps been imparted by the personal character of the Confessor, his virtues, and even his failings. Yet let it be recollected that many of his failings resulted from his great love of peace. His passive and tranquil disposition, which prevented his exerting his authority against those who were usurping his rights, also rendered these usurpers less inclined to disturb an authority which they scarcely felt, and which they knew must, at no distant period, expire.

Influence of the Confessor.

§ 7. The ancient kingdoms of the so-called Heptarchy, had merged in the three great divisions of Wessex, Mercia, and the Danelagh. They were not merged or united into one kingdom, but connected by a common policy: whether each had at this period an assembly, which, by a conventional term, we call the Witenagemot, is not certain. Wessex was the chief or ruling portion of the empire, yet under the Confessor,

Existing divisions of England at date of Conquest.

Wessex the chief.

though Winchester might still be reckoned as the constitutional capital, yet Westminster had become the residence of the monarch, the Basileus of the empire. Such a change of residence is always very significant, and indicative of a great change of policy in a government. The removal of the Czar from Moscow to St. Petersburgh, marked the total change of the fortunes of the Sclavonian race. Charles V., at Madrid, subverted the ancient authorities of Castile and Arragon, and made the first step towards the real consolidation of the principalities and kingdoms of the peninsula, into the monarchy of Spain and the Indies. Yet the severance of the different states of Britain was very distinctly marked: it was the custom that the Basileus should wear his crown in each; and though the ceremony of the royal ordination could be but once performed by the ministration of the Metropolitan of Britain, still it should seem that he needed to be distinctly inaugurated, at least in the three principal states of which the kingdom was composed.

Capital practically removed to Westminster.

The Danish invasions had entirely dislocated the kingdom. Force and violence, as employed by those barbarian invaders, had occasioned much evil; but even more harm ensued from the moral deterioration occasioned by their conquests. In their own country, and amongst their own people, they appear to have been deficient even in what are usually considered

Evil results of the Danish invasions,

as the virtues of the savage. The *Danelagh* was filled with a new population, who had dispossessed a great portion of the original inhabitants. The names of places, as is well known, afford the most cogent proofs how the population had been changed; and full as harshly as was subsequently effected by the Romanized Danes whom we call Normans. We do not know, for example, the Englishman expelled from the Norfolk village now called Ormsby, by the *Serpent*, for such is the meaning of *orm*, or worm; but we cannot doubt that he went out full as unwillingly as if he had been chased away by a Norman Trussebot, or a Breton Botevilain, in the subsequent age. We shall shortly have occasion to mention a very remarkable fact, proving the subsisting and secret influence of the Danish kings. Under the Danish influence also—for though the system had been perfected under Canute, it had begun at an earlier period—the old English policy had been altered by the parcelling of the empire into Earldoms. Mr. Hallam has well observed that these Earldoms had much similarity to the Duchies and Counties of the Carlovingian Empire: and important considerations arise from this fact, which his great sagacity first discovered.

§ 8. The constitution of the Carlovingian Empire is better known than that of Britain, but which became the model of the other? Whether the disciple of Alcuin might not have learned from him some principles of government, cannot be affirmed, but might perhaps be conjectured; and the extraordinary and otherwise inexplicable phenomenon of the French form of royal consecration having been textually borrowed from that of England, may lend some support to the opinion which we have intimated, though we may not venture to give it further advocacy.

Was the Saxon constitution copied by Charlemagne?

These governments were portioned out with some relation to the boundaries of the ancient kingdoms: most closely so in Northumbria. The *Earldom* had not absolutely settled into a definite hereditary right, but the claims of blood and lineage in the same family seem generally to have been respected. Towards the conclusion of the Confessor's reign, the fortunes of the house of Godwin prevailed. If, as it was said, he was really the son of a cow-herd, such an ancestry would have had as good traditionary repute as that ascribed to the first of the Capets—"*figliol fui d' un beccaio di Parigi.*" Harold, with his earldoms, extending from the Land's End to the German Sea—West Wales and Wessex, Sussex, Kent, and his portions of the Danelagh, and Mercia along the Thames, and beyond; Essex and Hertford, Middlesex, Oxford and Berks—was more of a king in reality than Edward himself; and, upon the peaceful death of the Confessor, Earl Harold became the King of the English, just as the

Enlarged power of the Earls.

Duke of Paris became King of the French, though with most unequal fortune: for whilst the dominion of Harold past away like a shadow, the power of Hugh Capet has been transmitted from man to man, by a special providence unparalleled in the annals of mankind.

[Oct. 1844.]

§ 9. Besides the Earldoms, the greater burghs formed a very important portion of the Anglo-Saxon Empire. Their powers, their constitution, their privileges, are enveloped in the greatest obscurity, and in many cases can only be conjectured, either by comparison with other bodies of a similar nature, or by the vestiges which, from continual usage and tradition, subsisted even until our own days. Their origin also was very diverse: some, unquestionably, were Roman; others were territorial communities: the only general characteristic which we can predicate with any degree of certainty, is, that there is no real foundation for the theory which placed them as the creation of a subsequent age,—an antagonism between commerce and feudality, between the shuttle and the spear, and as the victors of industry and civilization over aristocratic pride. At this period they were communities standing between dependent and independent authority, verging, in some instances, to the state of free communities. Many were enclavures, surrounded by the Earldoms, yet, nominally at least, dependent only upon the sovereign.

Obscure origin of the burghs.

Not antagonistic to feudality.

Analogies abroad.

Such a state of things was not uncommon upon the continent. Take one example out of many. Tournai, in the midst of Flanders, owed no obedience to the Count. Baldwin could make no *joyeuse entrée* within the walls. Saving its own rights and privileges, it acknowledged only the king of the Franks; but that *saving* was a very large one; his sovereignty did not amount to much more, than that they acknowledged him when his protection was desired.

Winchester was the proper constitutional capital of the Empire. Far more extensive was the city than at the present day; being one of the few localities which not only have escaped the general plethora, but have even fallen away. *Caer-Guent*, for the Saxons fully recollected its British name, retained the insignia of government. There was the royal treasury; and many a tradition was attached to the antient castle in which Arthur had held his court—traditions fully living in mind and memory, before they became the subjects of written romance or history. We are not unwilling to believe that the round table suspended in the hall—until recently mistaken for the chapel—of the castle, may have existed before Geoffry of Monmouth gave that form to the British legends which diffused them amongst so many distant nations and tongues.

Traditions of Winchester.

London.

London possessed the character of a free city. Its constitution had, however, sustained some alteration in the days of Canute. It should seem that the Danes had engrafted a colony of their own upon the English community. So large a number of the *Lithsmen*, or Danish soldiers, established themselves there, that one of the municipal courts acquired the Danish name of the *Husting;* a term, which in the devious course of language has been so entirely diverted from its primitive signification as to mean, not the court, but any scaffold or *dais* where elections are held. Of the interior government of London city, we can only say that the distinctions between the *rectores* or aldermen, and the commonalty, are distinctly marked. Proud and warlike, and defended by the Roman wall, of which the last fragment has just been saved from destruction, the citizens rejoiced in their privileges, rendering them a species of independent, though subordinate, community. Amongst other rights, London acted apart from Wessex or Mercia in electing or recognising the king. Of this right an exceedingly curious vestige remains in force to the present day, the Lord Mayor and Aldermen being always required to concur, as essential parties, in the act of recognising and proclaiming the accession of the new monarch.

Affected by Danish settlers.

Privileges of the city.

We have no direct notice in the Anglo-Saxon annals of the privileges or rights of the Cinque Ports; but the Anglo-Saxon constitution of their Court of Guestling, their Parlia-

Cinque Ports. ment if we may so call it, the naval services which they rendered, and the great and independent privileges which they enjoyed, as soon as our legal history properly begins, can scarcely leave any doubt but that, at this period, they formed a federative community.

§ 10. When Canute assumed the government, he appears to have retained the kingdom of Wessex more immediately in his own hands; but before the close of his reign, it had become the Earldom of Godwin. Possibly, however, under the Danish king, he did not hold it with *Diversity of races in Wessex.* what may be termed a uniform authority. This great dominion consisted of three integral portions, all designated as Wessex in ordinary language, but governed with some diversity as to rights, and more arising from the variety of races it contained. A large proportion, towards the west, was yet British, very unbroken and unmixed in the extreme west, but shading off as you travelled eastward, ceasing, perhaps, on the borders of Dorset and Somerset. Until the battle of Gavelford, the Britons had been able to make a steady resistance, and the British line of Princes of Dyvnaint, or Devonshire, *Independence of old population.* and Cernau, or Cornwall, can be traced from Geraint ap Erbin, lamented in the elegy of Llewarch Hén, to the reign of Athelstan, when the Regulus of West Wales became the liegeman of the Basileus of Britain. It is, of course, quite impossible to discover the exact boundaries and the different dominions, but perhaps even at a later period, the boundary between the two nations was the river Exe, on this side English land, on the other Wales.

Exeter enjoyed privileges nearly equal to London; it appears that others of the cities were scarcely inferior, and that no taxation could be levied upon them, unless they jointly assented to the grant. Perhaps the burghs of Wessex and others formed a league. In the north, there was certainly a powerful association, called the *five* or the *seven* burghs— Lincoln, Nottingham, Derby, Leicester, and Stamford—to which York and Chester were afterwards added. It seems, as before noticed, that this federation originally consisted of five; but when two others were conjoined, they were generally called by their nominal number of *Five Boroughs*, and sometimes *Seven Boroughs*, according to their real one. The *Cinque* ports afford a familiar example of the retention of an appellation derived from number, after it has ceased to be strictly appropriate. Lincoln, the chief of the five burghs, was governed by twelve hereditary *Lawmen*. This is a Danish term, and shows a Danish local government, which subsisted throughout the whole of the reign of the Conqueror. It is more remarkable, that, notwithstanding the political cessation of the Danish authority, and in spite of the Conquest, the inhabitants of Lincoln continued in alliance with the Danish kings, so much so that a treasure belonging to the Scandinavian monarch was permanently deposited there—either concealed from the Norman, or so well guarded that the Norman dared not attack the hoard.

§ 11. At the other extremity of Wessex, Kent retained its ancient boundaries since the first foundation of the kingdom; and even the division of the country into East and West Kent, or rather into the countries of the East Kentish men and West Kentish men, has existed from immemorial antiquity, though probably not exactly according to the modern boundary. A species of peculiar dignity seems to have been attached to this first seat of Anglo-Saxon power. From the reign of Egbert, the kingdom of Kent became an integral portion of the empire of Wessex, forming, nevertheless, an apanage held by the heir apparent to the crown; a separate, though subordinate kingdom, accepting the laws of Wessex upon such terms as appeared expedient to its own legislature, and, without doubt, retaining also all those traditional customs which formed the great basis of its common law. Surrey, or the Suthriga, which may be obscurely but distinctly traced as a separate kingdom, (though the foundation charter of Chertsey Abbey alone testifies the existence of Frithewald, its first known Subregulus,) and the adjoining kingdom of the South Saxons, seem to have become, in some degree, annexed to Kent; the traditions of history, if not its more authentic memorials, seem to point out that the Earldom of Kent was the earliest, and, as it were, the favourite dignity which Godwin possessed. Of the other portions of Wessex Proper, Hampshire, peopled by the Jutes and Goths, Berks, and Wilts, and Somerset, we can, anterior to the Danish Conquests, ascertain that they were subject to subordinate chieftains; but these had all disappeared, and Godwin ruled with immediate authority over this, the centre of the Earldom.

Hampshire.

§ 12. When we speak of Northumbria, we must, in the first instance, entirely divest ourselves of the idea of the modern county bearing that name, and consider the country so designated, as extending from the Trent and Humber up to the Firth of Forth on the north, and to the boundaries of Mercia and the kingdom of Strath-Clyde on the west. Upon the first settlement of the Angles, it became divided into Deira, which included modern Yorkshire, and possibly the bishoprick of Durham, and Bernicia, all to the north of the Tees. Both became subjected to Ethelfrith, but they never seem to have been united into one sovereignty. The indiscriminate employment by the early historians of the term Northumbria, to designate both portions of the country, throws great obscurity upon a history, of which, after the

Meaning of the term Northumbria.

bright era of Bede, so few memorials are preserved. A line of Danish Kings became firmly established: in no portion of England did their race become more predominant, and it always continued more distinctly separated than any other from the rest of the empire. As an earldom, the succession began after the death of Eric, and Oswulf appears as the first Earl of Bernicia, or Northumbria, north of the Tyne. Upon the death of Oswulf, Edgar, with the assent of the great council, divided his earldom into two: from the Humber to the Tees was bestowed upon Oslac, who was girt with the sword of the earldom: from the Tees, northward, as it should seem, perhaps to the Firth of Forth, was bestowed upon Eadulf Evilchild; whilst Lothian was granted to Kenneth, King of the Scots, to be held by homage, —a transaction of which more hereafter.

Establishment of Earldoms in the North.

Uchtred, married to Elfgiva, the daughter of King Ethelred, received the investiture of the whole of his father's earldom from the king, who added thereto the Earldom of York; but upon his death they became divided. Northumbria proper ultimately vested in Oswulf, whilst Deira became the Earldom of Siward, in right of Elfleda, the daughter of Aldred, Uchtred's eldest son. The fabulous genealogies of the north describe Siward as the son of a bear, a myth which at least describes his prowess and his ferocity. A Dane he certainly was, but, as we shall afterwards see, he showed great

Division of Northumbria.

fidelity to the Confessor. The remoteness of these earldoms from the seat of government, and the rugged character of the country itself, encouraged the national spirit of independence. The obedience rendered to the king was perhaps little more than nominal, and if the Conquest had not soon transferred the supremacy into more vigorous hands, it is probable that Northumbria, like Scotland, would again have become a realm claiming independence, and rivalling the supreme monarch of the empire. *Independence of this region.*

York, the birthplace of Constantine, evidences now, even by the one mult-angular tower, its Roman dignity; but we believe that in case of all the burghs, the Danish influence was very overwhelming. They became nationalized as Danes, and of this also we find a singular proof in the privileges enjoyed by the Danish Burgh of Grimsby. However difficult it may be to discover amidst the traditions of romance the real history of its founder, Grime, and the protection given by him to Havelok, the child of the Danish King, this now deserted port, which, in the twelfth century, was still the great emporium of the Baltic trade, enjoys, even at this moment, an exemption from toll at the port of Elsinore, in proof and testimony of its antient Danish consanguinity. *York. Relics of the Danes at Grimsby.*

§ 13. Legends and poems are almost the only memorials we possess of East Anglia. The Danes, under Guthrun, effecting a complete conquest, divided the land, and settled *East Anglia.*

the country; and concurrently with the memorable treaty which fixed the boundaries of the Danelagh, Guthrun, or Gorp, was confirmed in the possession of East Anglia, to be held as a *laen* of the crown of Wessex. After the cessation of the line of Danish Kings, we find it held by Athelstan, distinguished either by the Anglo-Saxon title of Ealdorman, or the designation of Semi-rex, descriptive, no doubt, of his great authority. Under Cnut it was erected into an earldom; Thurkell, upon whom he bestowed it, appears as the most successful and the most ferocious of the Danish chieftains. The pirates of Jomsburg were celebrated for their stern and unsparing valour, and Thurkell did not belie the reputation of his compeers.

Made an Earldom.

Divided state of Scotland.

§ 14. In speaking of Scotland, it is very important, in the first place, to recollect that at this period no such country properly existed. The Anglo-Saxon or English kingdom of Bernicia included the whole of the Lothians; and the royal seat of Kenneth M'Alpine, over whatever dominions he may have ruled, was beyond the Tweed. Colonies of Scandinavians were established in Caithness and Sutherland, and, as before mentioned, the British kingdom of Strath-Clyde extended, as its name indeed imports, to the river from which it is denominated, far into the heart of the modern Scotland. From the reign of Athelstan, we find the Kings of Scotland as the liegemen of the monarchs of

Britain, a tie often disputed, but never entirely cast off. The rebellion of the Scots, which drew down upon them the vengeance of Canute, was speedily followed by the submission of the Scottish Reguli. Malcolm and two other kings, described by the obscure and probably corrupted appellations of Maelboethe and Jemarch, performed homage to the Dane, who effected a total subjugation of the Scottish race and country. *Conquest by the Danes.*

I shall not here deduce with minuteness the transmission of exerted authority and obedience rendered, nor the difficulties which have been raised against the Scottish subjection to the British Crown, nor the answers which can be fairly given to the objections suggested by feelings which must in every way be honoured and respected, however unsupported by the facts of history; but the last transactions between an Anglo-Saxon monarch and the Scots are those which perhaps display most clearly the relations between the two crowns. Edward the Confessor, in the popular elegy which laments his death, was celebrated as the exalted ruler of heroes, the lord of the Britons, the Welsh, and the Scots; and the authority of the most pacific of our English monarchs was never disputed by his vassals. The throne of Scotland had been usurped by Macbeth, to the prejudice of Malcolm Canmore. He claimed the aid of his superior, which was readily *Political dependence of the King of the Scots.* *Macbeth.*

granted; a fleet and army, despatched by the Confessor, under the command of Siward, Earl of Northumberland, advanced to the north. Macbeth was powerfully aided by the Northmen; but the English forces gained the victory, and the result of the expedition enabled the Earl of Northumbria to fulfil the behest of his sovereign. Malcolm was appointed King of the Scots, pursuant to the commands of Edward, and from his lord he received investiture of Scotland, to hold under the Anglo-Saxon Crown.

Malcolm.

§ 15. From the Dee to the Clyde constituted the kingdom of Cumbria, or the Northern Britons. Strath-Clyde, properly so called, extended from the Upper Forth and Loch Lomond on the north, to the Kirshope, the Eden, and the Solway on the south; and from the Irish Sea and Firth of Clyde, which washed its western shores, it ranged eastward to the limits of the Merse and Lothian, including Galloway, or the country of the Southern Picts, the latter being, however, a distinct though subject dominion. The Southern Cumbria included the modern Cumberland, Westmoreland, and a portion of Yorkshire, Leeds being the original frontier town between the British and Anglo-Danish territories. This, the ancient and most brilliant seat of the British power, is almost effaced from our annals. Here, in Reged and Strath-Clyde, we must locate the fabled Court

Strath-Clyde.

South Cumbria.

of Arthur; and the traditions still floating in the recollections of the last generation, and the tales ascribed to the earthworks and fortresses where the Round Table was held, alone connects the country with the race which has entirely disappeared. Alcluid, or Dumbarton, continued to be the seat of a British monarchy, until the repeated incursions of the Danes involved the northern Cymri in the same misfortunes which had been sustained by their Saxon enemies. Alliance by marriage as well as conquests subjected the northern Cumbria to the Scottish Kings. Of these princes, Eocha, whose name is softened into Eugenius, and in whom we must, under either disguise, discover the more familiar name of Owen, appears in the most memorable battle of Brunnaburgh, when the combined Reguli of the north endeavoured to free themselves from their dependence upon the Anglo-Saxon empire. Athelstan triumphed; but instigated by the Danes, the Scoto-Cumbrian Kings continued their attempts to release themselves from the Saxons. In these conflicts they failed: the victory gained by Edmund over Donald, the son of Eugenius, placed Strath-Clyde, wasted and depopulated, entirely in his power. *Union of North Cumbria and Scotland.*

The transactions which ensued afford a most important insight into the policy of the Anglo-Saxon empire. Master of the vacant throne, Edmund might have retained possession, or *Conduct of the English King.*

granted Strath-Clyde to a favourite or a follower; but, yielding to the principle of lineage and blood, he restored the crown to the Scottish dynasty. Cumbria was re-granted to Malcolm I. as a benefice, upon condition that he should co-operate with the monarch of Britain by sea and land, and most particularly against the Danes. This engagement was ratified by an oath of fealty; but a singular rule of succession, established at an earlier period, received a new sanction. Cumbria was immediately vested in the Tanaist, or the son, designated in the lifetime of his father as his successor. For it had been established that the dominion of the Scots and of the Cumbrians should never be united in the same person, although the kingdoms should remain in the same family : Cumbria thus bearing the same relation to the Scottish crown which Wales, nominally at least, bears to the kingdom of England.

Disposition of Cumbria.

The refusal of Malcolm III. to contribute to the payment of the Danegeld, alleging that he was only bound to render military service, was punished by the ravages of Ethelred. The accession of Canute afforded to Duncan, the Regulus of Cumbria, a reason for throwing off his allegiance to the English crown. But the Dane invaded Scotland : a peace was concluded upon condition that the Regulus of Cumbria should perform homage to the sovereign of Britain and his successors. Malcolm Canmore

Relation of the Danes to Scotland.

became King of Cumbria, when his father Duncan obtained the Scottish crown. In his person, until the birth and majority of Prince David, the antient rule of succession was suspended; and under the reign of the Confessor, the whole of these territories were vested in the Scottish Sovereign, whose distance from the seat of government, as well as his power, tempted him to be the rival rather than the subject of the Anglo-Saxon King.

Chapter VIII.

THE CONQUEROR, FROM HASTINGS TO THE CORONATION.

1066.

<small>1066

Anarchical position of the country.</small>

§ 1. Upon Harold's death, the several component members of the Anglo-Saxon monarchy reverted to that species of constitutional independence, which in every case ensued upon the vacancy of the crown; but, of course, with the aggravation resulting from the previous condition of the realm. The community of interest, imperfect even in prosperous times, had been greatly diminished by adversity. Poverty weakens all moral authority, even the powers of affection and of love. Northumbria, which had gradually been drifting away from the Basileus, scarcely ever recognized the son of Godwin. In Mercia, loyalty was not ardent; and of Wessex, and that portion of the Danelagh annexed thereto, we can speak more positively. A large party amongst the English considered that they had obtained their liberation from a usurper; and the first immediate consequence resulting from the battle of Hastings, was, at least in appearance, the restoration of the right royal line.

Whether Edwin and Morcar were actually

engaged in the fatal conflict, cannot be ascertained. At all events, they drew off their forces immediately, and advanced to London. Unquestionably the strength and importance of the city tended to protect its constitutional rights; but it is remarkable that the pre-eminence of the citizens, in having the right of making the first choice, does not seem to have been contested. Immediately upon their arrival, the earls, or one of them, for the details of their conduct are involved in perplexity, laboured to obtain the throne. Claims to the royal authority, as it has been held by the line of Cerdic, these Mercian Earls had none: like Harold, they would have been usurpers, and yet usurpers from necessity; but they were wise and valiant, fair to behold, and pleasant in speech, possessing the strong arm and the liberal hand, with some of the good, and many of the specious qualities which reap the immediate harvest of popularity. They tried their chance, but failed. Edgar Atheling was safe within the city. What the age of the child was, we have no exact account. We can ascertain, however, from authentic records, that distinguished, recognized, and respected by the Normans as the Atheling, he was alive ninety-three years after the date of the Conquest. At this period, therefore, could he be more than ten years old? Infant as he was, however, he was proclaimed Basileus of England by the authority of the

Rectores and Potentes then in the city; an obscure hint, but indicating, when compared with other conflicting accounts, the great difference of opinion which subsisted.

The Atheling's party prevails.

It should seem that the Proceres, properly so called, in whose rank Edwin and Morcar were included, would have opposed the choice; but the Bishops, including the two Primates, Stigand of Canterbury and Aldred of York, as well as William the Bishop of London, all advocated the Atheling, and succeeded. In after life, Edgar exhibited a singular combination of courage and humility, of rashness and wisdom; but now what could he be otherwise than the shadow of a king? and the royal authority, at a time when, of all others, it required personal efficacy and energy, could only have been exercised by Regents in his name. Yet that name afforded the means of embodying the sentiments

His popularity.

of hope and expectation. The fragment of the old ballad calls him England's darling: it was the common belief that he would win the land; and, from the first moment of his proclamation, he was acknowledged, at least, throughout the whole of the Danelagh. Fidelity and unity of purpose might, humanly speaking, even still have averted the immediate subjugation of the English; but their measures were so unwise, so feeble, that even the black monks of Peterborough, that great stronghold of old English feeling, bear record with sorrow, that their further spirit of opposition to William was a visitation for their sins. Every effort they made to extricate themselves from the meshes of the net, only entangled them more and more.

margin: 1066

§ 2. Military operations, always difficult portions of historical narrative, if it be desired to give a distinct and clear idea of their succession, are peculiarly so during the middle ages. Where a science exists, you may connect insulated facts, and correct discrepancies by its theory, but there was then no science of war. The predatory character of the warfare renders the line of march undefined. The want of accurate topographical knowledge in the Chroniclers, encreases the obscurity; for no one can clearly describe any transaction connected with topography, unless he clearly understands the country which he describes.

margin: Evidence for William's campaigns.

I shall, therefore, in this narrative, relate the military transactions of this reign, after instituting the best comparison I can effect between the different sources, some of which are evidently derived from oral tradition, proceeding from those who had engaged in the conflict; many of these warriors wore out their old age in the convent of St. Evroul; and we receive the tale as modified by the imperfect recollection of the old, and the ignorance, perhaps, of the youth by whom it was transmitted to us. Many points must remain open to doubt, and particularly as to the order of events; but their

margin: Whence derived.

general nature seems to have been preserved with truth and sincerity.

§ 3. It must have been very evident to William, from the first moment of success, that the defeat of Harold was not the conquest of the kingdom. He had no maps, no itineraries, no personal knowledge of the land, no friends whom he knew of amongst the English, no guides whom he could trust. All before him was lost in distance and darkness, but he fully appreciated his difficulties, and felt that, whether success or discomfiture awaited him, the first and most important step which he had to adopt, was to secure an easy access to Normandy, and, in particular, to and from the ports at his command; the river of Dieppe, (the town then not existing,) the mouth of the Seine, and Barfleur: the latter the most distant, but which has been found by experience to offer the readiest passage to the Isle of Wight, the outwork, as it were, to the continent Island of Britain. He, therefore, immediately established a military position in Sussex; then, probably, at once devising that territorial division, whose aspect differs altogether from that prevailing in other portions of England. In the next place, ignorant as he was in other respects, of the resources of England, and, perhaps, even of its means of defence, he well knew that the great body of Harold's troops engaged in the conflict, had been drawn from Harold's own earldom, and more particularly from its southern portions; and that, consequently, the slaughter which had ensued had deprived these districts of their natural defenders. Hence, he would know that, besides Sussex, the shires of Hants, Kent, Surrey, Middlesex, Hertford, Berks, and Oxford would be peculiarly open to his attacks; and these constitute the scene of his first campaign.

He began his operations against Romney: it might be important to dislodge the English from this position, protected by the marshes; but he had another object besides. The men of Romney had defeated and slain a detached party of his troops, and he punished them for this act with great ferocity, which, without doubt, had its moral influence in inspiring alarm. Proud in the recollection of their old English blood, the men of Kent seemed fully prepared to resist the Conqueror. Not one of the seven sons of Godwin was there to lead them, but they assembled in great numbers in and about Dover. Harold had added to the original Roman fortifications: the castle, one of the very few then subsisting in England, was deemed impregnable; but the spirit of the English was broken. Appalled at William's approach, the garrison proposed to surrender. Before, however, they could bring forth the keys, the town was wrapt in flames,—their roofs of thatch and frames of timber were

1066

Dover taken.

blazing. It is said that the Norman soldiers, eager for prey and rapine, had cast in the burning brands; and so extensive was the conflagration, that even towards the close of William's reign, when Domesday was compiled, the burgesses were unable to pay the valued rents of their properties. If this destruction were accidental, it, nevertheless, served William well. By clearing the ground below, it rendered the castle more defensible, and prevented a sturdy population from again engaging in opposition to his authority. Dover was also the chief of the maritime stations, from which vessels might come forth and harass him in time of trouble. All these chances of danger were quelled by the fire.

State of Canterbury.

§ 4. William's troops suffered greatly from sickness whilst at Dover: his advance altogether had been tardy. Canterbury had full time to prepare for defence. As yet no Norman forces whatever had approached London. Archbishop Stigand had returned to his cathedral. Agelnoth, a man of great influence, and possibly one of the Godwin family, commanded in the city. A third individual of great importance was Ægelsine, abbot of St. Augustine's. He had recently obtained, from Pope Alexander, the mitre which exempted him from episcopal jurisdiction: perhaps, the earliest example of this mischievous innovation in England, which, subsequently, involved both See and Abbey in dissensions, greatly to their common detriment.

1066

It does not seem that Canterbury was very defensible. William had already excited great terror: the opulent citizens, (and they are distinguished as such,) dreaded pillage, and without waiting for the approach of William, they proffered their submission, and did homage to the Conqueror. They gave the bad precedent of being the first community which had made a formal and uncoerced submission, of their own free will, and unenforced by the sword. The transaction, therefore, was of great importance, and produced a corresponding effect, and very many flocked in to make their terms with their future Sovereign. But Abbot Ægelsine had been no party to this transaction; on the contrary, he exhorted the English to die in the defence of their country, like the Macchabees of old, rather than to submit. William advanced till within a day's march of London. Not far from the River Thames, below the reach of Greenhithe, is a tract still protected by marshes, and exhibiting the remains of woodland, in the centre of which is the ancient station of Swanscombe. Here Sweno, the Dane, had encamped amidst the mounds and fortifications of an earlier age, but which, thenceforth, received their name from his occupation of the locality. According to the tradition, so long the pride of Kent, as William advanced,

The City yields.

William advances towards London.

1066

Kent yields without bloodshed.

he saw the wood, like another Birnam, moving towards him; and when the branches were thrown down, he beheld the men of Kent in battle array, headed by the Abbot Ægelsine. How was William, so little expecting opposition, appalled at this array, threatening not only difficulty but danger! A parley took place; the men of Kent, Stigand being amongst them, demanded the preservation of their ancient liberties. William assented to the terms, and entering Rochester, conducted by the confederates, he was acknowledged by the kingdom of Kent as their legitimate ruler. The poetry in this tradition must not induce us to reject its substantive truth; nor must we any longer consign the incident to the romance of history. It is to this treaty that the men of Kent ascribe the territorial privileges which their county still enjoys; the immunity which protects the land from forfeiture, or, according to the old rhyme, "the father to the bough, the son to the plough," and possibly the equal division of the land amongst the male issue. The first of these rights appears always to have been peculiar to Kent; the latter prevailed to a very large extent in other parts of England, in different customary tenures, and still exists in the immediate vicinity of London. The hamlet of Kentish Town, now merged in the metropolis, perhaps commemorates some migration of an antient community. The his-

Kentish privileges.

tory of Gavelkind is one of the most vexed questions amongst our legal antiquaries, and I shall not pursue it; contenting myself with the observation, that, taking the transactions of the wood of Swanscombe at their lowest value, they fully evidence the main fact, that the Kentish men, having awed the Conqueror into an unwilling pacification, received from the beginning that greater share of indulgence which allowed them to retain a large portion of their antient usages undisturbed.

1066

Derived from the surrender to William.

§ 5. From Rochester, William, sending out a detachment to begin the siege of London, crossed the country to Winchester. The city had been assigned in dowry to Editha. William, claiming as the heir and kinsman of the Confessor, was bound to respect his widow. He therefore entered not within the walls, but required that the citizens, as elsewhere, should render tribute and proper fealty; and consulting with the queen, they assented. Still sending on forces to London, William proceeded through Surrey and Berks, not attempting to cross the Thames until he passed over at Wallingford. This point was said by the great Duke of Marlborough to be peculiarly defensible, and it subsequently became of much importance in the civil wars. William chose it, without doubt, for the purpose of defending London from attacks on the Mercian side. Here he was followed by Archbishop Stigand, who now

William at Winchester.

Moves again on London.

sought the king's peace, and abandoning the cause of the Atheling, proffered his homage; and William, on his part, made a show of accepting him, in the words of the chronicle, as his spiritual father. In the meanwhile, London still continued untouched; but William now advanced, and his forces spread all around the stubborn city. When stationed on the walls of London, the burghers might see the circling horizon glowing with red flame.

William, when he began to conduct the siege in person, occupied two points, and chose for his own stations Barking on the east, and the ancient Palace of Westminster on the west. The siege now began in earnest. Catapult and Balista cast their showers upon the dwellings; and the old Roman walls, ascribed to Julius Cæsar, or to Constantine, shook before the repeated blows of the battering-rams. So strong was the city, that it defied the attack; it was long before the citizens would acknowledge that they felt terror; and here also were those men of most renown, the Northern Thanes, the men of Anglo-Danish race, together with their metropolitan, Aldred, determined upon resistance. Singleness of counsel might even yet have prevailed, but Stigand had set the example of defection, and the Normans had many lurking friends. There was a citizen of note, one Ansgard, who in former battles had received so many wounds that he was unable to walk, and was borne about the narrow streets in a litter. A secret negotiation was opened between him and William. Ansgard summoned the rulers of the city, expatiated upon the threatening dangers, and exhorted them to submit to William's authority, as King Edward's lawful heir. They assented to the proposal, and Ansgard repaired to the presence of the Conqueror. With fair words and fairer promises was the Elderman received; and on his return, he addressed the full folkmoot of council and citizens, *senatus et vulgus*,—for the two orders are distinctly marked,—expatiating upon William's magnificence and glory, "wise as Solomon, bountiful as Charlemagne, ready in fight like the great Alexander." All resistance vanished. Edwin and Morcar, who seem at first to have hovered about London, and then returned to it, were amongst the first who gave in their adhesion to the Norman. Archbishop Aldred and Wolfstan of Worcester followed their example; the Londoners renounced Edgar as lightly as they had accepted him; throwing open their gates, they proceeded as suppliants to the presence of the Norman, bearing with them the keys of the city, and delivering to him the person of his infant competitor. William was holding his court in the palace where the Confessor had been accustomed to wear his crown. Courteously did he greet the Atheling: he kissed the child;

and harsh as his character may have been, he never deviated from kindness towards the descendant of Cerdic, often as he was provoked, often as Edgar disdained his protection, or rose against his power.

§ 6. None of these submissions made William king; and now ensued those transactions which really placed him on the throne, the assumption of the crown, in which we have to consider whether William acted with crafty policy, or the English, blindly, ignorantly, or influenced by culpable servility. When discussing William's assumption of the royal authority, it is needful to consider in this action both the personal character of the man, and the nature of his office. It is in the latter point that the chief difficulty lies. To identify William at the period of his accession, to understand the true sentiments of the parties, we must guard against the deception exercised by titles of dignity, and recollect that though the symbol continues the same, the value annexed to it has sustained the greatest change. The first proposition that William should assume the title of king proceeded from the English themselves, the bishops declaring, on the part of the people, that they were accustomed to be ruled by none but regal authority; a suggestion ascribed to the corruption of his gifts, or the terror excited by his power. Yet, are such representations correct? Do they not rather exhibit the prepossession of the modern writer than the facts and feelings of the eleventh century? Surely the influence of the prelates over the people was legitimate. They were the chief members of the great council, the parliament, if you choose so to call it, who could then be assembled; and with respect to the general conduct of the English, a closer examination of the principles still existing in our constitution will show that self-preservation at this juncture prompted them to take refuge under the Norman sceptre as their only protection against anarchy, and in the conviction that by thus acting, they best served their country's cause.

Submission not blameworthy.

Unless William assumed the supreme authority, they must seek out another king; even Sweno of Denmark would have been welcomed. Without a king, they had no chance of security in hearth or home. Our feeling with regard to the royal authority is very different to that which then prevailed. With us, royalty is the realization of a theory: with the Anglo-Saxons, royalty was a necessity. It was not a mere prejudice or prestige which influenced the various ranks and orders to urge that William should be anointed and crowned, but the most cogent sense of immediate need. We may respect the royal office, we may appreciate that exalted station, we may truly be pervaded with loyalty, we may entertain affection for the sovereign's person; but, in our present state of society, and

Necessity for a king.

<small>1066</small> still more under our present imperial form of government, we do not in the least appreciate how an Anglo-Saxon was compelled to be constantly thinking of the king, as much as every soldier thinks of his general, every child of his parent, every servant of his master. Without a king, the body politic was paralyzed: they required a king *de facto*, an active king, a reality: one who could sit on the judicial bench, judge the offender, decide the controversy, bear the <small>Edgar barred by his youth.</small> shield, wield the sword. Edgar, the effigy of a king, was disqualified, not by the meanness of his capacity, an imputation which, in spite of the partial testimony of the monkish flatterer of the Norman line, is contradicted by the whole tenor of his life, but by helpless infancy. All this resulted from the peculiarities of the Anglo-Saxon constitution: a period during which there was a mutual balance of the powers of subject and sovereign; effected not so much by the means of any national legislature or assembly, as by the division of authority between the courts of the people, the folk-courts, and the prerogative jurisdiction of the king's court, both being essential to the well being of the community.

§ 7. When the first burst of enthusiasm excited by the proclamation of the Atheling had subsided, then the English were roused to a full sense of their impending danger. They were appalled by the absence of a king. Rarely delegating his powers to others, no veil of etiquette, no train of attendants, no mist of forms and ceremonies concealed the sovereign from the people: his hall was open; the king presided in his own court, listened to the complaints of his people on the throne, at the gate, beneath the tree, commanded his own soldiers, pronounced the sentence upon the traitor, spoke out his favours, invested his prelates, opened his own purse with his own hands. All the active powers of the commonwealth sprang from the very person of the king, as the visible centre of unity, the centre around which every sphere revolved. Those who are acquainted with the affairs of the United Provinces, are aware how many of the needful powers of government were in abeyance during the non-existence of a Stadtholder, and how much therefore the appointment of such a head was recommended under any circumstances of political danger, and this in communities which, severally, possessed sovereign power. But the closest approximation to the condition of the Anglo-Saxon commonwealth, wanting a king, may be obtained by considering what would have been the state of England, if, upon the abdication of James, William of Orange had not proceeded to take possession of the throne; and Parliament, repudiating the Stewarts, and yet not daring to supply the royal authority by any power of their own, or by any fiction

In those days, the king must govern as well as reign.

Analogous cases of vacancy.

§ 1006

Abeyance of law during Interregna.

of law, an absolute interregnum had ensued. What then would have been the state of England? The king is the source of all justice: the judges are merely his delegates. With the death of the king, all the powers which he has granted by his commissions of every description expire. Borough and manerial courts continue to subsist, and may continue to punish such offences as are within their local cognizance; but none of the offences requiring the jurisdiction of Sessions or Quarter Sessions, Assize, or Oyer and Terminer, or jail delivery, can be redressed. No judgment can be given in Westminster Hall; King's Bench, Common Pleas, Exchequer, are all defunct: no chiefs or *puisne* justices, no Lord Chancellor to administer equity; no *capias* can be issued, no writ of execution sealed; none of the public revenues can be lawfully collected. All the sources of discretionary grace and favour are dried up; the recorder has passed sentence, but the mayor cannot pardon; no tenant of crown-lands can obtain a renewal of his lease; no dignity can be granted, no bishopric bestowed; yet more, the army, the navy, are entirely disbanded: no one can dare to give the word of command. In short, all the branches of public and national administration and jurisdiction would have come to an end.

§ 8. Moreover, the powers of ruling as the sovereign of the Anglo-Saxon empire were deemed to be so completely inherent in the king, the sworn king, the anointed king, the crowned king, as to render it impossible to supply the royal authority by any other chief magistrate or form of government. It is well known how strongly the same sentiments prevailed in England during the Commonwealth and Protectorate, and how much they contributed towards the restoration of the monarchy. Men felt that the value, the efficacy, the sanctity of the title of king could not be transferred or annexed to any other name of dignity. Had Cromwell boldly acceded to the humble Petition and advice, England never would have seen Charles Stuart on the throne. So innate and inveterate was the opinion, that no republican lawyer, Daniel Axtell himself, could ever well understand how it was possible to arrest John Doe unless by the king's writ of *capias*, or to imprison the petty larcener unless the offence was duly laid in the indictment as a breach of the king's peace, and against his crown and dignity. But let us consider the subject further. Let us endeavour to cause our thoughts to answer the Anglo-Saxon thoughts, and the more will the invincible reasons for the restoration of the royal dignity open upon us. An Anglo-Saxon King was, as all his successors ever have been, a responsible functionary. He holds his supreme dignity upon condition; he must answer for himself if need be. Concurrent with

1066

Constitutional limitations to the Royal power.

the inauguration of the Anglo-Saxon King was his covenant with his subjects: his throne was founded upon justice. Magna Charta did not create the compact between king and people; the Petition of Right did not create the compact between king and people; the Bill of Rights did not create the compact between king and people; the Act of Settlement did not create the compact between king and people; that doctrine prevailed long before. The king engaged to govern according to law, and sealed the compact before the altar. Those who only know the name of Archbishop Dunstan in connexion with an idle legend, or an exaggerated and perverted history, or a poetical distortion of his character, will be surprised to learn that he was the individual who dictated the pact, defining the extent, and limiting the abuse of sovereign power. He penned the coronation oath; and the coronation oath developed became the British Constitution.

William hesitates to assume the legal position.

Unless William consented to wear the crown as Ethelred had done, all these constitutional securities would be for ever lost. William hesitated, and consulted with his Norman baronage. "Great troubles still prevail," said he. He desired tranquillity rather than glory. Should he attain and be confirmed in the high dignity of royalty, he wished that Matilda should wear the crown by his side. His advisers reiterated their request. Still he demurred, until Aymery of Thouars took up the discussion: he urged William not to delay, and all about him were unanimous in the same sentiments; and, certainly, if the English had good reasons for seeking to induce the Conqueror to declare himself the legitimate successor of the Confessor, his own followers must have very sincerely concurred in that desire. By so doing, all the laws, all the usages of England, would be preserved, and be their guarantee for their rights, their possessions, and their liberties. National pride, the honour of the Norman name, may have had some share, self-interest more. Shrewd and sound reasoners were the Normans in all things of law and government. William had long since promised his barons land and fee in England. If he made his grants to them without any definition of his own authority, without any certain law, they would have had no law to defend them. Duke William was almost a despot in Normandy; what would he be if ruling as the victor in England?

§ 9. Furthermore, William, in assuming the royal title and in conforming to the constitution upon the postulation of the English, acted with entire consistency. He had always asserted a legal right: ostensibly, he had sought nothing more. Godwin himself testified against Harold: the father accused the usurpation of the son. William might and did assert that he had offered to submit the decision of his claim to an adjudication, according to the course, either of English or of Norman law. Harold had appealed to the battle field: the event of the ordeal won for the victor the rights of the usurper; but the Conquest was not to give him the mere military right of ruling over England. Such, at least, was the theoretical principle of William's first acquisition of the crown, a theory never forgotten, though soon destined to be counteracted by sorrow and misfortune.

William's promise to maintain law.

This compact was made with the English; but William asserted a far wider claim, and promulgated his charter to the whole of his empire. One faith to be kept, peace and security, concord, justice, and judgment to be observed and defended amongst Englishman and Norman, Frenchman and Breton, Wales and Cornwall, Picts and Scots of Albany, and throughout every island, province, or country, constituting the Empire of Albion; and all throughout that empire were to be faithful to William, and defend him against his enemies; all the free men, throughout the empire, were to hold their possessions in quietness and in peace, free from all exactions and all unjust talliage, so that nothing should be taken from them, and nought exacted except their free service, due by law, and as it should be enacted by the common council of the realm.

With respect to William's reluctance, represented, as it has often been, as the result of dissimulation and feigned humility, its causes are ambiguous. Possibly some witty Jongleur had even then put into jingle the statesman's apophthegm, *la parole a été donné à l'homme pour couvrir ses penseés:* William hesitated, like Cromwell and Cæsar; but his hesitation, unlike theirs, was the preliminary to assent; a disclaimer, followed by an acceptance, claims no great credit for its sincerity, and yet it might be sincere. William himself may have seen that his acceptance of the title of king would limit his authority. Moreover, when any object, long and anxiously sought, is obtained, we accept it with more fear than joy, shrinking instinctively from that which we have coveted, and saddened by the forebodings that the fulfilment of human wishes will never satisfy the desires of the human heart.

§ 10. Preparations were now to be made for the coronation: the right of administering the oath, performing the ordination, and placing the crown on the king's head, belonged to none but the Archbishop of Canterbury, as the representative of the community. Stigand had already become William's homager, and had forwarded his cause; but William repelled him at once from the office, and upon the ground, that, having obtained his elevation by unlawful means, he was unworthy to perform the sacred office; and Aldred, Archbishop of York, without any precedent, and contrary to every privilege, was appointed to officiate in his stead. As in the case of his predecessor, the coronation was prepared to be celebrated in the Abbey of Westminster. William caused the monastery to be surrounded by Norman soldiery: their ranks closed around,—the objects of curiosity, perhaps, of fear, to the surrounding crowds. This precaution might seem to indicate apprehension of attack, though none was declared. Archbishop Aldred opened the proceedings. He presented William to the English who filled the interior of the building. At an earlier period, the king would have been inaugurated beneath the open sky. Aldred was celebrated for his eloquence. After a proper and fitting discourse, grave and well composed, addressed to the English in their own English tongue, he presented William to the multitude, and asked the people, as of old, if they acknowledged him as their king. Gosfried, Bishop of Coutances, turning to the Normans, enquired of them, in like manner, if they were willing that their duke should assume the royal authority. All assent, and the loudest shouts of gladness rend the air. Next followed the solemn ritual: the prayers began, but the very ceremony of the compact which William was concluding with the people over whom he was called to rule, became the means of destroying the mutual confidence of the sovereign and the community. Cloud and storm are not more uncontroullable by human foresight than the movements of a multitude. It is an awful feeling to stand without a building wherein any important event is taking place, the impassive walls enclosing so much passion within. When the shouts, testifying the acceptance of William as a sovereign, burst from the Abbey, the Norman soldiery, ignorant of their import, or purposely misconstruing them, assumed the acclaim to be the token of insurrection and treason. They immediately fired the adjoining buildings; all, without doubt, of timber, and thatched with reeds or straw. The conflagration spread with so much rapidity, as to be quickly seen within the Abbey, and all the crowd there, of every rank and degree, the clergy excepted, rushed out in terror. Amidst this alarm the service proceeded. William was anointed with the holy oil. He took the oath upon the Gospel-book, kissing the golden cross, and swore that he would defend Holy Church, forbid all rapine, and rule the people committed to his charge, according to the law. Yet such was the contagion of the panic, that the officiating clergy could scarcely proceed. William himself, who never before had known apprehension, trembled with very fear; and thus was the diadem placed upon his head by Aldred, when he was confirmed as sovereign of the Island Empire. The victor of Hastings was agued with terror when receiving his prize.

[sidenotes: 1066; Alarm of Normans: the fire.]

Effect of ill omens on similar occasions.

From the first moment, this incident was accepted by the English as a portent of calamity, and it was permitted to work its accomplishment. The mischance was imputed to Norman fraud or cruelty: and these suspicions were followed by plans of vengeance. This portent darkened the first paragraph, as it were, in William's reign; and how strangely, in our subsequent history, did such apparently fortuitous events become realities! It was in that Abbey that Charles, altering, without assignable cause, the colour of his royal robe, appropriated to himself the prophecies which told the misfortune of the White King. When he thus came to the throne, could people forget, how, as Prince of Wales, the thunderbolt had struck down the ostrich plumes? and when the royal standard, at Nottingham, was cast down by the winds of heaven as soon as raised, did it ever wave again in prosperity?

William withdraws.

§ 11. This interruption to the ceremony seems to have postponed a most important portion of the transaction, the receipt of the homages. Immediately after the coronation, William quitted Westminster, and returned again to Barking, sheltering himself in the forest, disporting with hawk and hound, and, at the same time, superintending the important works already commenced under the direction of his clerk, Gundulph, towards the eastern extremity of

London. Here the English chieftains repaired to him, few in number, for few were surviving, and none of those who had partaken in the conflict of Hastings. Edwin and Morcar, who had abandoned Harold in the fight; Copsi, from the north, bearing with him the fame of honour and valour and truth; Thurkill, of Limesi, one of the few English who afterwards retained their possessions under the new dynasty; Siward and Aldred, the sons of Ethelgar, King Edward's nephew; Edric, the wild, as much a Cymric as an English lord; and some others of inferior degree, came forth and submitted, seeking his grace and favour, and having taken the oaths of fealty, received back their possessions from his hands. Yet this proceeding must not be construed into a restoration of forfeitures incurred by resistance: on the contrary, it was an acknowledgment of their previous right: it was that renovation of the bond of homage which became necessary, as the recognition of the new lord or sovereign, when death had dissolved the previous engagement; and down to our own day, the repetition of the same ceremony by prelates and peers, upon the accession of the sovereign, attests that most antient principle of our monarchy.

Tranquillity now outwardly prevailed again. It was a lurid calm; yet all seemed quiet. William, however, fully knew the extent of his dangers, and they were such as required the utmost exertion of every talent, as well of the statesman as of the warrior. His situation was most complicated: he had assumed the crown, not in the character of an ambitious invader, but as a lawful sovereign asserting his legitimate rights. He was, if possible, to forget the existence of the party by whom he had been opposed; and, exercising merely so much rigour as was needful for the purpose of shewing his confidence in his own cause, to abstain from any appearance of revenge.

§ 12. Claiming as the national king, he was bound to govern upon national principles, to conciliate public opinion, and to fulfil the compact which had placed him upon the throne, a peaceful sovereign, governing according to law. But, as Duke of Normandy, he was under great and heavy engagements towards those who had assisted him in the enterprize, all volunteers, not one of whom he could have compelled to cross the channel against his own free will,—all who had expected, and many who had been promised, to be guerdoned by the riches of England. All who had fitted out the ships which conveyed his troops, all who had assisted him in council at Lillebonne, or at Hastings in the field, and this not alone to his own liegemen, but to the mixed and mingled multitude, Bretons, Flemings, Poitevins, all who had joined in the enterprize.—All, whether of high or low degree, were equally expectant. Not only barons, knights, and vavassours, but the churls, the peasants, the menials, the craftsmen, the varlets, who had formed a part of the host: all that rascal rout, the followers of the army, bearing the same relation to the more noble robbers, that cur and jackal do to the lion,—butchers, cooks, jugglers, barbers, bakers, long-bowmen and cross-bowmen, monks who had wandered from the cloister, and priests neglectful of their vows, all mingled together, and all ravenous for the prey and depredation of England. It was a hard matter, indeed, to reconcile these most discordant characters, of King of England and Duke of Normandy, and the slightest indiscretion might either bring on a national resistance on the part of the English, or a rebellion of the Norman soldiery. And had there been no other cause of apprehension, still William would have found it most arduous to preserve the station in which alone success could be expected, that of watching for every occasion, and profiting by all.

marginalia: 1066. Mixed character of those who came over with the Conqueror.

§ 13. In truth, however, the Conquest had hardly begun: William had gained nothing beyond a portion of Harold's earldom: the Northumbrians would acknowledge no earl except one of their own choice, and how imperfect would be the obedience of such an earl to the King at Winchester or Westminster. In the districts beyond the marsh-lands, so near to the spot

marginalia: Limits of William's sovereignty.

where he then was stationed, and yet so inaccessible, Edgar Atheling was still recognized; the west had given no token of obedience: the Kings of the Scots and of the Britons were to be coerced into obedience; but, above all, how was he to withstand that enemy, which, occupying so large a portion of the island, encircled him, as it were, on every side? From the first moment of his accession, to the end of his reign, the battle-axe of the Dane was glittering before him. He learned to defy the convulsive efforts of the English: he disdained the anger of the King of the French, but the Dane never allowed him to rest.

Almost from the Thames to the Firths of Scotland, there was a Danish population of more or less density, Danish Earldoms in the far north and in the Isles, Erin overcome by the Danish strength, Jutland and the Isles of the Baltic preparing to send forth their forces; and the sea, not a protection against the invaders, but their path, their home.

When it was first heard in Denmark how William had invaded England, the intelligence excited the most hostile and angry feeling. What the Danes once had held they never abandoned, never deemed their right to be barred. William's enterprize was viewed as an invasion, not made upon Harold, but upon their own inheritance. There was no longer any national sympathy between the Northmen and the Normans. The exploits of Earl Rollo, Rudo-jarl, might become the subject of a Saga, but his descendants were Frenchmen, now speaking a strange tongue, and entirely severed from their antient kinsmen in Scandinavia; and there was no feeling of sympathy or community of interest by which hostility could be restrained. When William was in the height of his exultation at his recent conquest, perhaps, on the very day of his coronation, a Danish knight appeared before him, bearing the defiance of the Danish King. "Let him render homage and tribute for his kingdom of England: if he refuses, let him expect that Sweno will forthwith deprive him both of crown and kingdom." The danger was in every way imminent: the arrival of Sweno, who would be supported by so large a number of his own race in England; and the whole coast, from the mouth of the Thames to the Humber,—Essex, Suffolk, Norfolk, Lincoln, and York, invited almost his invasion. But William had fully prepared himself, and organized his plans; and he pursued them from the first moment of his landing, to the conclusion of his reign; and this rendered him the founder of the British Empire.

§ 14. William began by fully demonstrating that he would enforce the supremacy of the law: as far as his power extended, he entirely restored tranquillity. He made a progress through the whole of that part of England which obeyed him, extending, probably, for we can only speak on imperfect notices, in a species of diagonal line from Oxford, or thereabouts, to the Humber; but yet including large districts which retained a species of virtual independence. Wherever he ruled, the highways were cleared from robbers. Watling Street and Ikenild Street were traversed as safely as they might have been in the days of Mulmutius. Foreign traders, the Dane, the Fleming, the German, resorted in safety to the ports, bringing profit to the dealer, and custom to the king. No taxes yet were levied, for William had just taken possession of the contents of the treasury. His soldiery were rigidly restrained from rapine and violence. Not a meal could be taken from an Englishman against his will, nor an insult offered to the daughters of the land. This was a wise policy on his part: it was good for the English people, but better even for the Norman invaders that they should be thus held in. Had they been allowed at this juncture to disperse themselves in the towns and over the provinces, how easily might they have been cut off and destroyed by any popular insurrection. There might have been another repetition of the massacre of St. Brice's day. He made no distinction of persons in the administration of justice, excepting, perhaps, that punishment fell heaviest upon his own followers if they offended. The usages of the country continued inviolate: he came as the heir of his cousin, the Confessor, and his cousin's laws continued the code of the land, simply because no other jurisprudence was recognized or introduced; and it is possible that that formal conformation [confirmation (?)] of them which now exists, may date from the commencement of William's reign.

London obtained a special covenant. "William the King, greets William the Bishop, Godfrey the Port-reeve, and all the burgesses within London, friendly. Ye shall be worthy to enjoy all the laws ye were worth in King Edward's days. Every child shall take to his father's inheritance after his father: no man shall do you any wrong."—Few words: this precious document, still perfect as the day when the pen passed upon the parchment, still in the Guildhall, still in the City archives, still in the very treasury of the successors of the old Port-reeves and burgesses, lies within the palm of your hand; but contains in its brief compass all that the citizens could or can require. William guarantees to them, not this jurisdiction or that franchise, nor does he set out their boundary or measure their houses and lands; but he secures them all: William the Conqueror secures to the citizens of London, collectively and individually, all the rights, all the freedom, which, amidst every chance and change, they alone, of all the burgher communities in England, nay, of all the municipalities in Christendom, have retained till the present day. In each charter granted by successive kings, by Normans and Plantagenets, York, Lancaster, and Stewart, the grant of William is repeated as the first chapter of their great book of civil liberties. Yet there was one to whom gratitude was due from London, besides William the King. It was William the Bishop whose influence aided in obtaining this special grant. Bishop William's tomb had been demolished during the general devastation of the memorials of ancient piety; yet, until the structure of St. Paul's was consumed, the Lord Mayor and aldermen, when on the "Scarlet Days" they resorted to the Cathedral, turned aside as they advanced up the nave, and visited the gravestone which covered his remains, as some small token, now that the lamps were extinguished, and the obit suppressed, and the dirge no longer sung, of their respect for Bishop William's memory.

§ 15. William furthermore employed this period in making the circuit of his dominions so far as he could venture; and during the whole of his reign he annually, whenever time allowed, wore his crown at the three great festivals of Christmas, Easter, and Whitsuntide, in three of the great cities, of Wessex, Mercia, and Danelagh. This was not a mere matter of state or policy. According to the Anglo-Saxon constitution, all remedial jurisdiction was annexed to the person of the king; and William, in order that he might the better be enabled, like his predecessors, to administer justice to the suitor, and to grant grace and mercy to those by whom it might be sought, endeavoured, perhaps promised, to learn the English tongue. This, however, was never accomplished by him: the excuse was found in the troubles and cares of royalty, and, as it was said, in the inaptitude of mature and advancing age.

1066

Tries to learn English.

Many of these measures had, without doubt, their full effect. It was by William's civil administration, however mixed with violence, that England, about to split into fragments, was knit and bound together, in order that it might become one realm, under one High Court of Parliament, one king. The Conquest did not give us our constitution, but prepared the way for the constitution, through many an age of turmoil and trouble; and for turmoil and trouble William was immediately prepared

Spirit of his administration.

§ 16. It was a notorious fact, to friend and foe, to Normans and English, that the paucity of defensible strongholds in England had contributed equally to the successes of the Danes as to William's own. Not that strongholds were entirely wanting. Some Roman fortifications still existed, and were strong and defensible. They had enabled the Londoners to resist William's forces: they had almost turned him at Dover. Exeter was confident in the

Fortifications.

power of resistance which the fortifications of the Cæsars would give. Colchester and Chester might equally have depended upon theirs; but some places which the Romans had fortified had become waste and desert, and there were no citadels in the most important points, which William's strategic genius showed him ought to be occupied against a foreign, or still more, an internal enemy. There was, at this moment, evidently no object more important than that of restraining the population, should it become discontented, and of preventing a multitude, brooding insurrection, from becoming an open enemy.

During William's residences at Barking, he had begun, as before mentioned, his works adjoining London. As the citizens looked at the trenches, broken by his pioneers, hard by the river Thames, they might, perhaps, at first doubt, or not be willing to understand, the intent of the builder. A royal palace the fabric was, and indeed still is, according to law, and here we may enter the great council chamber, supported by pillars of oak, hard as iron, and the royal chapel, whose massy columns and circular apse remind you of the Norman Basilica. The builder, as it seems, was one Gundulph, a monk of Bec, a friend of Lanfranc, and who seems to have obtained the rank of chaplain in William's court. But the building was also a palace of defence: the fosse became deeper, and the flood gates were made and opened which let in the water of the river as it rose and fell with the tide, and the walls grew higher and higher, and the works now known as the Tower rapidly arose under the direction of the master mason who stood by. The model of this building was found in William's own birth-place, Falaise, no other alteration having been made except what was necessary from the difference of locality: our Tower upon the low banks of a great stream, Falaise with the living rock for its core. A monument of foreign domination was therefore now constantly before the Barons of London: yet it is remarkable that the King, yielding either to respect for the rights of that powerful, unruly, and jealous community, or to apprehension of the indignation which he might excite by their infringement, encroached as little as possible upon the city ground. He erected it over the old Roman wall, of which a portion may yet be traced within the building. More than one half, therefore, of the Arx Palatina, as it was proudly called, was and is in Middlesex: and whilst an ample circuit of the hamlets in the shire land on the eastern side of the boundary was placed under the authority of the Royal Constable, his jurisdiction in the municipal territory does not extend beyond the very gates of the fortress. Even on the shore of the river, this military

margin: 1066. Falaise Castle the model for the White Tower. Its position.

jurisdiction, important as it must have been, was ill-defined:—and because William hesitated in his usurpations of 1067, the extent of the powers derived from his acts is at this day contested by the magistracy against a warrior more distinguished than the Conqueror, to whose hand the crown has now intrusted the keys of the fortress.

William dreaded the citizens, and dared not himself confront them within their city. But he gained this object by other means, not less effectual, and yet without offending their pride. Through the intervention, as incidental circumstances,—for history is silent,—enable us to collect, of the Bishop of London, Ralph Baynard obtained the ancient soke or jurisdiction far within the city, but like the Tower, on the shores of the Thames, upon which he erected the castle which bore his name. It became the head of his extensive barony, which included fifty lordships and more, in Essex, in Suffolk, in Norfolk, in Hertfordshire, rendering him one of the most powerful of the Norman Baronage. Great were the privileges and honours held in London by Ralph Baynard; he and his heirs bore the Banner of the City, and in time of war, he came forth from the great door of the Metropolitan Cathedral, and received from the hands of the Port-reeve and the Aldermen the sign, "bearing thereon the semblance of the Patron Saint in silver and in gold," which he was to wave for the honour and service of the community. [1066] And many other were the privileges of Baynard in time of war and of peace: above all, that when the citizens held their Great Council, he was ever to attend the same, and to sit on the hustings next to the chief magistrate; whilst all the judgments given were pronounced by his mouth, and "according to his memorial" there to be recorded. Wise in this was the policy of the Conqueror, ingrafting the highest of the Norman lineages upon the ancient Saxon stock, and thus binding the conquering and the conquered race by a unity of interest, privilege, and power. Nor was this wisdom unrewarded, for whatever troubles disturbed the land, so long as the Conqueror and his children reigned, London never swerved from her fidelity. *Loyalty of London.*

§ 17. William steadily pursued his system of over-awing the country with castles;—in proportion as his power extended, the square, tall Donjon towers arose, all formed upon the same type, bespeaking their origin, palaces at once and castles, trophies at once of royal forethought and of unsparing power. *Other fortifications erected during the course of William's reign.*

The defence of the coast had been the subject of William's consideration from the moment when he landed on it. It was needful for him not only to provide for the means of advance, but also for retreat, in case of adverse fortune. If the reader will take up the map, he will observe in Sussex a territorial division, whose aspect differs altogether from that which prevails elsewhere in England. In most of the other shires, it may be observed, that the Hundreds are compact divisions, often marked even now by natural boundaries, by streams and waters, and probably much more distinctly before the disturbance of the ancient demarcations—a process which appears often to have gone on silently, for the purposes at once of jurisdiction and of fiscal management. In Kent the Hundreds are much smaller in proportion than in East Anglia; but they are, as it were, bound up into larger divisions, called Lathes or Lastes: the latter generally with a reference to natural boundaries. In the West of England, in Somerset or Dorset, the Hundreds are small, irregular, and apparently broken up in different parts of the shire. We may, however, be certain, that the Hundred or the Lathe arose from two main causes: the natural dispersion of races and tribes over the country, and the consolidation of detached tracts or townships under one authority or lord. But we look in vain for any trace of system, except in Sussex alone; here we find a territorial division, bearing its own peculiar name, and displaying a scheme of partition skilfully planned to sustain the empire of the Conqueror. The Normans were a hard people: wherever they conquered, they conquered outright. Plunderers they were, and they acted consistently: they divided the land by measurement, by the "rope" as it was called,—a process which singularly marked the native violence of their character. For in such allotments, they neglected and despised the natural relations previously existing amongst the people they had subdued. Now, this is the process which William effected in Sussex; the county is divided into six districts, extending right down from the northern border, each possessing a frontage towards the sea, each affording a ready communication with Normandy, and constituting, as it were, six military high roads to William's paternal Duchy. But few Norwegian or Teutonic terms can comparatively be found preserved amongst the Normans, but the "hreppar" seems to have been retained almost unaltered amongst them. Hence these demarcations were and still are termed *rapes*. Each possessed within its bounds some one castle, or other important station for defence or protection, and each appears to have been placed under one military commander. All the original Anglo-Saxon divisions are noticed in the Anglo-Saxon laws, and possessed an Anglo-Saxon tribunal; the rape is not noticed in any Anglo-Saxon law, and does not possess an Anglo-Saxon tribunal. Sussex sustained this great territorial alteration alone, being dealt with from the first moment entirely as a conquered territory. The adjoining shire of Kent was equally placed in a state of defence, by being assigned, as a Palatine Earldom, to Odo of Bayeux, and to him was entrusted the general government of the south of the Thames. One reason without doubt for placing this warlike prelate as a species of sovereign in Kent, was equally for the purpose of awing the Kentish men, and neutralizing the influence of Stigand, whom William greatly mistrusted, but could not immediately remove.

Negotiations with Sweno.

§ 18. A more complicated and far more difficult policy was required for the protection of the north, where, in addition to the obstacles of a discontented population, the coast was far more open to the threatened invasion of the Danes. It was there that most peril was to be apprehended. When Sweno gave his challenge, William did not allow his pride to overcome his prudence; he did not take up the gauntlet either literally or metaphorically; he met the defiance by craft and policy, and laboured to delay, if he could not avert, the impending storm. A temporary truce could always be purchased from the Danes: a most unwise expedient this in the weak, from whom more and more could be gained by terror; but William knew his own strength, and had fully settled how far he would trust to this expedient; as a negotiator, he chose Egelsine, the Abbot of St. Augustine's, who had been the means of winning or negotiating the Kentish capitulation. Others of distinction were adjoined in the embassy, bearing a store of money. They were well received in Denmark, and the gifts they brought being accepted by Sweno as the earnest of further tribute, hostilities were stayed. William, however, put no trust in this purchased pacification; sooner or later they would return insatiate for ravage and plunder. William therefore was imperatively called upon to consider how he could best organize the coast defence. Northumbria and East Anglia, from their position on the wide German sea, and from the affinity of the population, would most probably invite and welcome the invaders. In the more distant parts, beyond the Humber, though submission had in a degree been proffered, William himself would not venture. Such an expedition, at a juncture when his affairs were yet so precarious, would have been an act of rashness, not of courage; but Copsi, the lord of large domains, feared for his valour, and honoured for his character, the friend of St. Cuthbert, whose See he had largely endowed, was empowered to assume the earldom under William's supremacy. It was a bold experiment in the Conqueror thus to trust an Englishman in a territory so striving for independence, and bolder still for Copsi to accept a dignity threatening its possessor with so much personal danger.

margin: 1066. Danes bribed for the present. William places the Saxon Copsi in Northumbria.

§ 19. When William was making his royal

progress, he might observe how carefully the Romans had laboured to defend that territory which even they so emphatically called the Saxon shore, from the pirates and marauders, the ancestors equally of William and of his Scandinavian enemies. Nowhere, perhaps, so evidently as in East Anglia; and amongst the many defences raised by them, the traces of some of which still subsist, none more remarkable than the fortified camp commanding the ancient settlement of the Iceni, of which an imperfect fragment of the vallum remains, a testimony of its former importance. The situation had been most wisely chosen by some commander about the age of Constantine, or somewhat later, when the encreasing weakness of the empire suggested more and more of those precautions, which, however well planned, were unable to avert its destiny. The Wensum, then wide and broad, offered the means of ready communication with the ocean, and the estuary beyond was at this time so deep and unencumbered by sand as to be reckoned an open sea. But when the island was abandoned by the Roman power, the station was gradually deserted; a new settlement was established, probably in the disturbed period after the martyrdom of Edmund, by a mixed population of English, Danes, and Norwegians, somewhat further up the river, at the Northwick, or bend; and the old traditional proverb,—

> "Caister was a city when Norwich was none,
> Norwich was built with Caister stone,"

1066

is without doubt a true record of its history; and thus arose the then new town of Norwich, so differing in its circular ground plan and tortuous streets from the cities built upon Roman foundations, and in which traces of their regular castrametation are always more or less to be observed.

Norwich: when built.

The place had acquired great importance; it was, like the rest of Harold's earldom, entirely in William's power, and he seems at once to have appreciated the advantages of this locality, and determined to render it his first advanced post towards the countries where his future operations would require most protection. He formed the plan of placing his castle in the very heart of the city, the better to controul a warlike and unruly population, "savage and perfidious," in the terms of the contemporary historian who very possibly accompanied him during the expedition, and whom he distrusted and feared as much as those of London. Availing himself of a small ridge of firm rising ground which protruded itself into the city, he separated the extremity or headland from the rest of the elevation, by a very deep ditch or fosse, thus obtaining a command over the city below, as effectually as if he had raised an artificial mound, which, if practicable, would have required enormous labour. *Blanche fleur*

The Castle built by William.

arose to the established Norman type, but circled by wide and extended fosses and ramparts, for which the soil was levelled; but not contented with this fortification, he directed, if he did not immediately execute it, the formation of a new borough, dependent upon the castle, and inhabited almost entirely by "Frenchmen." It is possible that, even in the days of the Confessor, some of these strangers may have settled there; but the conquest gave this new foreign settlement such extension, that it required two new parish churches, the one dedicated to St. Giles, and the other to St. Peter, which still exist according to their original consecration: and here Roger Fitz-Osbern was left as commander, with authority extending over the whole north of the realm.

§ 20. Very closely connected with all immediate measures of precaution and defence, but still more with William's whole frame of government at all future times, was the great financial scheme of paying his followers by English land. How great was the caution and judgment which this operation would require! Unquestionably the English must have been fully prepared for some great transfer. They probably tried to be cheerful. William at present was as benign as his stern nature admitted of; they enjoyed a real and present good, and evils might be hastened by anticipating them; yet it was impossible that they could forget the assembly at Lillebonne: they could not drive away the recollection that even some of the prelates, who had passed over with William, had, as it was reported, refused to perform this supererogatory service unless land and fee were granted to them in the country they were to win. Moreover, their ancestors had experienced exactly the same bitterness of spoliation from the Danes; and we cannot doubt but that when the Englishman was expelled from the township now called Ormsby by the Serpent,— for such is the meaning of Orm or Worm,—he went out full as unwillingly as if he had been chased away by a Norman Trussebot, or a Breton Botevilain. William had no choice but to fulfil his promises sooner or later, for his empire entirely depended upon it; but he was in a very different position from the Danes: the claimant who supported his title as heir to the Confessor, could not exert any open violence; and the first instalment, at least, which he had to make to his followers, was to be regulated by principles, which, though going to the full extent of the law, did not pass beyond.

According to the universal principle, there might be want of clemency, but no positive injustice in considering, that the domains of all who had been slain when actually bearing arms against him in the battle of Hastings, should be confiscated to the Crown. This at once gave him an enormous fund, so to speak, to draw upon. However acquired, the Godwin family were the largest landed proprietors in England, and the private domains of Harold are very carefully distinguished in the great survey from the demesnes of the Crown. A very large proportion of these estates were situated exactly in those districts where it was most convenient for William to appropriate them,—Sussex, Surrey, Kent, Middlesex, Essex, Suffolk, and Norfolk. Furthermore, the army at Hastings, being chiefly drawn from Harold's own Earldom, the slaughter cleared away whole families, fathers and sons, who perished in the field. All these estates were open to William's distribution, and he bestowed them with a most bounteous hand.

§ 21. In the next place it should seem that there was another royal prerogative, such as had been enjoyed by the Confessor, which also strengthened his right of disposal. We can collect, amidst the obscurity of the Anglo-Saxon tenures, that a great deal of land was held according to a system existing in certain customary holdings at the present day. The owner had the power of transmitting the possession to an heir by bequest, by *quothing* or speaking forth the name of his intended successor to the lord. Supposing any of those who died at Hastings were innocent of treason, yet this was a lapse of which the sovereign could lawfully avail himself, if he did not choose to exercise especial grace and favour.

Furthermore, whatever grants were made, the Norman was to hold the land exactly as his Anglo-Saxon predecessor had done, neither better nor worse, rendering neither less nor more to the sovereign, nor exerting, so far as William authorized or restrained him, either less or more dominion over the cultivators of the land. The same relief for the Earl, eight horses bridled and saddled, four hauberks, four helmets, four shields, four lances and four swords; the Baron's relief, four horses, two bridled and saddled, two hauberks, two helmets, two shields, two lances, two swords. The Vavasour's relief, his father's horse as his father rode it, or his helmet and his shield, his hauberk, his lance, and his sword; the Villein's relief, his best piece of cattle, his horse or his ox or his cow; but so long as he rendered his dues and performed his right service, never was he to be amoved from the land. And for the Danegeld, when Danegeld was to be paid, two shillings for each hide of land, nothing less and nothing more. And if any one was impleaded for rent or due or service, it was to be tried and judged by the law, as the law was *tempore regis Edwardi*, nothing less and nothing more; and no one was to enter upon the land without the king's writ, testifying his possession was legal, and if he had no writ he had no legal right to the land.

Under such conditions, it should seem that extremely ample endowments were made during the first seizin of the Conquest. Of gifts made to Churches in Normandy or in Flanders, we cannot here speak; but Odo, not as Bishop of Bayeux, but as Count Palatine of Kent, and in that secular capacity which rendered him his brother's officer as well as Baron, received a very large portion of the county. Another was given to Hugh, the son of Thurstan de Bastenberg, Hugh with the beard, who generally however was called Hugh de Montfort, and who was immediately received into William's full confidence. A third, to Eustace Earl of Boulogne; a fourth to Richard de Clare, who, bringing over with him the rope which had measured the ambit of the octroi of his town and castle at Brionne, was authorized by the Conqueror to measure the same circuit round Tunbridge and the castle which he built there, becoming, what still is called the lawy or leucata, the municipal boundary of the town. Another share was given to Hamo Dapifer; and these, together with a chaplain, one Albert, of whom nothing else is known, and the prelates and ecclesiastical communities, had the whole superiority of the shire. Sussex was divided in the same manner. Roger de Montgomery, the Norman of the Normans, styled, if not created Earl of Chichester and Arundel, or Sussex, William de Briosa, Robert de Mortaigne Count of Eu, William's brother, and William de Warrenne, divided the rapes between them. The Isle of Wight was given to Fitz-Osbern. All these subsequently obtained much more extensive baronies, as William's power and means advanced and encreased. It is not practicable to ascertain the others who received their rewards by Vavassories or Subtenancies. We only know that they were made to such an extent as to satisfy William's followers that he was not inclined to depart from his promise: whilst at the same time his eulogists might declare, with somewhat ostentatious truth, "Nulli tamen Gallo datum est quod Anglo cuiquam injustè fuerit ablatum."

§ 22. But there was another promise which remained to be fulfilled: the vow which he had made during the conflict of Hastings, that, on the spot where the victory was gained, he would raise the Abbey in veneration of St. Martin, the Apostle of the Gauls; and to place therein the monks of Marmoutier, whose prayers might make amends for the perpetrated slaughter. So dreadful had been the carnage, that the Normans gave the name of Sang-lac to the heath; and here William proceeded to raise the structure, marking out the site of the High Altar on the spot, where, as it was thought, the corpse of Harold had been found.

"King William bethought him also of that folk that was forlore
  And slain also through him in the battle before.
And there as the battle was, an Abbey he let rear
  Of Saint Martin, for the souls that there slain were.
And the Monks well enough feoffed without fayle,
  That is called in England, Abbey of Bataile."

The territory, for one league around the

1066

Commemorative character of the foundation.

Church, was granted to the monks with all the king's rights and prerogatives, as free as he held the same. Within this circuit arose the borough of Battle upon the old English scheme of territorial organization; and the name of Montjoie, by which one of the four wards or burghs is known, commemorates the locality where William remounting his battle steed, rode up in triumph. Furthermore, in the plenary exercise of his royal authority, William declared that the Church of St. Martin of Battle was to be exempted from all episcopal jurisdiction: the Abbot was to be as supreme as the Primate of Canterbury. But Stigand, Bishop of the South-Saxons, did not assent to this grant. Exemption from the jurisdiction of the ordinary had hitherto been exceedingly rare in England; and if any grant can be produced which is free from suspicion, there is none which has not been the subject of contest. William was peremptory: the monks of Mar-

Special privileges of the Abbey.

moutier were there: Goisfrid was appointed Abbot; and Battle emulated the discipline of the parent monastery. When Goisfrid sought consecration, Stigand required, that, according to the canons, he would repair to his real mother Church, to Chichester, and proffer his due obedience. William heeded not the canons, and commanded the Bishop to repair to the Abbey, and give the benediction before the altar of St. Martin; and to remove the all pretence of episcopal jurisdiction, the Conqueror also prohibited the Bishop and his train from lodging in the monastery, or even taking a meal there. The first contest was thus between the Norman and the English prelate, and the latter succumbed; but when Norman prelates succeeded, they used every endeavour to retain and regain all the rights which they had enjoyed in the old English Church; and the privileges granted to Battle Abbey, to the detriment of the Diocesan, occasioned the greatest discontent and jealousy. Constant litigation ensued, nor has the dispute been terminated by the extinction of the monastery. The Abbot of Battle has given place to the Dean of Battle, who claims the same exemption, and the Bishop, at the present day, opposes the immunity as the successor of Stigand.

1066

Donations and grants were accumulated upon this favoured foundation, perhaps, the only seat in England of Norman nationality. Here the monks unrolled, before a Degville or a Darcy, a Pigot or a Percy, a Bruce or a Despenser, a Balliol or a Bondeville, a Mowbray or a Morville, a Fichet or a Trivet, the roll containing the honoured names of the companions of the Conqueror, from whom they deduced their lineages and their names; and in after times, in the days of York and Lancaster, of the White Rose and the Red Rose, when time had obliterated the distinctions of race, and hallowed and softened the recollection of the past, when community of interests and participation

Acquisitions of the Abbey.

The Roll.

in the same sufferings, and in the same prosperity, had united the English into one people, Battle Abbey became the proud and pleasurable monument of antient prowess and glory. Not so when raised: it was intended far less as a trophy of victory and exultation, than as the retreat of sadness and repentance. Where the heather had been burned, it shot up again: and where the elastic herbage had been trampled away in the battle strife, it sprung up afresh; but men said, that whenever the fertilizing rain watered the ground, you might see the crumbly soil resume the colour of recent gore. Report exaggerates the most common events, still more those affecting the imagination or the feelings; but the fact is positively affirmed, and there is no reason to doubt, that there was a period when it was substantially true. Chemical analysis can no more account for the singularly indelible stain, resulting from the vital fluid, than for any of the other mysterious properties imparted to it; and we, in our own times, have witnessed the same appearance.

Chapter IX.

WILLIAM RETURNS TO NORMANDY—HIS TRIUMPHANT RECEPTION—OPPRESSIONS EXERCISED IN ENGLAND BY ODO OF BAYEUX AND FITZ-OSBERN—GREAT TROUBLES—THE ENGLISH INVITE EUSTACE OF BOULOGNE—WILLIAM RETURNS TO ENGLAND—REBELLION OF THE WEST—DEATH OF COPSI—WILLIAM SUBDUES THE INSURRECTION—MATILDA IN ENGLAND.

1067—1068

§ 1. DURING these transactions, William had been providently preparing for his return to Normandy. It must have been a source of great internal comfort to him, always to be able to place entire confidence in Matilda. No Sovereign ever appears to have been more happy in his wife. During his absence, she had governed the Duchy with entire prudence, assisted by the advice of Roger de Montgomery, the Norman of the Normans, and Ralph de Beaumont. Robert, young as he was, had been associated to her in the government of the Duchy, of which he had been declared the heir; and William had no reason to fear the extinction of his male lineage, there being two stout and healthy brothers, William and Richard, in whom the old family name was revived. Nevertheless, William, fully conscious of the chances to which Normandy was exposed, whe-

Government of Normandy during the Duke's absence.

ther on the side of Anjou or of France, could not think it safe to remain away after the great effort, which must, in some degree, have exhausted the Duchy; and the cautions with which he had made his arrangements, enabled him to do so consistently, with the foresight of the statesman and of the general.

William's conduct towards the Saxon Royal line.

In all William's conduct towards the English, whilst going to the very verge of rigour, he had avoided all measures which could be construed into an affront to the feelings of the higher classes. To the late royal family he paid, consistently, great respect and honour. Winchester was occupied by him like London; but Editha remained there so long as she lived, in tranquillity and honour. Githa, Godwin's widow, continued as yet to enjoy her great possessions. Agatha, the widow of Edward the Outlaw, and mother of the Atheling, remained under William's protection with her daughters, Margaret and Cristina; foreign names, and bespeaking the place of their nativity—the eldest being even then as remarkable for her beauty as she was afterwards for her talents and her piety. It was commonly reported that her kinsman, Edward the Confessor, had promised her in marriage to Malcolm Canmore, king of the Picts and Scots; and that he had covenanted to give or confirm the Lothians as her dowry. If such a betrothal really had taken place, May Margaret must have been in her earliest infancy. This circumstance in itself would not render the story incredible; but no heed was taken of it by William; and the Hungarian mother and her daughters resided probably at Romsey in Hampshire, where Cristina afterwards professed.

In order to supply his place by an effective government, William appointed Odo his brother and Fitz-Osbern, regents of the kingdom during his absence, associating also Grandmesnil in some of the powers of administration. They would watch, and vigilantly, against all who were to be coerced by the sword; but those who were to be dealt with more gently, William gradually and quietly brought closer and closer about his court and person; as well those who might become the unwilling agents, as the active causes of resistance. Of these, the first was the Atheling, always treated by him with kindness and affection. Notwithstanding the slur which had been cast upon Stigand's character, William continued to treat the primate and metropolitan of the British Islands with all the outward veneration appertaining to his high dignity, though inwardly there was none whose "perfidy" the king more feared. Agelnoth, the "Satrap" of Canterbury, was also under suspicion. Every effort was made by William to conciliate Edwin and Morcar; they had fully yielded, and William had promised his daughter, probably Constance, in marriage to the elder of these brothers, as the reward of having obtained the apparently cordial submission of the younger. Waltheof also was much courted by William, and the subsequent marriage of the Anglo-Danish chieftain with Judith, the Conqueror's niece, shews how intimate was the alliance which had been formed. Yet, notwithstanding this, all were more or less dreaded by William; and when he took them with him, and embarked at Pevensey, although they ostensibly appeared as his visitors, they probably were themselves aware that they were taken as hostages, if not as prisoners. Thus they proceeded through Kent, indignantly pacified: thus through Sussex, wasted and desolated, a desolation from which the country did not recover even till the conclusion of William's reign. Thus they passed the lake of blood, and the rising walls of the expiatory monastery; thus they reached Pevensey, where William had landed as the Duke of Normandy, where he had defied the adverse omen, and where he now embarked to return to his own land as a triumphant king.

§ 2. William's progress in Normandy, through town and burgh, and more particularly his entry into Rouen, was celebrated by the people, animated by all the contagion of enthusiasm. They compare him to those Roman Emperors whom they idealized as the types of human grandeur. Beloved as Vespasian, admired as Pompey;—but above all they paralleled him to the hero, who, in the romantic traditions of the country, emphatically *Romantic*, was deemed to be the paragon of nobility and valour. The popular veneration which had been rendered to Cæsar, was transferred to William: he now even shares with Cæsar in the lingering local traditions, testifying the impression made upon the popular mind; and whilst the peasant tells you that every grass-grown rampart is Cæsar's camp, so does he point out every stately Abbey as the foundation of the "Duc Guillaume," the monument of his piety and power. And those who more extolled him declared how prouder than the triumphal train of Cæsar was that which followed their sovereign. Cæsar only brought forth his prisoners in chains; but our Duke is followed by the most venerated of the priesthood, the best blood of the nobility of England.

But it was during the Paschal Feast at Fécamp that the great display was made. Here were exhibited the choicest treasures of the English kings: the results of foreign commerce and national industry, which had rendered England so flourishing amidst every calamity. William had invited to this feast a host of the nobles of France, who, mingled with Normans, and Bretons, and Flemings, were the spectators of his honour and glory. The guests raised with wonder as they quaffed from them the huge buffalo horns, tipped with gold and silver, often emptied before at the carouses at Westminster and Winchester. Lamps and coronals, which Bagdad and Byzantium might have prized, bespoke the skill of the craftsmen of London or Canterbury. Curtains and tapestries which had decked the halls of the Confessor or the bower of his Queen; robes and garments heavy with embroidery, worked by those who were now weeping for the husband or the son. "More wealth has the Duke brought over from England" was the general exclamation, "than could be found in thrice the extent of Gaul;" and the learned priest declared how England might be called another Araby for gold, and the very granary of Ceres for fertility. But the wealth of England scarcely excited so much general interest as the aspect of the more youthful among the strangers : their race still retaining that personal beauty, the long tresses of flowing auburn hair, which first led the great Gregory to seek their conversion.

§ 3. This era was certainly the culminating point of William's worldly prosperity. He was enjoying all the first fresh pleasure of success, as yet unalloyed by its inevitable chastening or punishment. Without being ostentatious, William was fully aware of the importance of extending his reputation, and the means which he employed were connected with what were considered as duties. To the Pope he sent the banner of Harold. Most ample gifts were bestowed upon the churches of Normandy, and the solemn dedication of the Abbey[s] of Dive and Jumièges prolonged the joyful solemnities. Furthermore, — 1067 — William continued and encreased his patronage of those who might well encrease his fame. His court had been long the resort of the learned. Here was Lanfranc, the great ornament of European literature. We collect also, that *Lanfranc.* amongst those who filled the high and confidential station of his chaplains, were many of distinguished talent, and he employed that talent for the celebration of his fame. William of *The Norman historians.* Poitiers may perhaps be reckoned among the first; the narrative of the deeds of his patron exhibits an attempt, not unsuccessful, [to imitate] the authors of classic Rome. Another was William of Jumièges, whose pages preserve many portions of the composition of his companion, which are lost in the original. A third was Guido, Bishop of Amiens, (especially retained by Matilda, who now was called Queen,) whose poem upon the battle of Hastings, a composition so long lost and so strangely recovered, furnishes some of the most remarkable details on the occupation of London.

A poem, written under these circumstances, *Guido's poem on Hastings.* possesses as much authenticity, considered as an historical composition, as any poem can possess. Addressed to Lanfranc, Guido, in his own generation, acquired the highest reputation: he was another Virgil in the opinion of his contemporaries. To us, plain prose would have been more satisfactory: yet, as a literary monument, and

1067 — as evidencing the current and course of opinion, the verse is most interesting and instructive. It was not by reviving the fading reminiscences of Scandinavia, or recurring to the deeds of the sea kings, that the eulogist now sought to win his Sovereign's favour: it was by the example of Rome's warriors and Rome's heroes that the instructor sought to form the character of the Norman warrior, and to exalt his praise. The encouragement thus given by William to learned men, his patronage, judiciously and liberally bestowed, produced lasting effects. Through these men he became known to us: a school of historians was formed, for whom no parallel can be found in that period of mediæval Europe, and from whom we derive those most abundant materials which enable us to pursue the history of the Conqueror and his times with so much comparative accuracy and facility.

Roman character of this poem.

William's stay in Normandy.

William continued in Normandy for upwards of nine months, attending closely to the administration of the country; well aware, without doubt, that his presence would soon be required again in England, for as yet the Normans had only military occupation: moreover, he was extremely desirous that Matilda should participate in his honour, and possess the real dignity as well as the name of Queen.

§ 4. In the meanwhile, his affairs were not so prosperous as at first; and the country had very rapidly passed from a state of apparent but deceitful quiescence, to declared insurrection. With the exception of London and some few of the adjoining shires, there was hardly a district which did not display either manifest discontent or actual resistance to the Norman power. Whilst William was present, his heavy hand restrained his own Normans as well as his newly acquired subjects, but no longer. The English had been stunned by the blow: they now began to feel the smart. Fitz-Osbern and Odo, proud, sullen, and violent, invested as Regents with royal authority, indulged in all the license of royal power, freed from royal responsibility. Even in the best settled states, it is usually the character of a Regency,—as great an internal calamity, short of civil war, as can befal a nation,—to exaggerate the vices and faults of the monarchy. It is a mode of government which has the smallest proportion of political conscience; and William's justiciars imbued themselves with his harshness and rigour, without acquiring his countervailing prudence, and his sense of the utility derived from the semblance at least of moderation and justice.

Their situation was certainly one of great difficulty. William, waiting his opportunity, had purposely abstained from exercising any direct authority in Northumbria. English Northumbria, Danish Northumbria, British Northumbria, Scottish Northumbria, none of which can be marked out by any very precise boundaries, but all possessing very different interests, would require great management, and he seems to have left it doubtful whether the country was or was not to continue under the government of English or Anglo-Danish Earls, ruling as Suzerains under his supremacy. The very ambiguous term of Procurator applied to Copsi, leaves us in doubt as to the authority which he was to possess. William, however, had obtained considerable influence. Archbishop Aldred, the northern Primate, whose spiritual authority extended, if they would allow him to exercise it, up to the furthest verge of the Orkneys, strenuously supported William; so did some powerful Thanes; but against Copsi there existed the strongest antipathy. On first entering Yorkshire, he expelled Oswulf, who wandered for a short time in the forest like an outlaw, but friends and followers joined him, and Copsi was slain by a sudden and general insurrection of the people. Northumbria reverted to his competitor, and as far as it extended, this was entirely an anti-Norman revolution;—and foreboded the greatest evil from the assistance it would render to the Danes.

Not less threatening, though more tranquil, was the situation of the West of England. William was here partially acknowledged by some of the great English land-holders, and cordially: amongst others by Eadnoth, the standard-bearer or marshal of the host of the Anglo-Saxon kings, a dignity attached to his possessions. Eudo, *1067* Count of Porthoet, one of the co-regents of Brittany, seems to have entered warmly into William's interests ; and one of his sons, Brian, commonly called Fitz-Count, seems to have passed over and occupied some position on the coast of Somerset or Devon. But Exeter would by *Independence of Exeter.* no means accept the Norman domination otherwise than upon conditions, even if the city would go so far ; but we infer from subsequent transactions that the men of Exeter and others had much more extensive plans, and that they were seeking to form a general league amongst the English Burghs against the common enemy. But a little more, and England might have become the first Federal Commonwealth in Christendom.

§ 5. Yet all these dangers were of small import, when compared with the mischief resulting *Bad conduct of the Regents.* to William's cause from the bad government of his deputies. He had, without doubt, wise captain as he was, given instruction to them to follow up his plans of occupation, and to direct their efforts against the remaining portions of Harold's Earldoms. These were particularly the districts which had belonged to his brother Sweyn : Herefordshire, Worcestershire, and the adjoining parts, much mixed up with the half independent and half subdued dominions of the British princes, and also not very accurately distinguished from the dominions of the sons of Algar. Fitz-Osbern stretched across the country, and

1067

Advance of Normans in the West.

occupied Hereford, being assisted by Richard Fitz-Scroop, who, as it will be recollected, was settled there in the Confessor's days. At Hereford, a strong castle was built and a garrison placed therein; and at this period many other castles were commenced, at least, by Fitz-Osbern, all rivetting the Norman power. In these operations, much warfare, much bloodshed, much desolation was inevitable; yet, divided as the English were, any incursion or injury offered in the way of war to any particular Thane, would not have been considered as a national injury. But Odo, so unworthy of the name of a Bishop, and Fitz-Osbern, were carried away by excessive pride: all justice was entirely denied. All the wise coercion of evil, of needless crime, which had been enforced by William, was entirely thrown aside. William had caused peace to be observed and the dwellings to be protected: the Regents gave them up to robbery. William had ensured safe conduct to the wayfarer: the Regents gave up the highways to robbery and rapine. Above all, William had most carefully and inexorably protected the honour of the female: the Regents encouraged and supported their followers in sin and violence. It seemed as if the Normans, released from all authority, all restraint, all fear of retaliation, were now determined to reduce the English nation into bodily servitude, and to drive them to despair. This subversion of all discipline, this universal

Injustice of the Regents.

anarchy, was on the point of becoming fatal to the Norman power.

<small>1067</small>

We possess very curious, and, it appears to me, conclusive evidence that William was kept in ignorance of these transactions, and that he was deceived by the reports transmitted to him by his brother and Fitz-Osbern. But, as throughout the whole of this stage of the conflict, the Normans were settled and confirmed in their authority, not so much by their own valour or their own prudence as by the moral visitation which had fallen upon the English. If the English could have been united under any one commander, or if they could have been united amongst themselves, they might yet have recovered their independence; but the spirit of the race was broken: emigration began. Very many of the younger abandoned their country and all thought of it, and proceeding to the South, entered the service of the Byzantine Emperor, where they became a mercenary band, fighting battles not their own, and enjoying the luxuries of the East, as the price of their venal fidelity. Some went back to the land of their forefathers, the antient seats of the "old Saxons" on the Elbe, and are dimly traced in the recollections of German history. All these were for ever lost to England.

<small>English emigrations.</small>

§ 6. But there were others who at least were more consistent, and who left the country, not in despair, not dreading the yoke of the Normans, and determined to make one effort more. Egelsine had returned from Denmark, leaving his gifts; but many of the English, including Harold's sons, had supplied his place at the Court of Sweno; and urged him to revenge his injuries and their own. The Danes were impatient for action: his brother, Jarl Osbern, his Bishops, were all ready for the war, and a ready and joyful assent was given to the English entreaties. A second body of Englishmen resorted to Malcolm Canmore. Egelric, the Bishop of Durham, Malcolm's Diocesan, probably was on their side, and Malcolm on his part raised large forces for the foray. Lastly the men of Kent sought a liberator in the person of one who had been the Conqueror's compeer, his ally in the battle of Hastings, and a fellow vassal of the Frankish king. This was Eustace, brother-in-law of the Confessor, Count of Boulogne, of Guisnes, of Terouenne—Terouenne which had withstood the power of Cæsar,—both courted and distrusted by William, who, keeping the son of Eustace as an hostage, had nevertheless bestowed upon him large Kentish domains.

Notwithstanding the injuries which the men of Kent had, in the preceding reign, received from Eustace, they nevertheless much respected this Sovereign, destined to become the grandfather of an English king; and they invited him as a liberator. The great object was to gain possession of Dover, strongly fortified and strongly manned, and usually commanded by the Bishop and Hugh de Montfort in person. Watching the opportunity, when they were absent beyond the Thames, the confederates gave notice of the favourable moment. A Kentish vessel bore Eustace across the narrow channel, and having quitted the Roman Pharos which crowned his own white cliffs, he landed at the foot of the tower from which signal, in the times of the Emperors, had answered to signal in Britain. The Kentish barks, which had been sent over for the service of Eustace, conveyed over his chosen band of knights. *[1067. Eustace crosses to Kent;]*

The whole country around was in a state of insurrection. He began the siege of Dover Castle: more and more of the English joined him, and could he have continued the siege for two days more, the fortress would have been compelled to surrender; and the chief access to England might have been closed against the Conqueror. But the news of the invasion had reached De Montfort and the Bishop, and they marched all their forces against Eustace. The garrison, however, had defended themselves valiantly: Eustace had begun to be discouraged, and, as it is said, had already given the signal of retreat. At this moment, the Bishop of Bayeux appeared at the head of his troops. Eustace and his men fled. Many were thrown down the cliffs, and he escaped with great difficulty. *[And invests Dover; But is defeated.]*

§ 7. In the meanwhile, the Normans were encountering a great and formidable opposition on the marches. The Cymri were tasting the bitterness of the Norman sword: the hereditary antipathy between them and the English had been fast diminishing: the common sympathy of suffering now united them. Edric the Wild threw off his enforced obedience, and refused to submit to the conquerors; probably they were attempting to dispossess him altogether. Fitz-Scroop, and the garrison of Hereford, ravaged his lands. Blethyn and Rhywallon, the princes of Dehubarth, joined their forces to Edric, and, entering Herefordshire, devastated the country, and returned in triumph, loaded with booty, the incentive and the reward of their hostility.

William continued in Normandy, and evil news thickened upon him; and worse was to be apprehended—the invasion of the Danes. Yet he lingered in his Duchy, not ineffectually, but providing for its good government; reducing it into perfect peace. At last he could stay no longer. He again confided the government to Matilda, not daring yet to fulfil his purpose of placing her as a crowned queen by his side, but directing that she should rule in the name of Robert—an act of which he did not foresee the future grief it would bring upon him. William embarked at Dieppe in the depth of winter. The day of sailing was the feast of St. Nicholas of Myra, a saint peculiarly invoked as the patron of sea-farers: the weather was extremely stormy; but he arrived in England safely, though he had well nigh perished in the tempest which lashed the dark and stormy sea.

§ 8. William was received with apparent gladness; and with his accustomed prudence and firmness, he held his Christmas court at Westminster with all due solemnity. He had brought with him a wise adviser, Roger de Montgomery, for whom he had appointed the Earldom of Arundel, and upon whom he also bestowed the Earldom of Shrewsbury. He thus placed one who would become the most formidable enemy against the Cymri on their borders, not, however, without some invasion of the rights of the Mercian Earls; but Edwin was still considered as William's future son-in-law; and the chronicler, though seldom adverting to such details of passion, gives us to understand that a sincere and encreasing affection subsisted between Edwin, whose personal beauty is always noticed with remarkable emphasis, and his future bride. The others, whom William had taken over with him to Normandy, either returned now, or in the course of the year; Stigand, it should seem, resuming his functions, though still under that species of cloud resulting from accusations publicly announced, and yet continuing undefined.

In his conduct, William shewed more than usual benignity, receiving all who resorted to him, listening to all suggestions, and employing himself, amongst other plans, in means of disuniting the Welsh and the English, whose union might well cause him great apprehension. As he proceeded cautiously from place to place, the English were awed into submission, and wherever he appeared, he fully regained that dominion which was beginning to escape from his grasp. Not so when he reached Exeter: here a spirit of resistance existed, far more dangerous than the turbulence of the wilder regions of the north. Should this one city be able to defy him, how soon would all the other communities of the same nature despise his power? The citizens hated the Normans; their river opened an easy access to the Irish Danes; their Roman walls and defences, then the noblest in England, gave them more than the usual means of resistance; and they probably knew, that dreaded as the Normans were in the open field, they were comparatively deficient when operating against the walls of a fortress. The patriotism of the men of Exeter invited those who shared the same feelings; their opulence enabled them to purchase the doubtful though formidable aid of mercenaries from the north; foreign countries had stored their city with the means of defence; and when William approached, and required the expected submission, the citizens peremptorily refused, closed the gates, manned the battlements, and defied the alien king. No oath of allegiance would they take; no entry should he make within their walls; but they were willing to make the same recognition of his supremacy over their Commonwealth which they had rendered to his predecessor in the empire: one half mark of gold, when London should pay its tribute, but no less and no more.

1068

William had respected the qualified privileges of London; but without doubt, he foresaw that if he permitted a community so powerful, possessing such moral as well as material strength, to retain those rights, the same emancipation would extend itself to the other cities. Imperial York, the birthplace of Constantine; Derby, filled with her Danish population; Lincoln, secretly acknowledging the northern king; Chester, like Exeter, still defended by the Roman ramparts, the last shadow of the Empire; Winchester, ennobled by the recollections of the fabled Arthur; and even London herself, though bound down by the fortresses planted within her precincts—all would rally, and like the Lombard cities,—like that Pavia which had given a Lanfranc to England,—would league themselves, and defy him, as those in Italy were now beginning to assert their liberty against the successors of the Cæsars. William therefore would listen to no terms.

William determines to refuse them.

§ 9. The men of Exeter were divided. The rulers, the senate, who had much to lose, dreaded the effects of resistance to their personal comforts; —they came forth, they knelt before the foreign sovereign—they promised implicit obedience,

Siege of Exeter.

and gave hostages to secure their dishonourable submission. But when the wealthy citizens re-entered the walls, they were no longer the senate; the indignant people would not confess themselves bound by the act of the selfish few: they guarded the gates, and refused to hear of surrender. William, after reconnoitering the city, advanced, and approaching the gate, brought forth one of his hostages and put out his eyes. But the embittered inhabitants still would not hear of surrender; and having no pity for their own unfortunate townsmen in William's hands, abandoned them to his cruelty. The siege was continued till resistance was hopeless; the battlements were beaten down, and the lofty white walls fell shattered upon the ground, the foundations being burrowed through by the miners. Clergy and laity came forth soliciting pardon. William displayed a politic clemency: he accepted the proffered allegiance of the citizens, and protected their property from spoil, preventing his soldiers from entering the city, whilst the fury and storm of victory was raging. He profited by this forbearance: the soldiery would have plundered on their own account, not his; and at this juncture his object was not to punish but to secure: he surveyed his conquest, and marked out the place for a very strong citadel: Rougemont, for such it was called, rose with the usual rapidity. Baldwin de Moeles was placed in command: a large garrison prevented the citizens from being tempted any more to assert their independence. From a republic, Exeter became a municipality; and William's forces extending along the peninsula, his dominion was established even to the Land's End.

§ 10. William allowed his army to return to their homes, and celebrated a peaceful and joyful Easter at Winchester. He could now fulfil his heart's desire: he sent a stately train to Normandy to bring over Matilda. She passed over with her court and courtiers, noble dames, prelates and barons; but none amongst these was more distinguished than Guido of Amiens, he by whom the victory of William had been so lately praised and sung, a grateful theme to Matilda, whose hands had just assisted in completing the tapestry in which she had laboured to commemorate her husband's deeds: that roll so frail and yet so enduring, which has outlasted many a castle, town and tower.

The coronation was now to take place; but Stigand was again repelled from his office, and the solemn rite was fulfilled by Aldred on the festival of Pentecost. Within the year, Matilda was delivered of her youngest son, who received the name of Henry, and who became the peculiar object of his father's care. William had not neglected the education of any of his children; but with Henry, there may have been more opportunity for improvement. Lanfranc was his instructor, and Henry received that instruction so willingly, that, at no period of his life did he neglect or lose his pleasure in the cultivation he had received. Beauclerc the boy was called, a name as appropriate to his form as to his mind, and though youngest in age, the English considered him highest in honour. He alone of all the Conqueror's children was the Porphyrogenitus, the son of a crowned king and a crowned queen; the son of a father and of a mother ordained to royalty, the only one upon whom, according to popular opinion, regality could descend: and many a prophecy of the British Merlin, now adopted by the English, testified the gladness with which they would view the accession of one whom they might consider as a national sovereign.

Chapter X.

WILLIAM'S POLICY—REVOLT OF EDWIN AND MORCAR—FIRST NORTHUMBRIAN CAMPAIGN—DEATH OF ROBERT COMYN—EDGAR ATHELING'S FLIGHT TO SCOTLAND—MALCOLM'S MARRIAGE WITH MARGARET—DANISH INVASION—THE ATHELING RECOGNIZED AS KING OF NORTHUMBRIA—WILLIAM'S SECOND NORTHUMBRIAN CAMPAIGN—FINAL REDUCTION OF THE NORTH—REVOLT OF HEREWARD AND EDWIN—FURTHER CONFISCATIONS—CHURCH MATTERS.

1068—1072.

§ 1. By the reduction of Exeter, William established tranquillity in Wessex: a temporary tranquillity, but which fully enabled him to mature his plans of government. He might well expect the attacks of the Danes. Abbot Elsi had returned, and from him he might learn that Sweno, fully engaged in warfare with the Norwegians and the Swedes, could not then resume his plans of English invasion. {1068. Interval of peace.}

In the meanwhile the country prospered: William's stern authority ensured the peace, and more amity began to prevail amongst the English and the Normans. The partiality for French manners and customs, so encouraged by the Confessor, continued to encrease; and in dress and habits, and even in language, the natives more and more turned to their recent invaders. {Assimilation of English and Normans.}

§ 2. The tranquillity of the country was dis-

VOL. III. F F

turbed, however, by Harold's son, Godwin, who had been assembling large forces in Ireland. The Somersetshire coast, where he expected co-operation, invited him. His fleet, in which without doubt, the larger portion of the crews consisted of Danes or Ostmen, entered the mouth of the Avon, ravaging the country. They advanced, and laid siege to Bristol. But the inhabitants of that great and opulent town withstood the marauders for their own sakes. They fought for goods and warehouses, wives and families, and beat the enemy off. However, much plunder had been gained, even in this expedition, which they secured on board their ships, and then spread themselves over the whole shire, doing great harm. Eadnoth, the standard-bearer of England: he who had been King Harold's standard-bearer, had no sympathy with Harold's sons: he raised the forces of the country and gave them battle. He himself was slain, but they were beat off with great loss, and compelled to re-embark, and the English said that Godwin was not entirely dissatisfied with the results, as he was thus released from a portion of the exorbitant demands which he expected they would make for their equipment and pay.

§ 3. The settlement of the country, meanwhile, was not intermitted. More and more lands, more and more domains, passed to Norman superiority. Geoffrey de Mowbray, Bishop of Coutances, he who had been so efficient in promoting the assumption of the royal authority,

had abandoned his See, for the purpose of be-   1068
coming one of the largest proprietors in England; and his possessions extended through Berkshire, Wiltshire, Dorset, Somerset, Devon, besides many shires to the north of the Thames. Robert, Earl of Mortaigne, was now also possessed of lordships as far as the Land's End; and he erected the strong Castle to which he gave the name of Mont-aigu from the abrupt and pointed hill upon which it was raised.

    William's favourite residence was at Win- *William in Wessex.*
chester: a preference given not merely from its political importance, but from the facilities which it offered for those pleasures which the Norman kings pursued with such inveteracy. The weald of Kent, Sussex, and Hampshire, still constituted an extensive and tangled forest, though interspersed with many a pleasant village and many an open glade; for the continuance of land as forest was not by any means incompatible with husbandry and cultivation; and the district, especially in Hampshire, was fully settled, abounding, even then, with parish churches, round which the people were congregated:—the rights of pasture which they possessed in the commonland, affording the means of subsistence to the herds of beasts and cattle, but more especially of swine, *The New Forest.*
which constituted so large a proportion of their sustenance. Here William committed that great act of injustice which brought the most lasting opprobrium upon his name. He seized a compass of territory not less than fifty miles in

circuit, which was henceforth to be appropriated to no other purpose than the chase. The inhabitants were expelled: the sacred structures destroyed, and the New Forest became the lasting monument of the Conqueror's tyranny.

Management of the North.

§ 4. As yet, William had never been seen in the northern parts of England. Two of the great Earldoms were still only partially placed under his authority, Mercia and Northumbria. It might have been William's intention to preserve to the sons of Algar the dominion which they possessed in the first of these great principalities, for such they were, and which their father had ruled with almost regal power. Chester, where Edgar had triumphed over the British kings, had encreased both in moral and military influence, during Algar's prosperous and beneficent authority. William had wisely planned to bring this Earldom into his family, by giving his daughter in marriage to Edwin. None so popular was there as Edwin in England: none so beautiful, none so bold; nor could any plan have been more considerately formed; not merely for promoting the political influence of the new dynasty, than for conciliating the affections of the people. But the jealousy of William's Norman counsellors, and we may infer that of Montgomery in particular, defeated the plan. William lingered to fulfil his promise; then refused, and Edwin, hot and irascible, quitted the court and rose in rebellion.

Edwin.

The influence of the two brothers, Edwin

and Morcar—for the one is never mentioned without the other until they were separated by death—was exceedingly extensive. The Northumbrians had wished for Edwin as their Earl: the great Earldom of Chester belonged to the sons; they were closely connected with the Cymri, and they were loved and respected and honoured by Blethyn, their nephew, the British king. Waltheof returned to his Earldom, or at least to his domain. A simultaneous insurrection was organized: the optimates of the northern English and the Britons assembled, and instigated the inhabitants of all Albion to join in liberating themselves from their common enemy.

margin: 1069. Anglo-Saxon insurrection.

§ 5. The war broke out most fiercely in Northumbria; moor and wood, marsh and glen, became the strongholds of the English. Large bodies encamped in the forests, and the name of wild men was contemptuously bestowed upon them by the invaders. They availed themselves equally of the fortification of the Burghs: the Scots assisted, as well as the Danish population, and Aldred endeavoured to restrain the hostility of the northern metropolis, but in vain; battle was the cry; and to rid themselves of oppression, they threw off all government.

margin: The North revolts.

This was not the mode to resist an experienced and wary foe; and William recommenced his operations with the same prudence and comprehensive view which he had already displayed. Fenced cities the English possessed. The men of York could be proud and confident in the great, many-angular tower, upon which the Labarum of Constantine had been displayed. Others were tolerably well protected by earthen ramparts and stockades; but they did not possess any compact points of defence, in which, instead of covering a large and motley population, useless for war, you could victual a well-chosen garrison of efficient soldiers; and the irregular bravery of the English therefore contributed not to the protection of the country, but to its devastation and destruction. William's policy, therefore, consisted in establishing regular lines of citadels as he advanced. Every station was marked by a new fortress, placed under an experienced commander. Warwick was occupied; and upon the site of the tower illustrated by the traditions of the hero Guy, the great opponent of the Danes, the castle was built, granted to Henry de Beaumont, who was created Earl of that large dismemberment of the Mercian territory.

This demonstration at once shewed to Edwin and Morcar what they had to expect, and that their resistance to William's authority would end in their total ruin. They came forward, therefore, and requested William's grace and favour: it was granted to them in appearance; but Warwick and its Earldom were not restored, and they parted from the King entirely alienated, whether in affection or in loyalty.

Nottingham was the next station; here a castle was built, and granted to William Peverel, represented by a doubtful tradition as an illegitimate son of the Conqueror.

marginal: 1069

§ 6. Shortly afterwards, the forces of William were seen before imperial York. Terror had preceded him, and no thought of resistance was entertained. The citizens came forth with the keys, and offered them to the Sovereign on the bended knee, proffering obedience and soliciting mercy. Archil, the great Thane, whose possessions were spread over Leicestershire and Warwick, and Lincolnshire, and the British Mercia, and South Northumbria, surrendered also to William's authority, and gave his son as an hostage. All this was well, but William immediately began to lay the foundations of a strong castle within the city walls; and as soon as the works were in anywise defensible, they were powerfully garrisoned, under the command of Robert Fitz-Richard. This tower gave a sufficient token of the citizens' submission, and the doubts entertained of their sincerity.

marginal: York submits. Archil. York Castle

Probably the resistance of the Northumbrians at this juncture would have been more determined, had not their cause been weakened by the unexpected defection of that near ally upon whose support they most reckoned. Malcolm had fully prepared to wage a desperate warfare against the Normans; but Egelric, Bishop of Durham, terrified at William's approach, now sought to conciliate his favour, and meditated a peace. The original character of the Celtic Gael, as described by Bede, when speaking of the first invasion of Ireland by the English, was distinguished by mildness, resulting, perhaps, in some measure, from indolence, but rendering them averse, except under strong provocation, from offensive war. The ferocity which the "Irishry," as the Highlanders were also called until the last century, exhibited in Erin, when worn and torn by the unmitigated spoil and oppression of successive centuries, is a fearful proof of the manner in which the temper of nations, as of individuals, may be maddened by despair, and the dispositions most susceptible of love and affection turned to exacerbated vengeance. A strong desire for religious contemplation and domestic tranquillity existed amongst the Gael of Albania. Malcolm's determination of submitting to William was received by the clans with the greatest joy—as a boon, and not an humiliation. His embassadors, accompanied by the Bishop of Durham, appeared before the Conqueror, and the oath of fealty, taken by proxy, renewed the bond of dependence between the Kings of the Scots and the Basileus of the British islands.

§ 7. William's first campaign was thus even more successful than he could have anticipated: he gained his object without any sacrifice of strength. He now, therefore, returned to his capital of

Winchester, taking another route, but equally with the same intention towards providing for the defence of the country. Lincoln, strong in its Roman walls, had a castle erected, emulating that of York. Another was raised at Cambridge, to keep in check the dangerous Marshlands, possessing stronger natural defences than any which the hand of man could raise: another at Huntingdon. With respect to Norfolk and Suffolk, these had been erected into an earldom, and granted to Ralph Guader, a Breton by birth, and therefore no favourite amongst the Normans, but supported by his powerful alliance with Fitz-Osbern, whose daughter he had espoused. Other castles were judiciously raised about this time, as it should seem, in the dismemberments of Mercia; Stafford, Shrewsbury, and many more: some upon defensible points, but the greater number in and within the towns.

<small>1069 — Castles built at Lincoln; Cambridge; In Mercia.</small>

These fortresses did not merely furnish important points of defence: they inspired terror. Each tall, square dungeon tower, with its fresh walls, harshly and coldly glittering in the sun, standing upon the ground of the habitations which had been demolished, and the gardens and homesteads which had been wasted, to give a site to the fortress in the midst of the people, bespoke the stern determination of the Sovereign. They were the trophies of the Conquest in the strictest sense of the term; warning, threatening the native race. England, wherever William or

<small>Moral effect of these fortifications.</small>

his Earls and Barons had settled themselves, was planted with these citadels, of which the ruins are seen here and there, some degraded to mean uses, others still more degraded, as mere curiosities: some, and the proudest of them, the prison of the vagrant and the felon; others, open to the whistling winds. Then were they all new and strong, and cruel in their strength. How the Englishman must have loathed the damp smell of the fresh mortar, and the sight of the heaps of rubble, and the chippings of the stone, and the blurring of the lime upon the green sward, as he passed by the Norman castle; and how hopeless must he have felt when the great gates opened and the wains were drawn in, heavily laden with the salted beeves, and the sacks of corn and meal furnished by the royal demesnes, the manors which had belonged to Edward the Confessor, now the spoil of the stranger: and, when he looked into the castle court, thronged with the soldiers in bright mail, and heard the carpenters working upon the ordnance,—every blow and stroke, even of the hammer or mallet, speaking the language of defiance.

§ 8. Future events fully manifested the wisdom of William's system; but he had yet many more struggles to make. England was not won, though three years had nearly elapsed since he had worn the royal crown. The English began to feel most acutely that they were conquered: and many a wild and desperate scheme did they form for their deliverance. It is said that a plot, or conspiracy was organized for a general massacre of the Normans; and that the time fixed for carrying it into effect was Ash-Wednesday, the day of penitence and prayer. Concerning this plot, the English writers are entirely silent, but during this period, they are remarkably succinct and broken, betraying, by their fragmentary and incomplete notices, the confusion which prevailed.

1069

Sullen submission of England.

Whether true or not, this alleged conspiracy furnished the reason, or the pretence for great severity. Many English of distinction were cast into prison: others put to death, and far more extensive seizures of land without doubt ensued. We have a remarkable proof indeed that William had now abandoned his former just and equitable policy. If any could claim [possession for] his heirs, or next of kin, supposing they were not strictly heirs, [it should have been] Eadnoth the standard-bearer, who had lost his life for William's cause; yet all the domains of this great Thane were divided amongst the Conqueror's Norman followers. With Waltheof, Merlesweyn, and Gospatric, William had been afraid or unable to meddle, and these last relics of the English nobility now were in dread, lest the same fate should befal them which had visited their compeers,—captivity or death; and they determined to seek refuge under the protection of the Scottish king. But they contemplated more than their own safety. They contemplated rescuing the deposed royal family

Further seizures of land.

See p. 432.

<small>1066</small>

<small>Saxon emigration to Scotland.</small>

from the invader:—nay more, the preservation of the royal authority, and its actual restoration in the antient right royal line. They therefore embarked with Edgar, the widowed Agatha, Margaret, and Cristina; and St. Margaret's Hope, on the banks of the Tweed, preserves by its traditionary name the memory of the spot where the fugitives touched the Scottish shore.

<small>Flight of the old Royal Family.</small>

§ 9. No fact in the history of the island is more prominent, for perhaps the event is even of more importance in the Scottish annals than in our own, than the flight of the Atheling, and the marriage of Margaret with the Scottish king; yet there are none in which the details are enveloped in greater uncertainty; but, when it is recollected that none of those who relate the event could have witnessed it, and that probably much precaution and some artifice may have been needed, to enable the children of England to escape from the Norman Conqueror, there will be less reason to be perplexed by discrepancies, which rather confirm than invalidate the general narrative. It is therefore not at all improbable, that there may be some foundation for the tale, that the Atheling, or rather his mother Agatha,—for he must certainly have been too young to form any plan for himself,—first spread the report that they intended to retire to Hungary, to a distance which would put an end to all suspicion of future rivalry; and the picture preserved of Malcolm meeting the maiden 1069 on the shore, was that species of embellishment which imagination gives to love in every age.

It is very credible that the royal family of England may have been received in the palatial abbey of Dumferline; and still more, that, whether betrothed or not by her kinsman the Confessor, Margaret may have hesitated to accept the hand of the Scottish king. It is quite consistent with her character to believe that she would far more willingly have dedicated herself as a virgin to the service of the Lord. But it was destined that she should perform that service more effectually as a wife and as a mother. The assent of Edgar, young as he was, was required. Upon the urgent request of Malcolm, Margaret assented, unwillingly and reluctantly; but the extreme affection of which she was the object soon dispelled this, and she entered on that high and dignified station, which rendered her, in the truest sense of the word, a blessing to the realm.

Margaret marries Malcolm.

§ 10. If any doubt could be entertained that the plan of the escape to Scotland was purposed and deliberate, it would be removed by considering how entirely it falls in with the plans which the English were forming for the liberation of their race and country. They had been diligently despatching messengers to Sweno, urging him to carry on the war against William. Abbot Egelsine, having incurred William's displeasure,

The English apply to Denmark.

had fled to Denmark, and was without doubt one who most urgently pressed the request.

The Danes prepare a great army.

Most willingly was it accepted. Sweno, and Sweno's brothers, Canute and Osbern: Sweno's Jarls and Sweno's Bishops, full as warlike as they, entered heart and soul into the enterprize. A most powerful army and armada was prepared; where the name of England scarcely conveyed a definite idea, the fame of England's riches would be fully appreciated; and the summons given by Sweno excited the greatest activity in the north. In the forests of Lithuania, where Thor, and Woden, and Freia were yet worshipped, the Letts and the Vandals were arming themselves with their staves and gisarmes for the invasion. The Sclavonians, who subsequently assumed the name of Poles, were equally preparing for the fight. Still more so in the nearer Frisia, whence Hengist and Horsa came of old, now again ready to send forth her swarms of warriors to Britain, whilst all the adjoining nations and districts contributed their aid. Some of these tribes had been vanquished by Sweno—others were his allies— they swelled his host and added to the terror which it inspired.

§ 11. The whole of the north of England was again in a state of insurrection. Since the death of Oswulf, Northumbria fully defied the power of the Conqueror. So did all the marches of Mercia; so did many of the remaining Thanes

GENERAL RISING IN THE NORTH. 445

of Yorkshire; so did the great fen country of Ely, in the heart of that portion of the kingdom which William might call his own; and even where the people dared not evince open hostility, the hostile feeling could not be concealed. It was much against William's interest that all the monasteries were the very strongholds of national feeling. They were truly English, and besides the influence which they possessed upon public opinion, they supported the native interest by those immunities, which as yet the Conqueror had not dared to attack: here the English had deposited much of that treasure with which, when occasion should serve, they might renew the war.

1069

Great hostility to the Normans.

So eminent and so apparent were these dangers to the Normans, that they now lost heart. Very many threw up their English possessions, and departed to their homes in Normandy; some of them never to return. William himself found it for once absolutely impracticable to govern: he could not enforce obedience to the laws. An extended and predatory warfare wasted and harassed both parties: sickness and scarcity prevailed: the soldiery became clamorous, and William, unwilling to be troubled, and perhaps endangered by a demoralized and discontented army, dismissed a large number of his retainers, but with munificent rewards.

They are discouraged.

Many fly.

§ 12. But whilst troubles were encreasing around him, William's discouragement, so unlike himself, passed away. He sent Matilda to Normandy: she was to preserve the Duchy for her son, and to help her husband by her prayers. No token could more clearly bespeak William's sense of his impending danger, and the need of his utmost exertion, than his thus parting with the dear companion whose presence he had so anxiously sought. His forces and followers seem to have rallied in consequence of his bounty, and many others appear to have come over; Flemings, Poitevins, Angevins, and Bretons, all swelled his ranks, and he prepared for that struggle which was to fix him upon the throne.

Another year of hard conflict must ensue before the Conqueror was truly king. William himself took the command of all the military operations to the north of the Thames; and throughout the whole of the victories and vicissitudes involved in this great and final campaign, he is always so prominent in the foreground, that others are cast into comparative insignificance. In Wessex, of which the subjugation was so nearly complete as to leave no great cause for anxiety, Geoffrey, Bishop of Coutances, as we collect, was the chief commander.

§ 13. Quite undeterred by their defeat at Bristol, the sons of Harold, assembling a larger force, again invaded Wessex, and sailing up the Tamar, and landing at its confluence with the Tavey, they marched against Exeter; but they were encountered by Bryan Fitz-Count. Two desperate conflicts took place on the same day: the Irish Danes were totally defeated: had not nightfall intervened, not a man would have escaped; and after this punishment, they never again ventured to insult the territory of the Conqueror.

_{1069. Irish Danes defeated.}

More dangerous, because connected with the general scheme of national liberation, was the great rising of the Somersetshire and Dorsetshire men, who expected without doubt, cooperation from their countrymen; but they were entirely disappointed: they attempted a siege of the new castle of Montacute, but fruitlessly: the Bishop of Coutances, at the head of the citizens of London, Winchester, and Salisbury, routed one body of the insurgents, who were cruelly treated by the victors. Another body attacked Exeter. Here they might well have expected favour, but the citizens had had too recent an experience of William's power to dare to be unfaithful; and Bryan Fitz-Count taking the command, the insurgents were completely routed, nor was the tranquillity of this extensive district ever again disturbed.

_{Wessex finally pacified.}

§ 14. But the great danger to William's power was the truly national insurrection of the North; the other portions of the English nations were awed by the Norman power: they defied it. Gospatric claimed the great Earldom of Bernicia or Northumbria, from the Tyne to the north of the Tweed; and Durham became the gathering point for all the northern English, who flocked

_{The North resists.}

thither from every side; and taking a lesson from the Normans, they began to raise a castle, intended as the centre of future resistance, and where they could await the co-operation of the Danish king.

It was of the greatest importance to William that this country should be thoroughly reduced. Copsi had perished in the desperate attempt; but a successor was easily found amongst William's followers. None were more tough, more adventurous than the Flemings, and Robert Comyn, or de Comines, accepted all that William could grant to him of the Earldom. The regular succession of the old lines of Earls had been so disturbed, that there was as little certainty in their dignity as in that of an Hospodar of Wallachia; but no attempt had ever yet been made to place an entire stranger, a man speaking a foreign tongue, over Northumbria. So hateful was the prospect of this foreign domination, and apparently now so irresistible,—for Comyn was advancing with a very large force,—that the Northumbrians prepared to abandon their homes, probably with the intention of retiring into the English Lothian, or of protecting themselves in the yet unsubdued wilds and fastnesses of Cumbria. But they could not. Winter set in with unusual severity: deep snow covered the soil: flight became impracticable; and they determined either to slay the invader or to fall.

Bishop Agelwine was very hostile to the

Conqueror; but either the fear of vengeance, or *1069* feelings of humanity, induced him to warn Comyn of the impending danger; for it seems that the Northumbrian soldiery had purposely abandoned Durham in order to allure him into the town. But Comyn either disregarded the *Comyn at Durham.* warning or despised the enemy. He entered the city, and the houses of the Burghers were forcibly occupied by his troops. Early in the morning the town was attacked on every side by the Landsfolk. A battle took place in the streets of the city. Comyn was burnt in the *Is killed.* house which he vainly endeavoured to defend: and so general was the slaughter, that, as it was said, only one man escaped to bear the intelligence to him, who might well now apprehend that he would lose the title of the Conqueror.

§ 15. The confederates, Merlesweyn and Gos- *The English now invest* patric, assisted, as we can infer, by Edwin and Mor- *York Castle.* car, as well as by the Northumbrian Thanes, now advanced boldly towards York. Countrymen and burghers everywhere joined them: they entered the city, supported by the universal friendship of the inhabitants. But William's policy was successful. Their attacks upon the castle were vain. Robert Fitz-Richard, who commanded the city, was killed; but the fortress under Mallet still held out against the forces by which it was invested. The insurgents were in complete possession of the city and all the surrounding country. Merlesweyn, Gospatric, the great

G G 2

1069

Thanes, Archil and Charles and Waltheof, all had joined the English cause, and Edgar Atheling was proclaimed King.

William rouses himself.

The scale now might seem to be turning most rapidly against William. He now had a true competitor, for the Danes would soon arrive in the Humber; and if they supported the Atheling, the Norman cause was lost. William seems about this time to have been in Mercia; he advanced immediately with a very large army, as large as he could muster.

Regains York.

King Edgar and his supporters and the men of York all were taken by surprise, so sudden was William's march: they fled: he spared none whom his sword could reach; a great slaughter ensued: the town was plundered, the cathedral and the other churches profaned: he began the devastation of the country, but the Atheling escaped in safety, and again found a refuge amongst the Scots.

Nearly reaches Durham.

William now endeavoured to pursue his success: the way was open, as it seemed, to Durham, and he determined to punish the country and revenge the death of Comyn. He advanced without opposition as far as Allerton: no enemy appeared, no sword was raised. Durham was close at hand, exposed to their vengeance; but on the following morning, there was neither dawning nor day, so thick was the darkness that surrounded them, so thick was the mist, so impervious, so impenetrable. A panic fear seized the invaders; and now one in the camp reminded the Normans to whom the land between Tyne and Tees belonged. Even as Rome belonged to St. Peter, so did Durham belong to St. Cuthbert;. and many a legend was related how the despoilers of his church had been stricken with palsy or afflicted with wild insanity, and that no attack upon him ever remained unrevenged ; and William returned to the South, ingloriously and without triumph, to Winchester; depressed, but yet preparing for the continuance of the conflict by which the kingdom was to be won.

§ 16. The havens of Denmark and Norway were now in full activity; and when the days had lengthened, the long threatened armada of Sweno began the voyage to England. The commanders of the expedition testified its importance. Canute and Harold, Sweno's sons, his Bishops and his Earls all joined: the vessels were crowded with the warriors of the North, and the whole array bespoke the intention of permanent conquest. From the direction which they took, it should seem that the haven of muster was on the Flemish coast; for the course of the armada was first directed to the southern parts of England. From the cliffs and towers of Dover the horizon was seen filled with sails: the Danish fleet was approaching; but the invaders knew that the country there was filled with Norman soldiery, that the castle was bristling with spears. Nevertheless they attempted a landing, but were repulsed with loss. Sandwich appeared less guarded:

another attempt was, however, equally unsuccessful: again they were repelled by the forces of the Norman King. They dared not attempt the estuary of the Thames, but they continued their voyage to the north; their barks filled the pleasant Orwell, and, landing, they attacked Ipswich and plundered the neighbouring country: but the inhabitants, whatever Danish blood they might possess, beat them off.

Danes land in Suffolk.

Norwich was next attacked; but Ralph Guader resisted them bravely. Many were drowned, others slain by the sword, and thus repulsed, they kept off from the land until they entered the mouth of the Humber. The Atheling, and Waltheof, and Siward, gathering their forces as they advanced, prepared to join them; but the garrison of Lincoln, being advised thereof, were on the alert, and nearly surprised the Atheling, who again escaped however in safety.

Are checked at Norwich.

The Danes now reached York: the whole country receiving them with alacrity and gladness. Gospatric had arrived, and surely his Northumbrians must have been all joyous and triumphant in Comyn's recent slaughter; Waltheof, son of the noble Siward, who before, as it was said, had alone with his battle-axe defended the gate of the city against the Norman invader; Merlesweyn; Ailnoth; Archil, casting off his enforced homage; the four sons of Karle, who, as it seems, had even preceded the mixed troop of Denmark and Norway and Sweden and Sarmatia and the Elbe;

Occupy York.

and excepting the tall dungeon keep upon which William Mallet still unfurled the Norman banner, the whole of Northumbria was again lost to the Norman King.

₁₀₆₉

§ 17. During these events, William was in Gloucestershire. No mental anxiety could restrain him from the toils or pleasures of the chase, and he was hunting the deer in the forest of Dean, when the intelligence arrived of the great invasion. He immediately sent a speedy messenger to York, urging Mallet to hold out, and assuring him that he would be ready to give assistance; and the messenger was able to enter York before it was occupied by the enemy, and to bring back the message from Mallet that the garrison could well defend themselves for a year—a vain boast. The united forces of the Danes and the English were overwhelming. As the houses which surrounded the castle protected the besiegers, the Norman garrison fired them by their missiles, and the conflagration extending itself, consumed all that remained of the city, including all the churches, all the monasteries: the Minster itself was reduced to ruin.

William sends instead of going.

Fire at York.

No one in the city of York felt so much horror, so much dismay, as Archbishop Aldred. It was he who had taken the responsibility of sanctioning the authority of the Conqueror, and that without any right to assume the office, without lawful calling to the exercise of that constitutional authority, which belonged not to him;

Death of Aldred.

and now the retribution had fallen upon him. All knew the wrong—all saw the punishment. Aldred had crowned the usurper Harold—Aldred had crowned the stranger William. Crazed and distracted by the calamities of which, in one sense, he might consider himself as the author, he died of alarm and remorse. His corpse was borne to the Minster; but a little while after, just when the octave of the funeral was completed, the towers and palaces of York, yet proud of the relics of Roman magnificence, as we have said, were wrapped in flames. This was the act of the Norman garrison.

More Danish vessels landed their crews: they stormed the castle. Three thousand of the Norman soldiery were killed; an unprecedented slaughter. William Mallet, his wife and children, escaped; but when the fugitives, at least those of the lower order, reached the Conqueror, then stationed at Stafford, he accused them of treachery, and by the most cruel mutilations, satiated in some measure his anger and revenge. Indeed he must at this moment have been worked up to the highest pitch of irritation, for a desperate insurrection was prevailing in Mercia and the Welsh Marches. He had just given battle to the insurgents, and he had thoroughly defeated them, yet dangers were renewing themselves on every side. However, as usual, he recovered his presence of mind, and advancing towards York, fully considered all needful plans, whether of policy or of war. He had stationed his brother-in-law, Robert of Mortaigne, as well as Robert of Eu, in Lyndesay, and they were able to beat off the increasing Danish forces which hovered in the Humber, it having been proclaimed by the Northmen that they would all celebrate their Yule at York.

§ 18. In the meanwhile William was advancing: his first station was at Nottingham: he next reached Kirkly [Castleford?], for the purpose of crossing the Aire, but the bridge over which they were to have passed was broken down; and the army continued at Pontefract for more than three weeks before they passed over. From the present aspect of the country, it appears difficult to understand how the waters could offer such an obstacle; but it is said, that three weeks elapsed before they could discover a convenient ford, the point of passage having been ascertained by Lisois de Musters. This part of the story is very obscurely told. It is said that he first crossed over at the head of sixty knights, and then returning, acted as guide to the rest of the army;—but it is also very probable that William was occupied in those secret negotiations with the false and treacherous Danes which he brought to so satisfactory a conclusion. Hence the way was entirely open to York, which he entered without opposition. The country, uncleared as it was, might have furnished the means of resistance, but none was offered: no enemy appeared, and thus in safety he arrived

at the northern metropolis. All had retreated:
where was Jarl Osbern and his fierce compeers?
They had abandoned the English to their fate,
and the English had fled. And if we ask how
this result had been effected, we shall read the
answer in the future judgment of the Danish
Law-moot. When Osbern returned to Denmark, he was outlawed. William had trusted
as much to gold as to steel; and the bribes
bestowed upon the false and greedy Northman
had caused him to betray the trust which he
owed, as well to his brother as to the nation
whose resistance he had encouraged, and whom
he now abandoned to the Conqueror's vengeance.

§ 19. William immediately repaired the castle,
and put it in a state of defence. All the Danes
had not been participators in the compact with
Osbern, and with these dispersed forces William
had yet to contend; and some opposition, but
very fruitless, was offered by the English, who
fought, as it were, in the agonies of death.
Hitherto William had shewn himself a stern
ruler and a pitiless warrior, but yet restrained
by that feeling which we call the laws of
war; but he now pursued a course hitherto
entirely unprecedented in his age. However
barbarous the warriors of the middle ages had
been, none of them, even the most ferocious,
the most savage, the most unchristian in nature,
the heathen themselves, Dane or Goth or Vandal,
had ever carried on that species of warfare

which, in the language of Scripture, is called 1069 destroying the life of the country; and the same precept which forbade the destruction of the palm and the olive and the fig tree, in those countries where they furnish the sustenance of men, prevented them from forming the deliberate intent, not only of destroying by hunger the enemy they had before them, but of inflicting all the evil in their power, and of starving generations yet unborn. But William determined to give the first example of a razzia, a term introduced in our age by one nation, but involving principles openly or tacitly adopted or tolerated by all who are joined by the bond of civilization. On every side the horizon was filled with smoke and smouldering flame: the growing crops were burned upon the field, the stores in the garner: the cattle houghed, and killed to feed the crow. All that had been given for the support and sustenance of human life was wasted and spoiled. All the habitations were razed, all the edifices which could give shelter to the people, were levelled with the ground: wandering and dispersed, the miserable inhabitants endeavoured to support life even by devouring the filthy vermin and the decaying carcase. Direful pestilence of course ensued. The same devastations were extended far beyond the Humber. During nine years subsequent, the whole tract between York and Durham continued idle and untilled. Of the former inhabi-

He wastes the country.

tants there would scarcely have been a trace, had it not been for the decaying corpse, lying by the road side, and some few, who, protected by the forests and rendered reckless by despair, occasionally attacked the new settlers. But so successful was William's policy, that even at the conclusion of his reign, many a wide and fertile tract still continued desolate, and York itself was surrounded by a wide circuit of ruins.

§ 20. William continued at York in gloomy pomp, determined to shew himself the Sovereign. He caused the regalia of the Confessor to be brought from Winchester, and solemnly wore his crown as king in Northumbria; thus manifesting his adherence to the antient constitutional principles of the British Empire; not the one kingdom of England, but an assemblage of States, ruled by one Imperial Sovereign. As upon his first coronation at Westminster, the moral effect of this ceremony soon became apparent, giving the English an excuse at least for submitting without dishonour. Edgar had retreated with Malcolm, his royalty entirely passed away; and whether in consequence of any specific act or declaration, or from the general tenor of his conduct, he was considered as having resigned his claims in favour of his sister Margaret and her descendants, who were thenceforth deemed the heirs of the old English crown. Great troubles still subsisted: as yet William's labours were most imperfectly performed, and required every exertion of talent, ability and prowess. But he was prepared for all; and to this period we must assign many of those acts of which the fruit appeared subsequently.

It was at York that he made the division of great part of the country to his followers: their dotations consisting in great measure of the possessions of Edwin and Morcar; thus destroying the power of his adversaries, and planting his own people as the superiors of the land. All Holdernesse was bestowed upon Drogo de Bevere, a knight of obscure lineage, but who at once took his surname from the great district which he obtained. To Roger de Busly was given the noble hall of Edwin at Loughton in Le Morthem, of which the traces still subsist, and from whence he could contemplate the rich territories which became his portion. A larger share of Edwin's lands and royalties was bestowed upon the Conqueror's nephew, Alan Fergant of Brittany, comprehending three entire wapentakes and more, which became the great honour of Richmond, the name given by the new possessor in the new language, to the old English soke of Gillyng, a name without doubt harsh and inharmonious in the Frenchmen's ears; and where the lofty castle was raised which still attests the Norman power. A hundred and ninety-six manors were bestowed upon Robert of Mortaigne; a comparatively small share to William Mallet. Robert Bruce, from Bruix in the

Côtentin, had a far larger measure. Other Barons received in proportion to their merits or their importunity. Archil, the Saxon Thane, who, after his revolt had again made his submission, received back three small manors, the remnants of about sixty which he had previously enjoyed. Some portions of Gospatric's lands were distributed, but many were reserved to induce or reward any future submission; and the whole of the possessions of Waltheof, he who had been so familiar with William, and so much loved and trusted by him, his hall of Hallam, now the industrious Sheffield, and his other large domains, were unappropriated, and might again be enjoyed by him.

§ 21. As soon as the coronation was over, and the festival of the Nativity closed, William was again in march. It was not the Danes who had kept their Yule at York; but although they had been partly bought off and partly beat away from the Humber, yet they had not in anywise quitted the coast of England. They continued their depredations lower down the coast, towards the South, probably acting very much in independent expeditions and parties, plundering much, yet suffering from want of provisions, but formidable and giving much disturbance. Some returned to Denmark, and brought the ill-tidings of their unsuccessful operations in Yorkshire to Sweno, who immediately began to prepare another expedition. A dangerous centre of opposition was now again forming against William in the fen-lands, dangerous, not alone from the inaccessibility of their position,—where the boat could scarcely float, and the soldier could not march except on some narrow causeway, where three could scarcely move abreast; but even more dangerous from the strong and contagious national feeling of the people.

William had in some measure endeavoured to counteract this influence. Brand, Abbot of Peterborough, he who had so long acknowledged Edgar Atheling as King after the accession of the Conqueror, was a great Lord, for the opulence of Goldenburgh, as Peterborough was also called, gave him great authority and power. Upon his death, which took place a little before William's entry into York, the King gave the Abbey to one Thorold, a Frenchman as he was called, and a stern Frenchman; but as yet he had not been enabled to take possession, and he remained stationed at Stamford with his Frenchmen, to whom he intended to grant part of his Abbey lands. Further advance he dared not: more and more of the English party took refuge in the district, and more particularly in the Isle of Ely, the strongest point of all. Morcar was probably amongst them, as we can collect from subsequent incidents; a tale pursued, however, with great difficulty, through narratives as confused and disturbed as the events to which they relate.

§.22. So much did the strength of the insurgent

patriots encrease, that they acted on the aggressive, but they were met by a Norman force, and an uncertain report reached William at York that the English had been defeated, though, nevertheless, the same report informed him that they were full of confidence and defied his power. All that Edwin and Morcar had held in Northumbria was lost: much also of their Mercian possessions. Roger de Beaumont was in possession of Edwin's castle of Warwick; but, nevertheless, the great Earldom of Chester proper was unsubdued. So also were the British kings or princes, so closely connected with the family of Algar. This must have been a great cause of anxiety and apprehension to William. Thames and Humber and Avon were well nigh secured against the Danes. London and York and Bristol were all occupied by his forces, and commanded by his citadels; but the Dee still opened the most ready access to the Northmen, whether from oppressed Ireland or the isles, or from Scandinavia itself, for the navigation round the island offered no difficulty to the Northmen. Furthermore the city of Legions was the proudest and most defensible of all the Roman fortresses. Cæsar's tower, yet marked out by a building of later age, rose in the centre of the castellated palace of the Earls, where Algitha was yet in safety. An implacable hostility to William animated all the inhabitants: the massacre of Yorkshire irritated, but did not deter them.

Cymri and English united in another desperate attempt to recover that which they now began to consider as their common country. The men of Chester and the Welsh, whether led on by Edwin or by Blethyn or Rhywallon, attacked Shrewsbury. Had it yielded, the loss might, even now, have given a dangerous if not a fatal blow to the Norman supremacy.

§ 23. William could not at this juncture give help on that side of England. His first object was the reduction of the remaining portions of Northumbria; and he advanced towards the North. He had to war against the elements; and in the rugged tracts and broken ground, in the wasted and starved country, where every step condemned his cruelty; now through deep cold valleys and amidst crags and rocks, which even in the brightest spring were often enveloped in the snow-storm, the Norman soldiers were led on by their Sovereign, toiling heavily until they reached the banks of the Tees.

Here he encamped for fifteen days: he did not cross the stream, but messengers had passed over, to and fro. The result was the pacification of Durham. Gospatric, then probably at Durham, and who had taken the oaths before William's embassadors, received a grant of the Earldom of Northumbria, not, however, without paying so large a sum as a relief, that it was represented as a species of sale. Waltheof presented himself in person, and was restored to his possessions. Again he entered the hall of Hallam, and at some subsequent, but not very remote period, became the husband of Judith, niece of the Conqueror.

> 1070
> Waltheof's marriage.

The march back to Hexham, through paths hitherto untried, offered greater difficulties than the advance. One night the cry was raised in the army that the King was lost. William was in safety; but he and six horsemen had wandered and strayed from the main body, which they did not rejoin till the following morning. The frost was intense. Many of the horses perished; general discouragement prevailed in the army: each cared only for himself; and had any attack been made upon them, they might have been entirely cut off. But William had profited by his policy: the country was a desert, and not a hand was raised against him.

> William moves South.

§ 24. Alert, indefatigable, William immediately caused the fortifications of York and all the adjoining strongholds, to be put in a complete state of defence. He felt entirely certain that the southern parts of England did not need his presence. London, Winchester, Bristol, Exeter, probably all the greater Burghs, were, in the common sense of the term, loyal: separated in interest from the country at large; their riches, and they were very rich, made them so. In great cities, there is always, in such emergencies, a consistent conduct: their first principle is an inclination to oppose authority: their second,

> Reaches York.

submission to authority when conducive to their own advantage, and so William found them. His object was now the complete reduction of the north-western parts. Shrewsbury had been hard pressed, but it had held out. William therefore determined to attack the enemy in their most important position,—Chester. The weather was most unfavourable, the rain falling in torrents. Regular road from York to the scene of action, there was none; and William marched across the country in a direction never before thought pervious to cavalry.

1070

Marches South-West.

We can only guess at his line by the difficulties which attended his march. His forces seem to have been entangled in the hills and forests of the Peak and the surrounding districts. William's followers had never before been exposed to such trials. Provisions failed. They began to dread the bold pertinacity of the natives. Angevines, Bretons, Manceaux, men of the south, all unaccustomed to the severity of an English climate, declared they would serve no longer, and came to the King desiring their discharge. Such a permission would have involved their own ruin, and could have been only asked for the purpose of imposing terms upon William, and compelling him to retreat with them; but the Conqueror acted, men said, as Julius Cæsar did, under the like emergency. He would use no entreaty, he would give no promise. Cowards, he replied, might depart if

Difficulties in Derbyshire.

1070

Reaches Chester.

they chose; and, encouraging his men, somewhat by words, but far more by example, the march was resumed. If his horse failed, he walked, always preceding his men: he was the first to climb the rock, or to trample through the marsh; and thus, safe and sound and unbroken, the whole army came before Chester, and completely appalled or subdued the entire territory. The fortifications of Chester were strengthened and enlarged by the Conqueror; and the Earldom was bestowed upon Gerbod, the countryman of Comyn. In this instance, however, as in the other, the choice was not fortunate: the Flemings, strong as they were, did not take root. Gerbod could not maintain his ground against the English and the Welsh, and he returned to Flanders. He was succeeded by Hugh de Avranches, Hugh Lupus, as he is more generally called, who, as we shall afterwards find, rendered his Earldom the great bulwark in those parts of the Anglo-Norman power.

Hugh Lupus, Earl of Chester.

§ 25. And now William turned towards the South, directing the building or progress of fortifications wherever needed; Stafford amongst others. At Old Sarum he finally took his station. He mustered his army in the great plain covered with the vestiges of the primeval population. Here he reviewed his troops, and bestowed his rewards upon them, endowing the leaders, and without doubt those also of inferior degree, with

William's triumphant return South.

the lands which they had won: great had been their exertions in this last conflict, and most munificent was the bounty, which, at the expense of the vanquished, he displayed. Those who had been faint-hearted, he punished. Lightly, for the punishment consisted only in retaining them forty days after their companions were discharged. The heaviest part of the castigation was, without doubt, the loss of the rewards which they otherwise would have obtained.

§ 26. Great as these victories had been, England was still not entirely subdued: the East and the North were still resisting, and preparing for further resistance. The insurgency in the fenlands was becoming more and more formidable, not alone from the real danger of allowing a district so near the capital and so open to the sea to continue in a state of defiance, but, even more, from the manner in which it was magnified by popular opinion. Here was now almost all that was left of the old nobility of England, save Waltheof, Gospatric, and some of the northern Thanes. Siward Barn was there. Edwin seems to have joined his brother Morcar, so also Egelwine, Bishop of Durham. But their chief leader, or at least he who acquired most reputation, was Hereward the Outlaw, nephew of Brand, abbot of Peterborough, and son of Leofric of Brunne. In his native town, it is said that he had been a great raiser of strife and dissension when young. He would have been termed a

Swash-buckler in the phraseology of the Elizabethan age. Leofric drove him from his house: Hereward collected a riotous troop and plundered his father; upon which, as it is said, Leofric complained to Edward the Confessor, who, at his father's request, declared him an outlaw and banished him from the land, and he was called Hereward the Outlaw for evermore.

It may or may not be that Hereward received the belt of knighthood from his uncle Abbot Brand, after returning from various adventures both in England and beyond the seas. He now appears to have joined the Danish invaders, to whom, from his knowledge of the country and its riches, he might be of peculiar utility.

During these transactions, Jarl Osbern, according to his agreement with William, had been wintering in the Humber; but now another Danish Armada appeared on the coast: Sweno himself; his vessels filled with a tremendous host of Huscarles.—Osbern seems to have co-operated with them. Whether from antipathy to the Normans or from apprehension of danger, many of the inhabitants came forth and submitted to the invaders. But in this irregular warfare, this mixture of attack and defence and insurrection, it is impossible to follow the train of events with accuracy, and it is equally evident that the parties frequently changed sides; the main principle of the Danes being none other but plunder,—and all the English who adhered to the Normans, being treated as enemies by their own countrymen.

margin: 1071

§ 27. Hereward himself guided the Danes to the plunder of Peterborough. The monks closed the gates, and prepared sturdily for defence. Hereward knew the locality, and by his direction the Danes set fire to the buildings which surrounded the monastery and partially protected it; and the outlaws (for Hereward appears to have had a large train of those who were the like of him) and the Danes rushed in over the burning ruins. The monks now came out, imploring mercy, but none was granted by Hereward and his companions. They swarmed into the church. Some ascended the rood loft, and began to demolish the great crucifix, and secured the golden crown which adorned it. The pallio of the altar, of gold, and adorned with precious stones — the counterpart, without doubt, of those which still exist at Venice and at Milan — had, together with many similar objects, been concealed by the monks in a chamber in the tower. But Hereward's men knew where to find it: all the valuables of every description were carried off. Books, vestments, shrines, processional crosses of good red gold and bright silver — so much treasure that none could tell. Goldenburgh no longer deserved, and for ever lost its name: and Hereward afterwards often swore that he had done this with the best possible intent; it was a righteous act, he said, inasmuch as he

margin: Hereward and Sweno.

margin: Plunder Peterborough.

Danish plundering.

1071 thought that his Danish allies would thereby be enabled to make war upon the Conqueror and regain the land; and that, at all events, it was better that the treasure should fall into the hands of the Danes, than be reserved for the French abbot and his Frenchmen. All the monks were driven out, except one sick man who was lying in the infirmary, and the church was burned. This, however, was not the result of design: it caught fire either during or after a drunken carouse which the Danes held in the sacred building. All the treasure they carried away, and deposited it safely in the Isle of Ely.

William buys off Sweno.

In the meanwhile, William had been negotiating a treaty with Sweno, in which it was agreed that the latter should be at liberty to carry off all the gold and silver which he had plundered—a part, without doubt, of the subsidy by which he bought them off, as before— and they sailed away for Denmark. But their gains profited them but little. A violent tempest arose; their fleet was dispersed; many were wrecked and lost, and only a small portion reached Denmark. This was the great altar-table, and some other of the ornaments; a sufficient specimen of what they had gained and lost.

Danes again, for the last time.

Another Danish fleet shortly afterwards entered the estuary of the Thames; but after continuing there during two days—or rather, according to the old phraseology, two nights—

they also returned to Denmark. Wherefore they thus suddenly withdrew is not told; but when we recollect in what manner William had on previous occasions averted Danish hostility, there can be no difficulty in conjecturing the arguments he employed. The English were thus, at length, entirely abandoned by the Danes; Hereward established himself in the Isle of Ely, and more and more of the English resorted to him. It was now that Bishop Egelwine and Siward Barn came from the North, there being a most ready access to the fen-lands from the sea. Great was their confidence in their leader and in their position, so inaccessible, and so well supplied with the means of subsistence,—the waters swarming with fish, and the numerous islands and eyots abounding with pasture; besides which, they had many ready means of communication with the adjoining country.

margin: 1071. English make a stand in the fens.

§ 28. William did not rush to the attack of a position which, difficult as it might be to reduce, could not, if well watched, be very dangerous; the very marshes which constituted their protection, equally cutting them off from the rest of England. But they were encircled by his troops and his dungeon towers, commanding the surrounding means of access; and he made use of the antient Rech-dyke, the rampart of the Giants, as a line of defence, manning it with his soldiery. During this pause, he contrived to place himself in communication with Morcar, and induced him

margin: William blockades them.

1071

Morcar captured.

to come forth from Ely; so doing, he was seized, sent to Normandy, and placed in custody in the castle of Roger de Beaumont, who kept him in hard prison, in chains and fetters, whilst his (Roger's) son Henry was lording it in Warwick, that noble portion of Morcar's inheritance.

Edwin.

Edwin now lived only to avenge his brother. He sought help everywhere, from Scots, from Cymri, from the English, instigating them against the stranger. Possibly he might yet have escaped; but English treachery surrendered him into the hands of his implacable enemies. Three Englishmen—three brothers, three of his most intimate followers—presented themselves before the Conqueror, bearing Edwin's gory head as an offering. It was they who had betrayed the fugitive, when he and a small and faithful band were hemmed in by a stream on the one side,

Is slain.

and the rising tide on the other. Edwin and those with him fought bravely, but all were slain. William, as it is said, wept bitterly when he gazed upon the disfigured features. Instead of rewarding the traitors, he punished them by exile; but their crime taught him no mercy: Morcar continued in chains and fetters; all the remaining possessions of the family of Algar were confiscated, and widely distributed. A sister, whom the Normans called Lucia — an appellation probably substituted for some baptismal name uncouth to their ears—was bestowed in marriage upon Ivo Talboys, Lord of Holland,

and thus the line of the Earls of Mercia passed into a Norman family soon destined to decay. ₁₀₇₁

§ 29. William, proceeding warily, now determined to crush the rebellion; he himself brought up all his disposable power against the insurgents, ships and engines, horse and foot, carrying on his operations by sea and by land. On the east, his navy closely blockaded the coast; his boats filled the streams, where there was sufficient water to float them. The operations began by the attempts which the besiegers made to pass the treacherous morass and shallow waters, for which purpose rafts and floating bridges were employed. This attempt was unsuccessful. Years afterwards, the bones and the armour found in the depths testified the failure of the devices employed. But the difficulty roused the skill of the Norman engineers: a causeway was stretched along the marshes, which brought the invaders close up to the isle and its castellated monastery. Refectories and cloisters were filled with warriors. Amongst themselves were no incompetent defenders. It seems, however, that provisions began to fail; escape was hopeless, and they all surrendered at the Conqueror's discretion, save Hereward alone, who escapes, as it were, from history into the mist of poetic fable; his form vanishing, as it were, amidst the giants and warriors of the mythic age. Did we not find, in the earliest and most authentic of our records, the dry, technical, legal entries of his oxgang of land in Kesteven, held by Hereward, "*die qua aufugiit,*" we might very plausibly maintain that the Hereward, the protector of the host, was entirely the creation of fancy, such as we are now taught to consider Numa or Romulus, the hero of an old song.

1072

Fate of Hereward.

§ 30. Troubles and sorrows were now rising in Normandy, occasioning political anxiety and great anguish of mind to Matilda; but William, however much he might wish to give her his comfort, could not yet venture to quit England, for the northern parts continued to threaten disturbance. Waltheof and Gospatric had been permitted to retain a considerable degree of influence and power; and there were even yet some other of the antient English nobles whom he could not immediately sweep away. And much might be dreaded from the influence of the English fugitives, Edgar and the many with him, now settling beyond the Tweed, and still more beyond the Forth, under the protection of the Scottish king, the husband of the lawful heiress of the English crown. Their influence, or more possibly, some depredations upon the borders, instigated the Scots to a desperate invasion. Malcolm's army, marching round through Cumberland, as yet his own territory, entered Northumbria proper, wasted and devastated Teesdale, Cleveland, and the greater portion of St. Cuthbert's territory. A great battle took place between him and the English, at the place called

The English unite with Malcolm,

Who enters England.

Hundredeskeld, not far from the Darwent, and so called from the numerous streams with which the vicinity abounds. The old story is told of the Scots throwing infants into the air, and receiving them on the points of their spears: this aggravation of cruelty is a mere tradition, often repeated,—a conventional mode, so to speak, of describing their excesses.

1072

Ravages of the Scots.

The incursion on the part of Malcolm was impolitic. Gospatric, who had been so lately received as a friend by Malcolm, retaliated by invading Cumberland, which he pillaged, carrying off his prey athwart the country, to his strong castle of Bamborough. Malcolm, on his part, carried off a great number of captives of every age, belonging to the class of the villeinage, so numerous, as it is said, that they formed a large proportion of the population of the land. Hostilities were stayed for a time; but, if William had endeavoured to play Gospatric off against Malcolm, by placing them as neighbours, no plan could have been better devised.

Gospatric's revenge.

Malcolm's hostility furnished, however, to William a sufficient reason for asserting his supreme authority over the antient vassal of the Anglo-Saxon crown. He invaded Scotland, both by land and by sea, conducting the army himself, and having Edric the Wild as the chief commander under him. Nothing whatever is told of the circumstances which caused Edric to adhere to the Conqueror, or the Conqueror

William retaliates by invading Scotland.

to receive him again into his apparent confidence. William had undertaken the expedition with the intention of entirely subduing Scotland. He was grievously offended at Malcolm's rebellion, and Malcolm dared in nowise to resist. The sea coast was beset by the ships, filling the firths and waters: his troops, Normans, Bretons, and Flemings, filled the land: and Malcolm, appearing before William at Abernethy, a locality which has exercised the ingenuity as well as the scepticism of our antiquaries, performed homage and took the oath of fealty, and became William's man; the supremacy of the Anglo-Norman crown was established without contradiction; and it is possible that the same ceremony was repeated at Westminster, and that Malcolm there, like the other vassals of the crown, bore the sword before his supreme Lord and Sovereign.

§ 31. William's task, however, of reducing the North, was as yet not completed. Northumbria had always displayed an obstinate elasticity of resistance, and William strove, by degrees, to break every spring. Gospatric, or his descendants, claiming by hereditary right, might release themselves from Anglo-Norman supremacy, or only acknowledge that nominal obedience more dangerous than none; and it became important that he should be removed. He was neither honoured nor trusted by his Sovereign, and there was no difficulty in finding causes of complaint. It was alleged, or insinuated, that he had received bribes from Malcolm, an accusation not inconsistent with their recent hostility. It was laid to his charge that he had instigated and aided Comyn's slaughter; and, lastly, he was accused of his old transgressions in aiding the Danes in the great Yorkshire invasion, and in the slaughter of the garrison of the castle of the northern metropolis. Gospatric might have pleaded with entire truth, that there was no one of these charges, not even the first, if grants of land were to be considered as bribes, which was not fully known to William, when the latter had received his relief, and granted to him the Earldom: yet the great Honour was declared to be forfeited.

1072. William becomes hostile.

Gospatric fled to Scotland, from whence he went to Flanders, most probably for the purpose of enlisting Flemish forces, whose swords were at the service of any pay-master, and from whence he returned to Scotland. Malcolm gladly welcomed him, and granted to him Dunbar with extensive territories in the Lothians: and his three sons, Dolphin, Waltheof, and Gospatric, became border chieftains, dangerous to the English King.

Gospatric joins Malcolm.

William now had the great Earldom of Bernicia at his disposal. The bitter resistance which the Northumbrians had made to Comyn shewed him that the time was not yet come when he could confer the dignity on a stranger, and it was needful to find some one who might hold it, until a better opportunity should arise. It was therefore conferred upon Waltheof, the son of Siward, who, like Gospatric, claimed it as his inheritance. He was almost the only English chieftain exempted from proscription, and the long projected marriage between him and Judith, the Conqueror's niece, and sister of Odo, of Champagne, Earl of Holderness, was completed. It was an ill assorted marriage. Judith's subsequent conduct is full evidence that she became a most unwilling wife to the English chieftain. As for Waltheof, his first thought was vengeance, and his first deed after his inauguration was the shedding of English blood. His grandfather Aldred had been slain in the fatal battle of Settrington; and Waltheof, assembling a large body of Northumbrians, avenged himself upon the four sons of Charles, by whom that grandsire had fallen. Such a local feud was but a usual incident, yet Waltheof's conduct was considered as stained by cruelty; and it strongly exemplifies the turbulence of the Anglo-Danish population, which, amongst other causes, prevented them, brave as they were, from making any resistance to the common enemy.

§ 32. Thus, after almost six years of constant conflict, we may view the authority of the Anglo-Normans as being nearly extended over the whole of the antient dominion of the Anglo-Saxon kings; nearly, though not completely, for the Welsh, in their fastnesses, had not entirely acknowledged the Norman power. But in the meanwhile, what was perhaps even more important, the ascendency of the Normans over the English as a people, became far more firmly established. Until the captivity and the death of Morcar and of Edwin, William had proceeded leniently in the distribution of the English lands; but now, the process advanced with fearful and accelerated rapidity. It is said that he divided the English into two classes: the first who, having borne arms against him, were to be completely disinherited; the others, to whom some small portion of their property was allowed, as an encouragement to future loyalty. Archil may be considered as belonging to the latter class; but it does not appear that any regular system was pursued, except that of shewing the smallest degree of forbearance to all the higher classes of the occupants of the soil.

William's new confiscations.

According to the common report, sixty thousand knights received their fees, or rather their livings, to use the old expression, from the Conqueror. This report is exaggerated as to number; but the race of the Anglo-Danish and English nobility and gentry, the Earls, and the greater Thanes, disappears; and with some exceptions, remarkable as exemplifying the general rule, all the superiorities of the English soil became vested in the Conqueror's Baronage. Men of a new race and order, men of strange manners

The soil changes owners.

and strange speech, ruled in England. There were, however, some great mitigations, and the very sufferings of the conquered were so inflicted as to become the ultimate means of national prosperity; but they were to be gone through, and to be attended by much present desolation and misery. The process was the more painful because it was now accompanied by so much degradation and contumely. The Anglo-Saxons seem to have had a very strong aristocratic feeling: a great respect for purity and dignity of blood. The Normans, or rather the host of adventurers whom we must of necessity comprehend under the name of Normans, had comparatively little; and not very many of the real old and powerful aristocracy, whether of Normandy or Brittany, settled in England. The great majority had been rude, and poor, and despicable in their own country: the rascalions of northern Gaul: these, suddenly enriched, lost all compass and bearing of mind; and no one circumstance vexed the spirit of the English more, than to see the fair and noble English maidens and widows compelled to accept these despicable adventurers as their husbands.—Of this we have an example in Lucia, the daughter of Algar, for Talboys seems to have been a person of the lowest degree.

§ 33. William at this juncture also,—for he afterwards recovered his solid, stern and consistent principle of government,—lost much of his former spirit of equity; and allowing his people full license, the English became as it were, aliens in the land of their forefathers, outcasts in their own homes. William shewed that if need of state required, he would respect no feeling, honour no privilege or immunity; and therefore, in order to carry his spoliations to the utmost, not perhaps without the further intention of shewing the extent of his authority, he seized all the treasures which the English had deposited in the monasteries. William Fitz-Osbern was his adviser to this act, adding thereby to the odium he had already so justly incurred, in consequence of his oppressive tyranny. But the responsibility of the act rested, nevertheless, with the Sovereign. William was preparing to crush hierarchy, nobles and people, and to grind them to the dust. He began with the same intention as the English conquerors of Ireland, but unlike Ireland, England was permitted to retain those institutions which rescued her from the slavery she afterwards imposed upon others.

Aliens in their own land, outcasts from their own homes—why should the English remain in that which was no longer their country,—England? About this time it is probable that the emigrations proceeded with encreased rapidity, more to Denmark, more to the Elbe, where some of their descendants were afterwards traced, high in power and famed for sanctity, but most of all to the South. When the patriarch of Constantinople proceeds

1072

To Byzantium.

in pomp, he is informed that a Saint hitherto unknown to the Eastern Church, is venerated in the imperial city. He enters the humble dwelling where he is received by the barbarian host. He is conducted into the domestic chapel, where the lamp burns before the image of the Hagios Agostinos whom the Byzantine artist has painted, the apostle of the English race, the remembrance which the exiles cherished as the memorial of

The English guard.

their country. The English were deemed the most trusty defenders of the eastern Emperor, honoured by the nobles, favoured by the Sovereign; and in the last age of the empire, even when the cross was about to sink before the crescent, their descendants retained their native language, and saluted the wearer of the purple in the speech with which they would have hailed the Anglo-Saxon King.

§ 34. During this long series of conflicts, William had carefully attended to the policy of the

1070

state in all its parts. Whilst engaged in the wilds of the North, the legation despatched at his request by Pope Alexander was proceeding towards

Church matters.

England;—Hermenfried, Bishop of Sion, he who had already visited England as Legate, in the time of the Confessor, when England for the first time saw the representative of the Papal power. Two Cardinals were joined to him in the mission, —Peter, who filled the office of Chancellor and Bibliothecarius or Keeper of the Records of the

Roman See, and John, who bore the title of Sta. Maria in Trastevere, a man of great experience, and who had previously filled the office of Legate at Milan, when the proceedings were taken for purifying that See from the simoniacal character by which it was so deeply stained. These had been invited for the purpose of enabling William to reorganize the government of the English church, in conformity with the new order of things, and also for the purpose of confirming him in the royal authority.

At Winchester, during the festival of Easter, William again received the crown from the Pope, through the hands of his representatives. This is a very singular proceeding; and it would be hard to say whether it should be considered as an honour or as a submission; but the ambiguous act, wholly passed over by the English historians, probably as being most distasteful to them, must receive its comment from William's general character, and no one can suppose that he intended it to indicate any subservience to the Pontiff beyond what his interest would require. No sovereign but the Emperor was crowned by the Pope. Not long afterwards, a report was spread and believed, that William intended to conquer the Empire. This report, though at the moment it caused great anxiety to the Emperor Henry, must have been destitute of foundation; but, if we are at liberty to draw any conclusions from a fact of which so little has been recorded, we may suppose that William did contemplate the accession thereby of some of those prerogatives, which, in the words of a later writer, might tend to melt the mitre into the crown.

§ 35. But though William's possession of the throne was thus sanctioned; though England was prostrated, his mind was ill at ease: his conscience may have already reproached him:—but now he was stricken by one of those public proceedings, which, although they tell the world no more than was fully known before, have the great effect of giving that stamp, as it were, of culpability which removes the pretence of ignorance of sin.

William's remorse.

And censure. A heavy ecclesiastical censure had just been passed upon him for the abuse of that power which had been given to him. It was the doctrine of the Church, though often slurred over, and most rarely asserted, that the necessity which extenuated warfare never justified the prosecution of hostilities for the purpose of profiting by the spoil: furthermore, though shedding of blood in battle might be a justifiable homicide, justifiable by the offences committed by man against man, still that it was an eternal offence against the commandment given to the whole human race. When William made his first compact at Lillebonne, it was possible that he concealed from himself the injustice that he must commit, —that he did not contemplate the full extent of slaughter and extermination, of fire and famine and of robbery, the robbery of a whole nation, which would be needful for the purpose of carrying it through. The wrong was now consummated: the hideous aspect of the Conquest was now unveiled, and all saw it, even they who had profited most by the iniquity in which they and their Sovereign were involved.

1072

At this juncture the prelates of Normandy gave that testimony against the unchristianity of war, so rarely afforded. By their decree, confirmed by the apostolic legates, they imposed a general penance upon all, from the highest to the lowest, who had perpetrated the deeds which had established William on the throne. Their decree or sentence involved all the acts resulting from the license of war, or committed in its prosecution; the spoliations, the violences, the profligacy, the lifting up the sword to give the blow, although that blow might fail, the arrow shot at random; and so on, unto the death of each enemy encountered in the field, all meted and measured out in their degree, according to the technicalities of the discipline of the Church, but all condemned; unequal in degree but not in kind; the pillage of the marauder and the prowess of the warrior included in the same ban; deeds such as are sung by the poet or figured on the canvass or trophied in marble, marked out as the subjects of contrition, humiliation and repentance.

Penance imposed on the Norman conquerors.

All the culpability of the Conquest was universally felt: the majority without doubt silenced

1079

The Conquest not universally thought justifiable.

the call of conscience, yet we may trace that many obeyed the warning: there were those amongst the Normans who absolutely refused to take any share in the donations which William would have bestowed, who renounced them, as bought with blood, and who, by their words, and still more by their actions, rebuked the ambition of their Sovereign. This feeling also was probably the cause of the bounteous donations made by the Normans or their immediate descendants for pious and charitable purposes, more foundations of that description having been established under the three kings of the Anglo-Norman dynasty than during the whole preceding or

Self-imposed penances.

subsequent period of English history. Very many also sought rest and consolation in the places of refuge from the world afforded by the Church. Interior remorse or sorrow could leave no token in history, except in the case of him who had been the great cause and originator of the wrong; the gratifications, the employments, and above all the heavy anxieties of royalty, might in some degree blunt his recollection of his own deeds when in health and vigour, but the whole came upon him with unutterable bitterness in the hour of death.

Chapter XI.

AFFAIRS OF FLANDERS—WILLIAM SUBDUES MAINE—DISTURBANCES IN ENGLAND—RALPH GUADER'S CONSPIRACY—EXECUTION OF WALTHEOF.

1073—1075.

§ 1. WILLIAM, during the transactoins narrated in the previous chapters, had been fully four years absent from Normandy. The Duchy had been governed, and well governed, by the faithful and prudent Matilda; but heavy sorrows were falling on her, and great troubles were arising, in which she required counsel and aid. For this purpose, her husband first sent over William Fitz-Osbern, but the absence of this powerful [baron], so redoubtable to the English and the Welsh from his bravery, and still more from his merciless cruelty, had probably incited much of the risings in the Welsh marches; and a further delay ensued before William could pass over, however urgently his presence may have been required. *Normandy: troubles there.*

§ 2. An unnatural and implacable warfare had been carried on in the family of Matilda's father, Baldwin the Good, who died during the first years of the Conquest. Baldwin had two sons; the elder bearing his father's name, and Robert. Both the brothers, sons of the sovereign of a flourishing and *Flanders: the family of Baldwin. 1067* wealthy country, had respectively acquired opulent possessions, forming frontiers to their paternal domains. Both had obtained their sovereignties by marriage with widows, and both had successfully wooed by combining what may be called love and war. Baldwin was meek and quiet, humble and devout, altogether given to works of piety, the protector of the stranger and the orphan. When at mass, he always had his poor about him, that they might help him by their prayers; and when he succeeded to the county of Flanders, such was the peace in his time, that the plough was left in the field, and the door of the cottage remained unclosed. Richilda, his wife, with whom he gained the county of Hainault, was of an entirely opposite disposition. Beautiful, courageous as a soldier, indomitable in her passions, sagacious and crafty, she was considered by the people to be skilled in magic—a reputation which, in that country, yet retaining a deep and inward tinge of the antient Teutonic paganism, seems almost to have been considered as a praise. Hereditary Countess of Hainault, the first of her three husbands was Herman (some say, of the family of the Counts of Ardennes; others say, a branch of the house of Saxony), by whom she had two children—Roger, lame and ill-favoured, and a daughter.

Upon the death of Herman, Richilda assumed the government of Hainault in right of her children: a stepmother she was to them, not by nature, but worse—by deed. Baldwin of Lisle, anxious to procure this rich marriage for his son, and yet knowing the difficulty which there might be in imposing a Fleming upon the Hainaulters, proud as their forefathers, the Nervians, of their nationality, invaded Hainault for the purpose of giving the unreluctant Richilda the means of justifying herself to her liege lord the Emperor, and her stubborn subjects, by accepting, as it were under compulsion, the young heir of Flanders, who henceforth, from his residence in the capital of Hainault, was usually called Baldwin of Mons. The fruit of this marriage was Arnolf the Simple and another Baldwin. Dearly loved were they by Richilda, who in order to secure the succession to her new family, placed her daughter in a monastery, and induced her son, lame Roger, to take holy orders, and afterwards procured for him the Bishoprick of Chalons. So much for the elder of Matilda's brothers. Robert, the younger, was the very opposite in character to Baldwin of Mons. Hard and rigid, powerful and impetuous, it is said that when young his father sent him abroad to seek his fortune as a sea king. Driven off by the Moors in Spain, he entered Constantinople in the disguise of a pilgrim; there he plotted with the Northmen, there settled in the Byzantine service, for the deposition of the Emperor. Here again he was unsuccessful, and deservedly; and his third attempt was upon Friezeland, by which we must understand that portion afterwards called Holland, from a very small district, whose name, by one of those accidents which render political nomenclatures of so much importance, soon extended itself to the exclusion of the antient denomination.

§ 3. Friezeland, for so we must still call it, was at this time governed by Gertrude of Saxony, the widow of Count Floris, or Florence, by whom she had one son, Thierry. It is supposed, and not unreasonably, that Robert had gained Gertrude's consent, and that she was as willing to accept a second mate as Richilda was. But as female sovereigns were rarely allowed a choice, it was needful also for her to appear to act under coercion, and the maritime war carried on by Robert afforded her the reason and the excuse for accepting his hand. However accomplished, the marriage was entirely successful to the State. His bold and sturdy disposition was congenial to that of Gertrude's subjects; he conformed himself to their habits and customs—so much so that he became, as it were, a Friezelander, and obtained the name of Robert the Frizon; a name grateful to the Teutonic portion of Flanders, but used somewhat contemptuously by those of the Roman tongue.

The right of succession to the Earldom of Flanders depended very much upon the will of the parent. Being composed of self-existing communities, each possessing a national individuality, it was easy to detach any of them as an apanage for a cadet. The county of Boulogne had been created in this manner. Latterly, however, it became evident that this process would morsel up the country, and Baldwin of Lisle had determined to avoid it, by appointing Baldwin of Mons his sole heir. But his power of making this appointment was not sufficiently confirmed to prevent the possibility of dissension, and Robert the Frizon was not of a temper to promise acquiescence in any disposition of the inheritance which he might consider as a wrong. Baldwin of Lisle, therefore, not long before his death, which he felt approaching, convened the prelates and the peers of Flanders —for Flanders had her twelve peers, like France —at Oudenarde, and giving Robert a large sum of money as a compensation, he induced him to swear that he would not disturb his brother Baldwin in the succession. And he kept the oath to the letter; for during the three years that Baldwin of Mons reigned in Flanders he was undisturbed.

Upon the death of Baldwin, Richilda assumed the government, ruling in the name of her son Arnolf, now titular Count of Flanders and of Hainault, the first by his father's, the other by his mother's side. Richilda had encreased the possessions of her husband and her children by fair means and foul. She had acquired great portion of the allodial property in Hainault, and, ruling in Flanders, she despised all rights and privileges. Besides the connection of blood, there was a strong inclination on her part towards France. Philip had received the order of knighthood from Baldwin of Lisle: Richilda belonged to the Gallican portion of Belgium. She called in French counsellors, and imposed heavy, illegal, and degrading taxes upon the free people of the free country—degrading, because one appears to have been a house-tax, which was charged upon every door, every window, and, if we read the chronicle rightly, every bed or counterpane, which of course involved those domiciliary inspections by the tax-gatherer, odious at all times, but more particularly in those where the officers of the Sovereign were so often protected in injustice. Richilda's misrule fell most heavily upon Flanders Flamingante. Ghent and Bruges, Furnes, Oudenburgh and Ardenburgh, and Ypres, all invited Robert. Even Lisle joined the party; and Robert entered the country, which submitted to him, though not without resistance on the part of the sturdy Richilda. Yet she knew she could not make a stand without aid, and she implored the assistance of her two liege lords, the Emperor and the King of France.

§ 4. These troubles were extending themselves into Normandy. The Normans were dividing into parties; some siding, as it seems, with Robert—some with Richilda. Gerbod, the late

Earl of Chester, gave his powerful help to Robert. William appears to have much distrusted the Frizon, for his Frizian territories put him in close connection with the Danes; and Robert was not to be trusted. He therefore sent over Fitz-Osbern to assist Matilda in her emergency. In itself, the cause of Richilda, considered as the guardian of her son Arnolf, was the right one, and Philip entered heartily into her cause, assembling a large army, and requiring, as it seems, William to give that aid which, as Duke of Normandy, he was bound, or supposed to be bound, to give in the host of his superior. This consisted only of ten knights; but at the head of them Fitz-Osbern marched to Flanders as merrily as to a May game. Well he might, for a courtship had begun between him and Richilda, and she joyfully accepted him as her third husband, to the great indignation of the Flemings.

margin: 1078 — 1071. William aids Richilda: Who marries Fitz-Osbern.

The armies encountered each other at Cassel, and the greatest battle ensued, on the feast of St. Peter in Cathedra, which ever yet had taken place in Flanders. Robert's troops were much discouraged, for the forces which had joined Richilda, and more particularly those brought by the King of the French, were overwhelming —nor, perhaps, were they without apprehension of Richilda's spells. The fortunes of the battle were as varied as if it had been a tale of romance. Robert the Frizon was taken prisoner,

margin: Battle of Cassel, 20 Feb. 1071.

and carried off to St. Omer. But men said that Richilda's spells literally recoiled upon her, and brought on herself that evil fortune which she sought to cast upon the enemy. She and her troops were entirely defeated. Young Arnolf fought bravely: two horses were killed under him, but he fell by the hand of Gerbod, his own liege-man. Fitz-Osbern, the bridegroom, was killed, to the great joy of all the Flemings, who might anticipate in him a grievous Sovereign; and even more to that of the English and the Welsh, who triumphed in being released from his atrocious tyranny. Richilda herself was also taken prisoner; but she was exchanged for Robert, and being received in Hainault, transmitted the dominion to her son Baldwin; and, afterwards entering a convent, she subjected herself to fearful penance.

Robert the Frizon, on his part, entered into the full government, which he ruled strenuously during thirty years. Great ill-will always subsisted between him and his brother-in-law. William withdrew the Feudum de Camera, the pension which he had paid to Baldwin; and Robert retaliated by troubling Normandy as much as he could. He formed an alliance, of all others the most distasteful to William, by giving his daughter in marriage to Canute, King of Denmark—a marriage the result of which will introduce us to another important chapter of Norman history.

§ 5. This trouble was scarcely at an end when another arose, touching William even more nearly. The Manceaux hated the Normans, their oppressors, and despised them as barbarians. The grant, such as it was, which had been made to him by Herbert, the son of Herbert Eveille-Chiens, was invalid; and whether truly formed or not, the opinion that William had acquired possession by crime,—by the poison administered to Gauthier and Biota,—continued to excite great detestation. The Manceaux watched their opportunity; and the first token which they gave of their determination to regain their independence was by proceeding to the election of a Bishop. Clergy and people both united in choosing Arnauld of Avranches to the vacant see.

Hatred of William in Maine.

A great attack was thus made upon the prerogatives claimed by William, and it was followed up by the most determined assertion of independence. The citizens of Le Mans rose with one accord and as of one mind. The adjoining towns and chatellaineries joined them: so also many of the common soldiery. William's fortresses, so skilfully raised, could not sustain the attack; neither Orbitel nor Mont Barbette could hold out. William's Norman commanders, Turgis de Tracy, and William de la Ferté, were killed; and those of the Conqueror's soldiery who did not come over to the insurgents, shared the same fate, or were slain or expelled. The

Le Mans revolts.

capital thus taking the lead, the insurrection spread simultaneously throughout the country, almost all the optimates joining; Geoffrey de Mayenne again coming forward actively as a leader, and assailing the Normans with all his influence and power.

Le Mans first seeks a Sovereign.

Having thus cast off the foreign yoke, the Manceaux had to select some chief under whose name they might rally. Republican as their traditions were, they did not venture, as had been done in Italy, to place themselves only under an elective Roman magistracy. Powerful enemies had they to apprehend:—Fulk of Anjou, who longed to reduce them again under his power, but who dared not, lest he should provoke William; and William, who, though absent amongst the troubles of England, would scarcely fail to re-assert his sovereignty. The male line of the antient comitial family was entirely extinct; but one of the nearest representatives in blood was Gersenda, whom some represent as the eldest daughter of Herbert Eveille-Chiens, but who in fact stood in the same relation to Hugh his son. Gersenda, divorced from Theobald, Count of Blois, had taken as her second husband Azzo, or Albert Azzo, himself a widower. Este and Rovigo, and the Lunigiana, constituted his dominions; and the title of Marquis of Italy bespeaks his power; yet so very scanty and imperfect are the memoirs of that country, during the ninth and tenth centuries,

They apply to Azzo, husband of Gersenda.

that the patient industry of the most learned and indefatigable of historical antiquaries, has been scarcely able to trace the family of Albert Azzo in the ascending line, though his descendants take the proudest place in the princely and royal genealogies of christendom. Paula, sister of Gersenda, was equally near; for though the younger, yet primogeniture, not much attended to even with regard to males, was wholly disregarded with respect to co-heiresses. She was married to Jean de Beaugenci, Lord of the Angevine Seignory of La Flèche. His son Hélias, under more favourable circumstances, might have rivalled the Conqueror in talent, and certainly excelled him in virtue; but if Hélias at this time had any thought of contending for his ancestorial rights, his father was firmly attached to the Norman cause, and the Manceaux invited the Marquis of Italy, or of Liguria, as they also called him, to accept the dominion.

§ 6. It seems strange that Albert Azzo should have been prevailed upon to quit the opulent and lovely Riviera, and the noble seats of his ancestors amidst the Eugubine hills, for the purpose of establishing himself in cold Northern Gaul; amongst people whom he would consider as barbarians, and where he would be sure to be harassed by powerful enemies. Yet the desire of acquisition, and the wish also probably of securing the apanage for his younger son, Hugh of Este, prevailed; and he came over.

1070—1073

But returns to Italy.

Azzo's munificence at first acquired for him universal favour amongst the Manceaux, but that favour diminished with his resources. His treasures and their fidelity failed at the same time. If they abandoned him lightly, he deserted them with equal facility, and not them alone, for, returning to Italy, he left his wife Gersenda and his son Hugh of Este under the protection, *sub tutelâ*, of Geoffrey of Mayenne.

Geoffrey then rules.

As soon as Azzo had departed, Geoffrey of Mayenne appeared to all the world as Gersenda's husband. He assumed the government of the country; perhaps not without ulterior views, being himself of the blood of the Counts of Maine. His conduct was in itself sufficient to excite much odium. He encreased it by his exactions, and the citizens of Maine now gave a further development to their principles by establishing a Communia.

Le Mans asserts independence.

§ 7. This event, an event of the greatest importance, was certainly an out-breaking of the spirit which had given rise to the Lombard republicks, and which slowly, yet steadily, encreasing, developed itself in the Eidgenossenschaft of the Swiss, and thence onward, encreasing until its present uncontroullable power. But though I fully admit that it assisted in forming the municipal institutions of the French monarchy, I doubt the correctness of the theory which assigns to them its origin. Le Mans certainly had its municipality from the Roman times, though this new league was intended to give it a sovereign energy. We learn from Mans that the connecting element of the Communia was the oath, by which the members bound themselves to mutual fidelity. No freedom of action, no flinching was allowed; those who did not belong to the Communia, those who were not engaged by its bond, were excluded from all protection. The Communists ruled by terror: the most cruel punishments were inflicted, either without any legal judgment, or worse, by judgments having the semblance of legal form, but without legal foundation or verity.

1070—1073

Despotic freedom.

The nobles, as in Italy, were compelled to incorporate themselves in the Communia, Geoffrey de Mayenne sorely against his will. Had he refused, he might have lost his eyes or swung upon the tree. So also the Bishop: at the beginning of the disturbances, Arnold escaped to England, bringing the tidings to the King, by whom he was received with honour and rewarded. He returned, evidently for the purpose of aiding the royal cause, therefore the angry citizens would not receive him within the walls; but when, by the ill-advised interference of the clergy, he was permitted to reassume his episcopal functions, the citizens compelled him to join their cause.

Discontent in the city.

§ 8. There was one noble, however, who, depending on the strength of his castle, entirely refused to join the Communia;—this was Hugh de

Sulley, who not merely refused to take the oath and enrol himself amongst the citizens, but acted aggressively against them. This was a dangerous example: they raised and roused all their forces, and compelled the Bishop and the parish priests to lead before them, with gonfanons displayed, and St. Julian's banner. The communists surrounded the castle of Sulley; Geoffrey of Mayenne rendering his coerced co-operation, encamped apart, secretly conferring with the besieged, and turning all his mind to consider how he might best deceive or betray the confederates. Sulley and his men came forth, and bullied and defied the communists; they were tumultuously preparing for the fight, when a report, probably originated by Geoffrey de Mayenne, spread through the motley crowd, that Le Mans was in the power of the Normans. A desperate panic ensued: all fled. Bishop Arnold was taken prisoner, but courteously treated and released. The citizens got back to Le Mans, having suffered great loss, and in the utmost confusion.

Geoffrey de Mayenne was now in such ill repute, equally from his scandalous connection with Gersenda, and also from his treachery, which was now well understood, that he dared not continue in Le Mans, but retreated to Château du Loire. Gersenda now had to take counsel how she should regain her paramour, and also restore him to power. Hugh of Este was sent back by his mother and his guardian to Italy.

The plans of the Countess were so far successful, that the great castle of Le Mans was betrayed to him. He filled it with his troops, and threatened the subjugation of the new republic. Fear overcame prudence: the citizens sought the aid of Fulk of Anjou: he gave it readily, and entered with his troops: the castle was very strong, and its position commanding. As usual, the city suffered much by the attempt to reduce the fortress: part was burned; at length Geoffrey de Mayenne was compelled to surrender, and Gersenda was forgotten in obscurity and shame.

§ 9. Such had been the urgent perils of England, that when William was first informed by Arnold of the revolt of Maine, he could not then make any endeavour to regain his power; but when Fulk of Anjou entered the country, he was enabled to adopt the needful measures for revenging the insult offered to his authority. This was just at the juncture when the long series of conflicts having been terminated by Malcolm's submission, all seemed quiet and secure in his realm. All the English chieftains whom he might have feared, were banished, or in the dungeon, or slain. Wales was kept quiet by Robert de Breteuil, to whom, upon the death of Fitz-Osbern, William had granted the great Earldom of Hereford, and who promised in every way to emulate his father. Waltheof, now a member of the Norman family, was established in Northumbria: the dangerous coast opposite to Denmark, well and effectually guarded by Ralph de Guader, the Earl of East Anglia: and he therefore determined to carry on the war in person against the insurgents.

Regents in England.

As Regents or Justiciars during his absence, he appointed William de Warrenne and Richard de Benefacta; but others whom he could well trust also had a share in command. Geoffrey de Mowbray,—whose title of Bishop of Coutances, can alone remind us of his ecclesiastical functions, which he seems entirely to have abandoned, —continued as commander-in-chief, at least of the soldiery of the southern districts. Odo of Bayeux had nearly the same disgraceful preeminence.

§ 10. All preparations made, William issued his summons to his lieges, commanding them to accompany him in his voyage royal. When he had crossed the channel and entered Normandy, his troops were estimated at sixty thousand men, unquestionably an exaggeration; but the force was very large, and the English constituted a very considerable proportion of the army. William advanced into Maine, but not rapidly, devastating the country as he proceeded, burning towns and villages, spoiling the crops and destroying the vineyards. This is the first time that Englishmen ever fought upon French ground, and they did their work heartily. No resistance of any importance could be offered. Fresnay surrendered: before its walls William conferred the degree of knighthood upon Robert, the son of Roger of Montgomery, heir also of Talvas, *1073* heir also of Belesme, which name or title he assumed, and who here began his career of cruelty and violence. Sulley next surrendered, and all the country as William advanced accepted his authority with seeming joyfulness. Fulk dared not wait his approach. William presented him- *Takes Mans.* self before Mans. He solemnly summoned the inhabitants to surrender, and thus avert the punishment otherwise prepared for them. One day's consultation determined them to submit. Mans saw her republic expire. Forth came the citizens bearing the keys, and humbly craving mercy: they were graciously received: William promised them the full enjoyment of their usages and customs, and the whole province followed the example of the capital.

Fulk, however, bearing for some short time, *Fulk resists.* but with great vexation, this success of the Normans, renewed his endeavours to re-possess himself of the Maine. He began by intriguing amongst the Baronage. Some willingly entered into his schemes; but John de la Flêche, who himself would have had a good and plausible reason for opposing William, adhered to him with the greatest fidelity, and therefore became the object of Fulk's inveterate hostility. The war began again. Hoel of Brittany came to the help of Fulk. William again raised the combined forces of the Normans and the English: the Angevines and the Bretons under Hoel and Fulk advanced

<small>1079</small>

<small>[1079, Art. de v. 1. dates.]</small>

<small>But Maine is secured to William.</small>

to meet the Anglo-Norman forces, but no actual conflict ensued. The Cardinal Legate mediated, and a treaty of peace was concluded at La Blanchelande. William's right over Maine was confirmed by Fulk, and he might again write himself "Dux Cœnomanensium" in his royal charters. But what was even more important, the right of Robert was confirmed in like manner. Betrothed as he had been to Margaret, it might have been said that the marriage never having been completed, his right had expired, but it was now solemnly acknowledged by his liege lord.

<small>William's sons.</small>

§ 11. William continued some time longer in Normandy, enjoying the return of prosperity. No object had he so much at heart as securing the succession of Robert to his French dominions. Robert, his first-born, was most particularly the object of his father's unwise fondness. Clever, but bold and turbulent, he had already shewn undutifulness towards his father; and great dissensions had risen between him and his two surviving brothers, William and Henry, though Robert had already attained manhood, and Henry was almost a child. Richard, who intervened between Robert and William, now commonly called Rufus, was dead: a youth of great promise, but who had been killed in some mysterious manner, which seemed to make people loth to speak even of the circumstance; and the very short and obscure notices of his death are

<small>Richard.</small>

the only matters recorded concerning him in history, though his name appears occasionally as a member of the great council, and as such attesting his father's charters.

1078-4

It seems that, even at this period, Robert Courthose put forth those pretensions which excited the envy of his brothers. He became the head of a party of young men of congenial disposition; and although William was yet very vigorous, there were many who began to be inclined to court the heir-apparent, and amongst them one who was much in William's favour, Robert de Belesme, who, if knighthood constituted, as has been supposed, a special obligation between the parties conferring and receiving the degree, was, so far, William's adopted son. When the Conqueror was told of the escapades which the heir-apparent committed, he was amused by these demonstrations of character. He took them as a joke, and said, with an oath, Courthose will become a good soldier as he grows older.

Robert.

Matilda viewed her sons' dissensions in a very different light; they occasioned to her great grief and sorrow: her mind was full of evil forebodings, and she consulted, as it is said, a holy man, a hermit on the Rhine, supposed to have the gift of prophecy, as to the destinies which would befal her children. After three days, he gave his answer; and such was the answer as ever thereafter to fill her heart with sorrow. Neither piety

Matilda's anxiety.

nor intellect, neither scepticism nor even infidelity, will restrain mankind from seeking the forbidden knowledge of futurity; and the history of nations, as well as that of individuals, testifies how remarkably these attempts to lift up the veil of futurity, whether begun in faith, or effected by demoniacal agency, or by mere juggling and delusion, have been punished by drawing down the curse and the misfortune.

§ 12. In other respects, William was in tranquillity: Normandy well governed and flourishing, and he and Matilda, amongst other works of piety, continued the erection of their two great monasteries, which although begun nearly ten years before, had proceeded but slowly. St. Etienne was however advancing towards completion, and it seems that even in this, intended to be a good work, William proceeded with his characteristic impetuosity and want of regard for the rights of others. The greater portion of the church and monastery was built upon his own domains, but there was a small piece of land upon which the eastern part of the Basilica was to stand which belonged to one Asceline. It occupied the space of the presbytery and choir. William was never deficient in liberality; but whether Asceline asked too large a price or otherwise offended the Conqueror, we know not; but whatever were the circumstances, William seized the land against the owner's will, and the usurped portion was enclosed within the consecrated walls.

§ 13. Whilst William was thus successful upon the main-land, he was again in most imminent danger of losing the kingdom he had won. His acquisition of the crown had been reprobated as an act of injustice; and if this were dubious, there were none who could deny the wrong he had inflicted upon the English as a nation, not even they who had profited the most by the spoil. Moreover, there was a great and general dissatisfaction prevailing amongst a large portion of the Anglo-Norman settlers. There was no principle upon which the land had been distributed, except William's absolute will and pleasure. They despised, or affected to despise, the sterile fields and wasted and depopulated domains, with which, as they alleged, their services had been mocked and not rewarded. No ruler who pays by confiscations ever earns the love of his dependants. If they are loyal to him, it is simply to the extent that his interests are united to their own. Heavy taxations had been repeatedly imposed by William, and in this respect, there was no immunity for the conquering race. The land was charged equally, by whomsoever it was held. In addition to the injuries resulting from the prosecution of the wars and insurrections which had raged in England, there had been a succession of unfavourable seasons. Indeed, during the whole of William's reign, murrain destroyed the cattle; storms and tempests wasted the immature harvests. There is no stage of society in which these afflictions have not a political influence.—To supply the fruits of the earth is beyond man's creative power, and the pestilence or the famine distract the plans of the wisest government, and cause both the heart and hand of man to fail.

§ 14. Amongst the conquering settlers, there were, as has been before observed, a great number of Bretons. In coming over to England, they had brought with them their dislike of the Normans, and the Normans continued to hate and despise them. They considered the Bretons as a foul race; and whether they were *Bretons bretonnants*, or *Bretons gallicants*, they were equally disliked. It was amongst them, largely as they had been rewarded, that the discontent began, and of this the chief and leader was Ralph Guader. Earl of East Anglia, he had rendered good service to William, but a cause of offence arose which extended itself to another most influential chieftain.

It seems that Fitz-Osbern's daughter had been promised in marriage to Guader, and upon the death of the Earl of Hereford, his son Roger carried the contract into effect by bestowing the maiden upon her betrothed. William was extremely offended by this alliance. The cause of his anger is not clearly understood, but if we can join the various and very discordant accounts, it should seem, that, having first fully sanctioned the marriage, he afterwards forbade it:—whether he fully possessed the prerogative of wardship over the daughters of his tenants *in capite*, and could therefore retract any license he had given, or whether he dreaded the union of two such powerful houses, cannot be ascertained; but he manifested his anger: and the two nobles, perhaps out of apprehension for themselves, determined to strike the first blow, and conspired to dethrone the King.

1075

The bridal feast was held at the now obscure village of Ixning, near the Rech-dyke, dividing the kingdoms of East Anglia and Mercia, on the borders of Guader's Earldom. As usual, there was a numerous and merry gathering, and amidst the wassail and the gleeman's song, the plot so fatal to its authors, was matured.

Meeting at the marriage.

Amongst the guests was one invited, not without deep purpose,—Waltheof. His government of Northumbria, notwithstanding his feuds, had continued encreasing in strength and popularity. This was owing in great measure to his thorough union of interest with the Bishop Walchere. In order that the Bishop might be the better able to dwell safely at Durham, Waltheof had encreased the fortifications, perhaps rebuilt the castle which Gospatric began; and when the Bishop held his synod, Waltheof sat humbly in a low place amongst the presbyters, concurring in every measure needed for the preservation of "Christianity" in the Earldom. Waltheof, who had joined the Earldom of North-

Waltheof invited.

1075

Waltheof's position in England.

ampton to Northumbria, was the last representative of the high nobility of old England. He alone remained in wealth and apparent prosperity. Yet Waltheof must have been always morally in solitude;—where could he look for his former peers? those who had been his companions in place, in power, and in dignity. Could he deem that he was walking safely?—and might not the suspicion sometimes cross his mind, that the proud young Norman damsel whom he had espoused in his old age, Judith, or Edith, as the English were pleased to call her, the Conqueror's niece, had been bestowed upon him to watch his fidelity towards the Norman King? All this must have been felt as well by the Normans as by himself: and if he, whose influence might be expected to draw over a large portion of the native English, could be induced to co-operate, the success of the enterprise might be considered as ensured.

A plot formed.

§ 15. The plot had been long maturing, not unobserved by those who represented William in command. It was first opened to Waltheof during the height of the marriage festivities: the discourse is said to have been artfully conducted; and, after expatiating upon William's certain crimes and grievous tyranny, and the many offences imputed to him by common fame, Guader and Fitz-Osbern disclosed to Waltheof their great plan for a division of the kingdom. It was now the time, they told him, when Albion might reassert her liberty. Two of them were to be dukes, the third the paramount king.

1075

Did Waltheof agree to this projected revolution? or are we to believe that he strenuously resisted the offer, testifying against the guilt of treason, and pointing out the punishment it would infallibly receive? or did he, his mind obscured by the potent contents of the circling horn, give an imperfect assent to the plot, which when the dawning light brought sobriety and recollection, overwhelmed him with dread and confusion? It is certain that whatever may have been his words or his silence on that fatal eve, he never concurred in any act testifying discontent or even approaching to rebellion. Whatever charge may afterwards have been brought against him for concurring in the conspiracy, must have been grounded upon suspicion or surmise, or collected from the scarcely less dubious testimony of those who were really guilty, and sought to involve him in their crime, or, worse than all, of those who betrayed any declaration he may have made in secret and familiar converse.

Doubts as to Waltheof's complicity.

Waltheof's opposition to the plot, for such seems to have been his real conduct, greatly troubled the confederates, but did not disconcert them. Aid had been invited from Denmark; from Canute, the son-in-law of Robert le Frizon, perhaps also from the Frizon himself, and was confidently expected. Roger de Breteuil marched

Progress the plot.

1075

Norman opposition.

without opposition to his Earldom of Hereford, where he collected a very large force and began to ravage the adjoining territories. But all these marchlands were filled with castles, well stored, well manned, and particularly that of Worcester. This was held by Urso de Abitot, who held the rank of Hereditary Sheriff, or rather Vicecount in Worcestershire, in which county he possessed very large domains. He was a bold man, and unsparing, and when building the castle, he bearded the monks, encroaching upon their cemetery, and raising the outworks upon consecrated ground.—

> "Hightest thou Urse,
> Have thou the curse,"

was the angry reply of the Archbishop of York, when the report of Abitot's encroachments was brought to him. Walter de Lacy, another very powerful Baron, and who held much land in and within de Breteuil's Earldom, was also unalterably faithful to the royal cause.

English against the plot.

§ 16. All this Norman opposition might however have been rendered fruitless, had Roger de Breteuil met with any encouragement from the English; but all the hatred which they had borne to Fitz-Osbern was transferred to his son, and they most cordially co-operated with the King's troops and the King's partizans, for the purpose of expelling the lineage of the oppressor.

In spite of the anathema passed upon Urse, old Bishop Wolfstan most cordially joined him in taking the lead against the insurgents, and raised, if he did not personally command, the forces of his bishoprick. So also did Aylwine, the Abbot of Evesham, and although they did not immediately succeed in capturing the Earl of Hereford, they entirely prevented his forming a junction, which he had intended to do, with the Earl of East Anglia.

1075

Ralph de Guader had, at the same time, advanced towards London; but Bishop Mowbray and Bishop Odo were fully on the alert, and with combined forces of Normans and of English, for Guader appears to have been almost as unpopular as Fitz-Osbern, they attacked him near Cambridge, where his forces were completely routed. All who fell into the power of the Bishops were treated with inexorable cruelty, but he escaped to Norwich, and entrusting the command of the castle to his young bride, embarked and escaped to Denmark.

Defeat of Guader.

Ida displayed the accustomed strenuousness of the Norman women, and, encouraged by her, her forces sturdily defended the wide circuit of the castle and the burgh, so bravely indeed as to enable them to make reasonable terms with the Norman forces, which were ratified by the King. They were to come forth, and not to suffer in life and limb. Ralph himself was to

Siege of Norwich Castle.

forfeit his honours and his lands; his followers were to quit the realm within forty days, but they might return with the King's license. Ida sailed to Brittany, where she was shortly afterwards joined by her husband. William de Warrenne and Robert Malet took possession of the castle with three hundred men-at-arms, which, with the proportionate number of light armed troops and other soldiery, probably constituted the largest garrison the castle ever held; and Lanfranc was able to announce to the Conqueror that England was again pacified.

§ 17. War had done its work, but imperfectly, and now the heavier terrors of judgment were to follow. Towards the close of the autumn, William, having taken order for the administration of Normandy, leaving Matilda, as it should seem, at Caen, and giving the command of the castle at Rouen to the chief butler [cupbearer] of Normandy, Roger de Ivry, passed over to England. Roger de Breteuil was summoned to answer for his crime. Defence, there was none: judgment was given against him according to the Norman law: all his lands were forfeited, and he was condemned to perpetual imprisonment. It should seem that William had somewhat relented in favour of his kinsman, the son of his old and trusty friend. Courtesy diminished the hardships of captivity; and when the Easter festival arrived, the royal servants entered into Roger's chamber, bearing a pile of costly garments, the silken vest, the furred robe, the ensigns of the dignity of the Earldom. Such tokens were significant; might they not tacitly convey a message of comfort? might they not indicate to the captive that he would be permitted to display them amongst the Proceres at the festival of the ensuing Pentecost? If any such mitigation was preparing for the son of Fitz-Osbern, his own spiteful impatience rivetted his chains. He cast the gifts into the flames, exclaiming that they were sent to him, not in kindness but in mockery. A more forgiving temper than that of William's might have been offended by this contumely. He was chafed and vexed to extreme anger, and vowed that so long as he lived, Roger de Breteuil should never quit his prison house—neither did William's death give any release to the captive, who expired in his dungeon.

Offends William.

The proscription was extended to all his family; his sons, Reginald and Roger, excelling in valour and distinguished by exemplary truth, faithful servants to Rufus, faithful servants to Beauclerc, they were nevertheless marked, so long as they lived, by the stern displeasure of each sovereign. Depressed, degraded, pining under the heart-sick expectation of some restoration to their ancestorial rank, they pined in vain; and it was remarked by the English as a memorable proof of retributive justice, that the progeny of William Fitz-Osbern, the Count

Punishment of his family.

of Hereford, the Count of Flanders, the High Steward of Normandy, the confidant, the friend, the sharer in the authority of the King, but who had so mercilessly tyrannized over the conquered, should be utterly eradicated from the country he had so unjustly won.

William's regents were so confident of success, that knowing the chances of disturbance in Normandy, of which there were many, they had exhorted him not to trouble himself by immediately repairing to England. Waltheof had, directly after his participation in the unhappy festivities of Ixning, visited Lanfranc, and, consulting him both in his sacerdotal and secular character, opened the matter to him. Lanfranc, entirely convinced of his innocence as to any intentional participation in the treason, advised him to go to Normandy, to acknowledge all that he had said or done, and to implore William's forgiveness. The Earl of Northumbria obeyed the counsel and crossed over; but William received him sternly, and proffered no forgiveness, and the reason was a most painful one. Judith had shamelessly accused her husband of direct intentional and active concurrence in the treason.

§ 18. Sad and sorrowful was the festival of the Nativity, celebrated in the palace and abbey of Westminster. Edgitha, the Confessor's widow, was borne to the grave, and placed in the tomb by the side of her husband, where their bones still rest undisturbed.

William wore his crown as usual, but sitting in his High Court of Justice; and now the judicial proceedings began. With the meaner criminals, justice was fearfully expeditious. Against many, sentence of perpetual banishment was passed: many suffered amputation of their limbs: many had their eyes pierced with a hot iron: many were hanged, hanged to their shame, for this was the disgraceful death reserved by the English law for the thief, or those guilty of infamous crimes. First, the King dealt with Waltheof: a partial hearing of his case began. Judith came forward as the witness against him. No one overt act could be alleged even by her malice, and he openly and freely acknowledged that which he never had attempted to deny, that he had been an unwary and incautious listener; but that he himself had never, in word or deed, contemplated rebellion or treason. Many of the Normans, longing for the spoil, for those honours and lands of which so large a portion afterwards passed to lame Simon de Senlize, were very anxious to procure his condemnation, but nevertheless the great council could not agree in passing such a sentence. It seems to have been doubted whether the facts admitted by Waltheof were sufficient to convict him, and perhaps also whether his prompt and unreserved confession was not in itself a testimony of his substantial innocence. Much also must be allowed for the natural revulsion of feeling in his favour; in favour of one the subject of such odious and wicked domestic treachery,—and he was therefore committed to prison in the castle of Winchester.

Waltheof at Winchester:

Waltheof awaited his judgment in the prison of Winchester for more than a year. His days and hours were wholly given to penitence and prayer: one portion of his devotional exercises being the repetition of the psalter, which his mother had taught him in early youth, every day. His case was repeatedly argued and discussed before the tribunal; till at length the influence of his adversaries prevailed, and he was condemned to die. Judged by the stern and rigid letter of the law, it cannot be denied that he had fallen within its danger. According to our existing jurisprudence, not differing probably much in this respect whether from the Anglo-Saxon or Anglo-Norman law, there are no gradations of guilt in treason. All are principals, and misprision of treason, that is to say the concealment of the crime, would subject the imprudent participator in the fatal knowledge to capital punishment at the present day. Yet Waltheof's misfortunes, his wife's baseness, his piety, his contrition, excited much sympathy even amongst the Normans, and universally

Case against him:

amongst the English. All believed him to be substantially guiltless of any crime. A rescue was therefore anticipated, and the mode of his execution attests the apprehension which prevailed. Very early, in the chill grey of the dawning morn, was Waltheof brought forth upon the rising ground beside Winchester, where the church of St. Giles was afterwards erected. He knelt before the block, and began to repeat the Lord's prayer, but before he could complete the petition "*ne nos inducas in tentationem*," the sword of the headsman swung; and when the citizens were coming forth to their daily labours, the train of priests and bedesmen, returning from the scaffold, informed them of the fate which the Earl of Northumbria had sustained.

§ 19. Where Waltheof had expired, they interred his remains: a grave hastily dug in the chalky soil received them; and, scantily shrouded by the green turf laid again, they were abandoned in the unconsecrated ground, as if he were the vilest criminal, and as if for the purpose of disgracing his memory. But William and Judith were soon brought to the feeling that this attempt to dishonour the dead recoiled upon themselves. By Judith's request, William permitted that the body of the last English Earl should be removed to St. Guthlac's monastery. Gladly did the monks of Croyland undertake the sacred and

1075

joyful charge of performing the solemn rites due to their benefactor. Fifteen days after the death of Waltheof, Ulfkettle and his brethren arrived at the capital of Wessex, and proceeding to the place of execution, they removed the fresh laid green sward and opened the new grave and uncovered the corpse. It seemed as if the blow had just been struck, so fresh was his countenance and so unchanged his mortal spoil: it was seen, men said, that he had died in the midst of prayer. The martyr's relics, for such Waltheof was already deemed, were deposited in the Chapter House of Croyland. Many tokens, as it was soon reported, were given of Waltheof's sanctity. Judith, abhorred as his murderess, appeared, seemingly penitent, before the tomb, and covered it with a costly silken pall; but the offering was repelled from the marble, as if driven away by the whirlwind; and the contumely, the disappointment, the poverty and the wretchedness, which pursued her unceasingly till her death, were noted as the warning testimonies of her crime.

Honours done to Waltheof after death.

William's jealousy.

William's suspicions were excited by the national feeling nourished at Croyland. Accusations were preferred against Abbot Ulfkettle, the Englishman. He was deposed, and banished to Glastonbury; Ingulph, another Englishman, was appointed by the Conqueror in his stead. As usual, he had begun his career as one of the Conqueror's chaplains, and having received the habit, and his foreign training and education, in the great Norman Abbey of Fontenel, was probably considered by his patron as detaching him from the English cause. Not so : the honours rendered to Waltheof encreased, and the more splendid shrine erected by the new Abbot near the High Altar of the church which he restored, attracted more and more votaries. Ingulph was entirely an Englishman at heart, and the legendary history which passes under his name, though interpolated and enlarged, may be considered, when compared with the brief but more authentic memorials preserved, as an exponent of his feelings. Ingulph was succeeded by Gosfrid of Orleans, who had professed in the monastery of St. Evreux. Learned and kind and liberal, he adopted, Frenchman as he was, all the *religio loci*. More and more did the veneration rendered to Waltheof encrease, and daily did the resort of English pilgrims become more and more numerous, and more and more were the miracles talked of which had been vouchsafed at the shrine. A Norman monk scoffed and scorned this devotion, offered at the tomb, as he said, of a traitor who had received condign punishment. Gosfrid reproved him kindly but solemnly. The sudden illness and speedy death of the reviler, and the vision which appeared to the Abbot, added still more to the national veneration.

Time passed on, till at length he who has preserved to us the living history of the times, Ordericus, visited the Abbey of Croyland. His talents were celebrated, and the epitaph which he was desired to compose, and which was inscribed upon the sarcophagus, perpetuated the remembrance of the injustice which the English nation had, in the person of Waltheof, sustained. Nor did William ever recover from the moral condemnation due to his injustice: and when the pilgrim brought his offerings to the shrine, he was told how William's good fortune deserted him from the day that Waltheof died. Never again during the remainder of his reign, did he enjoy peace; never did he prosper. He resisted his enemies as boldly as ever, for his prowess was undiminished, his mind unclouded; but his bow was broken, his sword was blunted: never again was he able to defeat the enemy in the field or to storm the beleaguered city, until that fatal success which brought him to the grave.

Chapter XII.

WILLIAM RETURNS TO THE CONTINENT.—SIEGE OF DÔL.—QUARRELS BETWEEN ROBERT AND HIS FATHER.—BATTLE OF GERBEROI.—ROBERT'S SECOND OUTBREAK.—DISTURBANCES IN NORTHUMBRIA.—BISHOP ODO'S IMPRISONMENT.—MATILDA'S DEATH.

1075—1083.

§ 1. THE escape of Ralph Guader from Norwich Castle gave further trouble to William. He arrived safely in Denmark. Canute assembled a large fleet, upon which he embarked with the sturdy Earl Haco. They entered the Humber, surprised York, plundered the Minster, and sailed away with ample spoil. They made for Flanders; some perished, apparently by a storm, but the success of the enterprize was sufficient, with the promised aid of Robert the Frizon, who continued to nourish an implacable enmity against his brother-in-law, to concert another and more formidable invasion.

Guader escapes and joins the Danes:

Ralph Guader returned to Brittany, where he occupied the city of Dôl. Much enmity was arising against William. Philip of France never was otherwise than inimical, though not always in active hostility. All the borders of Normandy were more or less disturbed or inclined to give disturbance. The late transac-

Thence to Brittany.

tions in England had revived the national antipathy between the Normans and the Bretons. Notwithstanding the ample patronage bestowed by William upon Alan le Roux, Earl of Richmond, they considered that they were entirely out of his good will. Upon the death of Conan II., Hoel, Count of Cornouailles and Nantes, had acquired, or attempted to acquire, the supremacy of the Duchy. By marriage with Hawisa, daughter of Duke Alan, he had acquired the county of Rennes. It was very doubtful whether the right could be transmitted through a female, and his authority was much contested. Ever since the Conquest, Hoel and Alan Fergant, his son, who acted as being conjoined to him in the sovereignty, had virtually cast off the Norman suzerainty.

The protection afforded to the rebel, Guader, gave William an additional incitement against Brittany; and soon after the execution of Waltheof, he crossed over. The Normans most willingly joined him: the war had in a manner become national. Dôl was surrounded by the invading army. William swore bitterly that he would not depart until the town had surrendered at discretion. The garrison were terrified at his threats. Success appeared certain, yet, nevertheless, William continued in his camp, threatening and making demonstrations, but without attempting to assault the city, for the siege was converted into a sluggish blockade.

The delay was fatal; Alan Fergant advanced with a large force, magnified by report to 15,000 men. He was supported by powerful reinforcements from France, led on by King Philip in person. The besieged knew nothing of the army advancing to their rescue, and were even gaining some advantages over William, not distinctly specified, but which probably consisted in their having captured some of his men in their sallies; for they were such as to necessitate his making terms with them before his retreat. This he did disgracefully. He abandoned camp, baggage, horses, treasure to the amount, as it was reckoned, of thousands of pounds sterling, all of which rewarded the victors.

§ 2. This check induced William to alter his policy towards Brittany, and he acted wisely, according to a policy which the Normans and the Norman dynasty had followed with considerable success. The daughters of William and of Matilda, like all the members of this remarkable family, were distinguished; and no higher testimony can be found of Matilda's cultivation, as well as of her prudence, than the results which appeared in the character of her daughters. Agatha, the betrothed of Harold, had been sought in marriage by Alphonso, King of Galicia; but she could not transfer the affection she had felt for her first betrothed, unworthy though he was, to the Spaniard; and when sent to the Peninsula under the escort of the embassadors, despatched by the Galician prince, she prayed that she might be delivered by death. Worn out by grief and anxiety, her prayer was granted: she never saw him, and her corpse was brought back to Normandy.

William's daughters:

Cecilia: Upon the day when the monastery of the Holy Trinity was founded at Caen by William and by Matilda, the babe Cecilia was placed by her parents upon the altar, and offered to the Church. She was educated by Matilda, the abbess, and, taking most earnestly and sincerely to her vocation, she had, at the period about which we are now writing, professed, and, not very long after, the abbess having resigned, became the second superior of the community.

Adelaide: Adelaide, the most beautiful of the family, had also, when she attained a marriageable age, renounced the world, and lived and died a recluse. There were therefore but two daughters remaining who could be disposed of in marriage; Con-

Constance marries Alan. 1075— [obit, 1085.] stance, tall, fair, and prudent, became the wife of Alan Fergant, to her father's exceeding joy, and they were married with great solemnity at Caen. Like her mother, Matilda, she had great talent for government. Constance promoted the welfare of the Bretons in every way during the fifteen years that she reigned over them as their duchess, and the alliance contributed very mainly to repress the national antipathy which had subsisted between them and the Norman sovereigns.

The marriage of Constance and Alan Fergant was followed by another, even of greater importance in the history of England. Of all the daughters, Adela was the one who partook most of her father's spirit, boldness and courage. Stephen of Blois, Count Palatine of Champagne, anxiously sought her in marriage: a powerful, and, in many respects, a meritorious sovereign, but who was remarkably distinguished by a deficiency in the qualities by which Adela was characterized. To William, this marriage was of considerable political importance, for the House of Blois was one of the greatest dependencies of the French crown north of the Loire; and this marriage also was happily celebrated at Chartres, one of Stephen's capitals.

1075. Adela marries Stephen. 1081.

§ 3. These were prosperous incidents, but quite inadequate to afford any compensation for the encreasing troubles and dissensions in the royal family, and these had arisen from William's over anxiety and improvident prudence for that which he had considered the welfare of his child. There must always have been some apprehension in William's mind lest his own illegitimacy should be considered as descending to his own issue, thus opening the succession of Normandy and its dependencies to some of those who could trace their ancestry to Rollo; remote, obscure, or even fabulous as their pedigree might be. Or the King of the French might claim the Duchy as an escheat to the sovereign: the kings of France were continually gaining in authority,

Doubts as to Norman succession.

though that authority could be rarely shewn. The prestige which gave the supremacy to the king who had been crowned at Rheims and consecrated with the sainte ampoule, was constantly encreasing; and not the less influentially because that encrease was silent. William's affection for his first-born was very strong, and the very mismanagement of this favourite son shows its intensity. And the difficulties which William himself had encountered in obtaining the Norman sovereignty, had encreased his natural anxiety for the perpetuation of the dominion in his race. Hence, the repeated homage which he had caused to be performed to Robert when an infant and to Robert when a child. Hence his labours to secure the obedience of reluctant Maine: hence the confirmation he had obtained from Philip of the right of the future heir.

None of these transactions implied any intention on the part of William that he would resign his authority to his son. Yet, even in a mind far better regulated than Robert's, they might have been otherwise construed. The transactions with Philip in particular put Robert close upon a level with his father, and there were very many who found it for their advantage to persuade him that his rights were withheld. His influence encreased: Robert seemed to be very full of courage, clever, jovial and prodigal; a good speaker, a pleasant companion;

and he rapidly assembled round him a large and influential party; some, disorderly and profligate, but others of considerable standing and influence, who found it for their interest to encourage the heir-apparent's pretensions. He emulated the state of his father, lorded it over his brothers, and began to urge his pretensions to the immediate possession of Normandy and of Maine. William of course refused: father and son continued wrangling and disputing, not to that extent as to occasion an open rupture, but sufficient to excite continual disquietude, and to the mother most of all. Rufus and Beauclerc were bitterly incensed at the pre-eminence assumed by Robert, and the first, great as were the defects of his character, always showed much filial affection, but one and all were equally violent. They had not even a sufficient sense of worldly decency to attempt to restrain themselves: what they felt, they shewed; and with such a progeny was William surrounded, whether in peace or in war.

§ 4. At this period the nucleus of Robert's party consisted of Robert de Belesmes, Count of Alençon, and his connexions, mostly the powerful and turbulent Lord Marchers of Maine. Belesme, as it will be recollected, had not long since received the degree of knighthood from the King; but he passed over to Robert, and we cannot hesitate to trace the malignant inveteracy with which Robert pursued his father to the influence of this truly wicked counsellor.

Belesme and Perche.

The head of the Belesme or Alençon family was Rotrou, Lord of the castle and town of Mortaigne, which must not be confounded with Mortaine, and of the territory which, under his long government began to be called the county of Perche. Under the old monarchy, Perche was considered as the smallest of the fiefs of France; but at this period it was nevertheless a territory of considerable importance. As the border-land between Maine and Normandy and the Pays Chartrain, it might annoy or influence many neighbours more powerful than itself. Belesme was a fief of Perche, and it contained within its circuit Domfront, Nogent, and other strongholds which became of great importance in that partizan warfare which constitutes so characteristic a portion of the history of the Conqueror's family. Guarin, the founder of this line, had treacherously murdered one of his most intimate friends: he died suddenly, and was believed to have been strangled by the Demon. As in the case of the Angevine family, such traditions are always the evidence of family character, and unhappily not without influence upon it.

Rotrou makes war on William.

Rotrou was a genuine descendant of Guarin, and instigated, as it should seem, either mediately or immediately by Robert, he engaged in war with William. Henceforward indeed the colour of his history becomes tarnished and dull: he is no longer the Conqueror, bearing his triumphant banner, flushed with victory, but a commander vexed in spirit, engaged in a series of petty and frequently unfortunate conflicts and inroads, which continued until the end of his life.

§ 5. Irritated by Rotrou, William entered the Corbonnais, a portion of the territory of Perche, but intersected by domains belonging to his own vassals. In this inroad, he was accompanied by his miserable family, Robert and Robert's partizans, and William and Beauclerc, the latter still a mere lad, and those who might be considered as their adherents. In the course of the expedition, William and his troops halted at the town of L'Aigle, or Aquila. It was traditionally said that when the first founder of this stronghold began his castle, he was guided to it by an eagle, which contrary to the usual habits of the bird, had built her nest in an oak. Aquila then belonged to Richer, the brother-in-law of Hugh, Earl of Chester, and whose descendants, obtaining Pevensey and other large domains, became Lords of the great Honour of Aquila, mentioned with much emphasis in our history.

William retaliates on Perche.

In the course of the night, William was roused from his bed by a riot; a furious, and in the words of the chronicler who relates it, a demoniacal quarrel had arisen between the brothers, so fell was their conduct and bearing. The two younger, with their companions, had

Quarrel of his sons.

gone uninvited to the house where Robert was quartered; and stationing themselves in an upper chamber, they occupied themselves in playing with the dice. Whether in the rude mirth of the gamblers, or in their squabbles, they made a great uproar, and some vessel containing dirty water, was thrown over. The water, trickling through 'the ill joined planks, rained upon the head of Robert and his party in the room below.—"Are ye a man, not to revenge this shameful insult?" was the outcry instantly raised by the two Grantesmesnils, Alberic and Ivo. Robert rushed upstairs as if he were mad, and began to attack his brothers. The tumult spread through the town. King William's sudden entry prevented more immediate mischief, but Robert was not to be appeased, and he resented his father's interference as a cruel injury. A day of plotting with his companions succeeded; on the following evening, Robert and his adherents rode out across the country and attacked Rouen.

§ 6. Without doubt, they could not have ventured upon such a desperate attempt, had not their forces encreased as they advanced. They occupied the castle and palace; but Roger de Ivry, who commanded the great dungeon tower, drove them out, and without proceeding to further extremities, sent to William to know how he should act. William immediately ordered that the offenders should be seized. The command [was partially carried out.] Some were taken prisoners, but Robert was strongly supported. He returned to the marchlands. Hugh de Neuchâtel, who was Lord of Remelard and other fortresses from whence Robert could annoy his father, strongly supported him, as well as the whole Belesme connection.

1075–1078

The insurrection now began to assume a very threatening aspect; and the party of the heir-apparent was quite becoming distinct and prominent as opposed to the party of the old King. All the surrounding countries and populations, Frenchmen and Bretons, Manceaux and Angevines, began now to consider which side would offer most advantage. William had recourse to a policy which he had so often found successful. He bribed Count Rotrou to abandon Robert's party, and by his help reduced the castles of Neuchâtel. Robert appears to have returned to a simulated and sullen obedience, and for a short time the outward dissensions were stayed.

Parties of William and Robert.

Very brief, however, was this respite. Robert's adherents continued urging him to assert his rightful claims. He was rushing more and more into vice. Alternations of violent excitement and licentious indolence consumed his time. Harlots, minstrels, trouveurs and jesters, mean hangers-on and parasites, composed his court,— but not such classes alone, for amongst his adherents were many boasting the best blood in

Robert's life.

1075—1078
Robert's friends.

Normandy: sons and kinsmen of the old stock, the Barons, whose advice had strengthened William in counsel and whose swords had defended him in the field; and many even of those who had recently served him most efficiently, such as Roger de Benefacta and William de Molines; nay even the Mowbray, the nephew of Gosfried, Bishop of Coutances, and whose expectations were the largest perhaps of any of the vassals of William's crown. All these for various reasons egged his son on to disobedience and rebellion.

His demands.
Robert repeated his demands more vehemently than before; and in the course of the argument, he insisted strongly upon the confirmation which he had received in his title from the King of the French; and it was a shrewd as well as a provoking portion of Robert's conduct thus to insist upon the power of interference possessed by one whom William was so unwilling to acknowledge as a superior. William sometimes argued, sometimes evaded the request, sometimes denied it; quoted all the examples he could recollect (and his reading was extensive and his memory good) of filial disobedience, and its condign punishment, as collected from sacred or profane history; advised him to consult with Lanfranc and other wise men; and spoke sometimes as a father. Robert answered most contemptuously. "Father," said he, "I do not come to hear a sermon: enough and more than enough of these wise sayings of which I have heard so

many, until I am sick of them, from my teachers: 1075—1078 answer me concerning my claim, that I may determine how to act. I will no longer serve any one in Normandy, meanly as a slave."

§ 7. William was as hard in his denial as Robert was peremptory in his asking. He would never surrender Normandy, his patrimony, or divide England, his conquest. Never would he suffer an equal or a superior in his realm. Robert raged as he departed from his father, and he and his partizans quitted Normandy altogether as William's declared enemies. In the first instance, many of the noblest of his retainers, the proudest, and the boldest, accompanied him. Large promises were made to them, and something was gained by plunder; but they seem shortly to have deserted him, and left him only with some few of the most needy and the most vile of his adherents. Robert first repaired to his uncle of Flanders. Robert the Frizon, full of rancour as he was against his brother-in-law, could not then aid his nephew, who next visited the court of Eudo, Archbishop of Treves. Hence he began a farther course of wandering, proceeding from castle to castle, and from region to region, defaming his father, seeking to excite public opinion against him: thus wandering as a noble and yet beggarly pretender, during a period of more than five years. He rambled from Lotharingia to the Rhineland and Suabia, to Aquitaine and to Gascony, till at length he crossed the Alps,

William refuses.

Robert leaves William.

His wanderings.

and was received by Bonifazio, Marquis of Montferrat.

Boniface of Montferrat:

The dominions of Boniface extended from the foot of the Alps to the shore of the Riviera; from Vercelli to Savona; and Parma and Cremona and Piacenza, all owned him as their Lord. The mother of Boniface, Helena, was an English Princess. The Italians call her Helen, daughter of a Duke of Gloucester; possibly of some Anglo-Saxon Earl of Mercia, who assumed the softer name to please the Italian ear. Robert courted the daughter of Boniface, and as it is said, with the wish to obtain the aid of this prince against his father. The manner in which Albert Azzo attempted to possess himself of Maine, shews, that, notwithstanding the distance and the difficulty of the journey, there might have been a possibility of exciting the Lombard to such an adventure; and there was such a general epidemic fermentation and unsettlement of men's minds at this period, that there was a chance for any desperate enterprize. But Robert was unsuccessful. The hand of Adelicia, a name which, even in this case, one is fain to consider as a title or an epithet, was reserved for Roger Guiscard.

Refuses his daughter to Robert.

From the compassion or the policy of the princes and nobles whom he sought, Robert frequently obtained ample pecuniary aid; but the gifts and donations bestowed by their generosity or extorted by his importunity, were lavished with unprincipled rapidity. Robert's debaucheries kept him miserably poor, and he was frequently reduced to the greatest distress: to borrow from the usurer, or to beg, when the usurer would not lend. Matilda's heart was constantly turned towards her absent and degraded child: knowing his exigencies, she constantly endeavoured to relieve him, and transmitted to him from time to time large sums of money, by the hands of Sampson, the Breton, a trusty and experienced messenger, who must have had to make his journeys with much peril as well as skill. These acts of tenderness she carefully concealed from her husband: he discovered them by chance, and burst out into a paroxysm of fury, accusing her of supporting his bitter enemy. Matilda fully acknowledged her act. "If Robert, my son, were buried seven feet below the ground, and I could bring him to life again by my heart's blood, how gladly would I shed it, to restore him to the light of day." William became yet paler with anger, and gave orders that the eyes of Sampson should be plucked out. He was enabled to escape, and fled to St. Evreul, where, taking the cowl, he lived to a good old age: the companion of the youth of that historian who constitutes our main guide through this period of our history.

§ 8. Robert, when he returned from Lombardy, which seems to have been his extreme point, renewed his applications to Philip, who received him zealously, and placed him in a position where he could most successfully annoy his father, in the castle of Gerberoi. This was a very strong border fortress in the Beaucassin, near the Norman frontier, and about five miles from Gournay. All such March fortresses were usually sufficiently lawless, but Gerberoi had, in this respect, as it were, a peculiar franchise. It was the privilege of Gerberoi that all outlaws or fugitives might be received there as a sanctuary. Helias the Vidam, welcomed the reckless Robert; and what locality could better suit him and his desperate fortune? Here he established his head quarters, and gathered round him a band of freebooters, making large promises, and giving them present payment, by permitting them to ravage Normandy, his own country, the country which he claimed. Unprincipled as this predatory warfare might be, the treachery by which it was accompanied rendered it the more base. Many of the Normans of the higher ranks, outwardly the most loyal to William, were in secret communication with his son, betraying and selling their own countrymen and their own kindred to the outlaws. Such a state of affairs was equally affronting to the monarch and to the father. William collected his forces, and accompanied by Rufus and by Beauclerc, occupied the adjoining territory and laid siege to the castle. Gerberoi was defended with great obstinacy. Three weeks elapsed, during which no progress was made by the besiegers. William fought in person amongst the besiegers, and it is remarkable that his body squire was an Englishman. The siege was ended by a decided battle. Rufus was wounded. William, engaged in single conflict with a knight belonging to the adverse party, was exposed to the utmost danger. His horse was killed under him: the esquire, bringing up another, was transpierced by a javelin. William himself was cut so desperately, that the agony extorted a cry of anguish. Robert, his assailant, stayed his hand.

1078

Robert and William fight.

Baffled, humiliated, and full of sorrow, it seemed as if William's genius had fled, and the defeated Conqueror retreated from the single donjon tower of Gerberoi within the distant walls of Rouen. The disorders of the country still continued: and the Proceres now proffered their help, for the purpose of ending this most unnatural conflict. William received their proposals with angry grief. Roger de Montgomery, Hugh Lupus, Hugh de Gournay, Grantesmesnil, and Beaumont, with his sons, were the principal mediators. Of some the loyalty was ambiguous. The clergy added their influence; so also did Hubert the Cardinal Legate; and Pope Gregory himself addressed the undutiful son. Peace was concluded. Normandy was again assured to Robert by William: and the prelates and barons confirmed the compact. But William had yielded to necessity grudgingly and angrily; anxious as he was to secure the succession to his progeny, he could

Proposals for family reconciliation.

not forgive the indignity which he had received: and from the same lips which made the donation proceeded that fatal imprecation which sought to make it void. For William in the bitterness of his heart had cursed his son, and the father's ban was fulfilled in the child's destruction.

Troubles as to Waltheof's earldom.

§ 9. No peace, no rest, no tranquillity was vouchsafed to William. Fresh troubles had arisen in England. After the execution of Waltheof, the unsettled right to the great Northumbrian earldom ought perhaps to have passed to Liulph, whose birth and possessions well entitled him to the designation of the Noble Thane: and whose excellence of character, his truth, his honesty, and piety, gave him a higher claim to dignity. William however granted the earldom,

Walchere.

or perhaps the government of it, to Walchere of Lorraine, the Bishop of Durham. The word bought is used: but we must not take this word in its more technical sense. The rights of the bishop over the patrimony of St. Cuthbert were unquestionable; but if we consider the powers of government as being what are commonly termed feudal, we know that even the heir by blood, in such cases, as the accession of a new lord, was compelled to bargain with the sovereign for the restoration of his inheritance. Walchere, who had enjoyed the friendship of the martyred Waltheof, was of a kind and benignant disposition, yet weak and unstable, and timid and slack in his rule. Hence his retainers had more than usual licence and impunity; but he found great support in the co-operation of one who might have been the most dangerous opponent, the claimant Liulph. The feeling which animated the noble Thane was higher than that of ordinary patriotism; he loved the country because he viewed it as the possession of his patron saint: and quietly and unobtrusively he assisted the bishop where aid was most needed. When Walchere held the great moot of the earldom, he who might have presided, was content to sit below as an assistant at the tribunal; and so wise and prudent was he, that men believed that Cuthbert himself gave true counsel in the judgments of his votary.

1079. Liulph supports Walchere.

Liulph therefore had in every respect well deserved the bishop's confidence; but it deeply excited the envy of those who considered themselves as more especially entitled to the bishop's favour. I may mention Gilbert—to whom some portion of the government was entrusted,—and his chaplain Leobwine, by whose private advice he was constantly guided. In fact, the state of parties was such as to impose considerable difficulties upon Walchere. A strong body-guard of Frenchmen and Flemings had been needed to clear the way when he was enthroned, and the unceasing feuds and dissensions amongst the chieftains, their septs and families, constantly exposed him to the danger of unwittingly affronting some one powerful leader, at whose bidding the whole

Disputes hence arising.

land from Tyne to Tees, might rise in insurrection. Thus, the disorders of the country encreased; the bishop's knights plundered and slew; the bishop's archdeacon robbed the Church: and men whispered that, like Eli, he allowed his children to sin, and would be visited with Eli's punishment.

1079

Hostility of Liulph and Leobwine.

Liulph and Leobwine, sitting in the same court, constantly testified their opposition both of principle and feeling by the contrariety of their opinions. The Thane was well versed in the laws and usages of Northumbria, and the spirit of equity guided his judgments. Leobwine would obstinately oppose the opinions of his coadjutor, and revile him in the very seat of justice with indecent and contumelious language. Fell was the anger thus excited, and they determined upon a base revenge. The usages which fully allowed each individual to avenge his real or supposed injuries before the light of day, without incurring any responsibility beyond that which could be compensated by the blood fines, forbade all treachery, and still more, the infliction of injury upon an enemy protected by the hour of rest and the sanctity of his hearth and home.

Murder of Liulph.

§ 10. Leobwine and Gilbert, disregarding the principles which marked the difference between manslaughter and murder, aided by some of the bishop's knights, attacked their competitor, the good Liulph, in the darkness of the night, and slew him and the whole of his household. Having perpetrated the deed, they repaired at once to the bishop, seeking his protection, and informing him of all their vengeance.—" Thou hast killed me and thyself and all who are ours, thou wicked and foolish Leobwine," exclaimed the bishop, as he tore the hood off his head and flung it on the ground in anger and despair; and truly did he augur the consequences. He immediately took refuge in that strong castle so recently raised by Waltheof, protecting the cathedral, and itself guarded by the sanctity of the ground. He closed the portals, and sent messengers all about and around Northumbria, declaring that he had neither art nor part in the slaughter, that Gilbert and all his associates were or should be outlawed from Northumbria, and how he, the bishop, would clear himself of all suspicion of guilt by solemn compurgation, according to the canon law. This great anxiety shewed how much the prelate dreaded the avengers of blood, and that he himself was conscious that he had incurred great suspicion. Indeed his acts had not corresponded with his words. Outlaws he had proclaimed the murderers to be; but he had received them, sheltered them, consorted with them, and at this very time they were protected within his walls.

As was usual in such cases, the offence had become a feud between men and between families, in which all participated who were involved in the act, whether as offenders or as sufferers. Adherents on either side swelled the dissension more and more. It was evident that the long prevailing discontents against the bishop were now coming to a crisis, and that the question to be decided at the tryst at Gateshead was whether the respective parties of national Northumbria or the French government of the Lotharingian bishop were to prevail. Walchere and the perpetrators of the great offence, Leobwine his archdeacon, Gilbert his seneschal, his clerks, and his knights, repaired thither; and there also had assembled the vast multitude from beyond the Tyne, prepared to assert or to avenge their complaints against their enemies. Pledges of peace had been given, and the pleadings were to begin according to law in the open air, upon the green turf and beneath the sky. But as the bishop looked round and beheld the angry multitude, his heart failed him. Would any pledge restrain the hands of those who already had declared him guilty? of what avail would the compurgators prove? the twelve, or the twenty-four, or the thirty-six priests and deacons, placing their hands on the Gospel-book, and swearing that they believed in the innocence of him whom the uncontrollable power of popular opinion had already condemned.

Walchere therefore refused to proceed with

the discussion otherwise than within the walls of the church. Into this humble and then secluded edifice he and the accused entered, accompanied by some portion of his meisné. Without, on the bleak and then desert banks of the Tyne, were assembled the roaring and yelling multitude. From the sanctuary, the bishop sent forth a deputation of those who were to propose the terms of pacification. The messengers never returned. They were immediately slaughtered, and the same fate befel the others of the bishop's party, who, trusting to the legal truce, had remained without, unsuspicious of any harm.

Walchere withdraws.

There was now no longer any doubt as to the mind of the Northumbrians. Peace they never had really sought with the bishop: their intent was his death, and the extermination of the foreign rulers. Could any sacrifice avert the fate of the prelate? could the blood of Gilbert be accepted as a sufficient expiation? Whether urged by conscience or driven out by the despair of those within the unavailing sanctuary, the seneschal came forth, and was instantly transfixed by the spears and weapons of the assailants. Loud cries were now raised for Leobwine; the bishop knew that no sacrifice would appease them except the death of the archdeacon, who was considered as the root of the whole calamity, and sought to purchase his own life by surrendering the offender. Leob-

Gilbert is killed.

wine shrunk from his fate. The attacks upon the building continued; the massy walls and iron-bound doors of the church at first resisted. Fire was threatened: the miserable Walchere came forth, and standing upon the threshold earnestly prayed for pardon. "Good rede, short rede, slay the bishop," was the pithy advice given by the outcry of a Waltheof, the most determined of the bishop's enemies. He wrapped his head in his garment and was slain. The church was fired. Leobwine madly rushed out, and was cut to pieces, and all within perished.

§ 11. The rebellion spread throughout the country: the insurgents attacked Durham, occupied the city, and laid siege to the castle; but after four days' blockade they were compelled to abandon this enterprize, though the whole country continued in a state of insurrection. But there was a governor in England fully able to punish them. Odo, at this period, was supreme in command. Whether acting by his own discretionary powers, or, as is more probable, by William's directions, he advanced to the north. Northumbria was completely devastated. Had the Earl of Northumbria been a layman, the offence against the civil authority would have deserved severe punishment, but the clerical character of the victim encreased the indignation excited by his murder, and furnished an excuse, and in some degree a reason

for the greatest severity. The country was
entirely desolated; the innocent, and they
were many, who had taken no part in the insurrection, were all subjected to the same
punishment; and those who opposed no resistance whatever to the Norman forces, were
either put to death or cruelly mutilated, a practice constantly and consistently employed by
the Normans, and which equally had the effect
of awing the people and of irritating them
against their oppressors.

1080. Odo's pacification.

Malcolm continued bound by the homage
rendered at Abernethy, only until he could disavow the engagement which he had formed.
He could not consider the Norman as his legitimate superior, and the miserable conflict
prevailing in Normandy between the father and
the son might well encourage all the enemies of
the new dynasty to anticipate that a family thus
divided was hastening to ruin. Malcolm crossed
the border, and penetrated as far as the Tyne.
The country was defenceless. Captives, cattle,
English sterling silver, rewarded the invaders,
and the spoil was carried off by Malcolm in
safety, and therefore with honour, to his own
land; and it is most probable that, at the same
period, the greater portion of Cumbria was regained by the Scottish sovereign.

Malcolm ravages England.

§ 12. Important affairs in Normandy: a council held at Lillebonne under William's presidency,
in which some of the best laws of the govern-

Normandy.

ment of the country were made, prevented his immediate return to England, and he took the opportunity of testifying his reconciliation with Robert, by appointing him commander of the forces intended to enforce the obedience of the Scottish sovereign. Robert, for the first time in his life, repaired to Britain. The measure had been wisely considered by William. It was a testimony to the people of mutual confidence, and the station and power thus assigned to the son so lately in parricidal rebellion, might be considered as the most sincere token of the pardon he had obtained, and that the enemies of William could no longer found their expectations of success upon family disunion. But whether from the want of conduct on the part of the commander, or of efficiency in the troops, the expedition was shamefully unsuccessful. Robert advanced as far as a place called by the chroniclers Eaglesuret, in which strange orthography there is little difficulty in recognizing the Celtic name of Bridekirk in Annandale. Further, he dared not go, and he returned again to the south; but the expedition was not entirely useless, nor without a most memorable monument, as he directed the building of the new castle upon the Tyne. When Robert again met his father, or whether they ever met again, is uncertain. The reconciliation was hollow and insincere: the dissensions were renewed: Robert broke away again from his father; and resorting, first to Flanders and then to France, resumed his course of disobedience, injuring and annoying his parent by all the means in his power, and encouraging and encouraged by that parent's most inveterate enemies.

1080

Though repressed by Odo's vigour, the spirit of the Northumbrian rebellion still rankled in the heart of the people, and what was of greater importance and threatening far greater danger, was the distrust with which William now began to regard his brother. Furthermore, the aspect of affairs in Denmark was lowering, and William, quitting Normandy, repaired to England. He was accompanied by sorrowing and declining Matilda. Both might now well need the help of each other's society, and she continued his efficient friend and counsellor to the last.

Difficulties of William.

§ 13. A new bishop and a good one, William de St. Carileph, was nominated by the King as the successor of Walchere. Wise, well-instructed and prudent, he applied himself wholly to the restoration of the desolated see. He properly considered this important object as the common concern: the nobles and laity of the country were consulted: the advice of the metropolitan of all England was sought; and all acted under the sanction of the sovereign and his consort. It appeared better for the future stability of the see that the communities dispersed at Wearmouth and at Jarrow should be united on the spot where the body of St. Cuthbert was deposited. Pope

Walchere's successor.

Gregory confirmed the union, which also received the sanction of the legislature: that stately cathedral arose which still subsists, as it were in solemn triumph, and Durham became the great ecclesiastical metropolis of the north.

St. Cuthbert, to use the familiar expression of the age, preserved all his territorial rights between Tyne and Tees; and in proportion as our jurisprudence became more matured, the progress and even the fictions of the law gave them greater stability, and the palatine rights of the bishop became as well defined as those of the crown. But William de St. Carileph was neither honoured nor troubled by being invested with the perilous administration of the Northumbrian earldom—the dignity which had brought his predecessor to destruction. It became needful to provide for this most important government: a border country, filled with an inimical population, but which nevertheless needed to be rendered a barrier against an enemy.

§ 14. Difficulties were now coming fast upon William, such as he had never known before. In the earlier years of his reign, he had the comfort and aid of many a wise counsellor and many a trusty friend; but they were dropping away apace: a new generation was arising from whom he was estranged: those nearest to him had become cold or treacherous, and amongst strangers he had to choose between rash and untried youth and waning and declining age. As Earl of Northumbria, he selected an Alberic, whom heralds place in the genealogy of the noble family of De Vere; but he gave no honour to the lineage. Disturbances arose in Northumbria: Alberic's mind was unsettled: some soothsayer had held out before him the vision that he should rule over Grecia. His incompetency became evident, and he was removed from his earldom. Robert Mowbray, the proud nephew of the proud Bishop of Coutances, was substituted in his stead; an ill-fated appointment, but of which the results did not become apparent till the subsequent reign.

1081
Alberic.

Mowbray.

Though no opposition to William had been very successful, still there never had been any blow so entirely decisive as to lead the desperate to despair of casting off the Norman power. William had formed a well-concerted scheme for keeping the Britons of Wales in subjection by stationing around them the three great Earls of Hereford, Shrewsbury and Chester. But the heir of Fitz-Osbern was in the dungeon. Roger de Montgomery, following the opinions of his son, Robert de Belesme, was secretly inclined to Courthose, and the Earl of Chester, and a very large body of William's knighthood, had engaged themselves in the service of Odo of Bayeux, for the purpose of aiding him in the extraordinary enterprize which now engaged his ambitious mind. Princes of more than ordinary vigour were at this time ruling over the Britons; and William, whether for the purpose of inspiring a salutary

Wales.

> 1081
> William in Wales.

terror or of punishing some act of resistance, invaded Dynevor with a mighty army. The Welsh fled before him, and neither their swiftness of foot nor their knowledge of the country enabled them to escape the Norman sword: yet when William reached the shrine of St. David's, he appeared in the guise of an humble pilgrim, making his offerings to the patron saint; and such encrease, if any, as was made to the Norman power, resulted from the enterprize of those adventurers who shortly afterwards became so eminent as the Lords Marchers, and not from the prowess of the sovereign.

> Odo.

§ 15. William must have quitted England (for he did now quit it for a short period) for the purpose of allowing his brother Odo to commit himself further in those designs which, however notorious, had not, as yet, acquired a sufficient degree of consistency to enable him to visit them with vengeance. Odo's plans had excited great apprehensions in William, and the more so from the mystery in which they were involved. He had, as before mentioned, been gathering together large forces, or rather seducing them from William's service, and more especially those on whom William had relied for the defence of the country against the Danes, whether of Ireland or of Scandinavia. Some say that Odo had been consulting whether his Holy Orders as a bishop would be an obstacle to his obtaining the royal authority, intimating his hope and expectation that he should yet live to be a king. Other projects, involving equal, perhaps greater, ambition, were attributed to him. Rome at this period was the seat of dark and mystic credulity. Amidst the monuments which testified the might of the great empire, strange superstitions were nourished, which the Church had no power to punish, though she might condemn. Here the sorcerer cast his lot, and the diviner worked his spell. Almost until our own times, a constant incentive to these endeavours has been found in the attempt to discover the prognostications declaring the name of future occupants of the Apostolic throne. The mystical distichs of Malachi of Armagh, the uncouth hieroglyphics of Abbot Joachim, the wheels and the circles, and the compound monsters, alluding to age, and name, and country, and device, have constantly been investigated by anxious credulity, and the frequent semblance of truth which these false prophecies have possessed, has encouraged the confidence placed in the revelations proceeding from the source of all delusion. The many enemies of Hildebrand would anxiously resort to these predictions, and the rites of the magicians had received the answer that one whose name might be read as Odo, would come after Gregory as the successor of St. Peter.

1081. Odo's aspirations. Mediæval prophecies.

The augury was widely spread, perhaps for

the purpose of ensuring its accomplishment. Odo accepted it. Forthwith he despatched his trusty men to the insatiate capital of the Christian world. A sumptuous palace was purchased for him, and filled with the display of wealth and luxury. Gifts in profusion were bestowed upon the senators: every pilgrim who could be trusted bore an epistle with a due enclosure of coin, concealed in his wallet, addressed to some needy Roman citizen, or needier noble, whose vote was thus to be secured; and the people, high and low, anticipated their approaching deliverance from Gregory's stern rectitude and rigid principle, and the advent of a more congenial sovereign. Such modes of courting the papacy were sufficiently common; but Odo, the Norman Odo, was preparing even to fight his way to the Quirinal, if it could not be won by gold. [For this] he had been raising those large forces which had excited William's anxiety. All had agreed to follow him into Italy, and were mustered in the south of England. Gregory was yet living. Was Odo preparing to eject him by violence? Without doubt, the Bishop of Bayeux participated in the vague delirium of adventurous conquest, which in one guise embodied itself in the approaching crusades. The passions of men, as well as their imaginative feelings, were at this era strangely combining for the same end. Had Odo succeeded, had the papal authority become vested in an active and experienced warrior, wielding at once the keys and the sword, another Julius, when the papal authority was in the fullest vigour, Europe might have sunk under a Latin caliphate.

Whatever may have been the enterprizes projected by Odo, William viewed them as fraught with great and impending danger. Odo had never shewn any want of fidelity towards his brother; but William's natural harshness was encreased by age, and still more by the repeated acts of opposition, treachery, and rebellion, which he had sustained. This harass of spirit had gone on encreasing since Waltheof's death: it seemed as if there were no one whom he could trust in the world. Odo had stationed himself in the Isle of Wight, preparing to cross over with his troops to Normandy, to Barfleur: here he was suddenly prevented by William, whose measures had been taken so secretly and so determinedly, as to be wholly unforeseen by him whose visions were to be at once irrevocably dispelled. Before the Proceres assembled in the royal hall, the King declared all the troubles he had received from kinsmen and from strangers, from son and from brother, from friend and from foe. It was an impassioned tale of the disappointments of ambition, so often felt and so seldom revealed: an outpouring of his bitter troubles. He charged Odo with misgovernment, cruelty, treachery; and asked them for counsel how he should deal with this great state offender. All were silent: none ventured either to acquiesce in the charges brought against one still so powerful, yet less to contradict the angry, the implacable sovereign. William commanded that his brother should be arrested; yet no one dared to attempt to secure Odo's person. Whatever his conduct may have been, he was still a bishop: they shrunk back, fearing the censures of the Church, and thus their hands were stayed. William himself was compelled to seize the offender. "I am a clerk," exclaimed Odo, "and without the judgment of the apostolic see, I am not to be condemned." "Nay, I judge not the bishop," replied William, "but I arrest my accountant and my minister." Odo was shipped off to Normandy, and immured in the castle of Rouen, imprisoned and degraded, adding another to the long list of captives, who pined for the death of their oppressor or their own.

§ 16. Matilda, whose strength had been rapidly declining, now rested from her sorrows, and was buried where her tomb is yet seen; in her own monastery of the Holy Trinity at Caen, between the altar and the choir. In the same manner as popular opinion had represented that William's rough courtship had won the young bride by force, now was it equally reported, but in a very different spirit, that the wife had died in consequence of the ill-treatment she received from her husband. In the strict sense of the word, the accusation is most improbable; but his great love for her did not prevent the heavy trials she sustained from his ungovernable violence and wrath, and these probably shortened her mortal existence. The gloom thickened round him: it seemed as if all his good fortune had finally departed. Anxieties and troubles continued encreasing upon him, and after he had lost Matilda, he never, as it were, looked up again.

1083

Afflictions of William.

Chapter XIII.

REVOLT IN MAINE.—STATE OF DENMARK.—DEATH OF CANUTE.—CONSEQUENCES OF THE THREATENED DANISH INVASION IN ENGLAND.—FORMATION OF THE DOMESDAY SURVEY.—GENERAL IMPOSITION OF THE OATH OF FEALTY.

1083—1086.

§ 1. ALTHOUGH William had been able, hitherto, to put down all the various attempts which had been made against his authority, conspiracies frustrated, rebels slaughtered, opponents punished by imprisonment or death, still the prestige of his character was gone, and every failure seemed to suggest another attempt against him from those who were suffering under his rule.

State of England: In England, his taxation had become excessive. Geld after geld had been exacted from the people, always pitilessly, often illegally; and there is no reason to suppose that the administration of his continental dominions was managed with greater mildness in this respect.

of Maine. To the Manceaux, Norman domination was peculiarly grievous; and when William was engaged on our side of the channel, they rose against him, and more than one half of the province and its marches, threw off his authority. A species of biography of the bishops of

Le Mans, is the only proper history of Maine which we possess, and consequently we have very few details; but though Hélias de la Flèche is not named as a leader, there can be little doubt that he took a prominent part in the attempt, ultimately so successful, which the Manceaux were now making to recover their independence.

1083

William, however, did not act with any degree of vigour; and instead of making a great effort against the insurgents, he engaged in a conflict which bore the appearance of a private quarrel, with Hubert, Viscount of Beaumont, and son-in-law of the Count of Nevers. Hubert was possessed of the town and castle of Ste. Susanne, strong in its defences, but stronger in its situation. In consequence of some dispute with William, Hubert defied him, and, with his wife, abandoning Beaumont and Fredernay, he took his station in this castle, in the border country, between Maine and Anjou, as William's declared enemy. Hence he constantly annoyed the Norman garrison of Le Mans, and ravaged that portion of the country which continued under William's allegiance. William assembled a large force: his son-in-law, Alan Fergant, joined him, together with such of the Manceaux as still continued in their fidelity; but Hubert was able to collect a much larger, for he could pay well and promise more.

William's war with Hubert.

1084

§2. William began the siege in person, and

1083—1086

Romantic incidents of the siege.

built a tower, or rather a block-house, for the purpose of commanding the castle; but disturbances in Normandy called him away. He quitted the field, leaving Count Alan in command; and the siege was turned into a blockade, but so ineffectual that the more it was protracted, the more did the garrison of Ste. Susanne encrease in prosperity, deriving good profit from the depredations which they committed upon William's territories, and more from the ransoms which they wrung from the Normans whom they captured in their sallies; an honourable mode of gaining wealth, as we are told by the chroniclers, for profit was the main object of war. Many a poem, many a *gest*, has been framed of far less ample materials than the siege of Ste. Susanne would afford. Had Hubert patronized his Trouveurs, we might have been told how knights flocked to receive his pay from Burgundy and Aquitaine; how the great Norman Baron, Richer de Aquila, was slain, yea by the little lad who hid himself in the thicket, and shot him in the eye; how the great Earl of Evreux was taken prisoner; and how Gilbert de Aquila and William de Warrenne and the flower of the Norman host, attempting to revenge their losses, might be seen with shame retreating from the castle walls. Here all the might of Normandy had passed away: the bravery which had gained a kingdom was foiled by one dungeon tower. During four years did this conflict continue, when the Norman commanders, seeing their forces drop away, stung by the disgrace, and feeling the strife to be hopeless, advised William to submit to a pacification. He whom we must still call Conqueror, was compelled to pardon all the past, and to favour and honour Hubert, the chief rebel, restoring to him every domain which his ancestors had held.

§ 3. During all these transactions, William had been more and more haunted by his fears of the Danish power. A large portion of the population of England still kept up a friendly and intimate relation with the Northmen; still did the faithful adherents of the Scandinavian power believe that the Sea Kings would reclaim their inheritance; and carefully did they guard the secret hoard at Lincoln until the treasure could be delivered to its lawful owner's hands. Much as the north of England had suffered by the Danish invasions, this did not diminish their seeking towards the Northmen. Plunderers they were, but the English would willingly pay that price for deliverance from the galling yoke by which they were now oppressed.

Great elements of mutation were at this time germinating in the north. Canute, the son of Sweno, was governing with much vigour and apparent power. Until the accession of Canute the Great, the Scandinavian realms could scarcely be considered as forming a portion of the Latin Commonwealth. Morally, even more than physically, they were almost beyond the verge of Christendom. From the period when the dominions of Britain, and the Baltic, and North Sea realms had been conjoined in the person of one monarch, some approximation to the general tone of European policy had been gradually advancing, but the progress was very slow. From the Moot-hill, the Lawmen still thundered the dooms of Odin. The kings ruled by wielding the battle-axe of the Vikinga. No saga was told, no lay was sung, except in the antient speech of the Asi; and, above all, Christianity was only very imperfectly introduced: established it scarcely was: the parochial organization was incomplete: the hierarchy hardly settled or endowed, and secretly the belief of large portions of the population still adhered to the foul and bloody deities whom their ancestors had worshipped.

§ 4. But the younger Canute, emulating the renown of his namesake and ancestor, qualified by intellect, instigated by ambition, and actuated by policy, and in some degree by conscience, was endeavouring with the greatest earnestness, to bring himself into fellowship with the sovereigns who had divided amongst them the dominions of the empire. Of his own authority, he invested himself with an imperial power, governing, as far as he could, according to the state doctrines which had descended from the Cæsars. His great seal exhibits him with crown and sceptre, and seated on the throne, copying the imagery and paraphrasing the legend employed by his rival the Anglo-Norman king. The seal was entrusted to a chancellor, an archbishop; a board of chaplains assisted in the administration of the law; and an entirely new course of business and vein of thought pervaded the court and the general management of public affairs. Every encouragement was given to the literature, hitherto unknown, of Christendom, and many are of opinion that now for the first time ink and parchment were substituted for the inscribed rock or the Runic stone. But, above all, Canute sought to unite himself to the most cultivated and noblest of the European families, disdaining the barbarian beauties of the princesses of his own nation: he had therefore courted and obtained the Atheliza, the daughter of Robert the Frizon. Her lineage ascended to Charlemagne, and the name of Charles, given to their eldest son, testified Canute's pride in the ancestry which the child, the heir, could claim.

margin: 1080–1085 Canute's reforms.

margin: His marriage.

Denmark at this period was rich and very populous. The Cimbric Chersonesus, and the islands which constituted the Danish kingdom, possessed so large a population as to muster more than a million of fighting men, soldiers as well as mariners, who worked the ship upon the waves, and fought the battle upon the land. Canute upon his accession deplored the waning of the Danish power. He possessed in his disposition the great element of a conqueror, not to be discouraged by reverse of fortune. He had, in his earlier age, been foiled by the ferocity of the savage tribes of the East; but undismayed, he attacked them again, and the Esthonians, and the Letts, and the Samogitians were compelled once more to become the tributaries of the Danish king. But these victories over the Easterlings afforded no compensation for the loss of Britain, the pride and honour of the Danish name. Three expeditions had been sent against the island by Sweno and by Canute: three times had they retreated, not without profit, but without permanent conquest or abiding honour.

§ 5. He now prepared himself for one mighty effort. Ailnoth of Canterbury was still resident at the Danish court. More and more frequent and urgent were the requests which proceeded from the English, inviting his aid. Canute was surrounded by a large and troublesome family of brothers: the cadets of Denmark had no apanages, and lived as a burthen upon the people. One of these, Olave, he selected as his friend and counsellor, honoured him in station, and remunerated his services by the government of Sleswick and a large stipend. With him Canute consulted, and Olave strenuously encouraged his brother to prosecute his glorious enterprize. The token of gathering, like the fiery cross of the Gael, was sent round through Denmark from herred to herred, and from island to island; each jarl and each chieftain obeyed, and a thousand "snakes of the sea," fully manned and equipped for war, were assembled in the firths and bays of the Baltic and the North Sea. Six hundred ships were promised by Robert the Frizon, whose rancour against William had neither been diminished by time nor softened by sympathy for his brother-in-law's troubles and afflictions. Norway, ruled by Olave, who had married the sister of Canute, contributed sixty vessels of very large size, and filled with chosen warriors; and very early in the spring, the fleets, of which the larger squadrons were assembled in the waters of Limfiord and Harboe, all ready for the voyage, awaited only the signal for departure.

1085

Fleet collected.

William was preparing most energetically for defence, equally against his foreign and his domestic enemies. Larger than the army by which he had accomplished the conquest of England, were the forces which he now raised for its protection against the commander who threatened to despoil him of his prize, and to retaliate upon him the injuries he had inflicted upon others. Stipendiary forces were hired from every country which spake the Romane tongue, from every province north of the Alps; and Hugo, Count of Vermandois, the

William's preparations for defence.

brother of the French king, shared in the service which William's lavish bounty and expenditure commanded. To provide for the sustenance of these soldiers, they were quartered upon and amongst all the landholders of England: none were exempted. The bishop, the earl, and the baron had to receive the strangers as guests; and the sheriffs to apportion them upon the knights, and vavassours, and churls, and all of lower degree. Grievous was the burthen and great the distress of England, and encreased by the cruel and yet perhaps necessary precautions adopted by William, who wasted the seabord country far and wide, for the purpose of starving out the Danes, should they land, and by which he also prevented the English from offering them, were they so inclined, aid and the means of subsistence.

§ 6. Months however passed away without any appearance of the dreaded enemy; no hostile sails were seen rising above the distant verge of the horizon: no alarm was sounded, no beacons fired: the year declined, and a portion of William's garrison army was disbanded. Men might speculate upon the causes which had delayed the enemy. Openly, William had only prepared for defence, yet it could be judged from his acts that he was gaining in courage and in confidence. A winter elapsed: still, though with diminished hope or diminished fear, did England await the formidable invaders.

Another season began. William continued to watch the land sedulously: earnest deliberations were taking place in the council: fortifications continued to be erected: garrisons were not withdrawn, but yet the lingering enemy kept off, and, at the end of the second year, it was universally known that the expedition so talked off, so formidable, was wholly abandoned. A contrary wind, sweeping without intermission across the main, as it was said, never varying from the adverse quarter, never slackening, had kept the vessels locked into the shores. Canute at first doubted whether this apparently preternatural obstacle, might not be a token which he was bound implicitly to obey; but soon he suspected, or was taught to suspect, that the vessels had in truth been spell-bound, and that the Runic lay murmured by the wise women had raised the adverse gales. The sorceresses were the consorts or kinswomen of his proudest chieftains; punish them he dared not, but he had nevertheless avenged himself by inflicting heavy penalties upon their husbands. Great discontents had arisen, and thus did it become impossible for him to pursue his scheme of conquest.

It matters little whether these tales were the inventions of the north or the gratuitous fancies of the English. They contained a small portion of truth, and very small. This armada, like those which had preceded it, had been in

[1086]

Canute's reforms cause discontent.

part frustrated by William's policy: but the frustration of the plans of conquest formed by Canute was the consequence as well as the cause of a great revolution in the state of Denmark. High discontents were prevailing amongst the subjects of the Danish crown. Canute, possessing much talent, was attempting to accelerate the progress, as we should now term it, of civilization. His people were estranged from the rest of Europe, by manners and customs and policy; and he attempted to bring them into the pale far more by severity than by conciliation. He was anxious, perhaps conscientiously, to suppress the turbulence and disorders of the Danes; but many of these disorders originated out of immemorial custom and law. That he should shew no favour or affection to the rank or station or consanguinity of the offender, was right; but in the administration of justice he set at nought every opinion, every prejudice, every law. His fiscal officers oppressed the people by their exactions, and most unwisely of all, he was anxious to enforce the payment of tythes hitherto entirely unknown. In other parts of Europe, although ecclesiastical and even civil law had in some cases begun to render this payment compulsory, yet it had arisen in great measure from the spontaneous feeling of the people, desirous of rendering to the service of God a portion of the gifts which they received, and believing that able-going was thereby earned. Nothing has been more injurious to the interests of Christianity, than the destruction of the grace accompanying the free-will offering, by rendering it the object of compulsion. Here it was as unwise as it was ill-timed: the Danes entirely rebelled against the payment. It was as odious to those who professed Christianity as to the greater number, who were still pagans in their heart; and though Canute and the other Norman sovereigns succeeded at last in placing the payment of tythes upon a legal foundation, there was always a grudge against it, which prevented the hierarchy from acquiring its due influence and hold upon the people's mind.

§ 7. In Olave, his brother, Canute had a secret, a crafty, and an inveterate enemy. Olave had, in the first instance, encouraged Canute to undertake the English invasion for the purpose of embroiling him with his subjects, and involving him in contests with them. Olave wished to accumulate unpopularity and hatred upon his brother's head, and having selected his associates, he planned his successful conspiracy. William, well aware of the state of feeling prevailing in Denmark, was dispersing his bribes amongst Canute's counsellors and commanders:—Olave, the king's own brother, Osbern, his foster-brother, Jarl Haco, Eyvind, and many others of renown, all or most of whom had been corrupted before.

1086

Olave's dealings discovered.

Canute at first believed that he was assisted by his brother, returning love for love. He now discovered that his brother was a rival seeking his ruin. At first he repelled his suspicions, till Olave, who was stationed in Sleswick, broke out into open rebellion. This was a portion of the scheme which had been contemplated for Canute's destruction. When the fleets were first assembled, the weather had been very adverse: this delay had enabled the discontented party to mature their plans, and as it should seem, to [dis]obey sailing commands when the season became more favourable. Canute advanced to Sleswick with a great force, and ordered his men to seize the traitor brother; but no one would dare to lay hands on him, so great was the veneration rendered by the Danes to the descendants of Odin. But another brother, Eric, had no such scruple: he seized the offender, and by Canute's command he was chained and fettered, and sent to Flanders, where he was kept in hard prison by Robert the Frizon.

Olave arrested.

The expedition broken up.

When Canute returned to the port of Haitheby, he found that the vessels contumaciously and rebelliously had left their moorings, and crews and commanders had returned to their homes. He inflicted, as by his prerogative he might be entitled to do, a heavy fine upon all the mutineers, high and low, but which he remitted in consideration of their agreeing to the odious impost which he established for the dubious benefit of the clergy. It is a remarkable proof [1086] of the absolute power possessed by the Scandinavian monarchs, that he succeeded in his decree, but, as might be expected, the act excited bitter indignation.

§ 8. Further insurrections arose. Jarl Osbern and Eyvind appeared amongst the leaders of the insurgents : more English money promoted their hostility. Canute's adherents diminished. He became distressed and appalled, and took refuge in Odensee. Jarl Osbern approached the town at the head of the rebels. Canute, yielding to cowardly and perhaps treacherous advice, took refuge in the church of St. Alban, an edifice in whose dedication to the protomartyr of Britain, we can discern the influence of some English missionary. Osbern and the assailants surrounded the building: they now neither venerated the dignity of Odin's race nor respected the Christian sanctuary's immunity, and Canute was slain before the altar ; another triumph, as was usually supposed, of the Conqueror's policy and state-craft. But the new theory of government introduced by Canute, timing in with the general state of Christendom, worked surely though slowly ; and brought the institutions of Scandinavia into entire conformity with the other states of the West. From this period, the Northmen lost their empire of the seas : their settlements in Ireland and in the Highlands and islands

A new rebellion.

Canute is slain. 10 July.

merged in the English and Scottish kingdoms. We hear occasionally of some predatory attempt made with a lingering recollection of their strength, like an old man buckling on his armour, but unable to sustain the heat of the fight: the battle of Largs was the last defeat which they received in the isle of Britain; and the Scandinavian kingdoms scarcely ever again become of any importance in the general tenor of mediæval history.

William's political administration.

§ 9. It was the constant policy of William to base his arbitrary power upon his legal prerogative: to establish his constitutional rights as firmly as possible upon the law, and then to take the utmost extent of margin, according to his arbitrary will. Despotic monarchs usually endeavour to confound the boundaries between such lawful restraints as the institutions and customs of the people may afford, with their absolute authority; but William was so confident in his own strength that he never seems to have cared to profit by such an ambiguity. Either way his principles became most effective in modelling the elements of our constitution, and none of his measures had a more permanent effect in guiding the future course of the government administration than those which he adopted pending the Danish invasion. Whilst the Danish fleet was wintering in Haitheby, during the Christmas festival, King William began his regal circuit, and wore his crown at Gloucester, and held his court for three days. Next followed a Synod: lastly, a new and unusual meeting: a Micklegethought most numerously attended, in which the King held deep consultation concerning the state of his land. Doubt did not long prevail as to the measures which William had adopted; and we have strong reasons for supposing that in the execution of them, Lanfranc was a useful adviser. *{Council held by the King, 1085}*

§ 10. Soon afterwards you might see in every city and good town in England, save and except the Bishopric, the three northern lands, and London, a worshipful company, such, for example, as proceeded to the West; Remigius, Bishop of Lincoln, the founder of the cathedral, Walter Gifford, Earl of Buckingham, Henry de Ferrers, and Adam the brother of Eudo Dapifer. These commissioners began their proceedings by holding a court, at which, with the exception of the diocesan, all the members of the Hundred-moot were required to attend. Come forward, Gerefa, sheriff, you the lieutenant of the earl, you the thanes of the shires, you the priests of each and every parish church, you the reeves and villains of each and every township; come forward and declare upon the halidome the truth of the matters into which our lord the King commands us to enquire, and give your answer to each and every question as we ask. What is the name of your township, *{Commissioners appointed.}*

be it City, Borough, Thorp, Haim, or Bye? Who was the lord thereof, archbishop, bishop, abbot, earl or thane, in the days of good King Edward, for of Harold the law knows nothing? How many thanes, how many commendated, how many freemen, how many sokemen, how many burgesses, how many churls, how many cottagers, how many thralls? how many hydes of land be there therein? how many plough lands in demesne? how many acres of wood, how many of meadow, how many of pasture, how many mills, how many fisheries? how much hath been added, how much taken away? how much worth in good King Edward's time, how much when King William gave it, and how much now? What hath each freeman, what each sokeman; how many oxen, how many cows, how many sheep, how many swine?

With some slight variations as to the points of enquiry, this valuation of land and capital was taken throughout the whole length and breadth of England, save and except the metropolis and the four northern shires. The commissioners made their several circuits, and the information which they collected was reduced into writing and duly transmitted to the King. It was afterwards methodized and abstracted, and fairly transcribed in the great volumes of Domesday, and deposited in the royal treasury at Winchester, amongst the other muniments of the realm. It still exists, fresh and perfect as when the scribe put pen to parchment, the oldest cadastre, or survey of a kingdom, now existing in the world. The colophon, "anno millesimo, octogesimo sexto ab incarnatione Domini, vigesimo vero regni Willielmi facta est ista descriptio," attests the date of this great record, and the diligence as well as the skill of those by whom it was completed. In the entries of the names of places, the inaccuracies and corruptions shew that the writers were not well acquainted with the Anglo-Saxon terminology, though in the more familiar designations of persons, fewer errors are observed. The caligraphy betrays an Italian hand, and leads to the supposition that it was under the inspection and direction of the lettered Lanfranc that the work was compiled. Great force is given to this supposition from the circumstance, that in Domesday we first find those abbreviations, afterwards so common in our legal documents, but which, in fact, are derived from the Tyronian notes of the Romans, until then unknown in England.

margin: 1086. Execution of the book.

§ 11. The formation of this survey occasioned universal discontent : such an enquiry had never been made before. The English considered it as an invasion almost of their natural rights. It was a shame, they said, that a King should direct such a prying into each man's means : a shame even to tell of such a tyranny.

margin: Unpopularity of Domesday.

¹⁰⁸⁶

The discontent ill-grounded.

Yet there was more of temper than of sound reason in this discontent. With whatever acts of oppression William may be charged, in this case there was none. The Danegelt, the tax of six shillings upon every plough-land, was both a lawful and a needful impost, and the first and main intent of the survey was to make a full and fair assessment of the charge. The unsettled state of affairs during the latter years of the Confessor's reign, the misfortunes attending the Conquest, and the transfer of the land to the new proprietors, might all be sufficient causes for such investigations; but even if the kingdom had continued in entire tranquillity, it would have been equally required. So long as the land remained untilled, no Danegelt was payable, but when the plough had been driven over it, then it became liable to the charge, and it is most probable that in many cases the assessment had been neglected or evaded. This, on the other hand, was counterbalanced by the lands which had become wasted by the misfortunes of the Conquest; and whilst the Domesday survey secured the rights of the crown, it also ensured a fair apportionment of the burthen amongst those by whom it was to be contributed. The enquiry was made by the royal officers and ministers, but the repartition was made by the people: the English taxed themselves.

§ 12. After the court at Gloucester, William

continued his progress through his realms. Easter, celebrated at Winchester, was followed by a splendid court held in the palace of Westminster during the Pentecostal festival, when Henry Beauclerc, the youngest of the royal family, received, perhaps precociously, the degree of knighthood from his father's hand. This was followed by an extraordinary assembly. It seemed as if William were, so to speak, impressed with the presentiment that he must terminate his business in this world, obtaining at least some prospect of tranquillity. He issued his summons, his writs, in the more familiar term of our law, commanding all his councillors, both his archbishops and all his bishops, his abbots, his earls, his barons, his sheriffs, all his knighthood, and all the landholders of the realm, to appear before him at Sarum on the first of August, Lammas-day. Such was the multitude, that they never could have been assembled within the now silent ramparts of the antient British city, but spread themselves without doubt over the plain. Here William imposed the oath of fealty upon every landholder without distinction of tenure. His men, the King's men, they all became, whosoever else might be their lord.

A heavy impost succeeded this transaction; but if William had sought to secure somewhat of rest and quietness, his expectations were vain. Troubles and sorrows encreased. England still continued heavily afflicted by those visitations of Providence which no prudence of government could avert, but which rendered the task of government the more difficult and grievous. Continual storms and tempests, crops blasted and blighted, murrain amongst the cattle, foul and direful sickness amongst men;—famine, as usual, was the accompaniment of these visitations, and filled up the measure of punishment; and the chronicler records the calamities, as the chastisement which the sins of the nation deserved. Robert continued to harass his father to the utmost of his power. Alan Fergant attempted to throw off his obedience to his father-in-law; and William, assembling his forces in the Isle of Wight, crossed over to Normandy, never to return.

Chapter XIV.

WILLIAM'S EXPEDITION AGAINST BRITTANY—THE SIEGE OF DÔL—DISPUTE WITH FRANCE ABOUT THE BEAUCASSIN—SIEGE OF MANTES—ILLNESS AND DEATH OF THE CONQUEROR.

1086—1087

§ 1. BRITTANY, notwithstanding the patronage bestowed by William upon Allan le-Roux, Earl of Richmond, was inclined to resist the Norman suzerainty. The nature of their subjection to Normandy is one of the most obscure points in the most obscure of histories,—that of the Armorican Bretons; but the Normans never renounced their claim, and William now determined to enforce their antient obedience. The occasion was opportune. Alan Fergant, who had succeeded to the Dukedom of Vannes, which, as it will be recollected, was the capital of Bretagne Bretonnante or Celtic Brittany, and as such considered to be the Duke of the regal Duchy, had been recently engaged in war with Geoffrey, the Count of Rennes. He had defeated his competitor and cast him into prison, where he died, but his dominion was scarcely settled: and William, having, as it seemed to him, no further anxiety for England,

Affairs of Brittany.

<small>1086—7</small>

determined to reassert his authority as the descendant of Rollo in Brittany.

<small>William enters Brittany:</small>

William might have rested, but he sought trouble, and for the last, and fatal time, he passed over to Normandy. He assembled his forces: the Normans entertained a great antipathy to all their neighbours, and willingly joined him. He laid siege to Dôl, and swore bitterly that he would never depart until he had compelled the town to surrender. The place was not strong, and there appeared little reason for this exasperation; yet his boast was vain, and he trusted in a power which he no longer possessed. Alan Fergant advanced towards him with a large force, magnified by report to 15,000 men. It is said that Philip of France supported him in person. The besieged knew nought of the army advancing to their rescue; and strangely must they have been surprised, when, from the

<small>Retreats.</small>

walls, they beheld the royal camp breaking up, and the Anglo-Norman army fleeing away. Such was the case: William had retreated at the apprehension of an unseen enemy: he had abandoned his camp, his baggage, his stores, to the amount, as it was reckoned, of fifteen thousand pounds sterling, all of which rewarded the Duke

<small>Peace with Fergant.</small>

of Brittany. William was glad to conclude a

<small>[Placed also in 1075, p. 526.]</small>

peace; and his daughter Constance, wise and virtuous, tall and fair, became the wife of Alan; and thus the old connexion was renewed, preparing the way for a further union of the powers.

§ 2. William became more and more weakened, more and more perplexed, partly by the encreasing affliction arising from his son's disobedience and ingratitude, partly by dissensions with his own Suzerain. Amongst the other troubles and causes of trouble, attached, like so many curses, to the inheritance of Rollo, was the still unsettled claim to the territory, afterwards called the Norman Vexin or Beaucassin. William had been unable to assert his right— a better and more just cause of quarrel than such pretensions usually are. Whether from policy or from apprehension, William had been loth to wage war, either against Henry or Philip. Indeed, every battle which the Duke of Normandy fought against the King of the French, might become an example of insubordination, recoiling upon the King of the English. But he now determined to recover this territory, not only as his own, but in consequence of its great importance. Like all border countries, it contained a turbulent and unquiet population, and in this instance Frenchmen both by race and interest, they were always ready to infest the Normans.

§ 3. The fatal opportunity now arose, which gave an excuse and an incitement to action. Without any assigned reason, though most probably instigated by Robert, the burgesses of Mantes declared a petty war against William, and crossing the Eure, with a disorderly body of marauders, they plundered the neighbourhood of Evreux, particularly the domains of William de Breteuil and Roger de Ivry. They made much spoil, and took many prisoners, and returned driving herds and flocks before them, and conducting the bound captives, from whom so good a profit was to be made, glorying equally in the gain, and in the affront thus offered to the pride of Normandy.

William was roused to great anger; he was offended by the insult of this foray, and, connecting Philip with the transaction, he demanded the cession of Mantes, Pont-Isare, and Chaumont, in addition to the whole of the Beaucassin territory thus unjustly withheld. Philip refused, raising many cavils unfairly, and instigated by the undutiful Robert;— evading rather than denying the claims. Coarse jests passed between the sovereigns, by which they were mutually embittered; and William, now no longer to be restrained, prepared to assert his rights by the sword.

§ 4. It is rare that the chroniclers become descriptive; in this instance, adopting the style of the Trouveurs, and most probably echoing some popular ballad of the day, they tell us how the harvest was ripening, the grape swelling on the stem, the fruits reddening on the bough, when William entered the fertile land. As he advanced, the corn was trodden down, the vineyards rooted up, the country havocked,

the gifts of Providence wastefully destroyed. *1087*
An imprudent sally of the inhabitants of Mantes, with the intention of saving their crops, enabled William to enter their town, which was fired by the soldiery. Churches and dwellings alike sunk in the flames, many of the inhabitants perished, even the recluses were burned in their cells.

Mantes on fire.

William, aged and unwieldy in body, yet impetuous and active in mind, cheered the desolation, and gallopped about and about through the burning ruins. His steed stumbled amidst the glowing embers : like the third sovereign who bore the name of William, the royal rider received a fatal injury from his fall. A lingering inflammation ensued, which the skill of his attendants could neither allay nor heal. He called in Gilbert Maminot, Bishop of Lisieux, and Gunthard, Abbot of Jumièges, both yet retaining their former leech-craft, and well competent to comfort him, if he could be comforted, in body and in mind. The noise, the disturbance, the tainted atmosphere of Rouen, became intolerable to the fevered sufferer, and he was painfully removed to the conventual buildings of St. Gervase, on the adjoining hill. The inward combustion spread so rapidly that no hope of recovery remained, and William knew that there was none.

William's accident.

Taken to Rouen.

§ 5. Firmly contemplating the end, and yet dreading its approach, he sent for Rufus and

1087

William's agony of mind.

Henry, his sons; and now ensued that conflict of feeling never entirely absent from the death bed, but sometimes so painfully visible, when, as personified in the symbolical paintings of old, we behold the good angel and the evil demon contending for the mastery of the departing soul: the clinging to earthly things with a deep consciousness of their worthlessness, self-condemnation, and self-deceit, repentance and obduracy, the scales of the balance trembling between heaven and hell. "No tongue can tell," said he, "the deeds of wickedness I have perpetrated in my weary pilgrimage of toil and care." He deplored his birth, born to warfare, polluted by bloodshed from his earliest years, his trials, the base ingratitude he had sustained. He also extolled his own virtues, praised his own conscientious appointments in the Church: expatiated upon his good deeds, his alms, and the monasteries and nunneries which under his reign had been founded by his munificence.

He divides his realms.

But Rufus and Henry are standing by that bedside, and who is to be the Conqueror's heir? How are his dominions to be divided? William must speak of his earthly authority; but every word relating to the object of his pride is uttered

Robert.

in agony. Robert, as first-born, is to take Normandy: it was granted to him before William met Harold in the field of the valley of blood. "Wretched," declared the King, "will be the country subjected to his rule; but he has received the homage of the barons, and the concession, once made, cannot be withdrawn. Of England, I will appoint no heir: let Him in whose hands are all things, provide according to His will." All the wide wasting wretchedness produced by his ambition rose up before him: it seemed as if the air around him was filled with the wailings of those who had perished at his behest, by the sword, by famine, and by fire. Bitterly lamenting his anger, his harshness, his crimes, he declared that he dared not bestow the realm he thus had won: and yet this reserve was almost a delusion: the natural feeling of a father prevailed, and he declared his hope that Rufus, who from youth upwards, whatever were his other defects of character, had been an obedient son, might succeed him. And what was Henry Beauclerc to inherit? A treasure of five thousand pounds of silver. Henry began to lament this unequal gift. "What will all this treasure profit me," exclaimed he, "if I have neither land, nor house, nor home?" William comforted his youngest son, and that strangely, by intimating his foreboding that Henry, becoming far greater than either brother, would one day possess far greater and ampler power.

But the very words which William had spoken, now excited his own apprehensions: the intimations he had thus given, might, by implying a doubt of his right to confer the succession, instigate rebellion. He turned him round in his weary bed, and directed that a writ should be prepared, addressed to Lanfranc, commanding him to place Rufus on the throne; and the dying man, he who had just vowed that he would not take thought concerning the sinful inheritance, affixed his royal signet to the instrument by which, in fact, he bequeathed the unlawful gain; and he forthwith delivered the same to Rufus, kissed him, and blessed him; and Rufus hastened away towards England, lest he should lose the blood-stained crown. Henry, too, departed, to secure his legacy, and to consider how he should best protect himself against the troubles which he might occasion or sustain.

§ 6. Both sons have now left their dying parent. More suspense, more agony. Those who surrounded him had heard of alms and of repentance, of contrition and of distribution of the wealth no longer his own. Some portions to make amends for the wrongs he had committed, some to the poor; the ample residue to his sons. But as yet no real charity; of forgiveness, nothing had been said by William, nothing of remission to the captives in the dungeon, upon whom the doom of perpetual imprisonment had been past. William assented to the remark, and yet justified himself for his severity. Morcar had been hardly treated, and yet how could he, William, restrain the fear which he had felt of his influence? Roger de Breteuil had shewn a fell revenge, yet let them be freed; Woolnoth, the brother of Harold, a child when he fell into the hands of the Conqueror, who had sternly kept him in bonds since the days of his infancy, and Siward of the North, were to be released; and William ended by commanding that all the prison doors in England and Normandy should be opened, except to one alone: except to Odo his brother. Much were those about William saddened by this hardness: many and urgent were the entreaties made, but above all by the third brother, Robert of Mortaigne. At length William relaxed his severity, but without relenting, declaring his unchangeable conviction of Odo's perfidy, and that he yielded against his will.

1087

He frees his political captives.

This act of grudging, coerced, extorted forgiveness was his last. A night of somewhat diminished suffering ensued, when the troubled and expiring body takes a dull, painful, unrestful rest before its last earthly repose. But as the cheerful, life-giving rays of the rising sun were darting above the horizon, across the sad apartment, and shedding brightness on its walls, William was half awakened from his imperfect slumbers by the measured, mellow, reverberating swelling tone of the great cathedral bell. "It is the hour of prime," replied the attendants in answer to his enquiry. Then were the priesthood welcoming with voices of thanksgiving the

Night and morning of death.

renewed gift of another day, and sending forth the choral prayer, that the hours might flow in holiness till blessed at their close:

> " Now that the sun is gleaming bright,
> Implore we, bending low,
> That He, the uncreated light,
> May guide us as we go.
>
> " No sinful word, nor deed of wrong,
> Nor thoughts that idly rove,
> But simple truth be on our tongue,
> And in our hearts be love.
>
> " And while the hours in order flow,
> O Christ, securely fence
> Our gates, beleaguered by the foe,
> The gate of every sense.
>
> " And grant that to thine honour, Lord,
> Our daily toil may tend;
> That we begin it at Thy word,
> And in Thy favour end."

But his time of labour and struggle, sin and repentance was past. William lifted up his hands in prayer and expired.

§ 7. As was very common in those times, the death of the great and rich was the signal for a scene of disgraceful neglect and confusion. Not that we are now more purified or softened in heart: even in our own days the degraded chamber of a departed monarch witnessed the vilest rapacity; but in earlier periods the eager greediness, now usually restrained from much outward demonstration by habits of decorum and dread of punishment, was displayed and

vented without hesitation, fear, or shame. His 1087
sons had already departed: all who remained
of higher degree rushed out to horse, each hastening to his home, for the purpose of protecting
his property against the dreaded confusion of
an interregnum, or preparing to augment it.
Those of meaner rank, the servants and ribalds *Plunder in the building.*
of the court, stripped the body, even of its last
garments, plundered every article within reach,
and then, all quitting him, left the poor diseased
body lying naked on the floor.

Consternation and apathy were, after some
hours, diminished. The clergy recollected their
duty, and offered up the prayers of the Church;
and the archbishop directed that the body
should be conveyed to Caen. But there was *The body is carried to Caen.*
no one to take charge of the obsequies, not one
of those who were connected with William by
consanguinity, or bound to him by blood or by
gratitude; and the duty was performed by the
care and charity of Herlouin, a knight of humble fortune, who himself defrayed the expenses,
grieved at the indignity to which the mortal
spoil of his Sovereign was exposed, and who, as
the only mourner, attended the coffin during its
conveyance to Caen.

§ 8. At the gates of Caen, clergy and laity came
forth to receive the body, but at that very time
flames arose, the streets were filled with heavy
smoke: a fire had broken out which destroyed
good part of the city: the procession was dis-

persed, and the monks alone remained. They brought the body to St. Stephen's monastery, and took order for the royal sepulture. The grave was dug deep in the presbytery, between altar and choir. All the bishops and abbots of Normandy assembled. After mass had been sung, Gilbert, Bishop of Evreux, addressed the people; and when he had magnified the fame of the departed, he asked them all to join in prayer for the sinful soul; and that each would pardon any injury he might have received from the monarch. A loud voice was now heard from the crowd. A poor man stood up before the bier, Asceline, the son of Arthur, who forbade that William's corpse should be received into the ground he had usurped by reckless violence.

The Bishop forthwith instituted an enquiry into the charge. They called up witnesses, and the fact having been ascertained, they treated with Asceline and paid the debt, the price of that narrow little plot of earth, the last bed of the Conqueror. Asceline withdrew his ban; but as the swollen corpse sank into the grave, it burst, filling the sacred edifice with corruption. The obsequies were hurried through, and thus was William the Conqueror gathered to his fathers, with loathing, disgust, and horror.

Chapter XV.

RESULTS OF THE CONQUEST.

NEW POLITICAL POSITION OF ENGLAND—SOME CHANGES CAUSED RATHER BY TIME THAN BY CONQUEST—CONTINUITY OF LAW IN ENGLAND—SO-CALLED FEUDAL SYSTEM—WILLIAM'S ADMINISTRATION: IN CHURCH MATTERS: IN THE LAW—MILITARY SERVICES—JUSTICE—EFFECTS OF WILLIAM'S IGNORANCE OF ENGLISH—HIS CHARACTER—POSITION AS LEGAL HEIR TO THE THRONE—FALSE IMPRESSIONS AS TO HIS INNOVATIONS: EXEMPLIFIED BY THE COURSE OF THE ENGLISH LANGUAGE—THE CHURCH IN ENGLAND—LANFRANC—MAMINOT—WILLIAM'S ECCLESIASTICAL APPOINTMENTS.

§ 1. WE have now arrived at the conclusion of the era of great individual and greater national suffering. *General necessity for the Conquest.* England was mercifully dealt with. Since the reign of Ethelred, the empire had been gradually losing all power of defence against foreign enemies, whilst the people, deeply corrupted, were exaggerating the faults and losing the virtues of their ancestors. In the same manner as the sins of the European community demanded the visitation of the French revolution, so did England require the discipline of the Norman sword. The sceptre was taken from the English race, and they were placed beneath the dominion of the alien, raised up to fill the throne, and to whom the power was transferred.

§ 2. One of the most prominent consequences resulting from the Conquest, was its effect upon the external relations of the kingdom. England was brought into a closer connexion with the general affairs of the Commonwealth of Western Christendom than had ever subsisted before. Of course, a previous degree of intercourse had always existed of necessity. The narrow seas might be crossed by the merchant : missionaries were sent forth from our island to the banks of the Rhine. As we rush along his waters, the gigantic towers of Maintz still attest the pious labours of Boniface. After the desolations of the Danes, holy men might be brought from Gaul to Glastonbury or to Malmesbury, for the purpose of renewing the chain of ecclesiastical tradition in the minster, which an Alfred's piety had raised again from the ground. Furthermore, the community of intellect continued, though in a limited degree. Alcuin, the friend and companion of Charlemagne, was known and praised as an Englishman. Bede was universally received as a father of the Church; and Duns Scotus, and some few other British names, were known in the libraries of Gaul and Germany. But notwithstanding all these links,—and we may moreover enumerate amongst them an occasional matrimonial alliance or a complimentary embassy,—the limited intercourse and connexion was gradually diminishing. England, enclosed within her four seas, always harassed by the fears or the presence of the still pagan Northmen, was becoming more and more foreign to the feelings and thoughts and interests of the rest of Western Christendom.

Had fallen off.

Perhaps there is no one fact which illustrates this severance more forcibly and more completely, than the circumstance that when Anselm attended the council of Rome (1098), the fathers were utterly unable to decide what place should be assigned to the insular prelate in that venerable assembly. In the reign of the Confessor, Anselm's predecessor had crossed the Alps to receive from the Pope the pallium by which he was confirmed in the primacy, but an Archbishop of Canterbury had never before been seen taking his seat in council amongst the other members of the western hierarchy. No person living, no not the oldest, had known such a thing. From their predecessors, the prelates present had heard nothing of the station amongst them of Anselm's predecessors: their records told them nothing: if they turned over the acts of preceding councils, they did not find one single signature of an English bishop or an English abbot. In other words, England had no representatives in what were, virtually, the Parliaments of Christendom.

England practically unknown at Rome.

Urban removed all difficulties of station and precedence, by giving to Anselm the highest place in the synod: he caused him to sit in the apse, where he himself was stationed, having already in the council of Bari, addressed him almost as a colleague—"Includamus hunc in orbe nostro, quasi alterius orbis Papam;" a most significant epithet, and in which, it should seem, that more than a mere complimentary honour was implied. It appears to have amounted almost to an acknowledgment that Britain was considered as a co-ordinate empire, such as it was when the Basileus of Albion appeared as sharer with Charlemagne in the sacred honours of royalty, when he and Charlemagne were, in fact, the only sovereigns in the Roman world.

Honours to Anselm at Rome.

Such had been the separation of Britain from the rest of the Christian Commonwealth, that, by the accession of the Conqueror and his dynasty, the political situation of England was entirely changed. The waters of the Channel still continued to divide the cliffs of Albion from the cliffs of Gaul, but the island and the firm land were compelled to be constantly in communication with each other, to be united by sympathies, and cognizant of each other by hostilities. Henceforward England and France were connected by domestic ties, whether conjoined in friendship or conflicting in the field. The same lineages spread over England and Normandy and Flanders: it was hard to say who was the foreigner. But perhaps even more

England now united with France.

influential than these ties and relationships were the influences of doctrine and opinion. England was now prevented, as it were, from drifting away. The theory at this period of the Western Commonwealth, was that of unity: a unity often disturbed in practice, but which, yielding a nominal supremacy to the empire, and a real, though contested, supremacy to the Pope, impressed the nations of Europe that they constituted one community. Rome became the common sensorium of Europe, and through Rome all the several portions of Latin Europe sympathized and felt with each other. Hence the great difficulty of writing the history of the middle ages. The history of the papacy enters as an element into the history of each state or kingdom, and at the same time that so much of that history must be brought in as is needful to illustrate your national transactions, you must avoid any exuberance of discussion or detail, which may perplex the course of events with which you are more immediately concerned. The geographer cannot complete the square of the map of England, unless he introduces an angle of the opposite coast; but much more must be done by the historian.

Enters into the political organization of Europe.

§ 3. I must now pass to the effects occasioned at home by the accession of the Norman king, and to the manner in which the bitterness of the lot of the English was mitigated, and the inevitable miseries of foreign conquest speedily overruled.

Its effects at home. Speedily: for, when three generations and four had passed away, so had its evils disappeared. It was a storm which purified the air: a flood which fertilized the soil.

It has been considered, in the words of the most popular of our historians, "that it would be difficult to find a revolution more destructive, or attended with a more complete subjection of the antient inhabitants." We are accustomed to lament over Harold as the last of the Anglo-Saxon kings, and to consider the acquisition of the crown by William as the destruction of independence and nationality, English independence and nationality; *Protest against phrase, "Anglo-Saxon."* and I must needs here pause, and substitute henceforward the true and antient word English for the unhistorical and conventional term Anglo-Saxon, an expression conveying a most false idea in our civil history. It disguises the continuity of affairs, and substitutes the appearance of a new formation in the place of a progressive *Specific effects overrated.* evolution. Granted,—for who would deny it? that the Norman Conquest did, in its first and immediate consequences, give a great shock to existing constitutions, that it divested a large class of the great landholders of their superiority, yet it must be considered rather as an event than an overwhelming catastrophe. Indeed, the most striking proof of the exaggerated opinion prevailing with respect to the subversions resulting from the Norman Conquest, is afforded by comparing England with other kindred nations, whose soil was not wasted by the sword of the stranger. Let us look back for this comparison, not to the age of the Plantagenets, not to the age of the Houses of York and of Lancaster, not to the age of the first of the Stuarts, but to a time comparatively of yesterday, the reign of good Queen Anne.

Now at this period there were several nations closely allied to the antient English, nay in a manner the same people, who had never been conquered by the stranger. Such was the state of Denmark. Here are Danes, fair-haired and blue-eyed, in unbroken, unmingled descent from the Hackarls of Canute, Angles and Jutes, tilling the very soil which belonged to Hengst and Horsa. Here has been no hostile invasion, but what has become of the language of the Asi? In the dialect of comparatively modern periods, our archaism is still more remarkable. In the Lord's Prayer, as translated by Pope Adrian, in the year one thousand one hundred and fifty-six, there is perhaps only a single word which in the year one thousand seven hundred and three can be said to have been obsolete; and our Nicholas Breakspear, still so plain and intelligible, was exactly the contemporary of the warlike historian Snorro Sturleson; he to whom we owe the preservation of the [traditions] of the Saxons of the North; but to whom even Olaus, Rubeck, or Bartholimus could not have spoken without an interpreter. Upon

Correlative changes in Denmark.

Linguistic changes.

this wide and very interesting subject,—the mutations of our speech, I will not at present enlarge. I shall only remark, that, in certain states of human society, there is a tendency to enrich the nomenclature and simplify the structure of language, sometimes arising from what, in common, though rather disagreeable, phrase, is termed the "national mind," and sometimes from external causes; and that both were beginning to be in operation in England before the Norman Conquest. But the comparative circumstances of Denmark and of England will assist in enabling us to understand how great an alteration might have taken place in our national [character] (of which language is so forcible a witness), supposing the great event about which we are discoursing had never come to pass.

Changes in Danish law. With respect to government and laws and institutions, the departure from the antient commonwealth was perhaps greater even than in language. The Gothic Nemda was the subject of an archæological essay. Hard servitude had fallen upon the descendants of the Bondes, the tillers of the soil, who in the age of Harold Harfager raised their bold helmetted heads around the sovereign in the Landzthing. Jarls were unknown in name and in deed. In short, with the exception of some portions of the criminal law, and rules regulating the rights of property, the whole platform (to use the word in its Elizabethan sense) of the Commonwealth, since the fifteenth century, has been as completely changed as if the Christian of Oldenburgh had gained the throne sword in hand. I doubt if they can shew any court, any institution, any essential portion of the state, which derived its regular succession from an earlier time.

§ 4. But in England, even so late as the recent period which I have named, after all our conquests and civil wars, after our reformation, after our revolution, there still existed, as it were, whole strata continuing only slightly altered. In our political constitution, much we can trace; for example, how the real territorial authority of Siward, Earl of Northumberland, gradually waned away into the title which the Percy claimed. The courts of the burgh, the hundred, and the shire had not changed, even in name. The whole customary tenure of land, over all the length and breadth of the island, was, and indeed is, purely and sincerely English. If any one of my readers should chance to renew his holding under the Bishop of Worcester, it will be *gebooked* to him for three lives, exactly as if good Wulstane was to receive the fine. Of aldermen it is unnecessary to speak: everybody knows their venerable antiquity; and, indeed, throughout the whole of our municipal institutions, the vitality of the old English customs and constitution was truly wonderful. Bring an ejectment for lands in the parish of Clapham or Chelsea, and Judge Holt would at once have non-suited you for not laying the venue in the Anglo-Saxon town. If the lord of the manor had, or indeed has to vindicate his franchise, he presses into his service, or more truly perhaps into the service of his attorney, sac and soc, infangthief and outfangthief, and whatsoever else he can find in King Ethelred's charter. And if the Hlafod who now holds the possession of [the Saxon owner], were to exert his rights, the inhabitants of Manchester Square would be compelled to appear at the court of the Lite as in the earliest age.

Surviving Saxon usages. [cir. 1845.]

I have attempted the comparison contained in the preceding paragraphs, in order to shew how small is the necessity of ascribing the great mutations which unquestionably took place in the laws and government of the country, to national subjugation and hostile influence: a much shorter road of shewing the error of those who ascribe such a radical, such an overwhelming change to the Conquest, would have been simply to appeal to the evidence. In the code bearing the title which I doubt not will be perfectly intelligible to the reader, of "Les leis et les custumes que li Reis William granted al pople de Engleterre apres la cunquest de la terre; iceles meimes que li Reis Edward sun

Other proofs.

cusin tint devant lui;" and in the custumal ascribed to Henry Beauclerc, but probably even of later date, we have an assured testimony that as far as direct and positive legislation is concerned, William effected the smallest possible innovation: and in [regard to] the assertion, that, in the very frame of his laws, he made a distinction between the Normans and English, [we may appeal to the fact, that they were received by the] nation, not only without reluctance, but with zealous joy; and thus the very means by which William was enabled to accomplish the Conquest, prevented him from ruling otherwise than as an English king.

William regrants Edward's laws.

§ 5. It is most certain that, after the accession of the Plantagenets, we find a very great similarity between the laws of Normandy and the laws of England. Both belonged to one active and powerful sovereign: one system of administration prevailed. It was after one and the same course of business that the money was counted out upon the chequered table, on either side of the sea. The bailiffs in the Norman baillages passed their accounts just as the sheriffs to whom the bailliwicks of the shires were granted in England; and the brieves by which the king administered the law, whether in the kingdom or the duchy, are most evidently germane to each other. In all these circumstances, I can find the most evident and cogent proof that a great revolution was effected, not

Similarity of English and Norman law.

by William, but by Henry Plantagenet. Where he found his precedents, where his councillors, we know not, and in which country the new system originated, which, in a manner, they held in common, we know not. Documentary evidence would go a great way in deciding the question. At present none satisfactory has been discovered by the researches of the antiquary. Glanville, the English justiciar, affords the earliest precedents of the writs "de morte antecessoris," and "de nova disseisina." Howard, the Norman jurist, publishes our Littleton and Bracton and Hela, as the most authentic monuments which he can find of the antient laws of the French; and the traditions of Normandy even attributed the formation of that which in the reign of Philippe Auguste was their national code, the "Grand Coutumier," to the equity and wisdom of Edward the Confessor. Nothing in all this amounts to proof that Henry II., King of England, legislated for the Duchy of Normandy; but at least it shews, that, from other causes than the immediate conquest, to which it is usually ascribed, the uniformity may have arisen.

Norman law certainly not the original.

§ 6. Probably most of my readers have been expecting, in the course of the preceding pages, to hear much upon some subjects which hold so conspicuous a station in our usual, I may almost say our conventional ideas of mediæval history;

I mean feudality and chivalry. If, using old-fashioned allegorical language, we were to say that Feudality and Chivalry, according to the popular notions of them, are phantoms who must be driven away before we can enter the Palace of Truth, we should hardly be using too strong language. A great living authority upon these subjects—perhaps the greatest—he who whilst I write these lines, is at the head of the councils of the Sovereign to whom, under Providence, the guidance of the destinies of France is confided, has said, and most truly, that never did the feudal system of regular subordination subsist in the forms assigned to it by jurists. Feudal society, in its supposed entirety, is an imaginary structure raised only by the fancy of the learned, and of which the materials only, incoherent and broken, have been found lying on the soil.

M. Guizot on Feudalism.

* * * * *

In considering the developments of the Conquest, the first question which always presents itself to the mind, is the state and condition of the English nation under their new masters; and this is inseparably connected with the supposed establishment of feudal tenures by the Conqueror. This is a very large question, which we must treat in this place on the smallest scale. A dull subject, many persons would say, but which must be discussed, on account of the

Feudal tenures.

prominent, and, we must add, we believe erroneous position which it takes, according to the usual views of mediæval history.

But notwithstanding all the assertions which historians have made, we have never been able to satisfy ourselves that such a feudal system ever existed. It reminds us of the feudal castle, rendered so familiar to our eyes and mind by worthy Captain Grose, of antiquarian and facetious memory; and which, multiplied and adopted in our encyclopædias and educational books, becomes the ideal form of architectural chivalry; and truly never was any representation better entitled to the old-fashioned *inv: et delin:* in the corner, the dungeon tower in the centre, the inner bailey round the dungeon, the outer baileys round the inner, all neat and concentric as the crust of a pie. Now, though you might find such a square dungeon tower in many places, the inner bailey in half-a-dozen, and the outer bailey perhaps in a single example, still whoever forms his ideas upon this type, will have adapted them to a model which never existed. The reason why such a castle never could have existed is this, that every real fortification was necessarily adapted to the site which it was to defend; and the plan adopted to guard the coast of Dover, would, of necessity, be entirely different from that employed in the plain of Vincennes; and therefore, whatever similarity of principle there may have been in the so-

Marginal note: The system never existed in its theoretical completeness.

called feudal institutions, they became infinitely varied by the nations amongst whom they were adopted; being, in fact, a transmission of Roman jurisprudence and Roman institutions, combined with the usages of Teutonic tribes.

Without entering therefore into details, we shall venture to point out the two great errors which render the views commonly expressed entirely incorrect. The first is confounding the feudal tenures of land with what is called feudal government; for however paradoxical it may appear, there was no government in mediæval Europe founded upon feudality. The other is in the extreme exaggeration of the state of the common people, and the ascribing it to the barbaric invasions. So far as their influence extended, the lot of the Coloni was alleviated and not aggravated by the transfer of the Roman authority to the new race of masters. With respect to England, with which we are more immediately concerned, we believe, that, previous to the Conquest, all land imposed upon the owner the duty of contributing to the defence of the state, according to its value. As the Conqueror found the land, so he gave it; and after a good deal of uncertainty, over-exactions on the part of the crown, demanding more than was due, and refusals on the part of the landholders to give what was really due, the territorial system settled, after the accession of

Feudal tenures are not feudal government.

Land tenures after the Conquest.

the House of Plantagenet, into a more definite form.

§ 7. It cannot be said, that, upon the face of William's laws, there was any systematic attempt to treat the English with insults or indignity as a race; for he declared that every Frenchman who had paid scot and lot in the time of the Confessor, should continue subjected to the English law. But, leaving the entire framework of the English law untouched, he kept the administration of it wholly in his own hands, acting either in his own person or by those who, responsible to him alone, exercised his authority. He made a complete difference between the rich and the poor: none of his barons or tenants could be punished for any crime except by his permission. They might commit incest or adultery or robbery or murder with impunity: no one could meddle with them unless William chose. This denial of justice he effected by a complete restriction upon all the authority of the Church. For the greater portion of such crimes could only be restrained by excommunication, or ecclesiastical censure, and no bishop was permitted to excommunicate or to censure, unless by his leave and license. The first impression which this statement makes upon the modern mind, is that the secular courts were, nevertheless, open to the suitor. But the answer is, that these courts were completely guided by the King's arbitrary will, and that

William's stern personal administration.

Restrains the clergy.

the ecclesiastical tribunals were the only ones in which any degree of independence could be found. In all criminal jurisdiction, his hand fell as heavily upon the Normans as upon the English. There was no privilege of nation allowed. The English might give more offence; but both were equally crushed by his heavy hand.

The power which he exercised of nominating the bishops, deprived the national legislature of any independence which it possessed. The bishops were his own men, more even than the earls or the barons; and his restraint of ecclesiastical liberty extinguished any species of national liberty. When the bishops were assembled in council, he would not permit any statutes or canons to be propounded by the archbishop, unless, having previously approved of the same, they were entirely conformable to his will. Therefore, no reform, whether in manners or morals, or in the extensive branch of jurisprudence, which could alone emanate from these councils, could be effected, unless conformably to his inclinations, and to suit his interests. The papal power, so far as it could be exercised in Britain, could extend no further than William chose. No Pope was recognized in Britain, not even Hildebrand himself, unless by William his election and choice was approved. No papal Bull to be executed, unless sanctioned by royal authority: in other words, William, the Basileus

He names his own Bishops:

Gives validity to Councils.

and Popes:

of Britain, assumed and exercised the imperial power; and in this he most evidently felt and saw how needful it was, according to his scheme of authority, to resist the efforts which Hildebrand was making for the general liberties of the Christian community. Had the liberty of election been restored to the English sees; had the power of the papal see in punishing simony and corruption, or in removing from the episcopate those unworthy to exercise its duties, been suffered to be exerted, William's autocracy would have been at an end.

The only direct innovation in the shape of law, affecting the rights of his subjects, is an ordinance imposing certain regulations as to the mode of deciding criminal cases by wager of battle. This has been considered, more especially by recent writers, as placing the Englishman and the Frenchman upon unequal terms. It would require a far deeper knowledge of the actual practice of the Anglo-Saxon law (I employ this term unwillingly, but for the purpose of preventing misapprehension) than we shall ever possess, to determine whether there was really any unfairness or inequality; but, at all events, if this right did belong, as a patrimonial law, to his Norman subjects, he could not well deprive them of it; and, at all events, it speedily became obsolete, and we cannot find even a trace of it beyond his reign.

§ 8. I have already noticed the popular opinion

that William introduced into England the feudal law. We are told, by the most popular of our historians, that he found this system already established in France and in Normandy, and that feudality was the foundation both of the stability and the disorders of most of the mediæval governments. This opinion involves the proposition that the "feudal system" was established on the Continent, and was not established in England. The observations which I have made on this subject on other occasions, will enable the reader to judge whether it be well founded or not.

It is, however, somewhat remarkable that the many who have adopted this theory almost implicitly, never stop to enquire how it happened that Britain, containing the same elements of population and jurisprudence as the rest of Western Christendom, and more particularly France and Germany, should not have possessed the same law. The Anglo-Saxons and the Lombards were close neighbours in their original seats in Germany; the Salic Franks and the Ripuarians were the borderers of the Jutes and Saxons; and if the feudal law arose, as Montesquieu says, and as Hume, no doubt, believed, in the forests of Germany, how did it happen that, in the occupation of England, it was left behind? Still more remarkable is it, that no one should have been startled at the total want of evidence. With respect to England, what William found, that he kept; and not only are

Difficulties in the popular view.

we destitute of any evidence whatever to shew that he made any change in the tenure of land, but we have the strongest evidence to the contrary. Take Domesday, the great record, which was to establish the relations between the King and his landholders—those lands, conferred, as Hume tells us, with the reservation of stated services and payments, on the most considerable of his adventurers; and you will not find any one service or payment reserved, except the pecuniary payments, the Danegeld, which had been rendered in the Anglo-Saxon age. If more land was brought into cultivation, more was paid: if less, less. Domesday, which was to fix all the territorial rights of the crown, is wholly silent upon the subject.

Domesday testifies to no change.

§ 9. That the rendering of a military service for lands held of the Sovereign, a usage derived from the Romans, existed in Britain long before the Conquest, I have elsewhere shewn. That this was retained by William, when the same lands passed to his soldiery or followers, is in the very nature of things. Whatever obligation the land was liable to "*tempore Regis Edwardi,*" it was equally liable to "*tempore Regis Willielmi;*" and in this manner alone can we explain a fact which otherwise might be perplexing, the total absence of any direct allusion to military tenure in the great record of Domesday. In support of the rights of the crown resulting from the tenure of land, Domesday shews nothing. It

Roman origin of military tenure.

only establishes a negative, and that in a very remarkable manner. Hugh Lupus, we are thereby informed, holds the earldom by the sword, as freely as the King holds by his crown. So also, without doubt, did, at this era, the several Lords Marchers. Matters altered entirely when we have overleaped the reign of Henry Plantagenet; but we are speaking of the rights or rather no rights of the respective parties before the generalizations of the law. The hereditary descent of the "Laen Lands" continued, as before the Conquest, a customary right of renewal to the son of his father's tenancy, which could not be enforced, but which, in the ordinary course of affairs, could not be denied.

William makes no alteration.

It is very certain that when our system of military tenures was fully established, in the reign of Henry III., it was a received opinion, popular in the nation, and an axiom in the courts of justice, that thirty-two thousand knights' fees had been created by the Conqueror; but at that period there was a wise officer of the Exchequer, one Alexander de Swereford, also Archdeacon of Salisbury, who, in the exercise of his duties, wished to find a certain account thereof; but, on seeking evidence, he could find none. Rolls or records of the age of the Conqueror, save and except that Domesday which we have, could he not discover. Nigel, Bishop of Ely, treasurer to

Later traditions ungrounded.

King Henry Beauclerc, he so deeply learned in all the science of the Exchequer, knew nothing of it, neither had Richard, the Bishop of London, he who had fully expounded the business of the Exchequer, stated anything concerning it; and, therefore, he comes to the conclusion that when Henry Fitz-Empress required, as we shall afterwards find, acknowledgments from all the tenants *in capite* of what was due, he was otherwise ignorant of the origin and amount of the rights of the crown; and whatever other inferences may be drawn from this very remarkable statement, we cannot refuse the conclusion that there was no one written document testifying to the creation of military tenures; and that, when we find them afterwards established, they were a development of customary usages: some gradually reduced into regularity by the decisions of courts of justice, others by compromise between the subject and the crown.

No documentary proof on the origin of military tenures.

It was brought as an accusation against William, that he had much infringed upon the liberties of the Church, by exacting military service from the prelates; that is to say, adopting the terms of a subsequent period, converting frank almoigne into military tenure. He does appear to have acted arbitrarily; and, as we know from Domesday, to have allowed portions of the Church property to be taken away from its rightful owners; but, for portions of the Church lands, a military service was certainly due in the Anglo-Saxon age: and when we find the military tenures reduced into a regular system, the amount of service due from the Church lands was but small, and even so late as the reign of Edward I., not very accurately defined. Upon every military muster there was a species of squabble between the Lord High Constable and the bishops as to the amount of men-at-arms that ought to appear for them; and, indeed, in spite of all the endeavours of the law officers of the crown, the services were, even then, somewhat undefined from the baronage in general. And it is the greatest drawback to all our symmetrical historical theories, that we find the summonses to take the order of knighthood extended to all persons holding land above a certain amount, no matter of whom—a qualification grounded upon amount of property, and not of tenure. *Church military tenures.*

§ 10. William's first intention was to administer justice even as his predecessors. The Basileus, like the Eastern Sovereign, was accessible to the people for the purpose of affording that high remedial justice which he could alone impart. He was to hear the complaints of the people: he was to exercise his transcendent powers of justice, lest right should fail. For this purpose, William endeavoured to qualify himself, by learning the language of the people, so that he might listen to them with his own ears, and make such order or decree as the case required, *William as judge.*

without the intervention of any minister, interposed between the subject and the throne. But William was wholly a Frenchman: he had not even a reminiscence of the language of his remote ancestors, once so nearly allied to our own: he could find neither grammar nor dictionary to aid him: the instructor might be awkward, or the scholar unapt; and William had as little success in endeavouring to learn to speak English, as Charlemagne had in trying to learn to write. Both the royal scholars gave up their lessons in despair.

William cannot learn English.

How great and important were the consequences which ensued from this inability! It seems as if, for the purpose of confounding human wisdom, we were sometimes permitted to discern how the most important consequences result, not from plan or forethought, but from tendencies, actions, or sentiments apparently the least adequate to the results developed in after time. If we attempt to examine what at this moment constitutes the peculiar attribute of our present form of government, and upon which its practical merits depend, it will be found, not in the visionary balance of power between the crown, the aristocracy, and the people, but in the relation between the crown and the functionaries by whom the power of the crown is exercised, leaving to the Sovereign every lawful influence, but preventing the Sovereign from falling into the danger of abusing

Results of this.

Sketch of the spirit of our constitution.

that power; and, considered in this point of view, we should say that the whole history of the Constitution depends upon its development through the three stages which it has thus assumed. The Sovereign exercising his powers as a judge in his own proper person; the delegation of these powers to functionaries subservient to his prerogative, but proceeding according to definite and established law; lastly, the conversion of these functionaries into ministers, apparently appointed by the crown, but with the assent, virtually given, of the legislature, to whom they become responsible for the exercise of the authority placed in their hands.

§ 11. Now, the reign of the Conqueror exhibits the germ of the second of these great changes; the completion of the last was reserved for our own times. William's ignorance of the English language, which would incapacitate him either for hearing the complaints of his subjects, or, in many cases, giving the needful directions, would throw him naturally upon the expediency of delegating these functions to others; and he found an establishment for that purpose ready made to his hand. This was the Chancery, of which the foundation having been laid at a very early period, [it] acquired a new development in the Confessor's reign. As a portion of the imperial establishment, the Referendarius drew or prepared all royal rescripts and charters, and was the keeper of the royal signet. In the Frankish

Origin of the Court of Chancery.

monarchy, the succession of these officers can be deduced from Clovis, the patrician king; and we find an officer bearing this title in the charters of Ethelbert. In the reign of the Confessor, the assumption of the great seal, as the means of declaring the King's intention, has been already noticed; and, under the Conqueror, the need of employing secretaries for the many purposes with which the King had hitherto dealt, *viva voce*, greatly encreased both the powers and the influence of the King's chapel, as this department was called. Those who are denominated the King's chaplains were the writing clerks constituting the Board, of which the Chancellor was the head. This officer may be termed the Secretary of State for all departments, and thus he continued during many generations, until his functions were gradually subdivided amongst the other officers of state, by whom they are now exercised. That such an office could alone be entrusted to an ecclesiastic, was a matter of course; and Arfastus, afterwards Bishop of Thetford, held it at a very early period of the Conqueror's reign.

Early stage of the court.

From this department emanated the gewrits, or letters, by which the Sovereign intimated his intentions; and those relating to the administration of remedial justice, constituted a large, and to the people in general, the most important portion. Varied as they were at first in form, according to the circumstances of each case,

It issues writs.

they are all grounded upon one principle—that right was to be done, lest further complaint of an unredressed grievance, should again reach the throne. The principle upon which they issued was a combination, so to speak, of an exertion of the King's grace and favour, united to his obligation of dispensing justice. What the King granted, he might withhold, either because the complaint was too unfounded or trivial to require the interposition of the supreme authority; or because the obscurity of the complainant or the influence of the defendant, or party accused, might stay the course of law.

How often either of these causes might operate, cannot be here discussed; but one point was gained. There was a regular office, to use the common phrase, to which the suitor might apply, and a regular body of officials, by whom the first process for obtaining justice could be issued. These officials, for their own convenience, would begin to collect something like a body of precedents, and hereby the first foundation was laid for a regular system of jurisprudence. The greater portion of our antient writs consist of the principles of the Anglo-Saxon law, embodied in an Anglo-Norman form; and, finding, as we do, the same forms first employed in England, and subsequently in Normandy, at least so far as can be ascertained from any evidence hitherto collected by archæological industry, are we not warranted in the

It becomes a subjects' court.

Its precedents.

inference that it was the King of England who introduced into Normandy the usages which were common to both realms?

Result of William's absences on the law.

§ 12. Whilst William's want of knowledge of the English language occasioned this great alteration in the formal method of dispensing remedial justice, a still greater change took place in consequence of the repeated absences of the Sovereign and his successors, from the island realm. At least more than half the time of days and months and years of the reign of William and his children, nay even till the final loss of the duchy, was passed beyond the seas. During these absences, it became needful to delegate the royal authority: it was put in commission, and entrusted to various regents; but so prominent was the judicial character of the Sovereign, that these regents were always called Justiciars: it was not for the purpose of coercing his English subjects, for coercion might have been effected by the sword, but for the purpose of administering justice to them, that the Sovereign's place was to be supplied; and hence, so permanent has been our course of usage, that, in the event of the Sovereign's absence from England, her representatives would be called Lords Justices at the present day. These justices were probably more accessible to the people than the one person of the Sovereign; and, inasmuch as it seems to have been considered that the remedial jurisdiction of the English King was inherent in the

Regent Justiciars.

crown, it became the usage to appoint Justiciars for the exercise of those functions of justice, which, even when royalty became more settled, were growing too burthensome for the ordinary leisure of the throne.

§ 13. In considering the progress of the English Government, we must, in the first place, endeavour to distinguish very carefully between the form and the spirit; not by any means attempting unwisely to depreciate the mode and manner by which our Constitution has been administered, or to slight, or to revile any institution which commands popular respect, even though that respect may, in some degree, result from misapplied appreciation of the importance of its object; not, on the other hand, attaching a bigotted or overweening importance to one principle, so as to neglect all countervailing influences, the danger to which political theorists, of all others, are most generally exposed. The English Constitution is not based so much upon liberty as upon law; it is the glory of our law to secure the liberty of the subject; yet the subject should value his liberty only to obtain the protection of the law. Let not our Parliament be considered as a Congress, a Political Assembly, but as a Tribunal, in which, whatever the question may be, the vote of the member is the exercise of his functions as a judge; a judge protecting his fellow-subjects—a judge advising the Sovereign—a judge, if need be, be-

General results of the Conquest on the constitution.

Real intention of Parliament.

tween the subject and the Sovereign. Whatever abuses may have existed, whatever wrongs may have been perpetrated under the name of right, whatever selfishness may have been disguised under the garb of patriotism, whatever unconscientiousness may have been exhibited by individuals or parties, this, and no other, has been the theory of all our conflicts and revolutions.

Strictly legal character of its development. Ours has not been a rude contest for the assertion of independence, but an attempt to obtain an adjudication upon our rights, a case, an adjudication, a precedent. We have never, hitherto, contended for abstract rights or for general principles; our Constitution has never yet degenerated into a charter of maxims and definitions, divided into chapters and articles, but it has resulted from definite remedies applied to definite grievances; and when it ceases to be so, our empire will complete its fall.

William reigns by law; § 14. As William the Conqueror assumed the royal power, as the lawful successor of Edward the Confessor, it followed, as a natural consequence, that he would support his own authority by respecting Edward the Confessor's law; this constituted what we may term the technical principle of his government. Every prescriptive right was to be held as it had been in the days of the Confessor: the laws of Edward the Confessor were to be observed in all respects except so far as he had caused them to be amended for the benefit of the English people; and, at first sight, there was no intentional innovation, or no change.

But whatever may have been the theory, far different was the practice: even as William had been an uncontroulled despot in Normandy, so did he attempt to be in England. "All things, divine and human," in the words of a cotemporary historian, were governed by his absolute will and pleasure, all subservient to his caprice or commands. The first point, and in which his hand fell heaviest, was on the affairs of the Church. In Normandy he appointed and deposed the bishop, without question, without check or controul. He found the same usages established in England, exercised by that Sovereign from whom he claimed the throne, and therefore it must have seemed to him that he had, as it were, a double right; and he used it, though very arbitrarily, yet with prudence and wisdom. We must not always confound despotism and injustice. William was not a wild, a cruel, or a blood-thirsty Conqueror; with but a small share of moral principle, he had no love for evil or sin as such. In an age of universal profligacy, more especially among the higher ranks, his continence is a voucher of what we may term his moral feeling. Historical parallels, though frequently very delusive from the efforts made to overstrain either the resemblance or the antithesis of the respective characters, do, never-

But administers despotically.

His stern nature.

theless, afford much help to the student; and, excepting in the violence of his temper, which, however, he could well restrain when it was his interest so to do, I should say that there was as near a resemblance between him and his third namesake as could well exist between two different individuals, placed so widely apart. It is, I believe, the popular opinion, as expressed by the words of Hume, that it would be difficult to find any revolution more destructive, or attended with a more complete subjugation of the antient inhabitants. Unquestionably the cup of bitterness was presented to the English, but it was not deep; and, amongst the many providences which so singularly and specially mark the destiny of the English nation, it is impossible to doubt but that the effect of the Conquest was in every respect to encrease its powers for good, to strengthen the national intellect, and also, if they be blessings, to give the greatest impulse to its worldly prosperity and glory.

Compared to William III.

§ 15. Whatever aspects William's policy assumed, he never departed from the principle that he had placed himself in the position of a legitimate Sovereign, asserting legitimate rights. William did not present himself as a barbarian stranger, a Sweyne, or a Canute, wielding his battle-axe, slaying old and young, thirsting for blood, greedy of gold, seeking rapine, pursuing revenge; but as a lawful claimant, contesting the inheritance withheld by an unjust adversary;

His legal position.

and, as will have appeared from the preceding transactions, it is hardly possible to deny but that, on constitutional grounds, he had a better grounded title than he who was vanquished by the battle-trial of Hastings. When, therefore, William, as such lawful claimant, obtained the dominion, the reign of the usurper was entirely blotted out from the legal and constitutional annals of England. In the same manner as the ordinances of the Commonwealth have no place in our statute-books, and the patents of the Protector are expunged from our records, so was the reign of Harold passed over, and never recognized by the law. Even as King *de facto*, he was not acknowledged. Domesday, which was to establish the territorial rights of the Conqueror, the record by which he was willing to be concluded, that great memorial, not of an arbitrary power, but of the principle of establishing the rights of the crown, so far as property was concerned, by an immutable law, always dates them "*tempore Regis Edwardi*." William wanted nothing more than what King Edward had; he would take nothing as from Harold; he ascended the throne not as the victor of the son of Godwin, but as succeeding the Confessor. Therefore, he was to be bound to the responsibility of the monarch of whom he claimed to be the adopted son, the constituted heir.

Much may be collected from signs and

tokens in an age when imagery constituted the book of the multitude; when, or where, the knowledge of writing is confined to the few, the picture, the statue, the banner, the device, become, as it were, for the multitude a species of necessity. With us the arts having for these purposes lost their use, they have also lost their reality. But it was not so in those ages. Look, therefore, at William's great seal, by which his will and pleasure, his grace and favour, or his enmity, was announced. Here we find the type of the new dynasty. On the reverse, the Duke of Normandy, mounted on his war steed, grasps the sword of Rollo, defended by shield and mail, his visage concealed by the iron helmet; but on the obverse, the *Rex Anglorum*, seated on the throne of justice, wears the crown of Alfred, and presents the sceptre surmounted by the peaceful dove; and these two representations are living types, as it were, of the two dynasties. And it is hardly needful to repeat that, when called to the throne, he entered into the very compact which bound the English King, the Basileus, whose state and power he had assumed.

William as duke:

And as king.

If I had to sum up the character of William as a king in one loose phrase, I should say that as a king, though cruel, he was not unnecessarily cruel, prudent, cunning, entirely unscrupulous as to the means he used whether to gain or to secure his power,—the sword, the axe, and, if universal rumour could be trusted, the poisoned cup, were all employed without reserve or compunction. Yet, in spite of plunder, cruelty, and devastation, he had more heart than the majority of the statists of a more civilized age; he interfered nowhere, except where he needed to interfere. If, according to the popular legend, the Englishman was compelled to put out fire and candle at the sound of the curfew; he was, nevertheless, so far as the state was concerned, left quiet within his home. William made no attempt to introduce a new religion, new language, new customs, new laws. He never strove to Normanize the English people. *His character.*

§ 16. It is so popularly believed that all these were the immediate effect of the Conquest, that it requires an effort to disengage ourselves from opinions which have grown up, as it were, without thought. It certainly may appear to have been the natural course of things, that William the Conqueror should have compelled the vanquished to accept his institutions and his laws. Unquestionably we find, at a subsequent period, the French or Romance language not only blended with our English, but the prevailing dialect of the court and of the tribunal, of the baronial castle and the merchant's counting-house; in short, to use a familiar phrase, the very token of gentility. It is equally unquestionable that we find a course of public administration of public affairs, more especially in the fiscal *Further errors as to the changes which he effected.*

branches, nearly identical both in England and in Normandy. Furthermore, the system of tenure, usually called feudal, which prevailed in the two countries, is closely analogous in each. Lastly, there is a very near relationship in certain portions of the technical procedures of the law; yet in all these great points of resemblance, I believe that though some of them resulted from the Norman invasion, yet that others were only accelerated by it. They were already proceeding, the fermentation had begun, but slowly and sluggishly, and the Conquest only afforded an additional, and perhaps more active leaven. On the whole, the most probable hypothesis is, that England borrowed less than England gave. The laws imposed by the Norman dynasty upon the English were reflected back upon the victors. England was the more powerful and the more opulent territory: institutions arose from the combination of the old English law with the measures needful for the government of a newly subjugated country, which imparted new vigour to the sovereign authority.

England in fact influenced Normandy.

William, and still more William's successors, practised in Normandy the stern and orderly jurisprudence of the English king. Upon the total want of any written evidence as to the antient Norman jurisprudence, I have already remarked, and it is almost a whimsical illustration of the force of theory, that the Institutes of

Littleton, English to the very core, were published and commented upon by one of the most learned advocates of the Parliament of Rouen, as the best evidence of the institutions prevailing in Normandy, previous to the Conquest. But the Normans of Normandy thought otherwise: the Grand Coutumier of Normandy does not deduce its origin from Rollo, but claims the Confessor as its founder in the first page and paragraph. From him did they assert that their wise usages were derived; nay more, even Magna Charta was claimed by them after they had become the immediate subjects of the Capetian dynasty, as the foundation of their franchises, and their best security against arbitrary power.

See p. 602, ante.

Except from its influence upon the imagination, it would be hardly worth while to notice the legend of the curfew-bell, so commonly supposed to have been imposed by William upon the English, as the token of degradation and slavery; but the "*squilla di lontano, che paja il giorno pianger che si muore,*" was a universal custom of police throughout the whole of mediæval Europe, not unconnected with devotional feeling.

The curfew.

§ 17. Far more important, since it is so deeply connected with legislation, is the supposition that William endeavoured to force on his subjects the language of Normandy. Hume tells us that William the Conqueror entertained the difficult project of totally abolish-

Language.

ing the English language, and for that purpose he ordered that in all schools throughout the kingdom the youth should be instructed in the French tongue. The pleadings in the supreme court of judicature were in French, the deeds were often drawn in the same language, the laws were composed in the same idiom. Now the plain answer to this assertion is this, that we have no one example of any pleadings in the courts of judicature in French, of any deeds or charters drawn in the same language, or any laws composed in that idiom, until the reign of Henry III. What William found, he kept: like his predecessors; his laws and charters were written either in English or in Latin, though the latter gradually prevailed. Yet the English continued in continuous use, and the last example of its employment is found also in the very reign of Henry III., when, as before observed, we find the first employment of the French tongue.

Popular error as to the English language.

No doubt whatever can be entertained of the fact that, in subsequent times, the Romance dialect greatly prevailed in England; but we cannot blame or praise the Conqueror for its introduction. Indeed would it not have been a strange thing if William the Conqueror had caused his laws to be written in French, seeing that none were ever composed in that dialect in his own country; or, rather, that none whatever exist? Anterior to the Conquest, the only

William did not bring French into England.

monuments of jurisprudence are the ecclesiastical proceedings of the councils; and, subsequently, the Grand Coutumier, composed, as it should seem, immediately before the loss of the duchy by John, was first written in Latin, the French version being not earlier than the fourteenth century. Every writ, every letter, every missive which he addressed to his trusty men—his Frenchmen or his Englishmen, was in Latin or in English; and for the assertion so confidently made, and still more confidently repeated, not a particle of historical evidence can properly be found. *No early English documents are in French.*

§ 18. Yet the opinion has some claim to antiquity, and has received its sanction from the pseudo-Ingulphus, a romance which still obstinately retains its place amongst the sources of our history. The code of laws so often quoted by French and English antiquaries, as the earliest specimen of the Norman dialect, is merely a translation from a Latin text, executed, as it should seem, about the conclusion of the reign of Henry III. *No valid evidence for the error.*

It is in this reign that the so-called Norman-French first makes its appearance in the monuments of our diplomacy and jurisprudence, continuing, with very little variation, till the reign of Edward III., when the more modern French of Paris materially affected the archaic dialect of our island. Previous to this period no authentic law, or deed, or charter, has ever been *Real introduction of Norman-French into England.*

Disuse of English.

discovered, except in Latin or in English. The traditionary employment of the language of Rome, however barbarized or corrupted, continued to be one of the links which connected the mediæval states with the fourth monarchy, and it possessed a vast preponderance as a written language; but the employment of the English was limited to some few charters, writs, or letters, gradually diminishing in number until the last—which occurs [before] the age of York and Lancaster, when the diplomatic employment of the English language revived; and this last document is the memorable proclamation, declaring how Henry, King of England, Lord of Ireland, and Duke of Normandy and Aquitaine, had assented to the restraints imposed upon him by those whose names so forcibly bespeak their Norman lineage. To this most remarkable English document, penned so near to the Anglo-Norman period, there is not an English name.

§ 19. The gradual formation of our present English, as contradistinguished from what is usually termed Anglo-Saxon, is a problem not to be solved by the one single cause of the Norman accession; for though that event accelerated the change, still we must be permitted to repeat what we conceive to be the guiding principle of our historical investigations—that the Conquest only accelerated a process which otherwise would have proceeded more slowly and more incompletely; but still, that it would have differed only in degree, and not in kind. And here again we must take the test of comparison, as supporting the assertion which we have made. We regret the loss of our "English undefiled." In grim despair the philologer pores over the strains of Beowulf, and, failing to solve the impenetrable enigmas of the lay, he weeps over the deleterious influence of the Conquest. But has the Gothic speech fared better in its own country? Shall we find, in essentials, very much more conformity to antiquity in Scandinavia? Alas! if Regner Lodbrok were to chaunt his deathsong in the streets of Copenhagen, nay, even of Drontheim, the Quida would be as little intelligible to his auditors, as if Cædmon, accompanying himself upon his harp, were to intonate his glee at an oratorio in Hanover Square. *Change of language in Scandinavia.*

Our readers will recollect that, in conformity with our denial of the real existence of an Anglo-Saxon nation, except as a convenient, though somewhat delusive mode of designating the English of the ante-Norman period, so also must we deny there being any Anglo-Saxon language. If you had asked Alfred what he had in his hand, he would have answered it was an Engliscboc, and have been wonderfully surprised if you had given it any other name. The distinction then between the language which, in compliance with inveterate habit, we will call Anglo-Saxon, and the English, anterior to the Reformation,— for that event had here, as well as in Germany, *No such language as "Anglo-Saxon."*

great influence upon language,—consists, first, in the adoption of foreign words, principally from the Romance dialect of France; and secondly, in the obliteration of many of the inflexions of Anglo-Saxon grammar, the loss of all the cases save one, the diminution of the nice distinction in the moods of verbs by means of the tones and semitones of the vowels, and the general simplification in the construction of the phrases; and both those changes, although unquestionably aided by political circumstances, arose from the wonderful manner in which speech adapts itself to the exigencies or desires of the mind. "Out of the abundance of the heart, the mouth speaketh," is one of those divine truths as fully applicable to the collective language of each branch of the human race, as to the fulness and fluency of discourse, which strong and intense feeling gives to the individual.

§ 20. About the period of the Conquest, the Romance dialects of France began to exert a very singular fascination, if such a term may be employed, which has continued to the present age, and which caused them to become, for many ages, a common link between the various nations of Western Christendom. "Son," says the Norwegian king, in his instructions to his heir, "learn Walske, (Welch,) for that goes widest in the world." And the Northmen, as soon as they came in contact with other nations, with the most singular readiness, assumed their speech, and neglected or forgot the customs, as well as the language of their Scandinavian ancestors. Very few localities in Normandy now bear any traces of Teutonism in their etymology. A few vestiges may be traced by the diligence of the antiquary. Falaise is so-called from the Fels, or rock, on which it stands; Oistreham, Ouestreham, speak for themselves: yet, even in these cases, it may be doubted whether these and some others of the same kind are not due to a still more remote population—to the Saxons who peopled the Saxon shore, or to the so-called Gauls; for when we recollect that the great Druidical temple was called Eisern-thor, because it had iron doors, it is difficult to deny but that a Belgic dialect was spoken there before its annexation to the Roman Empire.

The Normans totally lose their original language,

Be this as it may, it is certain that when the Northmen occupied Neustria they found a population entirely Romanized, and the country full of Roman recollections and associations, still looking to the venerable shade of Rome as the mistress of the world. This Romanism the Northmen adopted with the utmost eagerness, and to such an extent, that when William the Conqueror was young, it was only a few old folks at Bayeux who could speak the Danish tongue. More singular, as evidencing the Roman impress given to the inhabitants of this region, is the fact, that, in Normandy, we find the earliest evidences of poetry in the Romance tongue.

And learn the Romance.

Yet the first jongleur whom we can quote as having chaunted the praise of the Emperor and his "doze peers," was Taillefer, at the battle of Hastings; for to suppose that the Chanson de Roland could have any reference to Rollo, is a theory as contrary to evidence as to the general tenor of Norman history. In Sicily, and in Apulia, the Greek and the Arabic were found as vernacular dialects by the Normans, and Roger assumed the diplomacy of Byzantium, and decorated his garments and his structures with the Cuphic scrolls of Bagdad. Yet here a Romance dialect preponderated; and the very name of Tancred de Hauteville shews how completely the Normans had become associated to the people whom they had subdued.

The Normans carry the Romance to Sicily.

Before the Conquest the same fashion was spreading. The palace of Edward the Confessor was filled with bishops and courtiers of Norman or Romance extraction. At an earlier period the Anglo-Saxons had begun to enrich their language by a macaronic intermixture of Greek and Latin, and so, in all probability, they now began to do with the more courteous phrases of the French or Romance tongues. The introduction, after the Conquest, of so many settlers of foreign origin, no doubt accelerated the process of intermixture. The Anglo-Saxon Chronicle shews how, even amidst the seclusion of Peterborough, Romance words began to become familiar. Yet in all this we can discern nothing of compulsion,

It reaches England under Edward:

but much of imitation, and of the influence resulting from intercourse and example; and thus, even in Scotland, the Romance became so prevalent, that an instance exists when the coronation oath was pronounced in the Norman or French language.

The great era, however, of the introduction of the Romance language in this country must be placed in the reign of Beauclerc; and the taste and examples of his two Queens—Matilda, and still more, Adeliza of Louvaine—gave an impulse to the employment of that dialect, which rendered it the language of secular literature. Yet other causes contributed, and amongst them, as we conjecture, were the needs of commerce. In London, certainly the most Anglo-Saxon portion of the realm, the earliest entries of their municipal records are in Romance French, and written with such remarkable purity and facility as to shew how thoroughly it must have been cultivated as the common language of intercourse in our metropolis; and the fashion continued to encrease in the court, as well as in the city. Whilst Edward III., by his legislation, prohibited the employment of the French language in the pleadings of the courts of justice, it was encouraged in the pleadings of the court of Love; and maintained its ground as exclusively amongst the higher classes as the French language in the court of Germany, in the days of Frederick the Great: and a whimsical, as well as an extraordinary proof of the influence thus acquired by habit, is found in the fact that the correspondence between George II. and the Prince of Wales, as laid before Parliament during their unhappy dissensions, is wholly in the French language.

§ 21. With respect to the grammatical alterations which the English sustained, we should be inclined to venture upon the following hypothesis, which we merely submit for the consideration of those who are better calculated to discuss it. Thorpe or Kemble, Halliwell or Wright, can alone investigate it with sufficient opportunity and knowledge. It seems, therefore, probable to us, that England before the Conquest possessed at least two, if not more, concurrent dialects, as in almost every part of Germany at the present day. The book language, we suspect, was not the vulgar tongue; it was fully understood by the common people, and yet not employed by them in common discourse; and after the higher classes were, if not wholly extirpated, yet much diminished in number and in influence, the vulgar dialect of the common people rose, as it were, to the surface, and, combining itself with the book language, formed the basis of the English which we now employ. If, for example, fifty years ago we can imagine a revolution which should have carried off the Adel, and the Burghers, and the Predigers of Holstein, and dispersed or destroyed the stores of literature, the Hoch-Deutsch would in great measure have disappeared: the Platt-Deutsch might have become the prevailing language; and in the course of years, Klopstock would, in his own country, have required the labours of the lexicographer, like our Anglo-Saxon remains. This is a rough comparison, but we believe it is the only one by which the development of our modern English can be explained.

* * * * * *

§ 22. According to the technical phraseology of some of our ecclesiastical historians, the tenth century is emphatically denominated the "*seculum obscurum.*" Towards its conclusion, a brighter light began to be seen on the verge of the horizon of the other portions of the Christian Commonwealth, until the period of the Conquest, but the darkness hung over England, perhaps even with encreasing shade. I do not speak merely of learning considered as an ornament. The attempts made by Alfred to give to the priesthood that knowledge needful for the discharge of their duty, failed. The bright days of the English Church had passed away, and her priesthood had settled upon the lees. It is with communities as with individuals; those who do not advance in goodness decline, and we seek in vain for any token of redeeming vitality.

The ecclesiastical synods, without which there can be neither the co-operation required for the administration of any human community, nor the gifts promised to those who assemble in

[marginal note: The Church system in England under the Saxons.]

the name of Him by whom the Church is guided, were almost entirely disused. When the clergy did meet, it was merely for secular concerns, and as a portion of the Witenagemot. They had practically become as effete as a Convocation. The abuses of the Church continued unrebuked and unrestrained, or what was worse, rebuked by the mockery of precepts not intended to restrain, as a clause in a mutiny act against duelling, a proclamation against vice and immorality. Learning had altogether decayed; and let it be recollected that in those days the theory, however imperfectly carried out, was that all learning should be directed to the service of God; so that this decay implies not alone a decline of cultivation and of intellect, but of sound doctrine and of holiness. He who could read Latin was talked of as a prodigy. With the decline of ecclesiastical discipline, morals had declined also: never can the one subsist without the other. The dusty rule of St. Benedict slumbered on the shelf, whilst rich fur and fine linen clothed the monk, and the savoury dishes smoked on the long table of the refectory. Scarcely could the priest at the altar, reeking from the debauch, stammer out the words of the Liturgy. Your English [clerk] was a glutton and a sot: of other vices we will not speak; it is sufficient to observe that they united the heat of passion to the most cold-blooded avarice. Without doubt, much of this degradation had been occasioned by the ceaseless Danish invasions, and equally so by the general breaking up of the Commonwealth, when the sceptre was wielded by Edward's powerless hand. But national misfortunes are judicial punishments, at once the evidence and the means of correction of national sins. The warnings were repeated, repeatedly disregarded, till at length they burst in vengeance.

§ 23. William in Normandy had shewn no great respect for the rights of the Church, when they were opposed to his will; and in England he soon shewed the extent which he gave to his regal power. Perhaps his first overt act was when he caused the monasteries to be searched for the property deposited in them by the English, a proceeding equally against good faith and the respect commonly rendered to the Catholic sanctuary. Heavy taxes were imposed without any mitigation upon the Church property, and large portions were violently seized and granted out to his followers. But these measures, though they might yield a certain degree of profit and advantage, did not accomplish the end which William's policy now openly sought,—the transfer of all the territorial supremacies to a new class of lords. This process, however, could not be effected entirely at his will and pleasure; but the vices of the Church of England afforded him the means of inflicting that punishment by which her strength was to be renewed. In the last era of the Anglo-Saxon state, besides the other sins of the clergy, the higher orders were most grievously stained with simony, the general corruption of the Western Church, but nowhere more apparent than in England—the simoniacal purchase of the sacred office, a sin against knowledge, equally detrimental to the Church and degrading to the hierarchy.

Trial of Stigand.

Of these prelates, no one was more defamed than Stigand, the Archbishop of Canterbury. But who was to sit in judgment upon the Primate? The problem was soon solved. Since the first settlement of the Anglo-Saxon Church, the Roman see had scarcely exercised any jurisdiction in England; and the connection which existed between this island and the patriarch of the West, seems to have been principally confined to the payment of Peter's pence, and the dues exacted for the pallium, the confirmation of the archiepiscopal authority. Now three papal legates are seen in England; Hermenfrid, Bishop of Sion, accompanied by two cardinals, dispatched upon the petition of William for the purpose of confirming him in the royal authority; but their further errand was immediately

before a council at Windsor.

disclosed. Convening a council,—it was held at Windsor for the purpose of extirpating the evils of the Church,—Stigand was canonically deposed from his archbishoprick, as well as from the bishoprick of Winchester. He was sentenced to the penance of perpetual imprisonment in the castle of Winchester: a scanty diet, insufficient for the wants of the old man, was allowed by the parsimony of the Exchequer. His friends advised him to provide himself with better food; he replied that he had not a penny. At last he died; and when they were stripping the shrunken corpse, they found a little key hung round his neck, and certain schedules of parchment containing an account of the treasure heaped up in the vault which that key opened, and to which he had thus clung to the very last. The blow thus struck was speedily followed up. Bishops and abbots were successively removed, many for sufficient cause, some perhaps unfairly; and this plan being consistently and steadily pursued, scarcely two more years had elapsed when Wulstan of Worcester was perhaps the only English bishop remaining in the realm; and for more than a generation, no Englishman was suffered to acquire any ecclesiastical dignity.

Other depositions.

§ 24. The constant overruling of the devices of man, is the perpetual key to the intricacies of human affairs. What sought William in the deposition of the English prelates? Why did he place the whole nation under a ban, rendering their name and race an exclusion from the Church of their fathers? His own pleasure, the security and consolidation of his own power. But the very measures which he employed worked against his own intent, and the wrong

William's reasons.

produced the remedy. Had the Conquest taken place a generation earlier, the irruption of the Normans would have been as injurious to the intellectual advancement of England as the invasions of the Danes, for under the first five dukes their own subjects neglected all useful learning. Fierce and untameable, they united the roughness of the barbarian to the heartlessness of partial civilization. But destined as the Normans were to effect a mighty change in the fortunes of Christendom, there was given to them the talent of seeking out the means of improvement. Of the eminent men who adorn the Norman annals, perhaps the smallest proportion were of Norman race. Discernment in the choice of talent, munificence in rewarding ability, may be justly ascribed to the Norman rulers. If in the Norman there was an entire absence of real national feeling, there was an equal absence of national jealousy; and at the same time that William was effecting the conquest of England, the way was prepared for rendering that conquest the means of introducing the teachers who were to reclaim the English Church from sloth and spiritual degeneracy.

These changes make way for abler men.

Lanfranc.

§ 25. Amongst those whose names the dying king enumerated, as testifying by their lives and conversations, that to the best of his power he had well exercised the trust for which he was now called to render an account, were those of Lanfranc and his successor Anselm. Of the second, we shall speak hereafter. [The career of the first we have traced to the period of William's marriage.] He had already refused the Archbishoprick of Rouen, offered to him upon the death of Maurellius, the Italian; and he equally shrunk from the acceptance of the see of Canterbury. In this dignity there was nothing which could tempt him. He delighted in the pleasant places in which his lot had been cast. Pursuing still with unabated zeal the studies which had raised him to eminence, and which were now giving him the more enduring gratification of the consciousness that he had been the means of training others to follow in the same good path, he was most loth to quit his solitude. But, yielding at length to the commands of the King and the solicitations of the Norman clergy, he accepted the unwelcome mitre, and was installed with more than usual solemnity in the metropolitan cathedral. He was most joyfully accepted by the people, who hailed him as a father; and henceforth Lanfranc deemed himself to be an Englishman, and identified himself entirely with the community to which he was now allied, but without in anywise departing from the fidelity which he was bound to render to his Sovereign. According to the old English constitution, the Archbishop of Canterbury was, as I have before observed, a species of tribune of the people. He was William's chief adviser. To this was added the authority of justiciar, or, as we should say, regent, which he exercised whenever William was absent from the realm; and pre-eminent as the station was which Lanfranc holds in the written history of the reigns of the Conqueror and of Rufus, it was the silent, or, at least, the unrecorded influence exercised by him as a statesman which rendered him most beneficial to the people. On Lanfranc, as Archbishop, we shall speak hereafter more particularly. In his mixed character, as the chief of the lords spiritual, he may be considered as the great supporter, in some respects the founder, of the constitution. His firm, but temperate defence of the rights of the Church, enabled his successors to be the defenders of the rights of the state. There is no true defender of one without the other. The crozier of Lanfranc, handed down by Anselm and Becket to Hubert and Langton, did more for Magna Charta than the sword.

Lanfranc's general conduct.

§ 26. It is the common error of all men to pride themselves upon their one good quality, which they consider as giving them a receipt in full for all the opposite failings and sins. William was clear of simony, the sin which, as I have before observed, corrupted the appointments of the Church in their very source, and in which almost all his compeers participated with the utmost gladness and greediness. Pope Gregory held him up, in this respect, as an example to others. But as the canonists lay down in grave technical aphorisms, what we all know from common sense—would that we did not from daily experience—the spirit of the prohibition may be fully violated, although the hard money may never have passed; and whilst William most religiously abstained from bestowing his prelacies in consequence of the "*munus a manu*," still he indemnified himself most amply by the "*munus a lingua*," and the "*munus ab obsequio*," deriving perhaps even more convenience and advantage from these considerations, than as if the preferment had been sold as the next presentation to an advowson is at the present day.

Gilbert Maminot was recommended by his great skill in medicine and also in astronomy. He was a court physician and court astrologer: felt the Conqueror's pulse and cast his horoscope. In the knowledge of a useful art there was nothing uncanonical; nor would the care of bodies have necessarily disqualified him for the care of souls; but what was the Bishop in other respects? The sports of the field, hunting and hawking, were his amusements. Science [also was his,]—for he was deeply learned according to the standard of the age, and one of his observations, accidentally preserved, forms an important link in the annals of the visible heavens. To these he added the habits of the camp. He was liberal and merry, fond of good

William's choice of prelates.

Maminot.

cheer and good fellowship. In his time the canons of Lisieux were as jovial as a mess-table, though, at the same time, he was most diligent in promoting secular learning. In short, he was fit for anything except his station. But no money had been paid, and William hugged himself in his virtue. Furicus, an Italian by birth, obtained the Abbey of Faringdon. He proved a worthy and diligent pastor; but William gave him this good piece of preferment for the same knowledge which had caused the appointment of Maminot,—medicine, and the result, whilst it diminished the evil to the Church, left the purity of William's intentions exactly as before. Remigius, the almoner of the monastery of Fécamp, when William was preparing for the expedition against Harold, marks himself down in the roll as furnishing a vessel with twenty full armed knights to man the bark; and thus with an easy conscience the wealthy see of Dorchester was bestowed by the grateful monarch upon the expectant. A bishop was bound to military service for his temporalities; and could the bargain made by Remigius, when he gave the seasonable aid, that he should receive an English diocese from his Sovereign, be reckoned simony? Certainly not: no money was paid; and were not the unpromoted actuated by a censorious spirit when they maintained that the death of Remigius, the very day before that upon which he had proposed to consecrate the sumptuous cathedral of Lincoln, the city to which he had removed his seat from the humble [Dorchester], was a judgment for his transgression? And the previous employments, as well as the characters of the majority of the prelates preferred by William, can leave little doubt that, though he may justly be exonerated from the grossest abuse, he was entirely obnoxious to the transgression of bestowing the holy office for the payment of secular advantage, a price neither less palpable nor less real than pecuniary corruption. The motive for their promotion was the belief that they would be entirely subservient to his will: they were to have no scruples, no opinions, no conscience where his authority was concerned. He was supreme in Church and State: his will was the only law.

* * * *

APPENDIX.

THE BARONIAL CASTLES
OF
THE COTENTIN, THE AVRANCHIN, AND THE BESSIN.

1. *Cherbourg.*—Originally a Roman station, held by Haigold or Harold the Dane (945), subsequently granted in dowry to the Adela, King Robert's daughter, by Richard III. In the grant it is designated as the *Castellum Carusbure.*

2. *Gonnville.*—In the eleventh century this castle belonged to the family of Rivers.—Vernon.

3. *Brasville.*—Only a mound is now subsisting. This situated between Cherbourg and Barfleur.

4. *Saint Pierre Eglise.*—Belonging to Robert of Glamorgan. The arms borne by the Glamorgan family are nearly the same in France as in England.

5. *Maupertius.* [*Maupertuis?*]—A Roman foundation.

6. *Martinvast.*—This castle passed to Richard de Martinvast, a Nottinghamshire Esquire. He did service with the commune of Cherbourg.

7. *Vauville.*—Richard de Vauville appears in the antient list of knights, who crossed over with the Conqueror. The Vauville family had also possessions in Septvents, or Septvaus. The name of this place affords a curious example of the fact, that in the black letter days, the old scribes could not always be certain of their own writing. One branch of the family read it as Sept vans, and gave seven

vans, or winnowing vans, as their bearing; while another branch read the word as *Sept vaus* or de *septem vallibus*, and bore seven hieroglyphics which stood for valleys according to the conventionalism of the Heralds' college.

8. *Greville.*—The name of Greville is enrolled in the list of the Conqueror's companions. There is another Greville ŏr Graville, in Normandy, but this is the original habitat.

9. *Château d'Adam.*—In the commune of Brix or Bruce, this unquestionably is the *Stamm Schloss* (as the Germans would say) of the Bruce family. The name of Adam was common in the early Bruce genealogies. A branch of the barons of Bruce continued in Normandy, and had a seat in the Exchequer, and the arms they quarter are the arms of Bruce of Annandale.

10. *La Luthumiere.*—Also in the district of Bruixes.

11. *Briquebec.*—This was Oslac's castle; Guillaume Bertram who held it, the son of Oslac, or perhaps the grandson, passed over with the Conqueror. From the Bertrams in the female line, descended the earls of Huntley and Dudley. From them also the Stutevilles, &c. It came afterwards to William de la Pôle. The Stutevilles also descended from the Stutevilles in the female line, and we find them amongst the leading baronage.

12. *Les Perques.*—This barony fell into the hands of the Briquebec family.

13. *Barneville.*—From Barneville came the Roger de Barneville, who is honoured by Tasso as a distinguished Crusader. We lose sight of this family in England, but they subsequently settled in the Scottish Lowlands.

14. *Carteret.*—Steady adherents of the English kings were the Carteret family. They afterwards settled in Jersey. The Carteret ranks as the premier baron of the island.

15. *Magneville.*—Magnaville took place amongst the proudest honors of the Cotentin. Altered by habit of

speech into the name of Mandeville. This family became of great importance also in England.

16. *Morville.*—Flourished in England, in Normandy, and in Scotland.

17. *Nehon.*—Originally a member of the Barony of Saint Sauveur, but dismembered by Neel in favour of his son and namesake. From Nihel, Neel, of Nehon, came the families of Rivers and Vernon.

18. *Saint Sauveur le Viscomte.*—Claimed to be the Premier Barony of Normandy. This lineage merged into the Tessons. "Tesson" signifies "badger," and it is said that the family acquired this name from always burrowing their way under ground so cleverly and cunningly that they acquired one-third of Normandy.

19. *Garnotote.*—This is one of the very few baronies in the Cotentin whose owners cannot be distinctly traced in England.

20. *Oglandis.*—Now or recently represented by the Oglander family of Nunwell in the Isle of Wight. Nunwell was granted to them at the Conquest.

21. *Beuzeville.*—Comparatively a modern castle. The history of the family is obscure.

22. *Amfreville.*—Hence came the Umfrevilles, the Avenels, and many more.

23. *La Fierete.*—Doubtful.

24. *Boutteville.*—The Bouttevilles came over with William the Conqueror, and settled in Somersetshire and Bedfordshire.

25. *Saint Marie-du-Mont.*—"Broad shoulders" became the epithet of this family; known in England, it is probable, by some other sobriquet.

26. *Freville.*—Settled in Cambridgeshire.

27. *Montebourg.*—Probably not erected before the fifteenth century.

28. *Tourville.*—Answers to the call of Battle Abbey Roll.

29. *Estres.*—Hence came the Estres of Dorchester. Coliford Estres retains the name of this family, which extended widely.

30. *Greneville* or *Grenville.*—Touches upon Estres. Unquestionably the cradle of the Grenvilles.

31. *La Hogue* or *Hague.*—Doubtful as to any castle.

32. *Barfleur.*—Harold lodged here. It may be noticed also that the Confessor when in Normandy started from Barfleur, when he made his first attempt to repass into England.

33. *Mont Farville.*—Hence the Foliot.

34. *Anne-ville.*—The Annevilles established themselves both in the Isle of Wight and the county of York. They came in with the Conqueror.

35. *Tamer-ville.*—This appears to have been held by the family of Siffrevast, so well known amongst our Baronage. They quartered Percy and Anneville.

36. *Valognes.*

LA MANCHE.

37. *Pierrepont.*—Robert the Lord came to England in the suite of William, Count of Warren. Hurst Pierrepont being the Norman designation, added to the old English locality, qualified him to perform the service of ten knights' fees. Holme Pierrepont in Nottinghamshire equally testifies the Conquest.

38. *Canville.*—From the owners of this castle came the Canvilles, and, in the female line, the Verduns.

39. *Varenquebec.*—Hence the family of Evreux or Gace, one of the trusty Guardians of the Conqueror. Rivers and Harcourts came from Varenquebec; hereditary constables of Normandy.

40. *Lithaire.*

41. *Bolleville.*—Bolleville passed with the Conqueror.

From this family came Eudo Dapifer, whose wide extended baronies are to be found in the south and in the east Essex, Southwark, Sussex, and Surrey. From them also the Mortimers. Hence also the Magnevilles or Mandevilles.

42. *La Haie-du-puits.*—Hence came the great Eudo Dapifer, who acquired, whether by force or favour, the largest proportions of robbery, called conquest, in the Counties of Sussex, Essex, and Suffolk. They expanded throughout England.

43. *Omonville-la-Foliot.*—Hence the great family of that name, amongst whose members Gilbert Foliot, the Bishop of London, is conspicuous; and Robert Foliot certified to fifteen knights' fees which his family had possessed since the Conquest. See also, Val de Saire, and Barfleur, Anneville and Morfarville.

44. *Plessis.*—This castle appertained to Grimoualde, who, in 1046, was the principal agent in the conspiracy intended to deprive the Conqueror of his States and his life, when Duke of Normandy. Grimoualde died in prison 1048. This castle seems afterwards to have passed to the Vernon family.

45. *Gorges.*—Very powerful did this family become in Dorsetshire and Somersetshire. Their bearing, a whirlpool, may be seen upon their sepulchral chapel at Cliefden.

46. *Aubigny.*—The Lord of Aubigny, when he passed over with William, was one of the great officers of the Duchy—the Pincerna, or butler. They afterwards assumed the name of Mowbray. D'Aubigny held great possessions in Norfolk, amongst others the Lordship of Bukenham. Neal or Nigel d'Aubigny greatly aided in the Conquest.

47. *Château de Lauve.*—The Lordship of Aubigny and the castle of Saint Clare are to the farthest east of the Cotentin.

48. *Pirou.*—They held much in Devonshire and Somer-

setshire. Stoke-pirou, in Devonshire, still commemorates their name.

49. *The Castle of Gratot.*
50. *The Castle of Agon.*—This was held by Duke Richard himself, who bestowed it in dowry upon his enigmatical wife Adela.
51. *Tourville.*—Not distinctly connected with England.
52.
53. *Muneville-le-Bingard.*—Settled in Kent.
54. *Camprond.*
55. *Cambernon.*—They settled at Modbury, in Devonshire; the name was anglicised as Chambernon or Champernoun.
56. *Orval.*—The d'Orvals came over with the Conqueror. They are found in Battle Abbey Roll.
57. *Saussey.*— The name appears in Battle Abbey Roll, but we have no farther account of the lineage in England.
58. *Trely.*—Two barons of this name appear in England, sub-tenants of the great Honour of Verdun.
59. *Quesnay.*—Great folks were they in England. They held great possessions in Dorset, Hertford, and Somerset, and produced a famous Bishop of Lincoln.
60. *Montchaton.*—We find no traces of their possessions in England, but they were much trusted by Henry Beauclerc.
61. *Regniéville.*—Not traceable before the sixteenth century.
62. *Brehal.*—Held by Fulke Pagnel. Within this Lordship we find the cradle of the Briquevilles, the Brevilles, the Carbonnels, the Chanteloups, the Montgomerys, the Mordacs, and the Pomerois.
63. *Carences.*—Appertaining to the ducal domain of Normandy, inasmuch as it was granted by Richard III. in dowry to his betrothed Adela; but it afterwards passed

to the Carbonnels, one of whom followed the Conqueror to England.

64. *Chanteloup or Canteloupe.*—They held great domains in Dorsetshire, and as far as Warwickshire, the parish of Aston Canteloupe. The second mentioned shire commemorates their barony.

65. *La Meuredraquière*, in England Mordrac, very amply endowed. Amongst the members must be reckoned the celebrated Archbishop of York, Henry Mordrac.

66. *La Pommeraye.*—The Cotentin family possessed upwards of fifty knights' fees in Devonshire. Bury Pommeroye and Stoke le Pommeroye still commemorate their name.

67. *Ver.*—In England *Vere;* and very illustrious English genealogists do not seem aware of their origin.

68. *Valence.*—Owed suit and service to the castle of Garray, a very noted family in England. No baron more illustrious than Aymer de Valence, whose tomb is one of the glories of the Abbey.

69. *Saint Denis-le-gast.*—His service commemorated in the Battle Abbey Roll. From the arms borne by the lords of this seignorie it should seem they are a branch of the Mordac family.

70. *Hamlye.*—Held by the Pagnels, amongst the most flourishing of our baronial families. Newport Pagnel, in Buckinghamshire, commemorates them.

71. *Château de Mauny.*—From this family came the celebrated Walter de Mauny.

72. *Gavray.*—Gavray, a royal castle. It was held as subtenants by the Amondevilles, the Montagues, and De Veres.

73. *Mesnil-Garnier.*—Almost a solitary exception as not having furnished any family to England.

74. *Montagu-les-bois.*—The lords of Montagu were subtenants of Mesnil-Garnier, but they furnished much to England. Drogo de Montagu came over with the Con-

queror, and the castle which he founded in Somersetshire retains the name of his Cotentin Castle, and appropriately.

75. *Hauteville le Guichard.*—Hence came the conquerors of Sicily.

76. *La Blontière.*—This castle seems to have been held by the founder of the family of Lord Rolle. They settled in Lincolnshire.

77. *La Lande d'Airou.*—This seems to have been originally called La Lande de Harold, but we cannot carry any English connexion farther.

78. *Beauchamp.*—Hugh Beauchamp came to England with the Conqueror, and obtained nearly the whole of the county of Bedford.

79. *Château Ganne.*—This name is attached to many places in Normandy; and it seems to be strangely but unaccountably connected with the romances of the cycle of Charlemagne, and wherever it occurs it is connected with some real or alleged act of treachery or treason. This was the case with this present castle during the minority of Saint Louis, when he was besieging the castle of Belesme. The Duke of Brittany, accompanied by a large force of English and Anglo-Normans, besieged this castle, which was delivered over to them by Fulke and William Pagnel, and twenty of the traitors belonged to that family. Many other stories are connected with this castle. In Haie Pagnel, the adjoining borough, there is a street called "La Rue Iscariote."

80. *Castle of the Berg*, of Haie Pagnel. This passed to the Fitz-John family.

81. *Château du Grippon.*—Between Avranches and Coutances. Its history is obscure, and not distinctly connected with England.

82. *Subligny.*—This name is found in Battle Abbey Roll, as well as among the Crusaders who followed Robert Courtehose.

83. *Saint Leger.*—They were first settled at Ulkham, in Kent, where they continued to the reign of Queen Elizabeth.

84. *Granville.*—Not to be confounded with Magneville or with Grenville.

85. *Saint Pair.*—It seems to have been held of the Dubois family, but there is some confusion about it. We find a Dubois, also called Sylvanus, who appears amongst the nobles of Normandy, following the Conquest.

86. *Champeaux.*—This is a Cotentin castle. William de Champeaux is noticed in the Red Book of the Exchequer.

87. *Saint Jean le Thomas.*—They became very important in the Cotentin under the Norman Dukes; from them came the Saint Jeans of Staunton Saint Jean in the county of Oxford. They married into the Hay family. Their name appears in all the lists of the Conquest. From them came the Bolingbrokes, the Saint Jeans of Bletso, of Staunton Saint Jean, and of Basing. The Mildmays also. We may see the genealogy of the family, or at least the genealogy could be seen in the choir of the church of Lediard Tregoy in Wiltshire.

88. *Genety.*—Doubtful.

89. *Saint Pierre Langer.*—Thence the Saint Pierre family, the Bunburys of Suffolk, and many others.

90. *Avranches.*—The boundary fortress. This became the domain of Richard Goz, the husband of Emma, the Conqueror's half sister, and sister in blood of the Count of Mortagne and of Odo, the too famous Bishop of Bayeux. The son of Goz was the renowned Hugh Lupus. He was Count of Avranches, and became the first Earl Palatine of Chester.

91. *Ducey.*—Little is known of this place in history. It is one of the very few of the Cotentin Castles which may be said to be inconsiderable.

92. *Pont Orson.*—Founded by Robert le-Diable, as a

check upon Brittany. During the singular contingency when Harold joined the Conqueror and they made an expedition into Brittany, Pont Orson was the Norman advanced post; and it was from Pont Orson, that they crossed the Coesnon. It was much the object of Henry the Second's care.

93. *Cheruel.*—The third in the chain of fortresses built by the Dukes of Normandy to restrain the Britons. This was the Castle Carroc of Guillaume de Jumièges. The family of Maresmenes came hence.

94. *Thany.*—Robert of Thony crossed over with William, and the family existed in great repute till the 15th century. As English Barons, they bore " argent six aiglettes."

95. *Ardeven.*—Occupied by the English during the famous siege by Rufus.

96. *Tombelain.*—This has some connexion with Tombland in Norwich.

97. *Montaigue.*—Connected with the Montague family, though not clearly.

98. *Argonges.*

99. *St. James de Beuvron.*—This castle was built by William the Conqueror, before the Conquest, and much importance was attached to it.

100. *Brecey.*—The family settled in Worcestershire, and the estates were recently held, and perhaps are, by the Lygon family.

Arrondissement of Mortaign. Very many of the inhabitants of this district went to Apulia. Others crossed over to England, having Robert, the Conqueror's son, as their leader. It is said that Robert held nine hundred and seventy-three Lordships in England.

101. *Biars.*—Hence the Avenels and the Vernons. This family became very illustrious in England, and still more in Scotland.

APPENDIX.

102. *Saint Hilaire.*

103. *Tilleul.*—King William appointed Humphrey de Tilleul commander of the castle of Hastings, but his wife teazed him until he returned to Normandy, and he lost his English possessions.

104. *Baronten.*—Hence came the great family of Verdun.

105. *Touchete.*—Hence the Touchetes Lords Audley.

106. *Mortaign.*—William Werelery was Count of Mortaign. His son succeeded him as Earl of Cornwall.

107. *Sourdeval.*—Château Gaune. The castle of Janelone di Maganza, the traitor of the Carlovingian cycle.

108. *Saint Mort des Bois.*—We find their name in Battle Abbey Roll—they are the Seymours.

109. *Roche Tesson.*

110. *Percy.*—In this remarkable canton are three very important castles, each appertaining to the head of a very powerful family, and pre-eminent amongst these powerful lineages, the Roche Tessons of that ilke. So extensive were their possessions, that it was said they held the third part of Normandy; or as was more tersely expressed, the tiers pied of Normandy.

The Tessons were descended from the Counts of Anjou. Raoul Tesson took a great part in the battle of the Val des Dunes. This castle, however, did not originally belong to the Tessons. It belonged to the Nigils of Saint Sauveur, and came to the Tessons by marriage. Two of the Tessons were in the battle of Hastings, but we hear next to nothing of them in England afterwards. It may be suspected that they were enemies of the Conqueror.

111. *Château de Montbray.*—Unquestionably to be identified with Mowbray, one of the strange tricks produced by the ambiguity of the form of the *n* and the *u* in antient manuscripts. It is very remarkable that in the old times, themselves, the very persons holding the names, either

from caprice or ignorance, confounded them. See No. 7, *Vauville.*

Roger de Mowbray attended the famous Parliament of Lillebonne; at the battle of Hastings Geoffrey de Mowbray, the brother of Roger, was the most prominent; but, alas, for consistency he was a Bishop, and much better fitted to lead a charge, than to celebrate mass, or sing a prayer. Often had he fought against the Danes, and the English, and two hundred lordships rewarded his piety. The last Mowbray who appears in history, was the son of the first Roger, and nephew of the too famous Geoffrey. To his father's patrimony he united the Earldom of Northumberland, and the plunder which descended to him from uncle Geoffrey. The remainder of his history falls into the reign of Rufus.

112. *Percy.*—A very extensive commune. It is a portion of the domains which Duke Richard III. granted to Adela, le notem Perci.

113. *Moyon or Mohun,* vulgarly corrupted into Moon. He was one of the greatest Barons of the Cotentin; five knights who held of him accompanied him to the battle of Hastings. The Barony passed afterwards to the Pagnels of Hamby and Brickbeck, where Her Majesty astonished the natives, as it is said, by telling them that she went to see it because it had once belonged to her family.

114. *Castle of Tregoz.*—The Lord of Tregoz appears in every list of the Conqueror's companions.

115. *Torigny.*—This castle was held by the famous Hamo Dentatus. Robert Fitz Hammond comes of this family.

116. *Castle of Brebeuf.*—This is not the name of a fief, but simply of the locality.

117. *Castle of Semilly.*—This was a favourite residence of Richard Cœur de Lion, and other Anglo-Norman kings. The name occurs in many of the Battle Abbey Rolls; they

afterwards passed to the Mathan family, whose descendants are still to be found at Neufchatel.

118. *Castle of Airel.*—Its owners are not known.

119. *Saint Lo.*—This castle is a Municipal castle; it was a castle out of which the town arose. It was raised by Charlemagne as a defence against the Danes. It became the possession of Geoffrey Plantagenet; after this we find no marked connexion with English history.

120. *Château de bon Fossé.*—This appears to have been held by Geoffrey de Mowbray; it has no other connexion with English history.

121. *Château de Soule.*—Under Henry II. it was held by Guillaume de Soule; a family of Soule subsists in England under the name of Sole.—(Soulis also?)

122. *Château de Canisy.*—Hubert de Canisy came with the Conqueror. It was held by the family of Carbonnel, subsisting both in Normandy and in England.

123. *Château de Marigny.*—It appears that the castle of Marigny was held by the family of Say, and it is thought that the Lord of Say was summoned under this or some other name to Parliament. Picot de Say is considered as the founder of the English branch; he was a baron in England during the Conqueror's reign, though he is not noticed as having come over with him.

124. *Castle of Egglandes.*—This castle was part of the dowry of the baby Adela.

125. *Castle of Graignes.*—The Mordracs seem to have held this castle.

126. *Castle of Hommet.*—The family of Hommet, amongst the most distinguished in Normandy, settled in England. From them came the great family of Rivers. The Hommets were constables of Normandy.

127. *Château de la Rivière.*—The barons who succeeded had no connexion with England.

128. *Château de Carentan.*—This was always a portion of the ducal domains, and became of much importance in the history of Normandy, though no known family settled there.

129. *Forteresse des Ponts d'Ouvres.*

130. *Château de Bohun.*—Hence the great family of the Bohuns.

131. *Château de Méautis.*—The Meautis family settled in England, and Sir Thomas Meautis is known as having built the tomb of Lord Bacon. He himself is interred at St. Albans.

END OF VOL. III.

CPSIA information can be obtained
at www.ICGtesting.com
Printed in the USA
LVHW111734170422
716440LV00004B/244

9 783752 592962